What Hides
in the Darkness

The Light Trilogy, Book One

K. L. Cottrell

Cover photo: JPagetRFPhotos/
http://www.shutterstock.com
Back cover design: Ellie Bockert Augsburger,
Creative Digital studios/
http://creativedigitalstudios.com
Cover/headings font: Dream Orphans

ISBN-13: 978-0996006606

Opening quote from Lucius Annaeus Seneca; "Death, be not proud" written by John Donne; *All's Well That Ends Well* written by William Shakespeare; "Hope" written by Emily Brontë; "The Raven" written by Edgar Allan Poe

"Shall I tell you what the real evil is? To cringe to the things that are called evils, to surrender to them our freedom...."

-Lucius Annaeus Seneca

Prologue

Evil is everywhere. It always has been. It always will be.

It dwells in murderers, bigots, thieves, rapists, terrorists and sadists. Sometimes it is stark and loud. Other times it is silent and conniving.

Sometimes evil in others can be sensed by those who do not possess it. Sometimes a person can look at someone else and intuitively know, with chill bumps on their arms and unease in their stomach, that they are not looking at someone who walks on the side of the righteous.

But sometimes evil does not smolder so close to the surface. Sometimes its face is easy on the eyes and its actions seem kind; sometimes it gains trust and makes friends and wears its disguise so well that no one knows what lies underneath until it is too late.

There are people who believe that Satan, God's eternal nemesis, is the reason evil exists. They believe Satan calls to those who do not hold God in their hearts and induces them to live against those who do.

There are those who believe that evil is learned. They think the details of one's childhood are what shape them into either a good person or a bad one. Perhaps a child's parents simply taught them that some people's lives are more valuable than others, or that violence is the way to get what they want.

Then there are people who believe that an evil mind is nothing more than a defective mind. They maintain that the fragility of the human brain is such that if it is deformed at all, whether in the womb or during life, it can result in numbness to the norms of society, or in dangerous insanity.

It does not really matter where evil comes from, though. What matters is that it is always at work, always lurking in shadowy places, always walking boldly in the sunlight. And that is where the real problem is discovered: evil is too vast to be stopped.

Too many people are full of hate. Too many people crave control. Too many people want to see others bleed. Too many people are self-seeking. Too many people see clearly-drawn lines and cross them with a sickening smile.

But what if one could detect malevolence in its most concentrated form? What if the evil that spans across so many people was visible—what if it could be *touched?* Could the splinters of it be removed from the world if they could be taken hold of one at a time?

Instead of just leaving the fight to higher beings or believing that some people are simply unfit to raise a child or that nature just sometimes creates sociopaths, what if there was the possibility of taking matters into one's own hands?

What if keeping the world from sinking into rampant wickedness was not impossible at all? What if just as blackness crawls through so many people, light flowed through someone else?

Well, the answer is simple.

What hides in the darkness could be found.

It could be challenged.

It could be destroyed.

1
Marienne

As I sit alone in an old tire swing in the backyard of a decimated home that stands at the dead end of an abandoned street called Grove Lane, staring at the cloudy sky and listening to two birds bitching at each other, it occurs to me that my life has not turned out the way I always thought it would.

'Change is inevitable.' 'Nothing stays the same.' 'God works in mysterious ways.' 'Expect the unexpected.' Et cetera. We've heard it all, every one of us. Even children know some of these sayings. The funny thing is that even though these words are everywhere and seemingly always have been, we forget all about them when shit starts hitting the fan for real. As soon as things start deviating from the path we know, we turn into a version of us we didn't think could exist.

Take for example my life Before. I was twenty-one and part of a wealthy family. My parents loved me and had been happily married for thirty years. My sister and I had figured out the perfect balance between being siblings and friends, and we even lived together. I had a great group of actual friends and among them were Audrey and Rafe, the best of the best. I'd known Audrey since first grade. I'd known Rafe since I was sixteen, and a couple of sunny months had gone by since we'd transitioned from being just friends to being a couple.

I wasn't expecting the unexpected. I was thinking everything would stay the way it was, the way it always had been: lovely, happy, fun, normal.

Then something bad happened, and it led to something even more terrible. No, not terrible—abominable. And just like that, I was a whole new Marienne Rose Connor.

Behold my life as it is now. I'm still twenty-one. I'm still part of a wealthy family, but it's fractured. My parents are no longer technically married because they're no longer alive. My sister Claire still splits the apartment with me, but I can feel her hatred of me even when we're not around each other. And instead of being out with all those friends I had, I'm by myself in a neighborhood that no one in Fayetteville, Arkansas gives a shit about anymore because it was torched years ago by some gang. In fact, it looks like those two particular friends I thought were the best in the world give as much of a shit about *me* as they do Grove Lane (not a single one).

And on top of all that, I've been seeing monsters.

Mmm, yes, that's right.

I don't mean I see them because they're ghostlike entities that 'visit' me or because I don't sleep well and my tired, overworked brain has started manufacturing imaginary beings with which to disturb me. I'm not crazy. No, in the two and a half months since the car accident that killed my parents and almost killed me I've been truly seeing, with my own two blue eyes, actual *monsters* where men should be.

I mean, it's not like they're everywhere. Don't get me wrong. They haven't taken over the entire male population. But they *are* there, somehow disguised as regular men. They walk around the mall, they flirt with girls, they drive cars, they have jobs. And when I say they're monsters, I mean that. They're horrendous-looking. They always look like they've just crawled straight out of hell. They vary in size, in height, in awfulness, but they're all fundamentally the same: unnatural.

Stranger yet is that, as far as I know, no one else can see them. I may not hang out with people anymore, but I do still go to the grocery store and stuff, so more than a few times have I been in public and spotted those creatures and found that no one seems to look at them the way I do. So I've gotten to where I just try to steer clear of them, or ignore them if we have to share space for some reason. They've never actively bothered me, though they do look at me sometimes like they would any other person.

But other people—I've definitely seen them interact with other people. I've even seen them...well, *lure in* other people. Like the girl at the bar at Applebee's last night.

I was by myself, of course, slumped over my rum and Coke. It was a Tuesday night, but everyone else at the bar was acting like it was Friday. I guessed it was the classic rock song pounding through the speakers. The power of music and all that.

The blonde girl on my right was scantily clad and telling some lame story to the guy on the other side of her.

"...and I was like, '*Mom, oh my God! I don't care if it's my birthday, I just got out of bed! I'm not even dressed! Put the camera away!*'" Her laugh was tinkling. "It was so embarrassing. I almost died."

No, you didn't, I thought bitterly.

(These days I don't have much of a sense of humor about things like death.)

The guy told her, "Wow, that's awful," and I could hear him smiling, but I knew he wasn't really amused. I knew that because 1) I wasn't inebriated like that blonde girl, and 2) I saw him for what he really was when I first got to the restaurant. He was one of those horrific, demonic-looking *things*. He had eyes that were red and skin that was gray and deeply fissured, like the cracked ground of the desert. His body was completely uncovered except for a sagging clump of chains around his waist.

That wasn't what the girl saw, of course, since he can somehow change his appearance to blend in with humans. Hell, I'd have mistaken him for a regular guy, too, if I hadn't spotted him before I got the rum in me. As it happened, I hadn't consumed my numbing agent yet, so I knew that fellow way better than the other girl thought she did.

They continued chatting and I continued drinking. The Coke fizzed down my throat and the taste of the rum lingered on my tongue, and I wondered what I'd be up to right then if things had gone differently with me—in turn, if alcohol affected me the way it used to, the way it's *supposed* to. I figured I'd be out with Audrey doing the same thing I was already doing. But I wouldn't know about the darker things in the world; I wouldn't see seven-foot-tall monsters with rotting mouths and razor-sharp fingernails where men should be. In fact, the girl next to me—talking to someone she thought was attractive, totally unaware of what lurked under that perfectly constructed mask—could have easily been my former best friend. She could have been the one flirting with danger.

Sickening.

I leaned back in my chair and tucked my long black hair behind my ear. I got a good look at the girl. Her loosely-curled hair tumbled down her back, which was bare for the most part because of her black halter top. Her denim miniskirt was fashionably faded and expensive-looking and the pumps on her feet were a glossy red. She didn't notice me looking at her because her attention was entirely on the guy.

He was leaning casually on the bar, seemingly absorbed by her. He had quite the façade worked up: smooth pale skin, clear blue eyes and brown hair gelled to perfection. Nice clothes, too: black button-up shirt, dark gray suit, sleek black shoes.

He turned his gaze on me then, and my skin prickled. His expression didn't change at all; he gave me the same 'interested' look he'd just been giving the other girl. Despite the discomfort weighing on me I stared back evenly. I wondered if he knew I could see what he really looked like.

He didn't look at me long enough to alarm the blonde nor long enough for me to determine what he did or didn't perceive about me. I wasn't terribly surprised by his turning away; her flashy halter and miniskirt were much more provocative than my jeans and lightweight hoodie. He straightened up and rolled his shoulders gracefully, drawing an appreciative sigh from the girl, and then held a hand out to her. Even though she took it nonchalantly I read excitement all over her. As she grabbed her coat she asked where they were going, managing to sound sweet and suggestive at the same time.

"Somewhere a little quieter," he told her in a voice that could only be described as enchanting.

And he had her just like that. I tossed back the rest of my drink and listened to her heels clicking on the floor as he led her away.

It wasn't my first time seeing one of those horrifying figures reel in some innocent person, yet a cold sorrow still seeped into my bones—does so even now, at Grove Lane, just at thinking about it. I don't actually know what the monsters do with people once they've gotten them alone, but they can't be of sound intent. I mean, that one was wearing *chains* instead of *clothes*.

My phone speaks up from where it sits in my lap to tell me someone's calling. I pick it up and see that it's Rafe. With a few too many angry punches of the button on the side of the phone, I silence the call.

So, yeah, as if that monster thing hadn't put enough of a damper on my mood last night, Rafe ended up being at Applebee's at the same time as me. Not a fun experience. He's probably calling me now to try to make me feel even worse about my reaction to seeing him. Or maybe he's calling to apologize. I have no intention of finding out why he's calling, though. If somehow he hadn't worn out his welcome with me the night of my car accident, he certainly wore it out last night.

I'd gotten started on a new drink at the bar when someone popped up beside me and said enthusiastically, "Hey, Mari!"

I almost choked on the drink—heart jumped into my throat and everything. I snapped my gaze toward the voice and instantly recognized its owner as Rafe.

I'd rather have seen *anyone else* standing next to my barstool.

Not a joke. I wished that instead of him I'd been face-to-face with that kid I used to babysit who declared his love for me on his fourteenth birthday and showed me the website he'd made in my honor, complete with pictures he'd taken and poems he'd written. He came to my house a week later while I was out with my friends and told my mom he had a late nineteenth-birthday gift for me. He ended up going into my room, hanging a huge '*I LOVE YOU*' sign on my wall, and stealing a pair of my panties.

Yeah, I suspected I'd find *his* company more pleasant than Rafe's.

Rafe, Betrayer of Hearts, Fucker of Best Friends.

He clearly found our encounter delightful, though, and said, "What's up? It's so good to see you!"

And it was funny to hear that since he lives a whopping arm's length away from me, in the apartment above the one I share with Claire. Or maybe it wasn't funny. Maybe it made sense given that I haven't seen much of him, or anyone, in months.

No, maybe what was *funny* was him acting like he's not part of the reason no one sees me anymore. It was funny that he'd dare to smile at me as if I never caught him having sex with Audrey in my bed while he and I were dating. It was funny that if only that hadn't happened, I wouldn't have witnessed it, wouldn't have stormed out of my own party, wouldn't have ended up driving the car that I wrecked just a short half-hour later, and wouldn't be the Marienne Rose Connor of the Now Times.

(A loner who inexplicably sees monsters in the places of random men.)

In fact, it was *hilarious* that Rafe was acting like nothing is very different when everything is—especially me.

But I didn't say that stuff to him because I didn't want to chat. So at my leisure I shrugged a shoulder and told the biggest lie of my life: "Not much."

He laughed and it was infuriating. "Not much, huh?" he echoed playfully. "Surely *something's* going on with you? Thinking of getting a haircut? Seen any good movies lately?"

"No," I said tonelessly.

"Well, that's exciting." He gave me the smile I used to love. I wanted to slap it off his face.

I suppose it's not hard to see why I liked him, though. He's a year younger than me, even down to the exact day, and something about me being slightly older but him being more attractive was just too interesting. He's more outgoing, more daring and more entertaining than me. Before that party he always knew just what to say to make me smile. He's also got eyes the likes of which I've never seen anywhere else in my life: they're a clear aquamarine color, and they offer a stunning contrast to his brown hair and tan skin. I always felt like the winner of the lottery when those eyes gazed into my less-interesting ones.

The gazing was going on at that particular moment, actually, but I didn't feel like a winner at all. I felt like a girl teetering on the wire between careful impassiveness and knocking the shit out of one poor bastard.

Rafe was oblivious. "So, do you want some company? My cousins aren't here yet. Or is someone on their way to you?"

I somehow managed not to laugh out loud at the idea of someone meeting up with me; my days of extracurricular socializing are over. Since the accident I've been keeping to the apartment complex and Grove Lane. The only reason I was out is because I went to Applebee's for a drink two Tuesdays ago and nothing awful happened, so I went back. I mean, one thing did happen: I realized alcohol doesn't treat me the way it used to. That was one hell of a shock, and a disappointment, really. But I figured out after a while what alcohol *does* do: it makes those awful monster men fade away. And I decided that's good enough for me.

It didn't mean I wanted anyone's company, though. Just because Rafe ran into me didn't mean I wanted to hang out. I've spotted Audrey twice recently, but that didn't inspire me to rekindle our friendship. So when I told him no one was joining me, I was trying to convey to him my interest in just keeping to myself.

But he told me, "Well, I'll sit with you for a minute." He got into the chair the blonde girl was in before and nodded at the bartender in his dude greeting way. Then he looked at me again. "So you're just out by yourself?"

Did I or did I not just say that? I thought crossly.

"We haven't seen you around. It's been a while since you've really done anything, right?"

Yep, because fuck you guys.

After another second he repeated, "Right?"

I just pulled the sleeves of my hoodie down over my hands and crossed my arms.

"So, what's the occasion tonight?" he pressed.

Finally I grumbled, "There's not one."

"Well, how's Claire?"

The talkative fuck wouldn't give it a rest.

"She still going out with that jackass who drives the yellow Corvette?"

I didn't answer him, but just the mention of Shaun—who, in fact, my sister was out with and who I still haven't even met to this day—made me roll my eyes, and Rafe noticed and laughed.

"Oh, Jesus! I've seen Claire go out with a bunch of different guys over the years, and out of all of them, that one is seriously the biggest waste of her time. I *swear* to that." He pressed a hand against his heart.

I didn't reply to that, either. I just turned my stare to my drink. With each passing second it grew more and more obvious that he wanted to act like there's no rift between us. He was joking around and acting adorable as usual, but I couldn't pretend for even two seconds that things haven't changed. I didn't want to talk about my sister or her date or *anything* with him.

"...guy wears sunglasses when it's dark outside," he was saying to an uninterested me. "He's worse than that guy with the 'rock band.'" I could hear the air-quotation-marks. God, he was trying so hard to charm me. And honestly, I wished I could fall for it. I wished I wasn't too angry and hurt to give him another chance.

But the truth is that the thing with Audrey hasn't been the only thing holding me back. I simply can't explain what's been going on with me. I can't say I've been seeing horrible creatures lurking around, that I can't get drunk anymore for some reason, that I dissect jokes normal people nonchalantly make about dying and wish I could just scream at them because it isn't funny. My only option has been to step back from the life I used to lead. Being alone hasn't been fun, but continuing on as usual would be impossible. On top of having to deal with my grief around a bunch of people who wouldn't get it, I think I'd eventually be tempted to bring up the fascinating new changes in my life. And...just no. There's no way. Alone is the way to go.

Rafe didn't catch on to my disinterest. "Do you remember him? The guy with the purple hair?" he asked. Then he laughed. "Wait, that's not right. He told us the color of his hair was *byzantium,* not *purple.*"

He sounded so much like his usual self that I felt like throwing up.

When he finally realized I wasn't amused at all, he turned imploring. "Come on, Mari. Smile. I've missed your smile."

"I bet."

My response rolled right off him. "Come hang out with us tonight. I can't just wander off and leave you by yourself once everyone gets here."

"Don't worry about me."

"Aw, come on. You don't really wanna sit here alone."

"I'm fine with being alone, Rafe."

"Oh, give me a break," he complained. "You're here and I'm here and no matter what you say, sitting by yourself isn't *fun.* Besides, your sister isn't home yet...."

"She could be." Not like it mattered, since Claire and I are on really bad terms. Needing to think about something else, I tried to give my thoughts over to the colorful bottles of liquor sitting behind the bar, but it didn't work worth a fuck. I could still hear him prattling on.

"She's not and we both know it. It's 9:30. That yellow Corvette guy isn't gonna let his only taker go home this early." By his tone I knew he was giving me his Don't Bullshit Me look, eyebrows lifted and everything. "You need to have some fun, so just hang out with us. You don't even have to talk to the guys if you don't want to. Just do it for me. Do it because I miss you. I mean, you haven't been the same since—since—"

I tensed up. I silently dared him to say I haven't been the same since the night I almost died and my parents *did*. To say I haven't been the same since I walked in on him and Audrey.

He didn't say those things. He didn't say shit.

Sad and incensed, I took a long, long drink of my rum and Coke.

Finally he told me, "Sorry."

I didn't know what to say, so I said nothing.

"I mean, I know it was a hard time for you—"

Ha.

"—it's in the past, so don't push people away. You need people. You need your friends. You need to talk to me again so we can work this whole thing out."

Before I could think of something to say that wasn't downright hateful, some guy yelled, "Yo, Rafe!"

It turned out to be Jeff, one of his cousins. I rolled my eyes at the muscle shirt he had on, because seriously, it's not June. It's the second week of October and the weather this year has been on the cold side already.

"What's up?" Rafe greeted him. They said a few guy things that I didn't care about whatsoever.

I was just getting back into my drink when Rafe touched a hand to my arm.

I glared at him and spat out, "What?"

"Hey, the guys got a table," he said as casually as he'd said everything else. "Are you gonna come chill with us?"

"No."

"I really wish you would."

"I can't."

"Of course you can."

"I *don't want to.*"

"Why not?"

I didn't deign to respond to that.

He interpreted my silence as me not having a good answer. "Okay, if you don't wanna hang out tonight, tell me when would be good for you. Tell me and then I'll be on my way."

I stared at him, growing more and more pissed off by the second. I was thinking, *What is this? He's not going to leave until I agree to hang out with him? That's ridiculous. I have the right to decline such an invitation after what he did.*

He stared back at me, looking resolute. "What do you think?"

"I think you should wander away and forget you ever saw me."

He chuckled because, haha, apparently I'm funny when I'm trying to threaten people. "Come on, I can't do that."

"Oh, it's not hard. I mean, walking got you over here, right? I guess you just forgot how it works. Let's go over it. Step One: turn your body in that direction." I pointed away from the bar.

"I don't—"

"Step Two," I cut him off, "is to put one foot forward and then put the other in front of it."

"There's no need to—"

"This helping you out any? It's a really simple process. You just keep putting one foot in front of the other until you find yourself in a place that doesn't have me in it. Bam, there you go—you've wandered away."

His eyebrows went up and under them his gaze was dark, finally void of the stupid playfulness. "Okay, why *the hell* are you doing this?"

I turned away from him. "I don't have time to explain your fuck-ups to you, Rafe."

Silence fell for a whole five seconds, and then he laughed. The sound was way off from its usual cheerfulness. After I got an earful of the weird laughter I heard, "Oh, I get it. I see what this is about."

It was about damn time.

"Why don't you tell me what I have to do to get you to stop feeling sorry for yourself?"

His words hit the air and hung there, unexpected and absurd, between us. They rendered me speechless. When I recovered I took a slow breath and then looked at him, my own eyes feeling dark. "I don't feel sorry for myself."

"Bullshit. You haven't done anything for two months but sit in the corner like an emo kid who lost her favorite black eyeliner."

My hand went up in a Stop Right There, Moron way. "You literally have *no idea* what you're talking about."

He turned incredulous. "Yes, I do! Look at you!"

He went on to complain about how I didn't care that that was the first time he'd seen me in forever. How unfair it was for me not to want to talk to him or even smile at him. How he guessed wallowing in self-pity is all I want to do anymore. Standard stuff.

But then he said, "People get cheated on and people die, okay? You're not the most victimized person in the world, and you acting like you are doesn't do anything but make you look like a pathetic fucking bitch."

And for the first time ever, I punched someone.

And then I got kicked out of Applebee's, which felt sadder to me than the fact that I'd just assaulted someone who used to be so important to me.

So, really, I guess Rafe is crazy for still trying to talk to me. If someone hit *me* in the face, I'd take extra special care to stay out of their life from that moment on. Indeed, as if he knows I'm thinking about how stupid he must be, he calls again. And I silence it again. Why the fuck would I want to talk to him after all that?

I spin around in the tire swing as a cold autumn breeze rustles the leaves of this giant tree. I let the stormy air move my hair around and send a chill down my spine. Despite Rafe polluting my thoughts, this moment is beautiful. I wish it didn't have to end.

But then lightning flashes and I know the moment has to end, like, now. The sun will be setting before long and I don't want to be caught outside in a storm when it does. So I drag my Too Old But Can't Be Trashed Because They Were A Gift From Mama And I Miss Her sneakers through the dull dirt and stop the swing. I extract myself from it with a sigh.

I trudge across the wide yard toward the blackened home it belongs (belonged?) to. Most of the privacy fence around the place is still standing, but it's open in a few spots and I leave through one such spot. Then I'm in the driveway, then next to the broken-down mailbox, then on my way down the road, making next to no noise as I walk in the direction of home.

Fayetteville is a lively city, so I find it odd that no one has gotten around to doing something with Grove Lane. I mean, really, it can't be that hard to clean up—everything was either burned to the ground or exists now in a very sad, very precarious fashion. Seems like it'd take no time at all to wipe my charred sanctuary off the map and put something else in its place. And it's not like I haven't heard people call what's left of this neighborhood things like *'depressing'* and *'dangerous'* and *'ugly.'*

I disagree wholeheartedly, of course, and I hope they leave this place here until the day *I* burn out.

When I reach the end of Grove Lane, I turn right onto Blossombranch Lane. It's an older, barely more populated residential area that doesn't give off quite the same vibe as the burned-down street does, though half of the houses within view are obviously uninhabited. The others are little homes to elderly people who never found the will to move after the gang attack. I'm thinking that the people who did move either had children to protect from more violence/keep from playing in a *'dangerous'* area, or they just didn't want to live so close to the ugly-fied Grove Lane.

In any case, this street is always quiet, always closed up. It offers me the chance to bid Grove Lane one last uninterrupted farewell until the next time I trot down this way.

So when I make it around the curve in the road after a few minutes, I'm startled to see there's a disturbance taking place on the faded asphalt not far from me.

And I go from being startled to being What In God's Name? surprised when I see one of the people involved is *glowing*.

Like really, seriously, swathed-in-gold, bright-like-the-sun glowing.

And then I'm five-feet-five-inches worth of horror when I see that the people fighting with the glowing person are not *people* at all. They're two of those monsters.

Yes, there are *two monsters* fighting *one glowing person* in the middle of this half-empty, half-old-people neighborhood.

And you know what? The glowing person is winning.

I practically fly toward the nearest tree so I can observe without being seen, because this is something I *have* to observe.

The glowing person moves with grace, with deadly precision. I quickly deduce that it must be a man. He's not as looming or burly as his enemies, but he looks taller than me and he's noticeably strong. And good God, is he fast. One second he's on his feet, fists shooting out at one monster, and in the next second he's crouched low, swinging a leg out under the other monster as it stands up from his most recent trip to the ground. Then the man is up again, stepping wide over his fallen opponent, pivoting back to the one still standing, sending a foot up to deliver a powerful kick to his face that knocks him down to the gray road, too.

My eyes widen and I gasp out loud, totally awed.

And somehow, the glowing man hears me.

I don't have time to duck back behind the tree before he looks my way, so I see it when he sees me—I see how his stance changes and gives away that surprise has taken the place of combat-readiness. I see it when, as the man stares toward me, the first monster to hit the ground finally gets to his feet and leaps onto his back. I see it when something luminous and slender falls from the man's form and clatters loudly onto the asphalt, and when he bends hastily to retrieve it. And when he is interrupted by the monster he kicked in the face angrily kicking the item.

Toward me.

The gleaming silver thing spins across the ground in shrieking circles *toward me* until it collides with the curb only feet away. I forget how to breathe as I jerk my gaze from the thing to the monsters, who I know are running toward me, livid and terrifying and murderous—

—except that they're taking the glowing man down to the ground, not sparing a single glance for me.

My eyes manage to widen even more.

They don't know I'm here.

They don't fucking know I'm here! The only person who saw me is the glowing man, who....

I watch the monsters tear at him. He's still moving, still fighting, but the odds have switched from somehow being in his favor to being really, really against him. As I watch, his opponents cover him with their horrible bodies and he disappears from my sight. He lets out a yell.

Holy fuck, he's going to die.

They're going to kill him because I distracted him.

Oh my God, no. No.

My mind doesn't catch up with what my body is doing until I'm halfway to the group, the silver object in my right hand. But that doesn't mean my mind isn't *working*. Indeed, it realized at one point or another that the object is a dagger, and that my hand needs to go around the handle like this, and that the blade needs to be angled in this way, and that the monster with his back to me has given me quite the opening.

I put all of my weight behind the dagger and drive it straight between his shoulder blades.

And I feel like the exact opposite of a pathetic fucking bitch.

2
Gabe

My rash decision to attack two Hellions alone has caught up to me. I'm about to die.

I find myself nearing the cold hands of death for the second time in my life, and the odds of me escaping them this time are infinitesimal. The Lightforce is about to lose the only Gatherer they have left in this area. Beatrix and Wes are about to lose the younger brother they never had.

And all I can really feel is embarrassment. All I can think about is the fact that a new Light person is watching all of this from just down the road, probably having no idea *what* he's even watching because I'm fighting a losing battle against a couple of Hellions instead of doing Gatherer things that don't involve fighting whatsoever.

A horrible scream erupts from the Hellion with his knees on my ribcage, surprising the hell out of me and damn near deafening me.

I'm confused as fuck as he staggers up and away from me, still screaming. The other Hellion moves his rock-hard forearm off my throat to back away, too, and when his comrade falls silent and starts crumbling, my confusion escalates. I know what a dying Hellion looks like, but I didn't do anything to fatally wound that one.

Then I tune in to a higher-pitched cry piercing the air and the person it belongs to swings out from behind the collapsing Hellion, glowing bright like a white-hot summer sun, my dagger in hand.

In...*her*...hand.

Oh my God. My very cells are jolted with my surprise. *That's the Light person I just saw, and it's not a guy. It's a girl. That is a* girl.

For a second I think my mind is going to explode.

It doesn't, of course. So I force myself to look away from her so I can see what the Hellion that isn't disintegrating into the stormy air is doing. He seems caught between going for me where I still lay on the ground and going for her, the nonthreatening-looking girl who just took down his cohort.

That brief uncertainty is his downfall.

When his numerous spider-like eyes turn toward me, the girl flings a surprisingly fierce kick at one of his shins. He wobbles from the unexpectedness of it. I throw my hands out and grab his ankles and jerk his feet out from under him, bringing him down to the ground with me.

Understanding that he's no longer on the winning side visibly crashes into him and fear takes over, transforms him into a frailer being. A jagged howl leaves him and he twists onto his stomach. He claws desperately at the asphalt despite the hold I've still got on his ankles, trying to get away because he knows what's coming.

I know what's coming, too, but I'm still goddamn astounded when the girl with the bright white Radiance of a Light person who's never been around others of their kind throws herself onto the Hellion's back and, with both hands, sinks my dagger into his putrid flesh.

He falls silent, goes still. She must have pierced his heart—and the first one's, too—because within seconds he turns from one solid being into chunks and flakes and ashes. He dies.

The girl drops my dagger. She skitters away from the Hellion's remains, sucking in air over and over and over as she stares at them, her pale face tinged with pink. And then she turns her gaze on me, light blue eyes sparking with intensity. I feel like it's the first time anyone has ever looked at me.

I stare at her.

She stares at me.

I stare at her.

She stares at me.

Neither of us says anything.

I'm so stunned that I *can't* say anything.

In all the years I've been working as a Gatherer, seeking out people like me who can detect Hellions after nearly dying, I've only found two new Light people whose age was within ten years of mine. Neither were females. I've found three new Light females, period—two didn't even believe me about the Lightforce, and the third is Beatrix.

And here I'm looking at a girl who has to be close to my age *and is still Light.* And she just jumped into my fight with two Hellions and took down both of them.

And she's fucking beautiful. *Oh,* she's beautiful.

Briefly I wonder if I got hit in the head during the fight and am either hallucinating or dead right now. But no. My mind never would have been able to dream up something like this.

I still can't figure out what the hell to say. Apparently, neither can she; all she does is return my fascinated look.

Thunder cracks around us and we both jump. And suddenly her eyes are bright with shock, not fascination. Shock and panic.

And then she's up and tearing away from me, long black hair flying wildly behind her.

"Hey—no! No, don't!" I exclaim, my voice returning to me all too late. "Don't run away! *Stop!*"

She ignores me.

But I'm very fast. The only way this girl is going to get away is if I want her to, and I don't. She has no hope of escaping me before I figure out how to ask her each and every one of the questions pounding riotously against my brain. *'What's your name?' 'How old are you?' 'How are you obviously a new Light person and yet so unafraid of Hellions?' 'Have you fought them before?' 'Are you seriously real?'*

Except that in the middle of flinging myself up onto my feet, a sharp pain spikes up my back and makes me shout out. I drop back to the ground, teeth gritted, remembering pretty abruptly that I sustained a few injuries during the fight—injuries that don't approve of me moving so quickly.

And just like that, the girl is gone.

Except fuck that.

I dig my phone out of my pocket. It appears to have somehow escaped the fight unscathed. I dial Beatrix's number and, very slowly, try to sit up so I can get out of the damn road.

When she picks up and says, "Hi, Gabe," her tone is way less cheerful than it usually is. I understand why almost immediately, but I quickly shove the knowledge into a dark corner of my mind. I don't want to think about it, especially not right now.

Panting against the rush of excitement in me and the throbbing in my back, I say, "B, holy shit."

"What?"

Upon swiping my dagger off the ground, pain zips through my body. My thoughts twist wildly around one another, and I groan as I stash the weapon in my jacket.

"What is it?" she asks quickly. "Are you okay?"

"I'm fine."

A little sharply, "Well, what was that greeting about?"

"I—hold on—" I manage to get on my feet, but my body screams in protest. For a moment I think I'm going to fall back down. Then I spot my Civic waiting a few houses down where I parked it earlier, and I tell my body we're done with the ground. "Where are you?" I ask as I head to the car.

"Driving to the Sanctum."

"*Where* are you, though? I've got to know where you are exactly. I really need your help. Something's—something's happened."

"Gabe," she says loudly, "I *just* asked if you're okay! Jesus, boy!" She sounds the way a real older sister might sound when her younger brother has done something stupid.

"It's not like I'm in pain or anything," I hear myself say defensively, and then I frown. "Okay, well, I'm in pain, but that's not the—"

"Oh my fu—"

"Just get over here and help me find her!" I cut her off. *God, could my car feel any farther away?*

A moment of silence. Then, "Who?"

"This girl I just found! She literally saved my life and then took off running and I was going to chase after her but I'm too—"

"You found a girl?" I hear her real question: *'You found a Light girl?'* Before I can answer either question she tacks on another one. "Okay, where are *you?*"

"Blossombranch Lane, right by that neighborhood that burned down."

I hear her tires squealing on the other end of the line. "What a coincidence. I'm about a minute from there."

I don't realize my chest is tight with tension until it loosens a little. "Awesome. Just drive up and down these streets around here and see if you can spot her. She's lit up like a star."

"And if I spot her, indeed?"

"I don't know, just—" My free hand jumps up to flatten against my hair. "Remember when you told me you saw Wes for the first time and just *knew* he was someone you wanted to be around?"

Beatrix is quiet and I know she's reliving that very moment, when she first met her husband. Then she laughs a little. "I remember."

"That's what I'm dealing with here, so if you find her, act accordingly."

She says, "Understood, darling. I'll call you back soon."

We hang up. I'm finally at my car, so I get in as fast as I can and start it. I've taken off even before my music starts back up from where I left it.

↶

My phone says it was 6:09 this evening when I first called Beatrix. It's currently 11:30 and I've only just now hobbled into my house. She and I spent every minute we had between 6:09 and now—what is actually 11:31, according to the clock on my microwave—looking for that girl's Radiance.

We never found it.

Disappointment lays like a stone pillar across my shoulders, cold and dense and heavy.

I've never seen anyone like her before, and I've been Light for eight years. I've been a Gatherer for seven. I've traveled all over Arkansas, and to Texas and Louisiana and Oklahoma. She's one of a kind.

And I don't just mean that I've never seen a Light girl close to my age before, even though, again, that is true. I also mean that I've never seen *any* new Light people attack a Hellion like she did.

Two Hellions. She got her hands on my weapon and then ambushed *two* Hellions.

And killed them.

And saved me.

I would do anything to be able to see her again.

Sad as it is to admit, though, if I do see her again it won't be tonight.

I realized at some point or another just how banged up I am from that fight. I'm not bleeding anywhere (the Hellions would've ditched me and bolted the millisecond they saw my blood, since that's what harms them) but I'm dirty and bruised pretty deep in some places. I desperately need to lie down, but first I need to get cleaned up. I'll probably fall out completely if I try to stand up long enough for a shower, so even though I'm not really a bath person, I run a hot one and sink into it. If my back could talk, it'd thank me.

I sit in the steaming water for so long that my thoughts eventually drift away from my wounds and the Hellions and the girl. It's not much of a relief, because they drift into much more painful territory.

Em.

The hot water does nothing for the ache that fills my chest.

Em's dead. The thought is somehow both dull and loud in my head.

Johnta Emilia, more commonly known as Em, was my Gathering mentor and the only other Gatherer working in Fayetteville besides me. He was the one who found me when I was sixteen, shortly after I turned Light. He was a tall, strong, smart African American man who was even better at Defender work than me. Like me, though, he had chosen to be a Gatherer. And in the years I'd known him, I'd never seen him falter.

The news of his death came as a shock to me, like the ground had fallen out from under my feet. I heard about it this afternoon. He died at the hands of Hellions somewhere in Dallas, Texas, but that's all I was told. That's all the Director of our Lightforce branch, Nick Grayhem, even knew.

I was summoned to the Sanctum after I got the unanticipated phone call because Grayhem wanted to talk in person. Once I got to his office he said, "I'd like to tell you what happened to Em, Gabe. Survivors should know these kinds of things. But we—we still don't quite *know* what happened. All we've got is evidence of Hellion involvement, and there's not even very much of that evidence." His mouth pressed into a thin line and his entire body seemed to sag. "There's just not much left of *Em.*"

That last sentence was the catalyst for me picking the fight with the two Hellions I saw on Blossombranch. It was all I could think about as I parked my car and snuck down the lonely road toward them. It was all I could think about as I made my first move, and then let the rage overtake me.

My back aches now as I think about the fight. It aches and pretend-says, *'Hey, thanks for trying to soothe me with this lava pool of a bath, but I think the bed is calling me.'*

I don't have it in me to argue.

Even after I lay down, though, I spend a long time trying to come to terms with Em's passing. I am wildly unsuccessful, of course. The failure both saddens me further and pisses me off, but that's the way it is. Grief doesn't just disappear, no matter how badly a person wants it to. Grief likes to stick around, cling to organs, trickle into thoughts like a noxious gas.

I turn to lay on my right side even though my back disagrees with me, and I see the time is 3:24 in the morning. Wonderful. Thunder seems to shake everything, even my bones, and makes me feel even more unsettled.

Em won't ever get to see storm clouds again. And the next time it snows, he won't be here to complain about the way other people drive. When I turn twenty-five, he won't be here to tease me about being a quarter of a century old. If I ever find that girl from earlier, I won't be able to share my excitement with him—or if I never find her, go to him for advice on how not to feel like total shit about it.

Here one second, gone the next.

Both of them.

∽

Even though Gatherer life isn't terribly exciting, I truly love my job. On those occasions when a new Light person accepts my invitation to join the Lightforce, I think I have the best job in the world. There's just something fulfilling about offering fellowship to people who've been thinking they no longer fit into society. There's something remarkable about seeing people who've been stumbling around, confused and scared, find that there is a whole new life waiting just for them. I may enjoy killing Hellions, may be skilled at it even after all these years of putting Defender work on the back burner (I hardly ever just fly off the handle like I did on Blossombranch), but Gathering…. Well, just as some people claim that being a parent is their calling, or being a teacher or a doctor, I think being a Gatherer is what I was always meant to do, even before I knew what the hell a Gatherer was.

But the next forty-eight-plus hours are total bullshit.

For one thing, I haven't found any new Light people since I found that girl—well, okay, since *she* found *me*. It's hardly a surprise, though, since Light people are so rare; I returned from my three-week-long traveling shift some days ago and she was the first person I'd spotted with white Radiance since before I even left Fayetteville. Still, with each hour that's passed without me so much as glimpsing a new Light person, I've grown more and more annoyed. For a minute I consider asking Grayhem to send me back out of town to search for white Radiances in another city. It wouldn't be that wild of a request, since all Gatherers are asked to spend a few weeks out of town every now and then specifically for a change of scenery. I just got back from mine, but Grayhem might not refuse me. He might let me go.

I don't ask him, though, because I know I don't actually want to be in a city that doesn't have that girl in it. And the fact is that it's my turn to be here, not somewhere else. Fayetteville needs me to stick around, unbeknownst to its inhabitants. I know the only thing I really want is to run away from Em's death, but as painful as it is...well, I just can't.

It's like a ripple was born from it. There's the thing at the center that sparked it all off—the raindrop on the placid surface of a pond, the unexpected death of my friend—and then other things spread out from that. Em died and he was my friend, and it hurt. He was also my only Gathering coworker, so I am now responsible for figuring out how to handle his part of our job. But he wasn't just my coworker—he was my superior, so now I'm in charge of things he was in charge of in that respect.

At least, that's the plan Grayhem told me about the other day when I met him at the Sanctum. And going along with it will only further confirm that Em is, in fact, gone for good.

After Grayhem offered me his condolences about Em, he said, "I have an offer for you."

"An offer?" I repeated.

"You and Em were the only Gatherers in the area. Three is the standard for a zone the size of ours—you know out in California and up in New York they've got as many as five or six in a zone like this—but you and Em were my best, so I didn't need a third." He held up his hands. "And now I've only got one guy and I'm looking at him."

"So," I deduced, "you need more Gatherers."

"I do, and my offer is this: decide on two Defenders to offer positions to and start considering yourself a superior, because—and I don't mean this flippantly, Gabe—you're the new Em."

What a thing to hear just an hour after receiving the news.

The words inspired in me a terrible mixture of sadness and responsibility. I told him, "Of course." Then, as an afterthought, "Thank you."

"You can handle it, can't you?"

"I can."

He wanted to know if I had any ideas on who I'd like to offer the positions to. I wasn't really sure why he asked, given that I'd had a whole ten seconds to think about it. But I kept that thought to myself and told him I didn't know, that I'd need some time to figure it out.

He seemed to understand. He knows Gathering can get slow for me, so I'm not in a huge rush, and he knows choosing new Gatherers shouldn't be taken too lightly. After all, they're the first representatives of the Lightforce that new Light people encounter. Can't pick just anyone for that kind of thing.

In any other situation I'd have had my shit together in a matter of hours. This time it took me two days to make up my mind. I won't lie: I put the thoughts at the back of my mind for as long as I could because lining them out equaled taking steps forward. And I didn't want to do that; I don't want to be *'the new Em.'* Not yet. Not like this.

But at last the lull in Gathering plus my reminiscing about my late mentor became too much for me. I decided to put my big boy pants on and do what needed to be done, even if it made me want to throw up at times. I made my choices and called both men to extend the offer to them. It wasn't too big of a hassle, since both accepted.

Phillip Janssen has been in the Lightforce almost as long as I have. He's in his fifties now, and it took me four years to figure out why I like him so much: he's a father figure. Of course, it was obvious from the start that he's a good man—likable, trustworthy, all that. He simply waited four years to tell any of us what the reason had been for his turning Light, and then it all made sense.

Janssen touched hearts like he did because he'd been the jubilant, affectionate father of triplets: three girls who all had the same bright blue eyes as their mother, his wife, the woman he'd loved since he was seventeen. He'd been a police officer before the shooting that killed all four of his girls and nearly fatally wounded him. Needless to say, once I found him and explained being Light to him, he was on board for helping destroy Hellions. And as it turned out, the guy who'd killed his family had been one such monster; he was discovered and killed by Janssen himself a year after the tragedy, which I think gave the man a lot of closure. Since then he has been both a strong Defender and a warm friend, someone who might sit you down with a bowl of homemade chili to give you advice on life just as naturally as he can stab a Hellion in the heart.

I think Janssen being one of the people who ease others into our lifestyle will be invaluable. He has a way of looking at you like he knows your thoughts and a way of talking to you that makes you feel like he knows exactly where you're coming from. And, really, I think it's so effective because he *does* understand. He knows both how high into the heavens you can fly on joy alone and how far into the depths of hell pain and anger can drag you.

The second man I've decided on is Alexander Wright. He's only been in the Lightforce for about two years and he's a fine Defender, but I think he will serve the Lightforce better as a Gatherer. He's a very serious ex-military man in his sixties, and he is unusual in that he seemingly has no sense of humor. His intentions are always made plain, thus he is clearly not a bullshitter. He wouldn't pull one over on someone to save his life, I don't think, and that could be useful for my line of work. People tend to think Radiance and Hellions and even me, though I'm obviously tangible, are a joke. It's my theory that one talk with Wright will turn an amused skeptic into an earnest believer in sixty seconds.

So it's late on Saturday night now, and I've been sitting at my tiny dining table for a while writing down key points and pieces of advice for Janssen and Wright. They're not really starting from the bottom rung of the Lightforce, but there are some pretty distinct differences between Gatherer life and Defender life. Case in point: my job, first and foremost, is to seek out Light people and propose they join the Lightforce. Only after that do I get to even *think* about getting sideways with a Hellion. Of course, the other day was different, but whatever.

That essential fact is the last thing I jot down: *'I remember making the transition from Defender to Gatherer a year after I joined the Lightforce. I know it will be a wild change for the two of you. However, the bottom line for a Gatherer is this: new Light people come first and Hellions come second. Always.'*

And then I think about that girl again. I've driven back to Blossombranch Lane several times since Beatrix and I searched around there Wednesday night, but never spotted her. It's only added to the pain and frustration already plaguing me.

If only I'd used my head and taken my own advice—if only I'd remembered that day that I'm a Gatherer, not a Defender, and had been doing my job instead of picking fights, I wouldn't have put myself through all of that. Wouldn't be sitting here now feeling like ass about glimpsing something so amazing and then watching it vanish, unable to do anything but beg it not to go.

But I wouldn't take it back even if I had the chance.

So before I lay my pen on the table and go drop down on my bed, I add a note to that last point. *'(New Light people are of utmost importance. Finding them wherever they may be hiding is what we do because without them— without their talents and the strength they bring to our cause—the bad things in the world will eventually overpower us. So find them.)'*

ᘓ

"I have one more thing to ask you," Grayhem had said to me. "Em's funeral is happening soon. Is there anything you'd like to be a part of? Anything you want to say about him?"

The first thing to pop into my head was uncertainty that I'd be able to pull off anything like that. Then, like all the other people in the world who have lost someone they cared about, I realized I would regret not trying. So I told Grayhem I did want to say a few words at Em's funeral.

That was on Wednesday, before I left the Sanctum. The funeral had been scheduled for Sunday because there was no real rush to get Em's body taken care of. There really was damn near nothing left of it.

It's Sunday now.

My daily routine is pretty standard: shower, brush my teeth, put on clothes, and leave the house. Even though none of these things are very exciting, today it seems wrong to do them the way I always do. Seems wrong to step out into the freezing morning once it's time to go and think that the leaves drifting down are a nice color, even though Em would've thought they looked nice, too. Seems wrong to listen to music on the way to the funeral home even though Em was also a music lover and I desperately want to think about something besides where I'm going.

When I arrive at the funeral home Beatrix and Wes are standing outside waiting for me, just like they said they'd be. It's a satisfying sight. It reminds me that not all of my friends are gone.

I get a rare hug and handshake from them when I walk up. It's appreciated but odd, because even though we're friends—more like the siblings none of us had in our previous lives—we never touch each other. Well, *they* touch each other because they're happily married, but I keep to myself. At some point in the past several years I got used to the fact that I don't have the social life of a regular twenty-four-year-old guy, and thus have no reason to touch people. So now it's kind of weird. And even though today's the day for comfort, I pull away from Beatrix and Wes after only a moment, hoping I don't seem rude at a time like this.

She says, "Hi, babydoll," her voice a little hoarse, and I know she doesn't think me rude. The cold wind blows her blonde-and-teal ponytail around, and she snuggles closer to Wes. "Doing okay?"

"I'm as okay as I can be," I tell her. "How are you guys?"

Wes runs the tattooed hand he doesn't have on Beatrix's waist through his short blonde hair. "Same. These things happen, but...damn...." He shakes his head. "Never thought we'd send Em off like this. Thought for sure he'd die at about ninety-nine."

Beatrix and I can only nod. I'd like to think I'd have been more prepared for this if Em had died sixty years from now. No sense in that kind of thinking, though, I don't suppose.

I draw a deep breath and let it out slowly. A thick white puff forms in the air in front of my face. "I guess we should go."

"Guess so," Wes agrees solemnly. He opens the door for his wife, and we follow her in.

I've been to a few Light funerals over the years. They're not any different from normal funerals, except that the attendees usually don't number the same. This one doesn't feel the way the others felt; it feels more stifling, more discomfiting. I guess it's because it's for Em, not for a Light person who'd died a month after I met them.

Things go quickly. Too quickly. Before I know it, the time has come for people to take their seats so things can get started. Then it's time for Grayhem to speak, and even though his speech is pretty long and detailed, it speeds by. Then two other authority figures in our branch—one of whom is Wes, who's in charge of Defender training—go up there and say what they want to say. And then it's my turn, and I feel like I *just* sat down in the pew.

It seems to take only one second for me to walk from my place in the second row to the front of the small gathering of Light people. Then my paper is out of my pocket, then somehow unfolded in front of me, and then the words to the John Donne poem fall out of my mouth.

"*'Death, be not proud, though some have called thee mighty and dreadful, for thou art not so; for those whom thou think'st thou dost overthrow die not....'*"

My voice echoes, faintly wobbly, around the room. If there are other noises being made—sniffles, sobs, sounds of agreement—I don't hear them. I read the poem, thinking Em would've liked it because he believed in leaving this world and going somewhere better. I never knew where he might end up going, or if *he* even had an idea of where he might go, but I know he wanted to go somewhere.

"*'One short sleep past, we wake eternally, and death shall be no more; death, thou shalt die.'*"

The poem is over. My turn to speak is over.

I turn to glance behind me at the closed casket. I think, *You're not out of mind, Em. Just out of sight.* And then I go back to my pew.

Only when a sniffling Beatrix hands me a tissue do I notice there are tears building in my own eyes. I think it's first time I've come close to crying since my mom died back when I turned Light.

It's not until later, though, when we're all watching Em's casket being lowered into the silent and uninviting ground that any of us really let any tears fall. Awful as the whole thing is, I feel a little closer to my comrades than I did before. Beatrix is the only female in attendance because she's the only female in the Lightforce for many towns around, so the rest of us are men. And even though no one likes to see a grown man cry, there's something strengthening about all of us doing it.

It truly is only during the hard times that you find out who your real friends are. And that revelation is the first thing to make me feel the least bit okay about life continuing on after we leave here.

After the ceremony a simple brunch is held at The Room, the club Grayhem owns underneath which the Sanctum sprawls in secret. It's a quiet event, but there are smiles here and there—people seem to have come to the same realization I did about being in this together. I hear a few people discussing Em and the funny things he used to say, and the old Beatles shirt he used to wear when he was having a bad day. At first I find actually being amused difficult, because this day sucks so much ass. But our memories of Em are good ones, and they *are* funny, and at one point someone brings up such a hilarious story that every person here laughs, including me.

Grayhem told us all at one point that we can have the rest of the day off if we want it. Some people like himself and Red from Armaments and Mark, our crippled receptionist, said they think they could use the easy time. Beatrix and Wes said they'd prefer going back out to work (we all knew they meant they'd prefer to go hunt down and annihilate some Hellions in Em's name). And Grayhem pulled me aside and told me the offer is for me, too, even though I'm the only trained Gatherer for the time being. But I'd already made up my mind: I need to try to find some new Light people. I need to make myself feel better by way of potentially making other people feel better.

"Call us if you need to," Beatrix tells me on our way to our vehicles. "Maybe we can get together for dinner."

"Yeah, man, I'd hate to see you sitting around alone tonight," Wes agrees.

"Dinner would probably be good," I say. "I'll talk to you guys later on."

Beatrix says, "Okay, sweetheart." Wes opens the passenger side door of his Jeep for her and she gets in. Then he and I nod at each other, and he gets behind the wheel. They're gone in moments.

Since *I* won't be killing any more Hellions in Em's name, I decide listening to the Beatles in his name will suffice. I turn the music on and leave the parking lot of The Room, too.

The first place I go in my quest to find new Light people is Blossombranch Lane. Call me crazy. Call me lame. These are things I've already thought about myself since the first-and-last time I saw the girl. The fact remains that she's someone I want to be around, just like I told

Beatrix—if not because she's the first girl to truly catch my attention in years, then because she's got some impressive raw talent when it comes to killing Hellions. I *cannot* pass up the chance to talk to her about the Lightforce, even if that chance seems ridiculously, laughably, sadly small.

The street, still as ever, has managed to feel lonelier than usual. There isn't even an animal in sight.

Yet another fruitless attempt.

I turn my car around in one of the sad driveways at the far end of the street, trying to decide if I want to go to the mall or possibly a park. As I maneuver slowly around a pothole in the road, I choose the latter option. I never know where I'll find a new Light person, and I think the air would do me some good.

In the brief silence between one Beatles song ending and the next beginning, I hear a faint yell from behind my car. Bewildered, I look in my rearview mirror to see who—

3
Marienne

He stomps on the brakes so fast that his tires squeal.

"Oh, thank God," I pant, slowing down. I'd been leaving Grove Lane when I saw his car and hadn't had enough time to hope he wasn't about to drive away when he started doing just that. So I ran after him as fast as I could, yelling and waving, desperate not to let him leave *again* without me talking to him.

Yeah, that's right. I know he's come down this way a few times since that one day. I've been hiding from him, though, too scared to say anything. Well, maybe not scared—maybe shy. I mean, I'd thrown myself headfirst into a tussle that looked downright perilous and didn't really involve me, then stared the guy down like my mom never taught me that staring is rude, then hauled ass away from him without so much as asking if he needed me to call an ambulance.

It'd taken me a few hours to calm down and convince myself I was still alive after all that. It took me many more hours to come to terms with the fact that I hadn't imagined him glowing—and God, what a sight that had been. All I could do was stare at him, at the details of the light that curved around his form and brushed against his clothes and skin. It was utterly divine. It was streaked with thin lines of molten gold around which glittering flecks seemed to swirl softly, like motes of dust in a beam of sunlight, only infinitely more beautiful. It was the most brilliant thing I've ever seen—and the most mystifying. It took me days to decide I want to talk to him about it.

The other times I'd watched him drive by from some hiding place or another, his glow had looked a little fainter than it'd been that first day. As he hurries over to me now, having practically leapt out of his car the second he was able, I see it's completely gone. Part of me is sad about it because the glow was so beautiful. Another part of me is glad he's apparently a normal enough guy not to be in a constant state of looking like he's on fucking fire.

And as he comes to a stop just feet from me, that latter part of me is also glad for the dimming because I'd kind of forgotten just how...how *right* this guy looks to me. Not having a golden glow taking up most of my attention does a lot to remind me. He's a good head taller than me, it looks like, and lean. His untidy hair is dark brown and where it isn't sticking up, it almost brushes his eyebrows. And under those eyebrows are green eyes that are openly staring at me.

I stare back, ignoring my manners yet again.

On that first day I saw him his outfit was plain but nice, except for how dirty and ripped-up it'd gotten during the thing with the monsters. It'd consisted of, like, jeans, a plain white shirt, a black stand-up-collar jacket and black shoes that may have been slip-on Vans. The clothes he has on now are different—all black and more sophisticated, like he's just come from somewhere important.

All this time I've been looking at him, he hasn't done anything but look back, appearing for all the world incapable of doing anything else. But I can't take any more silence. I have to say something.

It ends up being, "I'm so, *so* sorry that I almost got you killed that day."

He blinks a few times. Gazes at me some more. Says nothing.

"I know you're probably mad at me for that and I don't blame you at all. I'm pretty embarrassed about it because it was totally careless. I mean, I was just trying to hide over there and watch you kick some ass, but it was too cool and I've never seen anything like it—" I suck in a breath, still too winded from running and the excitement of seeing him to be babbling like this. I drape my arms over the top of my head to try and calm my pulse down.

After what feels like forever he tells me simply, "My name is Gabe."

A reluctant smile pulls at my lips. I like the way his voice sounds. "I'm Marienne."

He smiles, too. "I have a lot to talk to you about, Marienne."

And, my God, he pronounced my name correctly. (mary-ENNE.)

I nod, my breathing less labored. "I'm all ears."

"Great. Let me do something with my car." He gestures behind him to where his silver Civic chills in the middle of the road, driver's door open. For the first time I notice there's music coming from the speaker. Pretty sure it's "Come Together," and that's awesome.

I don't mention it, though. I just head over to the driveway of the nearest abandoned house while he goes to his car. He moves it to the curb in front of the house and I settle down on the cold stretch of concrete. When he rejoins me, he sits down an arm's length away from me.

"I accept your apology for the other day," he tells me, "but I definitely want to thank you for not letting me die after all."

A flush spreads across my skin just at the memory of me screaming like a wild woman.

He notices my embarrassment. "What's wrong?"

"I didn't know what the hell I was doing."

"I know you didn't. Or," he shrugs one shoulder, "I *figured* you didn't, I guess I should say."

"How's that?" I feel a little stung by his reply even though he was just agreeing with me. I guess some little tiny part of me had held out hope that I'd looked like a skilled badass and he'd been in awe of me like I'd been of him.

I should fuck off with that right now. Of course he knew I was flying by the seat of my pants. There's no way I looked as awesome as he did.

At length he speaks, but not to answer my question. "Was I glowing when you first saw me?"

Though not patronizing, the tone of his voice tells me he feels sure that he was. Mine goes a little bit quiet when I say, "Yeah, you looked like the sun."

He smiles a little. "Gold?"

I nod.

"Well, you were glowing, too."

My eyebrows go up. "Huh?"

"And you still are."

I turn my head to the side a little and cut him a look. He just said I'm *glowing*, didn't he? He did.

His smile grows.

"You kidding me, Gabe?" I ask.

His gaze drifts around me, like mine did with him that day. "No, I'm not kidding. I wouldn't—" he shakes his head, smile fading, "—I *couldn't* make that up. I promise you that."

How is that possible?

Okay, fine, it's possible. He *glows, doesn't he? Plus there are honest-to-God monsters roaming around. Glowing is not the weirdest thing I've ever heard of.*

Wonder what I look like to him.

"Am I gold, too?" I want to know.

He shakes his head again. "No, your Radiance is white, which means you haven't been around other Light people before. That's why I assumed you didn't really know how to fight Hellions. You're new to being Light."

I've never heard anyone say things like that before. Although I can deduce what Radiance is and what Hellions are, I'm a little lost on what he means by *'being Light.'*

But the way he says it...it's *easy.* Relaxed. Like it's a good thing and there's no reason to be afraid of it.

"Light?" I echo, my voice suddenly soft.

"Yes. That's what we are, you and me." He gestures between us, something brightening in his eyes. "And others, too."

I decide right here and now that whatever being Light is, if it's the answer to why I am what I am now, I'm on board with it. To hell with fearing it—I want to throw my arms around it and kiss it with gratitude. I've been hiding away, trying to ignore the unsettling differences in myself and in my life because I don't understand them. And I don't want to do it anymore if I don't have to.

"Okay," I say. "What does it mean?"

"Being Light is a rare state some people find themselves in after nearly dying."

Well, *there's* something I don't want to think about. Some of my buoyancy fades away. "Oh."

As if he can tell, his eyes turn more sympathetic. But he keeps talking and I appreciate it. "One of two things happens when people face death. They're either claimed by it or given more time in the living world, but some of the people who are given more time aren't the same after their encounter with death. We call them Light people because they gain Radiance and are granted the ability to detect Hellions." He straightens up some. "That's what we call the monsters you saw me fighting—the ones you killed. How long have you been seeing them?"

"Since the beginning of August," I say a little numbly.

He frowns. "That's quite a long time to go without someone finding you."

"Haven't exactly felt like taking the town by storm," I admit.

His expression is untroubled again, even a little bit amused. "That makes sense. Anyway, the Hellions are evil, I'm sure you've noticed. They harm humans and turn them away from decency. The worst kinds of people on Earth are Hellions in disguise, or strongly influenced by them. But they go unnoticed by people who haven't come in contact with death, or by people who have who simply returned to this world as normal as they ever were."

I wet my lips. "Okaaaay. So what determines who turns into a Light person, other than...the dying thing?"

"I don't know," he says, looking apologetic. "There are really only guesses regarding that. I'm pretty sure no

Light person is younger than fifteen, but other than that there doesn't seem to be anything specific connecting all of us." He narrows his eyes thoughtfully. "I've been Light since I was sixteen and a Gatherer since I was seventeen, and I've located people of various—"

"How old are you now?" falls out of my mouth and he stops talking, looking surprised.

Heat seeps into my face, down my neck, even along my spine. I look away and clear my throat, make sure my hair is tucked behind my ears. *Smooth, Marienne, I think in a mutter, you damn fool.*

"I'm twenty-four," he answers.

Good to know, good to know. Only three years older than me. I want to punch myself. As if his age makes a fuck. He's probably in a relationship. Or just isn't interested in me.

Nodding way too many times, I say, "I see." I stuff my hands into the pockets of my gray pea coat. "I'm sorry, please continue."

"Wait—Marienne, how old are you?"

My pulse skips.

Shut up, he's just asking to be polite.

"Twenty-one."

I hear him say rather distractedly, "That's incredible."

Now equal parts delighted and puzzled, I look at him again. "Is it?"

"Uh, yeah, but anyway," he says hastily, looking like *he's* embarrassed, "I've encountered people of relatively different ages and sizes and colors and religions and genders. There don't seem to be any noticeable common denominators. There's no real way for us to know yet why one person becomes Light and another doesn't."

Interesting. "Hmm."

He nods. "So, there are more people than just you and I who are Light. We're all part of a clandestine operation called the Lightforce, and we've..." he inhales deeply, "...well, we've all got a purpose."

I get that comforted feeling I got when he talked about being Light before. It turns my voice soft again when I ask, "What's that?"

"Got any guesses?"

I look at him for several moments, racking my brain. *Critical thinking, Marienne. What's he been talking about all this time? Did anything sound particularly important?*

The monsters, I realize. *The Hellions.*

"Are we supposed to kill Hellions?" I ask carefully.

One corner of Gabe's mouth turns up. "That's exactly it. If you join the Lightforce, your job will be to help kill Hellions in one way or another."

"Oh, wow." I laugh once, and it's a breathless sound. "That's what I did the other day, right?"

A fuller laugh escapes him. "In no uncertain terms."

"And you do that *every day?*" Again I feel awed.

He shakes his head. "Actually, being a Gatherer means my job is to find new Light people like you and explain things. There are other people in the Lightforce whose first concern is killing Hellions."

"Wow," I say again.

"Yeah...." He rubs at his jaw for a moment. "So, now that I've officially told you about the Lightforce, I'm supposed to leave you alone for a little while so you can think about everything."

I cross my arms against a cold wind that sweeps up out of nowhere. "Okay."

"There are no obligations," he says, "but it's important that you know this: the reason you are the way you are is so you can fight Hellions. You were chosen for this just like I was, just like the others were. It's a big deal, but whether or not you want to join the Lightforce is ultimately up to you. And let me mention that you won't be able to kill Hellions without special weaponry, so you can't really go rogue or anything."

I chuckle and say, "Okay," again. "So how much time do you have to give me?"

"Twenty-four hours minimum." He pulls his phone out. "It's about noon. If you want to meet back here tomorrow at this time, we can."

"Yes," I say without needing to ponder it.

He smiles at me. It's fantastic. "Great."

"Great," I repeat. Then I wonder something. "Why aren't you glowing anymore?"

For a brief moment he looks pained, like he's had a thought that he wishes he didn't. Then he clears his throat. "If you're in the presence of another Light person for long enough, your Radiance will fade away from the air. Today we buried one of our guys, so there were a lot of us in one place and that probably sped the dimming along. But I generally don't spend a whole lot of time around other Light people. Defenders have their own work to do, and I spend most of my time looking for white Radiances. So when you saw me the first time I'd been by myself for a while."

Ah, shit, a funeral. No wonder he looks so prim.

He also looks like he doesn't want to discuss it right now, so I ask, "And why can't I tell I'm glowing?"

Looking a little relieved, indeed, he shrugs. "Just can't."

I can't help but feel disappointed.

"But," he says, holding up a finger, "when your Radiance fades away you'll get a mark on your wrist." He tugs his right shirt sleeve up and leans toward me, hand out, palm up. "Can you see mine?"

I bend closer. It takes some leaning around—and some almost touching his hand with my nose—but I finally gasp because I *can* see it...barely. The shimmery gold circle on his slightly tan skin is very faint. It's not something I'd ever have noticed without invading his personal space; not like the ostentatious Golden Gleam Body Cream I got one Christmas from Audrey (that whore).

"Wow," I breathe. "It's wonderful."

He looks a little surprised. "Yeah?"

"Yeah, it's proof that you're like me without your...what's the glow called? Radiance?"

"Yes."

"Mmhmm," I hum. "Your Radiance was—well, it was gorgeous, but Jesus, was it bright."

"I'm sorry."

I lean back from him again and scoff a little. "Don't apologize to me. I still feel like a jerk about nearly getting you killed."

"They didn't kill me, though, because you killed them first," he reminds me.

"I...yeah," I say slowly.

"I've been doing this for a long time and I've never seen anything like that." He sounds like he's impressed with me or something.

And that is laughable. Barring the other night with Rafe, I've never been a violent person. So I tell him in a Don't Go Thinking Too Highly Of My Combat Skills tone, "I've never *done* anything like that." And then the image of the Hellions tearing into him flashes back into my head, and I feel the distress all over again. "I just—you were—I couldn't let them...I had to *try* to...."

He looks at me like he's waiting for me to finish my sentence, and at the same time, like he already knows what I'm trying to say.

It's nice.

I clear my throat. "Okay, anyway, I know you said you need to get going, so I just want you to know that this whole thing has been kind of odd, but it's really—it's really *welcome*. I was pretty sure I hadn't lost my mind or anything, but walking around thinking I'm the only person who's like this was just bleak."

"I know," he tells me, and I know he means it.

"So thank you. I guess it's just your job, but thank you."

Gabe smiles brightly and stands up. "No, you're welcome, Marienne."

I stand up, too. "Thanks," I repeat stupidly.

He chuckles. "You're welcome," he repeats, not sounding stupid at all.

I give a little nod. "So...see you tomorrow."

"Okay. Have a good day."

"You have that, too." I curtsey, and then walk down the driveway and back toward Grove Lane.

And for the first time in quite a while, I feel pleased with the turn things have taken.

$\backsim$

'There's a place and means for every man alive.'

After I graduated from high school I spent a few semesters at the University of Arkansas. That line (taken from a Shakespeare play I can't remember the name of) met my ears on the first day of some poetry class I enrolled in because I loved reading and wanted to try for something other than books. I knew who Shakespeare was, of course, but all I'd read from him was *Romeo & Juliet* and I thought it was just okay. Then there I was that day, looking over the random selection of poems and lines from plays my professor printed out for the class, and suddenly I felt like I was truly understanding words for the first time in my life.

That line is on repeat inside my head as I stand waiting for Gabe in the driveway I left him in yesterday. The words remind me of the situation I've found myself in; they seem to say, *'Marienne, there is a time and a place for stepping out of your box, and they are upon you.'* I also think the poem's stuck in my head because the way I felt when I first heard it is how I felt when Gabe told me about being Light: just *yes.* It was just *right,* and it had lifted some weight off of me. It felt like I'd found a smidgen of sense amidst all the bullshit.

I spent much of the twenty-four-hour period he gave me to think about what he said wondering where the hell these answers had been for the past two and a half months. Eventually I remembered, duh, I'd been hiding from the world nearly that entire time, so I shouldn't feel too annoyed about having missed out on things. So then I moved on to thinking about killing those Hellions. Even though it'd very nearly ended badly for Gabe and could've been the last thing I ever did, I can't help feeling...well, proud of myself. It feels *good* to have been part of something bigger. What I did was, albeit impulsive and hazardous, infinitely better than simply ignoring the horrid creatures I've been seeing since my car accident. Part of me wonders if it wasn't better than any other thing I've done in my life.

I shiver and bounce on the balls of my feet. It's colder outside today than it was yesterday, and the sky is full of low gray clouds. I heard on the TV that snow is expected to blow through today. I'm rather excited about it, except that it'll probably make walking hither and thither a little more difficult.

(Observe one of the woes of not having a car because I wrecked it and in doing so killed my parents, meaning Claire doesn't pity my no-car-having ass and doesn't feel like I deserve to be chauffeured around. And I'll admit that I agree with her on both counts.)

When I hear the hum of an approaching car, I lift my gaze from a crack in the driveway I've apparently been staring at. It's Gabe's Civic. He doesn't look at me as he parks along the curb, and I'm grateful for the chance to take a deep, steadying breath. I notice him doing the same just before he gets out.

'There's a place and means for every man alive,' I think for the two-hundredth time.

He closes the car door behind him and starts walking my way. When he finally looks at me his expression seems nervous.

"Hi," my voice cuts through the frigid air.

He puts his hands in his jacket pockets and stops a fair distance from me. He hesitates before he says, "Hi, Marienne." Yep, something's bothering him.

Weirdly, his stance and the way he's regarding me leave me with the distinct feeling that *I've* got something to do with his unease. It's bizarre. He's a badass—what could I possibly be doing to make him nervous? He could take me out in about two seconds if he thought he had to.

I'm too intrigued not to ask. "Got something on your mind?"

His teeth worry his bottom lip, and he nods.

"Is it me?" I ask before I realize that's not quite what I wanted to say.

His eyebrows go up.

I rub my fingertips against one side of my face. "I mean...you look uncomfortable."

"And you think you're making me uncomfortable?"

I pucker my lips, feeling a little self-conscious. And then I'm like, *Fuck it,* and I admit, "Well, kind of, yeah."

He smiles, but it doesn't reach his eyes. I feel sure he's going to ask me why I think that—in a supercilious manner, no doubt, even though he hasn't acted superciliously thus far. That's just the kind of tone people take when they ask things like that.

Instead of asking that, though, he says very quietly, "Well, you're right."

"Why?" I ask. I tuck my hair behind both ears and then pull it forward again. My hands drift down the length of it. "I don't want to do that. I'm sorry."

"There's nothing to be sorry about."

I frown, bemused.

He doesn't elaborate, just asks, "Have you decided how you feel about what we talked about?"

"Yes." I decided approximately one minute after I left him yesterday.

'There's a place and means for every man alive.'

Gabe straightens up, lifts his chin a little. Despite his odd apprehension, the guy looks like he'd be on the edge of his seat if he were in one.

He fascinates me.

I tell him, "I've decided to do it."

"You've decided to join the Lightforce?" he clarifies.

"Correct."

He looks away and takes in a deep breath. Then it comes bursting back out in the form of a laugh, and when he looks at me again his eyes are bright. Just like that.

I cross my arms, unable to fend off suspicion. "What?"

His shoulders are actually shaking, he's laughing so much. Even though I'm perplexed as hell, it's hard for me to keep from smiling, too. God, don't get me started on the way he smiles.

"What's funny?" I ask more sharply. "Are you laughing at *me?*"

"No." He draws another deep breath and takes a few moments to calm himself. "I was trying to prepare for you saying you don't want to join, but you didn't say that, so I...." He shakes his head, still smiling. "Your answer just makes me happy, Marienne. That's all."

Oh. Well, that explains how aloof he was acting before. I imagine my answer *does* make him happy, since recruiting people for the Lightforce is his job. I think I'd be pretty pissed off if I had only one responsibility and couldn't carry it out.

Less indignantly I say, "Right, well, that makes sense. So, um—" a gust of wind rushes around me and makes me tense up, "—um, what's next?"

"Well, there's a form you need to fill out at the Sanctum. That's the closest home base for the Lightforce, just fifteen minutes away or something. It's where new people go to train, and there's a club above it that the Director owns. Sometimes we hold little events there for Light people."

"Oh," I say slowly, "so there's actually a—a whole *base* for Light people hiding right here in Fayetteville?"

He nods. "Yep."

"That..." I sigh, "...that probably shouldn't surprise me."

"Probably not." He chuckles and then stops rather quickly. "There's something you should know, though, Marienne."

"What?"

He regards me seriously. "As I'm sure you can imagine, the Sanctum isn't a public place. It's only for Light people, so only Light people can know about it. And like I said, it's not even easy to find because it's underneath a club Nick Grayhem owns. So at this point in the process, I usually take new members there myself."

Good on you, Gabe, because Marienne Rose has no vehicle.

"But I don't think I should this time."

I peer at him. "Hmm?" Why does he think that? Does he expect me to meet him there or something? Has the time already arrived for me to admit that I don't have a car? And to think I was doing so well not drawing his attention to the fact that every time he's seen me, I've been on foot.

He scratches the back of his neck as his eyes drift away from me. "Well, I was thinking I'd get my friend Beatrix to take you to the Sanctum for me. Just so you feel a little more comfortable, you know, since you're both Light girls."

"Oh." That does sound nice, honestly, even though Gabe doesn't frighten me. Maybe this Beatrix and I will even get along—my first female Light friend. The thought actually makes me smile a little. "Okay. Thank you. Sounds lovely."

"Yeah, I think you'll get along great." He narrows his eyes, still not looking at me. "But that's not all I want to tell you."

I lift my eyebrows in acknowledgement. Then I remember he's got his eyes on the gray sky above us and not my face, so I say, "Okay."

"I hope you don't get upset. Just want you to know the truth, you know? I think you should be aware of something like this."

Well, now he's got me feeling nervous.

How bad is it?

Oh, please, God, don't tell me this whole thing is a sham. The Lightforce stuff makes so much sense. It feels so good, like I'm—

"You and Beatrix are kind of the only girls in the Lightforce around here."

Oh. "Really?"

He nods.

Well, shit. That's not half as soul-crushing as I thought it was going to be.

Still I wonder, "How is that?"

He shuts his eyes and rubs a hand over them. "Well, not everyone who almost dies becomes Light, right? So there aren't that many of us to begin with. Most think they went insane after their brush with death and that we and the Hellions are all imaginary. And out of *those* people, half end up committing suicide to escape it all. So the people who are left who actually join, just...most are men...." He shrugs and reopens his eyes, finally looking at me again. "Don't get me wrong, it's not like I don't come across Light females on occasion. The Director down in Austin, Texas is married to one and I found two older women a long time ago, but they weren't very receptive. And there's Beatrix, of course."

He looks so nervous about this that I feel bad.

Before I can tell him it's all right, he speaks again. "Does this affect your decision?" His expression says he's not sure he really wants to know the answer.

My answer's not any different than it was, though, so I tell him, "Actually, it doesn't."

"Are you sure?" he replies promptly. "I understand if it freaks you out. Really, I do."

"Well, it's a little weird, but it's not your fault and it's not the worst thing I've ever heard. I mean, before I met you I'd been getting used to not having any friends at all, so...."

He nods as he looks at me. "Okay. Okay, then."

"Okay."

"I can still get Beatrix to take you to the Sanctum, though. She's pretty excited to meet you."

I smile. "I'm excited, too. When will that be happening?"

He's finally starting to look like he believes that I'm not going to bolt over this news. "We were thinking tomorrow afternoon, if that's good for you."

"Sure."

He gives me Beatrix's number so I can call her later and tell her where I live. Then he says, "Thank you, Marienne. For not shutting me down about the Lightforce, I mean."

Still can't get over how he says my name. Like I've not noticed that, though, I lift a shoulder and say, "Thank you for telling me about it."

We quiet and look at each other; honestly, I'm starting to think he's the most attractive guy I've ever seen. It's kind of weird, though, because he doesn't look like a model or anything. I don't really know how to explain it.

But we can't stand here forever while I contemplate it, because the wind is really cold and I'm not sure the tiny flecks of white drifting down around Gabe's head are figments of my imagination. So I say, "I guess I'll see you tomorrow. Or, uh, whenever." *Dumbass. Just because you're going to see Beatrix doesn't mean you're going to see him.*

"Probably tomorrow," he agrees. He looks like he's trying not to smile.

"Okay." I wave at him and hurry away before I start giggling or something.

Soon I hear him start his car, and then I hear him drive away. Silence falls after he goes, the only sound that of the cold wind blowing dead leaves across the empty road. But after a few moments I hear footsteps.

They're coming from behind me—coming *toward* me. Footsteps that don't sound small enough to belong to a child, light enough to belong to a female, or graceful enough to belong to Gabe.

Dread shudders through me, but I have no time to think anything beyond, *Oh, God Almighty,* before the person says, "Mari, you wanna explain to me what the fuck that was about?"

Still on edge and now dumbfounded, I whirl around and find Rafe coming up fast.

Wait, what? "What the hell?" I ask, shocked. "What are you doing here?"

"I've been following you since you left the apartment," he says, his aquamarine eyes angry. "What are *you* doing here, and who was *that?*"

4
Gabe

"When did you say you're going over there?" I ask Beatrix over lunch the next day.

She lifts an eyebrow at me, her hazel eyes amused. "After lunch, I said. Which is after I leave here. Which is the same as what I told you half an hour ago."

I nod. "Oh, right."

"And two hours before that."

"Yeah, okay."

"And when I spoke to you last night after I talked to Mari on the phone."

Wes chuckles from beside her. "Baby, don't give him a hard time."

She smiles. Her rhinestone labret piercing glints in the light hanging low above our table. "You serious? This is all new territory for him, which means it's all new territory for me. I have to tease him a *little*."

He places a kiss on her cheek. "Well, make fun of his hair or something, not the fact that he's somehow found himself a girl to like. Happened to me once, you know."

Her smile softens, and she turns her head to kiss him on the mouth. Then she concedes, "Mmkay, you have a point."

"And what point is that?" I tease around a mouthful of club sandwich. "That something's wrong with my hair?"

They both turn back to me. "Well, I don't know if I'd say something's *wrong* with it," she says, "but it does kind of do whatever it wants."

"No joke." My hair's rather unruly, it's true. I haven't thought much about it lately, though, because it's not long enough to really bother me yet. Eventually I'll go get a haircut.

"What is Mari's hair like?"

I chuckle. "What kind of question is that? And why're you calling her Mari?"

"It's a *girl* question because, hello, she's the only other girl around here and she seems adorable, so I care. And I'm calling her Mari because she told me I could." Beatrix tosses her own colorful hair back proudly.

Wes and I laugh, even though I have to wonder why Marienne didn't tell *me* that, too.

"What?" she asks.

"Brag much?" he grins. "We see you over there, flinging your hair around because you have permission to use her nickname."

"Don't know what you're talking about, love." She winks at him. Then she asks me, "But really, what's her hair like?"

I don't actually have a problem with recalling the way Marienne looks. Oh, who am I kidding? There's no *recalling* going on here. She's stayed in my head since the first time I saw her. Finally I answer the question. "It's long."

"How long?"

"To the middle of her back, I guess."

"What color is it?"

"Black."

"Straight or curly?"

"Uh...straight-ish? I don't know. It just...*is*." In my head I can see her smoothing her windblown hair behind her ears all over again.

"I bet it's so pretty," Beatrix muses.

Grinning in agreement, I take another bite of my sandwich.

"She seems funny, too."

I nod. After I swallow my food I say, "Yeah, she actually curtsied the other day."

Beatrix's eyes widen. "Can't wait to meet her. Seriously."

Wes looks happy about her seeming happy. "Soon."

"Soon," I agree.

"Soon," she sighs, touching her food for the first time since I mentioned her picking up Marienne.

Ten minutes later, when we walk out into the snow that's been drifting prettily from the sky since last night, she goes back to being excited. "I'm going now!" She puts her arms around Wes's shoulders. "Until we meet again, my love," she says in an elegant, actress-y voice.

He grabs her waist and sweeps her forward theatrically. "The next hour will seem a week." They kiss rather chastely for having exchanged such fancy farewells.

These are my friends.

I chuckle. "We'll see you at the Sanctum, B."

She extracts herself from Wes's arms and heads over to her black Saturn Sky, waving as she goes. "See you guys in a bit. Drive carefully." She ducks into her car, and mere moments pass before I can hear heavy rock music pounding through it.

Wes has been riding shotgun in her car all day, so now that she's going to get Marienne he rides with me. For the first few minutes of our journey nothing happens, other than him commending me on a song choice. But then we spot a Hellion pulling a cheerful-looking Latina girl into an alley behind a run-down building.

We decide to take care of him for a number of reasons. Firstly, it's become instinct for Wes to kill any Hellion he sees. Secondly, there's still anger deep in my chest over Em being killed—being dismembered, really— by a group of Hellions that none of us have the opportunity to fight. Thirdly, the Hellion's got a young girl with him as opposed to just wandering around alone. And lastly, Beatrix and Marienne won't be at the Sanctum this soon, so they're not waiting on us or anything.

After I park a safe distance away from where we spotted the pair, we pick our way around parked cars and dumpsters until we locate them again. The girl is standing between the Hellion and the bricked side of the building in the otherwise empty alley. His torso and arms are naked but completely covered in huge, oozing, infected-looking sores that I can actually smell from where I stand. It's a worse odor than what was wafting out of the dumpsters we passed.

The girl doesn't have a clue that anything is out of the ordinary, though. The Hellion's got her fooled completely. She can't fathom who she's really looking up at, smiling with, standing on her tiptoes to whisper to, and it's sad. And nauseating.

As if Wes can read my mind, he mutters, "Fucking vile, isn't it?"

I make a noise of agreement. And then we whip up a plan.

We need to get the girl away from the Hellion without her seeing our faces. It's *crucial* that she doesn't see us when we attack him, because to her he's probably a good-looking boy and any harm that befalls him in front of her eyes will send her screaming for help. And if she runs off telling people what the two guys who murdered her boyfriend look like, it'll turn into anything from a hassle to a really bad situation.

Ultimately we decide there is really only one thing we can do: wait for our moment. We watch while the Hellion flirts with the girl. After a minute he steps closer so her arms can go around his sore-ridden body. We wait another minute and then watch him lift his fetid hands to her face, watch her bright eyes close, watch him put his jawless mouth on hers, black tongue lolling. They are, in a manner of speaking, lost in the beauty of their stolen kiss. And our chance has arrived.

It takes us less than ten seconds. We sweep up on either side of the Hellion and slip our daggers between him and the girl. Silently and expertly we both slit his throat, me moving my blade from left to right, Wes going from right to left. And then we disappear again.

It's not easy to walk away so quickly. A Light person should always confirm that any Hellion they attack is floating away in pieces and particles before they leave the scene. But that can't happen today. We've used our quickest move and now it's time to go. If we stay, we risk being spotted by the girl.

Luckily, Hellions don't bleed. We hear no screams of horror from the girl as we make our way back to my car.

When Hellions die they simply disintegrate, so the only thing she's left with is confusion, or maybe alarm, as to how she'd just been making out with a guy and now is totally alone. But there are no answers to be offered to her; if the situation was different I'd feel bad for her.

As it happens, I feel bad for *us* for having witnessed the utterly repulsive kiss unfold between such an unsuspecting girl and a monster.

The Sanctum is located on a far edge of Fayetteville. Like I told Marienne, The Room is only for Light people, so I have never seen it very busy; sometimes it's used for birthday or holiday celebrations (or funeral services), and every now and then Lightforce members from other places will visit and Grayhem will put the club to use. The main entrance into the Sanctum is through The Room, though, so even if people don't really sit around and waste time in the club, they do pass through.

Today Wes and I will be going through the club's back entrance, so it's unlikely we'll see anyone who might be in there. I park in the lot tucked behind the building and we go through the passcode-only door. On the left side of the narrow hallway is a heavy door requiring another code, and beyond it is a wide staircase that only leads down. The space is cold like the air outside, so we leap impatiently down the four flights of stairs until we make it to the bottom floor, where Wes types in the code for the door on the right, labeled *Number 2*. Then we enter the receiving room of the Sanctum.

The carpeted room is large but perpetually plain. Evenly-spaced wooden chairs line the walls on either side of us, a desk and two doors line the opposite wall, and the fourth wall holds this entrance and a flat-screen TV. The

TV is currently muted because Mark, a balding man who nearly died in a construction accident five years ago and then was crippled in a car wreck on his way home from the hospital, is on the phone behind the desk. He offers us a distracted wave while he continues his murmured conversation.

"Guess we got here first," Wes says, dropping into a chair. "You see the remote anywhere?"

"Mark probably has it." I nod toward the desk as I sit down, too.

Wes looks that way and stretches his arms above his head. "Ah, well, I don't wanna bother him," he yawns. "Guess we'll just watch the news in silence."

"There's never anything good on there, anyway," I murmur as my eyes catch part of the scrolling text at the bottom of the screen: '...*THE SPORTS STAR SAYS HE DID NOT FEEL INTOXICATED BEFORE HE GOT BEHIND THE WHEEL OF THE CAR....*'

"I'm thinking about getting that dragon earring for B," Wes says. "For her birthday."

"That's a good idea." I'm not much for piercings, but Beatrix has managed to make the ones she has look all right. She's got both earlobes, her labret and her left nostril pierced, and all she wears in any of them are tiny rhinestone studs. She hasn't gone into overdrive with it, so it's not discomfiting to look at her. Now having spotted in the mall a long silver cuff shaped like a dragon, she wants her ear cartilage pierced.

"Yeah, I know she wants it bad," Wes agrees. "She drools every time she thinks about it."

I chuckle because I know he's right. Every now and then he and I will be talking about something and look over to see her staring off into space. One of us will ask what's on her mind and she'll say wistfully, "The dragon."

Across the room Mark hangs up the phone and says, "Afternoon, guys. Where's the missus, Wes?"

My stomach does something funny when he says, "She's on her way over with a Light girl Gabe found the other day."

"Well, that's great," Mark says, nodding at me appreciatively. "New faces are always welcome."

"New faces *and* new talents," Wes says. "This girl actually ran up and killed two Hellions that were about to kill Gabe."

Mark raises his eyebrows. "What? Just out of the blue with no training?" He doesn't ever engage in combat with Hellions because he's been physically unfit to fight since he joined the Lightforce, but he still knows how dangerous they are. He knows that the only people who ever walk away from a fight with them are those who have been trained to kill them.

Wes and I nod, still sharing in his disbelief.

"Well, we're even more blessed to have her than I realized, huh?"

Before either of us can reply, the opening of *Number 2* distracts us.

Beatrix walks in saying, "Here we have the receiving room." She stops in front of Wes and me and gestures toward Mark, then glances at us. Excitement almost as bright as Radiance shines in her eyes. "Over at the desk is Mark, our receptionist."

I snap my gaze to Marienne as she comes to a stop next to Beatrix. "Hi, Mark," she says, fluttering her fingers in a little wave.

Mark smiles and waves back. "Hello, there. And how are you today, Beatrix?"

"Doing splendidly. You?"

Marienne's eyes flicker to me. One corner of her mouth turns up shyly when she spots me looking at her, and I immediately return the little smile.

The desk phone rings and Mark stops talking to Beatrix to answer it. She touches a hand to Marienne's shoulder and turns her smile on Wes. "This is my husband Wes. Baby, this is Mary-Anne."

I frown. *Mary-Anne?*

Wes nods at her. "Nice to meet you, Mary-Anne."

That's not quite right, is it?

Indeed, she looks a little disappointed before she smiles at Wes and tells him, "It's nice to meet you, too. Please, call me Mari."

Oh, so that's *why Beatrix gets to use her nickname.*

I actually laugh out loud.

Marienne's eyes find me again and she looks at me knowingly. "Afternoon, Gabe," she finally greets me.

"Afternoon," I say with a chuckle, barely refraining from tacking a correctly-enunciated, *'Marienne,'* onto the end.

"Oh, yeah, and of course you know Gabe," Beatrix chirps. "So, Mari, are you ready to fill out this form and take the tour?"

"Yep," she replies, still looking at me.

"Cool. I'll grab the stuff." Beatrix starts toward the front desk, and Wes leaps up from his chair to run after her and smack her on the ass.

"Feel like sitting down?" I ask Marienne.

"Yeah, okay." She tucks her hair behind her ears and takes the empty seat on my left. "How do you feel about this snow?"

"I like it."

"Me, too." She picks up one end of her purple scarf and studies it. "I'm a cold-weather person."

"So am I."

Across the room I hear Beatrix whisper-yell, "Weston, if you don't quit grabbing my ass in front of people, I swear...."

I look over and see him smirking at her. "What? Are you gonna teach me a lesson?"

"Mark doesn't want to see it," she insists, albeit with a smile. She goes back to digging around in a desk drawer. "Or Mari or Gabe or anyone else in Fayetteville."

He bends over and whispers something in her ear, and she bursts out laughing. Then she claps a hand over her mouth and glances at Mark, who's still on the phone. She mumbles something back to Wes that makes him laugh, too.

"She mentioned him about sixty times on the way here," Marienne tells me. "It was hilarious."

Nodding, I say, "I believe that."

"Everything we passed reminded her of him. Buildings. Cars. Street signs." She laughs softly.

I look at her and smile. "They were made for each other and they don't let any of us forget it, so prepare yourself for that."

"I'll prepare myself."

I clear my throat a little and gesture toward her. "Well, you...you look really nice today." I think about hastily adding that she looked really nice the other times I saw her, too, but I don't want her to think I'm a bumbling idiot, so I keep my mouth shut.

"Oh—really? Thank you," she murmurs, glancing down at her outfit. Indeed, like the others she's worn it's basic and not very revealing: jeans, white shirt, scarf, flat black boots, coat. I think it's awesome. She straightens her legs and lifts her boots off the floor, then puts them back down and looks over at my clothes. "You look really nice, too. I like that shirt."

I look down at myself. I only chose this black and white plaid button-down because it was the last clean long-sleeved shirt in my closet. "Do you?" I ask, suddenly glad that I've been putting off doing laundry for the past several days.

Before she can respond, footsteps approach us. We look up and see Beatrix holding a pen and clipboard. "Here we are, doll. Fill the top one out. The other is a list of rules for you to keep."

It takes Marienne a few minutes to fill out the information sheet. When she's done, Beatrix returns it to the front desk for Mark to file and then we're ready to walk her around the place. We double back into the stairwell and go through *Number 1* first.

"Well, you've got a place to stay already, but this is the residential hall," Beatrix says. "The rooms go from A to Z, so they go around this corner down here." She leads us away from the entrance to the hall and we go around the corner on our left. She stops and motions toward a door. "Here we have a lounge."

Marienne goes over and peers into the room. I don't have to look into it to know it holds two couches, a table and set of chairs, and kitchen appliances. There's a

TV hanging on the wall with both a DVD player and a VCR sitting on a shelf under it. However, despite all these furnishings the room has always felt rather lonely to me. It's probably because no one really uses it, since about two people live down here.

Beatrix heads to the next door down. "This is the laundry room."

Marienne peeks in there, too. Like the lounge, it's pretty well-stocked. In addition to several washers and dryers, there should be everything from detergent to empty hangers to an iron and ironing board in there.

We continue on. "Here's an extra bathroom, and the rest of these rooms are just bedrooms. Down here at the end of the hall are a telephone and a fire extinguisher. Actually, there are fire extinguishers all over this hallway." Beatrix takes care to point each one out as we walk back the way we came.

We're almost back to *Number 1* when Marienne asks me, "Do I need to know the codes to get through these doors?"

"Yes," I nod. "The one into the back of the club—" I point above us, "—is 3141. The one into the stairwell is 5926. *Number 1* is 5358, and *Number 2* is 9793. There's an emergency exit out of the Sanctum and the code for that is 2384. Also known as the first twenty digits of pi."

Her eyes widen and she snorts.

I know what that means: she's not a math person. "I'll write them down for you," I chuckle.

"Thank you. Truly."

Back in the receiving room I write the codes down for her, and then Beatrix lets Wes take over the tour. He presses his hand against the shiny wooden door on the right side of the wall behind Mark's desk. "Behind this door you'll find a conference room and a handful of offices. Grayhem's is at the end of the hall on the left. The others belong to me and Red, the man who handles weaponry." He glances at me and clears his throat, and I wonder if he's going to mention that one of the offices belongs to me, too, now that Em's gone. He doesn't, and I'm grateful. "So, if you need to speak with Grayhem in private, you can just go through this door. The rest of us only spend a little bit of time in our offices."

"All right," Marienne says.

He leads us to the left where the other, plainer door stands. We file through it into a hallway that's not nearly as long as the residential one or the one upstairs. There is one door on our left side, one at the far end of the hall, and three on our right side. Wes goes to the left and walks through the door, shadowed by Beatrix. Marienne and I follow, and as soon as the light comes on she gasps. "Wow."

The word echoes around the enormous rectangular room. I still remember the way I felt when I first saw it, so I know how wild it looks to her—hell, I still think it's pretty cool. Spotless mirrors encompass the entire left wall, from end to end and floor to ceiling. The floor itself is made of four different materials: plain white vinyl tile right beside us, sleek wood next to that, blue springboard beyond that, and gravel against the far wall. Lots of things have been arranged against the wall to our right: full-body dummies, exercise equipment, benches, a water stand, a cabinet with a stereo on it, a table holding towels and mats, a rack supporting dumbbells, and a rack for weapons.

"This is the training room," Wes states. "You'll be brought in pretty soon."

Another, "Wow," is all Marienne manages.

He chuckles. "Here in a few days you'll be dropping that first 'w.' Don't let my wife fool you. She can kick ass as well as any guy, and she'll teach you to do the same." As an afterthought, "She'll hone your skills, anyway. Apparently you can already kick ass."

Marienne finally takes her eyes off the room and looks at Beatrix. "Oh, you're going to train me?" she asks with a smile.

Beatrix nods but looks like she'd rather be clapping or jumping for joy. "I thought it'd be appropriate...and fun."

"I agree."

Wes smiles at Beatrix before he addresses Marienne again. "Ready to keep going?"

"Yeah, of course."

He leads the way out the door, his hand finding his wife's so he can pull her along.

Marienne follows, but she looks back at me. "I like this place."

"It's neat," I agree as I catch up with her, "and it's practically a fortress. It's the safest place for any of us to be."

She nods thoughtfully and looks forward again. "Yeah, I can feel that. It's cool." After a beat she adds, "Thank you for walking around with us. It's nice and I'm sure you've got other things you need to do."

"It's no problem, Marienne." I think I hear a quiet laugh leave her, and I'll bet it's the name thing. I fight the urge to laugh at my friends' expenses yet again, and gesture to the other side of the hallway. "This first door is a bathroom." I point at the second door. "And this is the infirmary."

"The infirmary," she echoes. "The mini hospital. Ugh."

"Yeah, well, you'll pay Dr. Roterra your share of visits."

She looks at me, nose wrinkled, and makes a noise of disfavor. It makes me smile.

When we come to the door to Red's domain, otherwise known as the last one on the right side of the hall, we find that Wes and Beatrix have already gone in. The latter turns away from her chat with the men when she hears us pass into the room.

"Here she is," she says cheerfully.

Red, outgoing as always, walks over and puts a strong hand out. "Hello, Mari. Name's Red." He shakes her hand and gestures with the other to his short-cropped red hair. "I know yer thinkin' my parents were imaginative, but they died when I was thirty-five so ya won't be able to meet 'em and gush to 'em about what a damn unique name they chose for me."

She laughs. "It's not the worst name ever, sir."

He grins toothily and releases her hand to point at her. "Ya know what? Yer right." He crosses his thick arms over his chest. "Did anyone fill ya in on what I do 'round here?"

She looks at him a little apologetically. "No, sir."

"All well and good, little lady. Well, ya've seen Hellions, right? So maybe ya've wondered how ya kill somethin' that appears to be dead already, and that's an important question. In our branch I'm the one in charge o' makin' the only instruments that can kill a Hellion. Gabe, son, can I see yer dagger?"

I draw it out of the padded pocket inside my jacket. I leave it sheathed and pass it to him, and he lifts it up to Marienne.

"This is what yer basic dagger looks like." He lays it out across his palms. "Simple, slender, and imbued with Light blood. I'll get one fixed up for ya before long."

She bends closer to inspect the brushed-silver handle. The rounded curves of it are made to fit my hand, so it looks and feels a little different than hers will, but I guess it didn't prove too big a problem on Blossombranch. A little distractedly, she asks, "There's blood in it?"

"Yes'm. Don't know if ya know this or not, but yer blood is special. It's what makes all Light people special. Our blood is different from other people's on a cellular level—it's why we can't get drunk anymore, for example, and it's why we can see Hellions at all. And that difference is their only weakness. Hellions are pure evil, and us bein' run through with life and light makes us their opposite. It's the only thing they can't stomach, so it's the only weapon we have against 'em."

"Holy *shit*," she mutters. I meet Wes's and Beatrix's eyes and we all grin, knowing how she feels.

"So we put our blood *into* our weapons," he continues. "It holds up well with metal, but it's also effective dried into a powder. Light blood in any form'll harm a Hellion, so sometimes throwin' the red powder is the best ya can do without slicin' yerself open just to get the upper hand. In order to really kill one, ya gotta be a bit more violent—" he winks, "—but I hear ya know that already. I'll let Mrs. Avery there explain it better on her own time." He starts unsheathing the dagger.

Marienne looks like she wants to respond, but then the sheath is off and the light above us dances like wildfire across the uncovered metal, and a little gasp is all that leaves her. I can imagine why. On top of it being a smooth, lustrous version of the handle, the blade shimmers faintly gold the way Light marks do. The thing is nearly luminous; it *looks* like it's infused with Light blood.

Red smiles. "It's somethin', ain't it?"

She nods and looks away from the dagger to smile, too...at me.

Too good.

I don't get a smile back before Red speaking again steals her attention. "Now I've said all that, sweetheart, I gotta be up-front and say I can't formally create yer weapons for ya until ya've undergone basic trainin'. I know ya grabbed this here dagger the other day and handled a couple Hellions real good with it, but rules are rules."

Color touches her cheeks and she finally gets some words out. "I understand."

"Well, don't get all embarrassed, now," he says with a hearty chuckle, noting her blush like I did. "What ya did ain't nothin' to be embarrassed about, k? I'm just goin' by the book here."

She smiles and nods, though her cheeks are still pink.

Red sheathes the dagger and gives it back to me. "Let's g'on and instruct ya in the ways o' Hellion killin' for a week or so—get ya some proper trainin' to go with that fearlessness ya got under that belt o' yours. Then we'll get ya back in here."

"Sounds like a plan," Beatrix speaks up. "Mari, do you think—?"

"Knock, knock," a voice calls from the door. We all look over and find Grayhem looking in at us.

"Hey, there, come on in," Red waves. "Just talkin' to our newest lady here."

"This is Mari," Beatrix introduces her before I can.

Marienne gives Grayhem a smile as he walks into the room. He returns it, looking more than a little surprised, probably at her age if I had to guess. "It's a sincere pleasure, young lady. Nick Grayhem, Director of the local Lightforce branch. Feel free to call me Grayhem."

"You, too, sir. Thank you."

"Well, guys and gals," Red says, "kindly pardon me and the boss man. We got a discussion what needs havin'."

Grayhem's expression turns grave, so we all hurry out, calling out our thanks and goodbyes.

After we point out the emergency exit at the end of the combat hall, we head back to the receiving room. Wes hunches his shoulders and takes in a deep breath. "Well, Mari," he exhales as he drops an arm around Beatrix's shoulders, "I hate to say it, but me and B gotta run. We've got Hellions to hunt down."

Beatrix smiles at Marienne. "Babydoll, this was so fun. Do you need me to pick you up in the—? Oh." Her smile drops away. "Oh, shit."

"What?" the rest of us ask.

"I don't have a backseat."

Mildly confused, I ask, "Are you just now realizing this?"

Wes chuckles. "Yeah, Gabe and I noticed it two years ago when you bought the car."

"Ha, yeah," Beatrix gives us both a look, "I mean that if Wes and I are leaving, I can't drive Mari home because I don't have a backseat."

Oh. *Oh.*

"Oh," Marienne and Wes say.

I look over at her. She's already watching me, and I feel sure she can see the idea forming in my mind. Still I tell her, "I'll drive you if you want me to." I don't know how I manage to say it sans nervousness.

She looks back at Beatrix and says easily, "Yeah, I'll go with him. It'll be fine."

Amusement is gradually replacing Beatrix's concern. "Well...you want me to come get you in the morning? I was thinking we could start training tomorrow. How's 9:00?"

"That would really be great."

Beatrix nods and reaches up to the hand Wes is dangling off her shoulder. She tangles their fingers together and says slowly, "Then I'll see both of you tomorrow."

"Okay," we say.

Wes nods as they walk past us. "Later, Gabe. Mari."

And then they're gone.

We stand in silence for a few moments before I say, "Whenever you're ready, I guess."

She nods. "Yeah, we should—yeah." She starts toward the door.

Outside, the snow is starting to build up. It makes everything look prettier than normal, and it fills me with a sense of calm that I welcome with open arms. The fact that I'm about to have Marienne in my car has me torn between anxiety and elation, and it's nerve-wracking. I'm not used to it.

Once we're in she says a little timidly, "Thank you for doing this. Really."

I turn down the old Matchbox Twenty song me and Wes were listening to. Despite my nerves I tell her sincerely, "You're welcome. I'm happy to help."

She sounds like she's smiling when she says, "You're too kind. And I love this song."

"Wow, seriously?" It's "You Won't Be Mine"—not a song that ever made it to the radio. Yet another point for her. And I feel slightly less awkward now, so that's a relief.

"Yep. It makes me sad, though."

"Me, too. Want to listen to it anyway?"

"Absolutely."

I restart the song. The only talking that goes on during our drive is her giving me directions to her home, and even then our words are quiet. It's nice.

It turns out that she lives in a nice apartment complex close to Blossombranch Lane. I park where she says to and turn the music down again.

"Thanks again," she says. "I really didn't want to walk, and I hate taxis."

Ha, like I'd have let her walk all the way here. "Not a problem."

After a beat she adds, "And thanks for saying my name correctly."

I shoot her a grin. "You know, at first I wondered why you didn't ask me to call you Mari, but now...."

She snickers. "I really don't care to be called that, but your friends—" she holds up her hands apologetically, "—I mean, it's not just them, it's most people—they just don't say my name right. I get tired of being called whatever variation of Marienne they come up with."

"So I shouldn't feel bad, huh?" I ask, drumming my fingers on the steering wheel as I look out at the falling snow.

"Not at all. But if you really want to call me that, you can. I know it's easier."

I shake my head unconcernedly. "I like Marienne."

"Cool. Is Gabe your actual name or is it short for something?"

My heartbeat seems to stumble and my fingers freeze mid-drum. Believe it or not, no one in the Lightforce has ever asked me that...something I didn't think was strange until this moment. I like that she asked. "Gabriel," I say diffidently.

"Oh, wow. Do people call you that?"

"No." I laugh a little. "I don't think anyone in the Lightforce knows that's my name."

She's quiet for a few moments, like she's considering that. Then, "I like it, personally."

I slide a look over to her and say sincerely, "Thank you."

She smiles and it makes me smile.

"So, you seem to be handling all of this stuff pretty well," I remark. "Are you good with it, really? Or are you going to start freaking out at some point?"

"No, I'm fine," she tells me easily. "I'm glad to be a part of it. The whole thing makes sense to me." Her shoulders lift a little. "If anything, I'm a tiny bit worried someone's going to jump out at me and scream, *Just kidding! Go back to your suckfest of a life now.*"

I laugh. "Well, that's funny, but you don't have to worry about it. I promise."

She laughs a little, too. "Okay. I believe you."

I suddenly feel like if I don't get her to keep talking to me, I'll go crazy. I want to know more about her. So I cross my arms and shift in my seat and ask, "Do you have a job or anything?"

I seem to have asked an unhappy question, though, because she grimaces. "Um, I did," she answers hesitantly. "I had one when the—before my—" She pauses and clears her throat. "The night I turned Light, I got banged up and had to take off work for a while. Embarrassing as it is to admit, once I was better I just...didn't go back. Things have been difficult since that night and I just didn't think I could...um...."

"Nah, I understand," I assure her.

She nods and looks out the windshield. "I've lived here with my older sister for a few years. We used to be really close. But now...." A soft, humorless laugh leaves her. "I guess I *wish* I had a job so I could reduce the occasions I see her from once or twice a day to zero times a day."

It sounds like she means that. I ask her gingerly, "Why?"

She inhales a little unsteadily. "Irreparable damage, Gabe. That's all." She takes a deeper, calmer breath and looks at me again. "So how does *your* job work, exactly? You get paid to just find people like me?"

I nod. "I get paid and I get free housing."

"Really?" She perks up. "What's your house like?"

"It's pretty great. It's kind of in the mountains."

She sighs, looking like she loves the idea. "That sounds wonderful."

"The house is nice, but the view is the best part," I admit. "The far edge of my backyard is actually a cliff, so I can just walk out there and look down into a valley full of nothing but trees."

"Dang," she murmurs. Her eyes narrow a little like she's trying to picture it in her head.

I give her a second, and then I say more seriously, "Yeah, but look. You'll get paid for being in the Lightforce, too. They'll train you to be a Defender because everyone needs to have those skills, but even if you end up being a Gatherer—or, hell, doing something like what Mark does— you'll get paid like for any other job." I glance at the apartment and then back to her. "If time away from here is what you want, you'll get it."

One side of her mouth turns up as she regards me. When she says, "Thank you," the words are earnest.

I didn't really do anything for her. Maybe she just appreciates that I don't think she's a bitch for not wanting to hang around her sister, but who am I to judge her for that, anyway? Wherever her gratitude comes from, I accept it with a little smile of my own.

Shortly she says, "I guess I should go, but I appreciate your..." she flutters her fingers around the car and in the general direction of the Sanctum, "...everything."

I nod once. "You're welcome."

She nods, too. "So I guess I'll see you...when I see you."

"I'll be at the Sanctum sometime tomorrow," I try to say nonchalantly. Would I normally visit the place while I'm working? No. Can I help wanting to do it now that she's around? No. Is it obvious to her? Probably. But whatever.

As she looks as me, color brightens her cheeks. Her fingertips smooth distractedly at the hair falling over her shoulders and she says, "I will be, too. What a coincidence." And I get that she definitely does understand I'll only be going to the Sanctum to see her—that it's not a coincidence at all. And I'm not sure she minds; I hope she doesn't.

But I don't manage to ask and make sure before she gets out of the car and shuts the door. So I just smile at her when she looks through the window to wave at me, and she smiles back pretty damn big before she turns and walks away.

I don't think tomorrow can get here fast enough.

5
Marienne

I feel rested when my eyes drift open in the morning. It's surprising; last night I was so wired over the Sanctum stuff that I got about four hours of sleep instead of my usual eight, and on top of that my rest wasn't a quiet one. I suffered through two nightmares that felt so real I can still see them as I stare at the blank white wall my bed is pressed against.

In the first, I relived last week's trip to Applebee's. The details of the place were cranked up: the copious colors, the clinking of glasses on tables and forks on plates, the lights on the ceiling, the vibration of "Stranglehold" through the building. The Hellion was there at the bar. Like he did in real life, he looked and sounded normal as he flirted with the blonde girl, but this time when he looked at me he crumpled back into his true self. Except for his eyes—he retained the stunning blue eyes of his human guise. They pierced mine while he gripped the chains hanging down his front, his smile terrible and his stance indecent. And he spoke to me. He actually said my name. His voice sounded like a rock scraping across glass.

A mere two minutes have passed since I left the other nightmare. I was in a pitch-black room with my hands bound behind me by something serrated, my body wracked with terror so strong it made my bones ache. After what could've been an hour or only a minute, a door opened and dim light spilled into the room. In the doorway stood the silhouette of something towering and powerful with long claws, from which a substance I couldn't identify was dripping. He shut himself into the room with me and moved with heavy steps through the thick darkness. He let out a rumbling laugh that promised something horrible. And for the first time, I wanted to go back to the night of my accident and die then, so I didn't have to die in that room.

I didn't die, of course. I just woke up. And, boy, was I thankful for the snow-brightened morning sunlight that was beginning to fill my bedroom. I needed that comfort.

Should probably get up, I tell myself now as I bury my face in my pillow and stretch my body. *Training with Beatrix today. Need to be ready for whatever the hell that might entail. Oh and yeah, I get to see Gabe again.* Even though that last thought is especially nice, I slump against my mattress with a sigh. My bed is too warm and comfy. I don't want to get out of it.

But I must.

I shut my eyes and rub them as I roll away from the wall. Once I'm sitting up, I drop my hands to untwist my long nightshirt from my body—

—and see the person standing beside my bed.

"*Fuck!*" I shriek, leaping away. I press back against the wall, my heart suddenly at a million miles an hour. And just as abruptly, I realize who it is.

It's Rafe.

Rafe has snuck up on me *again.*

But this time we're not out in the day. We're in my bedroom, alone, and I've just woken up. I've barely got clothes on. And he's not across the room in my little desk chair. He's standing by my bed.

"What in *God's* name are you doing?" I shout at him.

Too calmly, he says, "We need to talk."

"Get out of my room!"

He lifts his hands and backs away. "That's fine. I'll be in the living room."

I slam my palms against the wall behind me. "Fucking whatever! Get *out!*" I don't care where he is as long as it's not twelve inches from my bed.

As soon as he steps into the hallway, I bolt to the door and slam it shut behind him. Then I lock it. Then I stomp into my bathroom and shut and lock that door, too.

I know I spend at least an hour in the shower. For quite a while I just stand under the hot water and try to get myself together. On the one hand, I want to be in a good mood when Beatrix gets here. On the other, I want to punch something because I can't wrap my mind around what I just woke up to.

How the hell did Rafe even get into my room? That's the most unbelievable thing I've ever experienced, and that includes seeing a monster at Applebee's and letting a guy who glows drive me home from a tour around an underground stronghold.

I'm still seething when I finally get out of the shower. Just to prolong Rafe's wait I take the time to clip my fingernails and toenails to the exact same lengths, and then I file them. Then I put a few q-tips to good use, brush and floss my teeth, dry my hair. I even pull out a bottle of lotion that's been sitting unopened in my cabinet for months and rub it on me.

And then I have to choose an outfit—yet another tedious task.

When I'm finally ready to go see what on God's green earth Rafe wants to talk about, the clock on my nightstand says the time is 8:46. It confirms just how early it was when I discovered he was in my room, and it pisses me off even more.

I walk into the living room and find him standing with his back against the wall opposite me, arms crossed and eyes on the ceiling. He blinks but doesn't look at me when I demand callously, "The fucking hell do you want? And how did you get in here?"

"Claire let me in because I wanna talk to you."

Fucking Claire! She sure is senseless for being almost thirty fucking years old. "Talk about what?"

He swallows hard, finally appearing to be something other than comfortable. After an age he says, "I think I've lost you."

"That's an astute observation."

"I want you back."

"No."

He closes his eyes. "What can I do to get you to change your mind?"

"My mind can't be changed."

A grimace creases his face. "I'll do anything."

"There's nothing you can do. Things are different now."

He opens his eyes and finally looks at me. "How I feel about you isn't different at all."

I frown. "So you still feel like I don't deserve a faithful boyfriend? I can live without that, Rafe. I really can."

"You do deserve a faithful boyfriend. You deserve the best things in the world."

"You say that...."

He shakes his head. "I *mean* that. I just didn't know how to give you all of those things before."

"You still don't know how to."

"I think I do," he disagrees.

"Okay, well, you said a lot of things at Applebee's and none of them indicated to me that you'd changed. Not for the better." I bite the inside of my cheek. "I didn't think you'd ever call me a pathetic bitch."

He clenches his jaw. "I was just mad that you—"

"*You* were mad?" I cut him off. "I'm not the one who slept with someone else while we were going out. That, by the way, is something else I never thought you'd do."

He stares at me, his expression turning bleak. "I'm sorry. Seriously, I'm sorry I hurt you like that."

I stare back at him until my eyes start to ache and I have to shut them. In a way I believe that he is sorry, but it's just not enough. The way I felt about him changed after what went on between him and Audrey. But even if I magically get over that, there will still be a chasm between us that can't be spanned. I'm...*this*. I'm Light. He's not.

A deep sorrow touches me through my anger. It's not just that I'm sad he cheated on me, or that I couldn't truly give him another chance even if I wanted to. What hurts the most about this whole thing is that I still remember the Rafe who used to be one of my best friends, the Rafe I knew before everything went downhill. He was sweet and fun to be around. He was protective of me. He could make me smile without trying.

I feel like *that* Rafe died on the same night my parents died. I feel like I'm not only lamenting the loss of my mom and dad, but also the loss of him. It's like even though his body is still walking around, the lovable boy who used to inhabit it is gone and can never be reclaimed.

My voice sounds dull when I say, "You should go. There's nothing for you here."

"Mari," he murmurs, "*please*—"

"This is just how it is now." After a few moments I open my eyes again, and I realize with a jolt that he's almost upon me.

"Look, I made a mistake with Audrey, but people just do that sometimes. It'll only wreck everything if you let it."

I step away to try to keep space between us, but I move too late. "What are you doing?" He's already close enough to touch me, and he lifts a hand to do just that. I tense up.

"I'm gonna show you that what we had isn't gone like you think it is." His fingers curl gently around my arm.

I wrench away before he can draw me closer to him. "You are not."

"We can still make this work," he insists. This time he reaches out and touches my cheek as he steps right up to me.

Again I move out of his reach. "Stop touching me," I warn him.

"Give me another chance," he implores me. "I can fix this. Just let me kiss you and prove it to you."

"Why would I let—? *Why?*" I exclaim, taking several more steps away from him. "You were with her in my house—in my room, in my bed! I don't want you kissing *me* ever again."

Rafe shakes his head. "Really, I'm sorry. I don't know why I did it."

"Please."

"I don't know why I did it," he repeats, "but I swear it wasn't because I didn't love you."

"That doesn't make any goddamn *sense!*" I bellow. "Just how *stupid* do you think I am?"

He holds his hands up, his eyes widening. "I don't think you're stupid, but are you listening to what I'm saying right now? I know I fucked up and I will do *anything* to prove to you that you can trust me again! I want you back, Mari! I'll do anything to make that happen!"

"There is no action you can take," I groan, "no word you can say, no—no gift you can give me, okay? There's no life you can swear on that can make me forget how I felt when I found you in there, Rafe." My chest hurts as the memory flashes into my head: him on top of her, moving between her bare legs, her hands in his hair, my sheets in a wild tangle underneath their bodies.

"Just try to forgive me," he pleads, totally unaware of the vivid memory wreaking havoc on my mind. "I know you, Mari. You're sweet. You've got a good heart. You're the best person I know."

"Then why did you do that to me? And don't the fuck tell me you don't know!"

He shrugs helplessly. "I just...I guess it was just that I'd been drinking and I was all—I mean, you and me hadn't had sex yet, you know, and Audrey hit on me. You know how she is. She's a huge flirt and she wants what she wants and—"

"Oh, for God's sake, don't blame this on her *or* on me," I interrupt him, shaking my head furiously. "Don't you dare look right at me and tell me you aren't responsible for your own actions."

"Okay, I don't know what to do. What do you want me to say? Everything I say is wrong!"

"*You* are wrong," I counter, pointing my finger at him. "You were wrong to cheat on me, and to approach me at Applebee's and insult me, and to follow me to Blossombranch the other day, and to show up like this and ask me to just forget everything! We can't go back to holding hands and skipping merrily across the bridge *that you burned to the fucking ground!*" By the end of this, I'm screaming.

Rafe has no time to respond before a knock sounds at the front door. I stomp over to it, fling it open, and find Beatrix standing on my front step.

"Oh, I—God, hi," I stammer breathlessly, trying not to direct my fury at her.

She doesn't look concerned, though. Honestly, she looks kind of amused. "Hey, doll."

I step away from the door. "Come in. I'm—I'm just—"

"Ripping someone a new asshole?" A smile spreads across her face as she steps inside.

My anger falters a little and I chuckle. I can't help it.

"I guess I showed up at a good time," she says, tossing her blonde hair over her shoulder so her teal ombré is out of sight. She winks at me. "I wouldn't be the only one upset by you disappearing into a jail cell."

I shake my head and sigh. "Let me just get rid of him." I turn away from her and fix my eyes on Rafe, who hasn't moved at all. I jerk my head toward the front door. "I'm done talking to you."

He glances at Beatrix. I don't know if he's intimidated by her (even in her heart-print coat, she has that I'm A Badass vibe) or if he wants to save face because he thinks she's sexy in that late-thirties-rocker-chick way, but he doesn't fight me. He does, however, take his time moving toward the door; he saunters past Beatrix and me so casually that my blood boils.

He looks at me once he steps off the front porch. "There are a few other things I wanted to tell you," he says, pausing in the falling snow, "really important things, but I guess now isn't a good time."

"I don't want to hear any more apologies—"

"Things about guys in run-down neighborhoods, Mari," he interrupts me, his expression turning stony. "Things you *need* to hear, whether you want to or not."

Oh, God.

When he confronted me on Blossombranch the other day, I almost lost it. I thought he overheard my conversation with Gabe, who I couldn't explain even if large amounts of money were being offered to me. I quickly realized, though, that Rafe hadn't overheard us, which was a huge relief; still, me talking to Gabe at all set him off and he wouldn't quit pestering me about it. All the way back to the apartment I evaded his questions by lecturing him on how unacceptable it was for him to have followed me like that, but I should've known he wasn't going to let it go.

"Not interested," I finally say, shutting the door.

"*Guys in run-down neighborhoods,*'" Beatrix repeats slowly. "Was that about Gabe, or...?"

"Yeah," I sigh. "I'll tell you about it in a minute. Are these clothes okay?" I gesture to my white long-sleeved shirt, black yoga pants and sneakers.

She confirms that they are okay, so after I locate my coat and purse, we leave.

Once we're in her car she wants to know everything about Rafe, so I tell her. At one point my stomach growls loudly and I realize I didn't get a chance to eat this morning, so we hit up a drive-thru for some breakfast and that only gives me more time to vent.

She's an excellent participant in my bitchfest—not just because she offers sufficiently obscene comments, but because I can tell she really does care. The things she says are well-put and insightful and welcome. However, they also touch on a more pained part of me: they make me realize how much I miss having another female to talk to, how badly I've been craving validation since Claire turned so cold. And by the time we park behind The Room, I'm trying to decide whether or not it'd be weird for me to hug her.

As soon as we're out of her car, though, she walks around through the snow and hugs me first. She pats my hair when she pulls back. "Mari, baby," she says, "I've got a good fifteen years on you, and I've learned a thing or two or ten about life while I've been on this planet. One of them is that sometimes—" she chuckles, "—well, *oftentimes* the best way to get over a guy is to get—"

"Please don't say it," I interrupt her. My cheeks burst into flame just at thinking about that popular saying. "That's not me." Not even with Gabe, and I think that man is my definition of Hot Damn.

Beatrix throws her head back and laughs. "—is to get *rid of your anger*," she finishes, looking at me again with shining eyes. She gestures toward The Room and, moreover, the Sanctum. "Training is good for that."

My blush deepens at my having assumed the wrong thing. "Oh. Yeah, that's probably...yeah."

We head to the back door and she links an arm through one of mine. "But while we're on the subject of shameless female behavior, let me tell you another one of those things I've learned in my time on the planet." She types in the passcode. "Skank bitches all treat guys the same way, from how they look at them to the things they say. So as Gabe's honorary big sister, I notice when he's gotten skank bitch attention. And you, little lady, do not treat him like you think the best way to get over a guy is to get under another one."

Embarrassed as I am, a little laugh leaves me.

She gains us access to the stairwell and releases my arm. Her bright hair bounces around her shoulders as she walks down the steps in front of me. "And that makes me happy, Mari. Makes Wes happy, too. Gabe is a guy of a different kind. I mean, he's *a guy* just like my husband—" she scoffs, "—all guys are *guys*, you know what I mean? I know he thinks you're gorgeous. But so far I haven't caught him looking at you in a way that's made me want to barf."

Part of me wants to laugh again, but a lot of me is concerned about something else, and it makes me stop walking. The words are out before I can decide whether or not I really want them to be. "Do you think he only notices me because of my Radiance?"

Beatrix stops walking and turns to look up at me, a frown forming on her face. Not an angry frown—it's one that says, *'Uh, wow, that's a sad thought.'*

I swallow hard. "He already told me that you and I are the only girls here. So...be honest."

Her face softens into a look of thoughtfulness as her eyes drift over me. "He notices your Radiance, sugar," she allows shortly. "It was the very first thing he noticed about you. That's part of his job, of course, but even if it wasn't, Radiance is impossible to ignore. It really is a sight to behold and it really does set a person apart from everyone else. But do I think yours is why he walked around the Sanctum with us yesterday, and went out of his way to drive you home, and then called to tell me you like some little-known Matchbox Twenty song he likes?" She meets my eyes and shakes her head. "You're special and you're a change for us, but he's not the desperate type. He's too smart. He wouldn't make something out of nothing with you just because he wants something new."

I believe her. I can't help it. Feeling relieved, I tuck my hair behind my ears and laugh a little. "Did he really call you?"

"He did." She laughs, too. "Don't tell him I told you, though."

"I won't." I give her a grateful smile and murmur, "Okay, well...thank you."

She starts gathering her hair into a ponytail. "You're welcome. That guy from your apartment is a disappointing ass, but not every guy is just like him, so don't worry. Even if it turns out that you and Gabe don't get along very well—" she gives me a skeptical look as she ties a rubber band into her hair, "—that'd be only two guys out of all the guys in the world. Know what I mean?"

"Yeah," I chortle.

"Great. So, speaking of that clown Rafe—you ready to go get rid of some anger?"

Thinking about the way he tried to kiss me, I wrinkle my nose. "Absolutely I am."

⌒

Four hours later, I feel better emotionally. Physically, though...well, that's a different story. See, I've learned something here today. It was quite a revelation, one everyone should be aware of: you might think you're in pretty good shape, but that *does not* mean you are.

Just look at me. I'm five-foot-five, slender with a few curves here and there, never had a problem with being under-or-overweight. But does that (and having taken some little zumba class at U of A while I was there) mean I'm in shape? No. If I were, I don't think simple things like stretching, working on an elliptical machine and jogging around the training room would have worn me out like this.

I'm currently lying flat on my back on the springboard, staring up at the ceiling. I'm sweaty as hell. Panting like some sort of wild animal. Wishing I had some water, but not wanting to get up and grab it.

But all things considered, I'm in a pretty good mood. Beatrix was right: this has been a good release for my anger. My frustration did a lot to fuel me as I practiced some high kicks and ran around the room and worked on the elliptical.

She seems to think I've done great even though I don't feel that I've done much of anything. In fact, I mentioned that to her. Then I learned a fun fact: everyone who turns Light starts positively responding to training really quickly, even if they previously weren't Exercise People. They think it's because fighting is so central to our existence, and that whatever chooses people to be Light chooses those with body types that can handle combat. So even though I'm beat today, apparently I really am doing fine, and in another day or two we can start on offensive and defensive tactics.

I'm interested to witness this for myself.

The volume of the music echoing around the room lowers. "Doing okay?" I hear her ask over the White Stripes song. I'm glad for the interruption, since I can't decide if I hate the hypnotic beat or enjoy it.

"Think so," I reply. "Just taking a breather."

"Hop up in a second and walk around some. That way you can catch your breath without cooling off too quickly."

But cooling off quickly sounds sooooo good.

I make myself sit up, and my body is already starting to bitch about the movement. I don't even want to think about how I'll feel tomorrow. I glance at the mirror and see that my appearance better matches how I feel physically rather than emotionally.

"I think this has been a reasonable lesson, huh?" Beatrix asks. "9:30 to, like, 1:30?"

"Whatever you think," I groan as I get to my feet.

In the mirror I can see her rolling her shoulders. When she took her coat and sweater off earlier and made visible her tank top, I noticed her shoulders are dotted with lots of tiny black star tattoos, and I was momentarily struck by the urge to get some badass tattoo myself. And then I remembered, *Ew, needles,* and changed my mind again.

Stretching my heavy arms above my head, I add, "If you want me to practice for several hours a day, I will. If you think I'll be okay with just a few, that's fine, too."

"This has been good so far. We'll see what the next few days look like."

"Deal." I drop my arms and roll my head around a few times.

The music cuts off completely. "Can I ask you something?"

"Sure."

"What the fuck made you decide to go after those Hellions the other day?"

My cool-down procedures come to a halt. My gaze stops on the floor. For many seconds I stare at the stiff blue springboard, suddenly grasping for something to say.

It's not that I don't know the answer. I just don't want to think about it, don't want to admit it.

But I like Beatrix. I like talking to her. I manage, "I couldn't let another person die because of me."

"What do you mean?"

I lift my eyes to the mirror again. Her reflection is regarding mine with curiosity, which is a lot better than the apprehension I was expecting. Still, the words don't quite want to leave my mouth. Not when they sound so bad in my head.

"Mari, sweetie?" she presses carefully after a little bit.

"I got—" My voice sounds strangled. I swallow hard and then do it again, but there's a painful lump in my throat, further encouraging me not to say it.

I want to be her friend, I remind myself. *And no one wants to be friends with people who won't be honest.*

Each word is a razorblade in my throat when I say, "I got my parents killed. My car went off a bridge. Just an accident, but...it could've been avoided."

If that son of a bitch hadn't cheated on me, I wouldn't have been reading his apology texts. The voice in my head is harsher and colder than before. *Reading his pleas for me to come back to the party so he could explain himself.*

"Is that how you became Light?" Beatrix's gentle question rips through my thoughts.

I nod, desperately not wanting to remember that night anymore. Thankfully, my mind conjures up images from the day I killed the Hellions instead. "When I came up on Gabe fighting those Hellions, I was just amazed—*he* was amazing. But I gasped or whatever and I don't know how he heard it, but he did. He looked up and saw me and the Hellions saw their chance and went after him and...." My shoulders lift and then drop back down. "I mean, I don't remember picking up the dagger. All I remember is realizing he was about to die because I distracted him, and then I was just there."

Some time passes before Beatrix says, "I never thanked you for that, so from the bottom of my heart, thanks for not letting him die. He's like family and...." Her voice sounds different than it did—frailer, like she's on the verge of crying. It's heart-wrenching. "You say you didn't process what you were doing until you were already in the middle of things, but you could've stopped then. You could've dropped that dagger and run like the wind. And you didn't." She laughs once, breathlessly.

I don't know what to say. Before I can try to come up with something, the door to the training room opens. Memories of car wrecks and Hellions disappear from my mind.

It's Wes. He strides into the room with a smile on his face, eyes on Beatrix. "Hi, love," I think I hear him say. When he reaches her he drops his hands onto her shoulders and presses a kiss to her cheek, murmurs something else. After she replies he looks over at me. "Hi, Mari. Having fun?"

"Absolutely." I smile, but I know it doesn't reach my eyes. Just in case he thinks I'm being sarcastic I add, "Beatrix is great and I've heard a lot of interesting music today. How are you?"

"Not bad." He turns around and glances at the door. "Gabe's behind me somewhere."

The thought cheers me. Then I remember where I am and what I've been doing and how I look, and I don't feel so enthused anymore. I make a blubbery noise with my lips and turn toward the mirror. My ponytail no longer passes for a ponytail and pieces of hair are stuck to my face and neck by sweat. My face is pink, and so is the skin above my shirt collar.

Are those sweat stains under there? I wonder, lifting up my arms. I drop them back down in displeasure. *Yep, and that's just great because they're* totally *not gross.*

I scowl at the floor and think more irritably, *Oh, who gives a shit. People sweat. Beatrix sweats, and so do Wes and Gabe.*

Except Gabe sweating probably isn't very unattractive.

Okay, let's not think about that.

Too late. My stupid brain is already wondering what he looks like without his shirt on. Since, you know, it was only logical for me to go straight there after how he might look with sweat—

"Hey, Marienne," I hear from beside me. "How are you today?"

Jesus. Christ.

I inhale deeply and close my eyes. Then I turn my head toward him, reopen my eyes, and put a smile on my face. "Hi, Gabe. Doing fine."

Concern creases those lovely features of his. "You sure? Your face is pretty red."

That's because I was thinking about you half-naked. "Mmmhmmm," I hum. "How are you? All right?"

"Yeah, I'm all right, thanks. So do you need some water, or...?"

I nod slowly, glad that he's unaware of my mortification. Still, I have to force my eyes to stay on his face because they want to wander (even though he's fully dressed—God, I'm getting worse). If I don't show them who's boss, they'll betray my dumbass thoughts and I'll have to snatch them out of my head. "I do think I need some water," I tell him.

He gives me half a smile, seeming amused but still concerned that I'm going to fall out any second. "Okay, well...I'll escort you to where the water is."

"That's gentlemanly of you."

"I try."

By the water stand, I hear Beatrix saying something to Wes about Rafe showing up in my room this morning. Once she realizes Gabe and I are close, though, she smiles at us and changes the subject. "So, any luck with white Radiances today, Gabe?"

"No, but I did see a Hellion father and child at the mall," he replies, filling a Styrofoam cup with water. "Had to call Wes over." He holds the cup out to me.

"I—huh?" I don't know which I was expecting less: him retrieving my water for me, or him saying he saw a *Hellion child* at the mall. "Hellions aren't only adults?" I take the water cup and smile my thanks.

He flashes a smile back to me, and then says seriously, "Unfortunately, no. They grow up just like regular kids. That's why you hear about some children committing heinous crimes."

"So they're still...?" I frown and glance at Beatrix and Wes. "I mean, we have to kill them?" They nod. I look at Gabe and he nods, too. "That is awful." It makes sense, but it's awful.

They all look at me sympathetically. Behind that sympathy is a knowing look, though, and I can tell what they're thinking: *'One of these days, she won't feel so bad about it.'*

The fucked-up thing is that I'm sure they're right.

Once I've pulled my hair back up, we all leave and Gabe offers to drive me home again. I recall him telling me back on Blossombranch that he doesn't usually spend time with people, and I just can't help feeling happy that he seems to be reconsidering that where I'm concerned. So I accept the ride—and, yeah, it's fun. We listen to Queen and talk about what we both did today. He tells me more about those two Hellions at the mall. I tell him how my training went and that I really do like Beatrix. We pass some reckless bastard getting pulled over by the police, and I learn that Gabe has never gotten a speeding ticket and that he's deathly afraid of driving without a seatbelt on. I completely get that because I, too, always have to have a seatbelt on. For a minute we talk about how horrifying it'd be to drive on the autobahn in Germany. Then "Bohemian Rhapsody" comes on and we both start singing along, which eventually turns into us drumming on whatever we can reach and singing loudly and proudly. No joke.

So, yeah, the best part of my day so far is my trip home.

When we pull up in front of the apartment I reach for my purse. "I'll give you some gas money." Least I can do, right?

He turns down the music. "No, don't worry about that."

"Um, I owe you that."

"I don't want your money."

"Well, call it a gift or something. I want you to have it." I take a ten-dollar bill from my wallet and hold it out to him. Then my eyes catch on something, and I gasp a little and take my hand back. "Gabe."

"What?" He sounds somewhat alarmed, like he thinks I've spotted a Hellion.

But I pull my right sleeve farther up and whisper, "Look. I can see my mark."

"Oh." He leans closer, but I still hold my arm out a little so he can get a good look. The faint gold circle seems to warm underneath his gaze, like it knows another Light person is looking at it. I start to ask if his mark ever does that, but I don't because he murmurs, "Very nice, Marienne. It looks good on you."

Be still, my hammering heart.

"Does the circle itself have some kind of meaning?" I ask.

He shrugs. "I'm not sure. I think it's just identification for other Light people's sakes. They're hard to see right off the bat, of course, but they react to nearby Light people—" (well, there's that) "—so it keeps us from having to walk around bright as hell all day, every day." He leans back into his seat.

"Oh, okay." I take a deep breath and tell myself, *All right, get it back together.* I hold out the money again. "Here we go."

He cracks a smile. "Keep it."

I gingerly lay the money on his right leg. "You said, *'Thanks for the money,'* wrong, but don't worry, I know what you meant. And you're welcome."

He chuckles. "Marienne, take this back."

"No."

"Yes."

"Or what?"

"Nothing." He puts the money on my lap now. "I just don't want it."

I give him a look. "You don't like free money, Gabe? Are you kidding?"

He laughs again. "Yeah, I like free money. But if you're going to give me a gift, I'd rather it be something of a little more value to me. Like information."

I tsk and start putting the money away. "Okay, then. What do you want to know?"

"Are you dating anybody?"

The quiet question has my heart trying to jump out of my chest. My hands go cold even though my face grows warm. And I realize something: going back in time actually is possible, because I may be twenty-one, but that question sends me right back to junior high.

"I—uh—" I stuff my wallet back into my purse and tuck my hair behind my ears. "I'm not. No. Do you have a girl—wife...person?" I curl my hands into fists and make myself look at him.

I swear to God he's blushing, but I don't know why and I have no time to ponder it because he smiles and says, "No."

My day is exponentially better than it was the last time he smiled at me.

I conquer my Junior High Syndrome enough to confess quietly, "I don't know why. You're something else."

His gaze is earnest, but he tells me simply, "I'm the same thing you are."

The sentiment sits warm in my mind for the rest of the day, even when Claire comes home later and, for the trillionth time since August, looks at me like she can't believe I've been blessed with another day on this earth.

6
Gabe

On Thursday, once Marienne and I have gotten in my car after her training I tell her, "Got a tiny little surprise for you."

She beams. "Really?"

I fish my phone out of my pocket and start tapping around on it. "It's not much, but I thought you might like it." I find the picture and hand her my phone. "That's what my backyard looked like this morning."

She gasps softly and breathes out, "Oh." Her eyes move over the valley full of snow-topped trees, and the mountains in the distance, and the soft color of the sky. "Oh, Gabe, it's awesome. I can't believe you woke up to this."

I smile. "Like it?"

"You have no idea. It's so much better than an apartment."

"Prettier for sure, but there's hardly anyone around."

"That's weird to me. I don't know why people aren't jumping at the chance to live on a mountain. I'd do it if I could." She gives my phone back. "Maybe I'll build a house on a mountain."

"Are you interested in architecture?" I ask as I start out of the parking lot.

"No. I mean, architecture is *interesting*, but could I make a profession out of it? No."

"Why not?"

"I would do an abominable job."

I chuckle. "I think if you like it, you can make it work."

She laughs a little, too. "My poor math skills beg to differ."

"Well, are you a good artist? Maybe you could just deal with concepts or something."

"I *can* draw, actually," she says, "but I'm better at small things than large things. Like, I can do eyes pretty well, but not a whole face."

I sigh. "I wish I could draw. My mother could. And, of course, I didn't really start wanting to learn until after she was gone."

"Yeah," she says kindly. "That's the way it goes, isn't it?"

"It is."

She hesitates before she asks, "What happened to her? Or is that not...?"

I murmur, "It's fine. I don't mind you asking." Still, the memory saddens me. "She died the night I turned Light. Our house got broken into and the burglars shot her."

"Ohhh, God, no," Marienne says softly.

"Yeah." I press a hand to my right ribcage. "They shot me, too. Just didn't kill me."

She tells me earnestly, "I'm sorry. I know it doesn't help anything, but still."

I look over at her and give her a grateful smile. "I appreciate it anyway. And I'm doing a lot better now than I was at first. Time really does help."

Something in her eyes shifts and she looks away, so I do, too. "I'm glad to hear that." She clears her throat and asks more lightly, "What do you like to do, then? In your free time?"

I inhale deeply and let it out slowly. "Um, I don't really know." And that's the truth. I've been focused on nothing but work for so long that I usually just sleep in my free time. Even when I'm having my meals I keep my eyes open for white Radiances. I spend time with Wes and Beatrix every now and then—not often enough to call it a hobby. Haven't had anything to do with a girl in years.

After a few moments she wonders, "Reading?"

I nod a little. "I like to read, but I don't do it often."

"What about writing?"

I shake my head. "I've never tried it."

"Hmm. Do you like playing video games?"

That one makes me laugh. "What guy doesn't?"

She chortles. "Yeah, okay. Well, what kind of games do you like? Mario?"

I grin. "I do like Mario, but I haven't played any games in a really long time."

"Oh." After a second, "Are you a good cook?"

I squint and ruminate for a second. "I think so? It's been a while since I cooked much of anything."

"All right...do you like movies?" She's starting to sound a little confused by my answers.

I tell her the truth even though it'll probably only puzzle her further. "Yeah, but it's been a while since I watched a movie, too."

She sits quietly for a minute, and when I pull up to a red light I look over at her. She looks back at me, her expression contemplative. "Do you spend most of your time working?" she finally asks.

Slowly, I nod and admit, "Yes."

A little smile comes onto her face now. "Do you love it?"

Out of the corner of my eye I see the car ahead of me already driving forward, so I face the front. I get us going again before I say, "Yeah, I do."

"What's your favorite part?"

"That I find people who feel like they don't belong anywhere." I'm definitely not used to being asked questions like that, but I drum my fingers on the steering wheel and decide to keep talking. "I'm good at Defender work, though. That's what I did for the first year I was in the Lightforce—and don't get me wrong, killing Hellions is important, *so* important. But the look that comes onto a person's face when they see me and realize they're not alone...it's...outstanding." I chew on the inside of my cheek. "I saw it with you, too—especially on the day you talked to me, but a little the first time I ever saw you. I think that day you were pretty stuck in combat mode."

She lets out a breathless laugh. "Yeah, that was a really chaotic minute for me."

I grin. "For me, too." I think back to how receptive she was the first day we talked. Some of the information surprised her a little, like me telling her she was glowing, but I could tell she wanted it. She looked at me that day like she wanted every syllable I had to offer her, like she'd wait all day for me to explain things if she had to. That's what I love the most about being a Gatherer: being able to save someone with a simple explanation.

Oh, fine. I also liked the fact that she wanted me to talk to her at all.

And I *really* like that she still does. I tell her, "I used to play the piano all the time. I liked that a lot."

"Really? I love the piano," she says. "I can't play it, though. Well, maybe I can play a tiny bit of 'Mary Had A Little Lamb.'"

"I'd say that I'll help you with it sometime, but I don't know where to find a piano."

"Yeah, I don't know that, either. But if you ever come across one, let me know. We can trade a piano lesson for a drawing lesson."

For some reason, that turns my already-bright mood incandescent. I actually hold a hand out to her. "Deal."

She shakes my hand and echoes, "Deal."

Oh my God, I already love touching her. I wonder if it shows—I wonder if she can tell that she's the first girl I've touched in forever, not counting hugging Beatrix at the funeral.

When she lets go of my hand she asks, "What's something you don't like?"

Looks like I didn't give myself away. "Country music," I say after a second.

"I'm with you on that one."

"I also don't like...soda."

She asks, "Oh? Why?"

"I mean, I used to like it, but once I started training and had to do a lot of fighting, I learned water is the best thing to drink when you're thirsty."

"Ah. Good point. Maybe I should start on that myself."

"I'm sure your body would appreciate it. It doesn't like being dehydrated."

She sounds like she's smiling when she says, "No. No, it doesn't." Then, "Who trained you back in the day?"

"Wes did. He'd been in the Lightforce for eleven years already."

"Jesus. So you really are like his little brother."

I nod. "Fifteen-year difference between us. I'm like the little brother his parents conceived on accident."

She laughs. "That's funny."

Not one of my more entertaining moments if you ask me, but if I'm making her smile, okay.

"What exactly made you want to be a Gatherer in the first place?" she asks. "If you were doing so well being a Defender?"

I draw a breath and hold it a second before I let it back out. "It was Em." It still hurts to think about him, but I don't think Marienne knows I'm on the same level as Wes as far as being a trainer goes, and it's kind of an important aspect of my job now. "Johnta Emilia is the man we buried recently. He was the Gatherer trainer around here—had been for a really long time. I just got to talking to him one day and I was curious about what his job entailed, you know. And everything he told me just sounded so rewarding that I wanted to try it out."

"And look at you now," she says softly.

I clear my throat. "Yeah, I'm—I'm actually what he was, now that he's gone. I'm in charge of the Gatherer stuff around here now."

Marienne gasps. "Really?"

"Really. He and I were the only two Gatherers in town because..." I frown a little, not wanting to sound conceited, "...well, we didn't need anyone else. But I can't do it all alone, so I've spoken with a couple of Defenders who are interested in making the switch."

"Wow," she says, sounding excited. "I mean, I can tell that you miss him, but I know you'll do a great job taking over for him."

A soft laugh leaves me. "You know that, do you?"

"Yes."

What a nice thing for her to say. "Well, thank you. It's going to be...strange. It already is, really."

"I'm sure, but you've got promise written all over you. You'll be great."

I can't help a smile. She sounds so confident in me that *I feel* more confident in myself.

When I pull up in front of her apartment I inform her, "I'm doing all the asking tomorrow."

"I will prepare myself," she says.

"You do that."

She nods once. "I'll do that."

I nod back. "Do it."

"I'll do it."

"Do." For some reason, I find myself grinning.

"I will." A smile makes its way onto her face, too, and she puts her hands on her cheeks like that'll make it go away. It's adorable how it doesn't work at all.

And then suddenly we're both laughing. My face actually hurts from it after just a few seconds. And I don't really even know what's tickled us so much.

"What's so funny?" I barely manage to ask her.

"I don't know." She opens her door. "I've given up on trying to figure myself out."

The frigid air feels good on my suddenly warm face, and it helps me calm down enough to speak clearly. "Maybe I'll follow suit. It's kind of fun."

She bends down to look at me. She's still smiling brightly and it's marvelous. "I feel like I'm probably a little stranger than I am fun, but whatever you think, Gabe."

One thing I do know is that I love hearing her say my name. I try to reel in the rush of boldness I'm getting from this weirdly exhilarating situation; instead of telling her, *'What I think is you're the most awesome girl ever and I wish I could hang out with you all fucking day,'* I say, "Our whole existence is strange, Marienne."

She nods. "Good point." Then she snorts and her eyebrows go up and she claps a hand over her mouth. Voice a little muffled, she says, "Okay, I'm going now."

"All right." I start laughing again just at remembering our ridiculous back-and-forth.

"See you tomorrow?"

Can't believe she'd double-check that. "Yes, tomorrow."

She shuts the car door and hurries away, laughing the whole time. I can hear the sound until the moment she closes herself into her apartment.

"Good God," I sigh to myself.

I head to the mall directly from her apartment. This afternoon marks my first time meeting up with Janssen and Wright for any semblance of Gatherer training. White Radiances aren't around every day, though, so we don't end up with much to do. Still the guys are patient, and they listen as I talk about the kinds of things I've learned to expect from new Light people.

When I first started out as a Gatherer, Em had a different conversation with me. He was a great mentor and friend, but he said, "Try it for yourself," a lot. Although that was a good lesson for me to learn, I'm working with men who have already seen years of straightforward action. I think it would benefit them to hear how the more subtle approaches have worked for me, even if they end up not using them.

I tell them new Light people will always be startled by us. They'll always stare at the Radiance if they can see it, and they'll always ask about it. Sometimes they'll freak out and run away, or start yelling or throwing punches because they don't think we're real.

Their initial reactions don't necessarily foretell how they're going to receive the whole speech—Em said when he found Wes, he almost took a punch to the stomach because his Radiance surprised Wes so greatly. But after Em said what he needed to say, Wes was way less hostile. So, barring the person trying to murder them in self-defense, a Gatherer should always try to push through whatever response they get at first.

After that, it can be a difficult thing to figure out. On the one hand, a little persistence can be a game-changer. We need as many people in the Lightforce as we can get because our numbers are so thin compared to those of the Hellions. On the other hand, some people don't react well to being entreated even the tiniest bit—like the guy I found last year who punched me in the mouth so hard I have a scar on my bottom lip now. Some people just want to be left alone to deal with their new life however they see fit. In such a case walking away feels like admitting defeat, but staying would only make things worse. New Light people need to have room in their heads for such extraordinary conversation, and if they don't have it...well, they just don't.

But you can't always tell who will have room and who won't. Sometimes the younger people are more open to the whole thing, and sometimes they think I'm playing some kind of elaborate joke on them because I'm pretty young myself. Some older people are stuck in their beliefs about what can and can't exist, and others say they've lived long enough to know there are things in the world that are real no matter how difficult they are to explain.

Sometimes the whole thing just goes perfectly: a Gatherer finds someone who is approachable and ready for answers. But it's nothing anyone should count on happening, and Janssen and Wright seem to accept that.

Not surprisingly, we go all the way through dinner without spotting anything of interest to us. We split up after that. The other day Janssen volunteered to take the night watches; he was already doing that as a Defender because he was used to life as a policeman. So after spending another couple of fruitless hours by myself, I head home for the night and leave Fayetteville in Janssen's hands.

I get there and get settled in, but I'm not tired enough to fall asleep. Instead of lying in bed anyway like I usually would, I decide to do something I haven't done in quite a while: turn on my TV.

Since I'm not too familiar with most of what's on, I settle for *The Breakfast Club.* My mom loved it, so I saw it more than a few times when I was younger. Watching it now saddens me. It also makes me laugh, though, because John Bender is too hilarious sometimes—maybe even funnier than usual with all the editing they had to do to put the movie on TV. And the movie makes me think about Marienne with a different sense of anticipation than usual, because tomorrow I'll be able to tell her I actually did something with my free time.

And really I'm excited about that, because although I love being Gatherer Gabe, I realized during her questioning that I've been seriously shorting myself on enjoying the things I like as regular Gabe.

⌒

I guess I fell asleep thinking about Marienne, which is weird because the thought of her doesn't fatigue me in the least. Case in point: I wake up in the morning at my usual time of 6:00 and once the thought of her stirs in my head, I'm wide awake. And cheerful. So cheerful that instead of being mad that there's some really annoying paid programming rolling on my TV (I fell asleep with it on, apparently), I actually listen to the lame script for a minute just in case the product isn't completely worthless.

It turns out to be completely worthless after all, but I'm still in a good mood.

I don't have much sustenance at my house since I don't spend a lot of time in it, so I swing by Starbucks every morning. It's usually pretty busy, which is good for looking for white Radiances, but today I see none. I do spot a Hellion, so I call Wes and let him know. He's pretty close by and makes it over before the Hellion leaves, so we talk for a minute and agree to catch lunch together, since we'll both be going to the Sanctum afterward. Then it's time for him to get in his first kill of the day, and I leave him to it.

While I mosey around Wal-Mart, I check in with Wright. He's got a whole lot of nothing just like me, but we agree that the day is young and full of potential, and remind one another to call if we find any new Light people.

Something else that is young and full of potential: the human child. I'm looking at a few CDs when I hear an adorable, shrieky giggle from the next aisle over. I look up, amused, but see nothing.

A guy starts talking from that direction, his voice overly deep and theatrical. "Charlotte is going to be late for kindergarten! Oh, bother! All she wanted to do was take *The Tigger Movie* to show-and-tell, but her baby sister spilled apple juice on the only copy she had! Now she's at the store getting another one, but time runs short! What can be done? Who can be called?" The words echo around the department.

An excited cheer pierces the air, I guess from Charlotte. "Daddy the Bullet!" she shrieks.

"That's right!" the guy booms. "Daddy the Bullet is here to safely and speedily transport darlings in distress to where they are needed most! Hold on tight—and go!"

I look toward the end of the aisle, and a second later a guy about my age sprints past with the elated little girl thrown over one shoulder, the DVD clutched in her small hands.

I laugh wholeheartedly. It's at times like this that I really wish I could have that.

I don't waste more than a few seconds on that wish, though, because it'll never be realized. I've known for a long time that no one with Light blood can reproduce, even if they try to do so with a normal human versus another Light person. Disheartening as it is, it makes sense. If a Light person created a human child, they'd want to tell them about Hellions but wouldn't really be able to. Even if they tried to raise the child with a simple belief in Light people, what good would it do the kid if they couldn't see Hellions for themselves? And it's impossible to birth a Light child. So it's a no-go all around.

After a few hours, once most of the stores in town are open, I decide to search out a birthday present for Beatrix while I work. She'll be most pleased with the dragon earring Wes mentioned the other day, so I don't feel like I need to spend too much time poring over my options. I end up at the mall because there are bazillions of possibilities, and I know I'm bound to find something.

Though it's not quite what I planned on finding at the mall this early, I spot two Hellions. So I call Wes for the second time this morning.

He's perfectly capable of handling them himself, but he still asks, "Wanna split the kills?" when he shows up. He nods at the monsters, which are walking a ways in front of us, looking rancid and out-of-place to no one but us two.

"It's up to you," I tell him unconcernedly. "We can knock them out together or you can have a little fun taking them on by yourself."

"Eh, well," he squints in mock-deliberation, "they *are* in a really public place...."

I nod thoughtfully, playing along. "More and more people are showing up by the minute."

"What kind of sick bastard would I look like should someone happen upon me gutting two seemingly normal fellas?"

"We should definitely be responsible," I say as the Hellions turn into the food court, "and kill them super fast."

"Super fast and super furious."

"Just like the other day, huh?"

Wes holds a strong fist up. "It's what we do best."

Well, it's what *he* does best, but whatever. I don't see any white Radiances around and, yeah, better to be efficient than insist he kill them alone.

The Hellions head toward two of the food stands closest to the restrooms. They seem to be debating something (could it really be food? To be honest, I'm not sure if they even eat food) when a young mother and her little girl step out of the women's restroom. The Hellions go still and openly stare. The mother is talking on her cell phone while the little girl trots along, but she takes a second to snap her fingers and command, "Hey, come back!" as her daughter approaches the Hellions.

She waves and yells, "Hi!"

Wes and I stop near the little group, feigning interest in the food stands as the mother ends her phone call and hurries over. "Trinity, quit bothering people!" She looks at the Hellions like she thinks they're attractive and is embarrassed that her kid is hollering at them.

If only she knew that the man bending down to see eye-to-eye with her daughter is actually completely skinless. "Oh, that's okay, Mommy," his voice rumbles loudly. "A girl this pretty is no bother."

The other has skin, but he's covered in jagged slashes like he was whipped with barbed wire. His human disguise must be the polar opposite, because he approaches the woman confidently and she doesn't back away whatsoever. He asks her coyly, "Does she get her gregariousness from her mother, or just her charm?"

The woman smiles in delight and her little girl squeals, "I'm four!"

The Hellion in front of her looks at his cohort. "Four is such a good age, isn't it?" The words are dripping with filthy pleasure. He looks at the woman and says, "Our families are extensive—children everywhere, and for some reason they all seem to be the most fun around this time."

Wes makes a faint noise of repugnance at the same time that my stomach turns unpleasantly. We know the truth: these sons of bitches have been around that many little children because they're pedophiles.

"Bathroom, then come back out?" Wes mumbles.

"Mmhmm."

We pretend to ignore the little group as we skirt past. After spending a minute in the restroom, we hear the skinless Hellion rumble less vociferously than before, "I like them. Wonderful child, oblivious mother."

They must be alone again. Wes and I look at one another. "Get that one," he mouths.

The other Hellion muses that he rather likes the woman. They're beginning to discuss how to get the pair somewhere more ideal for abduction than the middle of the mall when Wes and I walk out.

It wouldn't be smart to yank them back into the restrooms to kill them because the people working at these food stands are sure to notice something like that, and also cameras would probably catch it. The safest option is to follow the pair as they head in what I assume is the direction the mother and child went in. Our opportunity arrives shortly, though. The Hellions follow their targets into JC Penney and decide to spy on them from behind a bunch of towering, cluttered-up merchandise. We check to make sure there aren't any people or cameras close by, and then we're right behind them...literally. They're too busy eyeballing the woman and child to notice us.

Once we're behind the slashed-up one, Wes gets right to it. He kneels down, produces his dagger and swipes it across the backs of the monster's knees, and he lets out a surprised screech.

The skinless Hellion's first reaction is to jump between the two of them, but after a second he realizes I'm with Wes and a danger to him. This revelation comes to him too late. My dagger is already drawn when he turns toward me, and he lunges right into the blade. He cries out in fury or pain or both, and while he does that I yank out my dagger and then sink it into his thigh. Now he's got two disintegrating wounds, making it even easier to drag him to the floor where Wes has just finished handling the other one.

In a matter of moments the total of flaky, dusty piles on the ground is two. We straighten our clothes, put our daggers away and leave with no one in the store suspecting anything. Humans can't hear Hellions' true voices, only the disguised voices they use and only when the Hellions want them to. When faced with such a sudden and weighty moment as this past one, the Hellions have no time to arrange their disguise. They're just themselves, so the only beings that know what's happening are them and us; no one else heard them screaming.

"I'm happy we got them," Wes says. "The ones that hurt kids are the fucking worst."

"They really are," I agree. I think back to the little girl from Wal-Mart—Charlotte. The idea of someone even considering harming her makes my blood boil. She has her father on her side and he clearly loves her, but even he might not stand a chance against a Hellion. Me, though? I stand a really good chance against the enemy. Maybe I'll never have what that guy has, but what I *will* have, until the day I die, is the ability to keep families like his safe. And I will accept that substitution gladly and with honor.

I can't wait to tell Marienne. I'm sure she'll be happy to hear that we prevented what was sure to be a heart-breaking, and probably gruesome, story from unfolding.

Wes and I decide to just stick together. He helps me pick out a funny birthday card for Beatrix, and he picks out a very sappy husband-to-wife one for himself. Then he says she'd probably like a gift card to Bath & Body Works, so I get her one and he finally buys the dragon earring.

"I bet you twenty bucks she cries," I say to him.

He looks at me contemplatively. "I bet you twenty bucks she screams *and* cries."

I nod. "It's on."

"On and on. And just in case you're wondering, I don't care if it's a whole twenty-dollar bill or if it's a couple of tens. Whatever. Just don't write me a check."

"I'll keep that in mind for the future, when I lose a bet to you that isn't this one. And who the hell writes checks?"

He chuckles. "People who think debit cards are manufactured in hell."

"Ridiculous. Checks have your address and stuff on them. Plastic is just your name and two inches' worth of numbers."

"No shit," he agrees, sounding like he really is bothered by people's continued use of checks.

I can't help but laugh.

A little while later, over lunch, he says, "So, B kind of loves Mari."

"Already?" I ask, even though I'm not that surprised.

"Okay, she *really* loves her," he amends. "I thought you and I were good friends to that crazy woman, but apparently having another girl around is top fun." He laughs a little and shakes his head.

"I understand that, I guess." I smile. "Marienne is great."

He nods. "Leaps and goddamn bounds better than that girl you liked way back when."

I know who he means—Ella—and I groan just at the thought of her. "She was fucking terrible. I didn't even *like* her, I just...." Embarrassed by the cheap relationship I had with her, I wave my hand around dismissively. "She doesn't deserve to even be compared to Marienne."

Wes laughs heartily now. "Nothing sucks like thinking back on your mistakes, huh?" He tsks and shakes his head. "Nah, I'm just giving you a hard time, dude. I know that was just one of those things we all go through in our lives."

"One of those humiliating, immature," I say slowly, "a-lesson-hard-learned things."

He absently cracks his knuckles. "Been there, done that, not going back."

"Not ever," I agree, taking a bite of my food.

"Okay, so, different subject. Kind of."

I nod my acknowledgement.

"B wants all four of us to hang out."

The statement both puzzles and cheers me. After I swallow my food I ask, "Really?"

He leans back in his chair and crosses his arms. "Yeah, really. I think she wants us all to be closer because of Em's sudden death, but like I said, she also enjoys being around Mari—and so do you. I told her I'd ask you about it, but that you and Mari aren't dating so I didn't know if it'd be weird. At least, I don't *think* you're dating each other."

I shake my head a little. "No, we're not, but...."

He raises an eyebrow. "Mmmhmmm."

"What?"

"You're not dating, buuut—" he rolls his head around in a dramatic circle before leveling a knowing look on me, "—you're pretty fucking interested."

I laugh. "Well-spotted."

"What can I say? I know what a guy looks like when he digs a girl." He holds up his left hand so I can see his black wedding band.

Still amused, I say, "Right."

He winks. "So I can tell B a group hang isn't completely out of the question?"

I shrug a shoulder. "It's fine with me."

"Sweet. Thanks."

"Yep. A happy Beatrix makes for a happy Weston, huh?"

He nods. "That's it." As he leans forward to go back to his food, he sighs. "We all deserve to be happy."

7
Marienne

I have almost completed my third full training session and I have to say that although the muscle soreness is rough, I kind of love all the exercise. I don't know why I've gone so many years without investing in some kind of routine physical activity, but I wish I'd started sooner than just this week. It's liberating.

Oh and yeah, Beatrix's expectation really is already coming true. It's only my third day doing this and I'm feeling spectacular. I feel awake and alive during these hours, and after they come to an end I feel like I've actually accomplished something. Even if that something is, for now, only getting myself into better shape, I know it'll help in the Hellion-killing department later. It'll help me save lives. And that is something I'm willing to work for...if you can even call it work. Like I said, I'm having a blast.

Today, near the end of our time together Beatrix and I slow down to some slow stretches so we can discuss the details of killing Hellions. She puts her left hand on her left hip and then leans her torso in that same direction, reaching her other arm over her head. "First thing I'm going to say: the quicker they die, the better."

I nod as I sink down into a lunge. "Got it."

"The best way to kill them quickly is to slice open a main vein—" she lowers her one hand briefly to draw a fingertip across her throat, "—or get Light blood directly into their hearts via stabbing. Any other wound from a Light weapon will definitely help you out, though, because the area around it will start decaying away immediately, which can leave them at a huge disadvantage." She straightens up and starts that same stretch on her other side. "For example, if you were to somehow sever one of their hands, the flesh going up his arm would crumble away starting at that place. If you throw red powder in his face, it'll start disintegrating where the powder touched it. But to kill him, you have to do more than just those kinds of things. Get what I'm saying?"

"Absolutely." I shift to lunge a different way.

"We almost always have control of the situation because they can't pick us out like we can them. They only know we're on to them if we give ourselves away." She stands up again and this time stretches both arms and her torso forward. Something on her pops and she makes a noise of satisfaction. "Still—and I don't mean any offense— you're new to this, so for your first official kills I'll have you incapacitate them with your red powder before you leap in for an execution. Then once you've better seen what their reflexes are like and how the build of your body affects your stealth, you'll be able to do what the rest of us do and just get in and get out."

I sit down on the floor and put my legs straight out in front of me. "I'm not offended. That sounds pretty smart." I stretch as far forward toward my toes as I can...which still isn't a very impressive extension, honestly.

"Well, you helped Gabe with those two, so I just want you to know I'm not discounting that. This is just what we do with new people."

I sit back up and mutter, "Oh, Lord." I fucking hate the prickling tightness in the backs of my legs. I know it'll get better the more I do this stretch, though, so I try it one more time and tell Beatrix, "I promise I don't feel insulted.

Those Hellions were completely preoccupied trying to kill him. I was almost cheating."

She laughs and I hear her walking over to me. "You know my thoughts on that, darling." I feel her pat me on the back. Then she adds, "Don't hate me, k?"

Before I can ask what I should be not-hating her for, she flattens both palms against my back and presses down. "Aw, fuck!" I gasp as my chest dips seriously close to my legs. "Not comfortable!"

"I love you! Don't hate me! Seven more seconds!"

"Ohhh, *I* don't hate you," I tell her, "but my legs might." When she lets me up, I can't help but laugh at the utter relief washing up and down my body. "I'm sure I'll thank you for that someday, but damn it."

"I know just how you feel," she tells me, and I believe her. "All of this gets easier, though, just like I told you. And you *will* thank me, just like I thanked Wes."

How romantic, I think as I work on standing up. I make a mental note to ask her someday about how the two of them got together. Right now I'm too busy ignoring my body's pleas to lay down flat on the floor and rest. Once I'm up I say, "It's already easier than it was on the first day."

Beatrix nods. "Kind of like magic, huh?"

Even as my legs wobble under my weight, completely pissed off about the strain I just put on them, I concur, "Totally like magic."

I'm glad when Gabe and Wes show up, because that means training is officially over and I'm about to enjoy some Gabe Time. He chuckles as we walk to the door behind the other two. "Are you okay?" Well, *he* walks. I've got more of a hobble going on.

I nod and give him a smile. "I'll be fine."

"Undoubtedly, but I haven't forgotten how this training feels at first."

"I'm starting to feel pretty good, but that first day it felt like someone beat me with a sack of oranges." I can't help but laugh a little at my next thought. "Not like being beaten with a sack of oranges would really bother me. Later I could get a giant jug of the juice from all the destroyed oranges, and all the pain would be worth it because orange juice is the best."

He laughs, too. I can't believe he seems to find me as funny as he does, but I don't question it out loud. His laugh is just too great a sound.

For the past few days, when the time came for me and Gabe to go one way and Wes and Beatrix to go another, she's given me an encouraging goodbye. There's always an endearment in there, too. Today it's, "You're doing awesome, Friend Bear! Tomorrow will be even better!"

I only manage a smile before Wes busts out laughing. "Did you just refer to Mari as a Carebear?"

She gives him a questioning look, like he's weird for asking that and she's totally normal. "Yes?" He laughs even harder, which turns her look into one of exasperation. "What? It's a compliment."

"A Carebear," he barely gets out through his laughter. I can't help a grin, and from beside me Gabe starts laughing, too.

I adore these people.

"Okay, whatever," Beatrix says, waving a hand dismissively.

Gabe says, "Only you would have the names of the Carebears memorized so you could use one in everyday conversation."

Wes doubles over, and even as a smile comes onto Beatrix's face she says, "Right, well, we're going now."

"Later."

I wave at them. "Bye."

Wes waves back at us, still laughing, as Beatrix drags him away asking, "Was it really that big of a surprise? You know who you married, right?"

It cracks me up pretty badly.

Once we're in the car Gabe says promptly, "Okay, so, questions?"

Getting started already, I see. No problem. I'm glad to know I'm not the only one of us who thought about this more than a little bit. "Yes. I'm listening."

"Have you always lived in Fayetteville?"

"Yep. Have you?"

"Nope. I lived in Hot Springs until my freshman year in high school. We moved because my mom got a good job offer."

"Ohh. At the start of high school. Wow."

"Yep. What do *you* like to do in your free time?"

Mmm," I say reflectively. "Listen to music. Read. Draw."

"Those are some nice hobbies."

I chuckle. "Well, a few months ago I might've added, *'having a drink with my friends,'* in there." I shake my head as I put my seatbelt on. "Not now, though."

"Yeah, alcohol is quite a hindrance to us now." His seatbelt clicks into place, too. "Do you miss them? Your friends?"

It takes me a few seconds to figure out my answer. "I don't think so. They haven't really turned out to be who I thought they were."

He nods slowly. "I can understand that."

I tilt my head to one side as I observe him. "Yeah?"

"Maybe, anyway."

I know today is supposed to be Interrogate Marienne Day, but I still ask, "What happened?"

He shrugs. "Nothing specific. Just that after I turned Light the number of people who wanted to be around me dropped to zero really fast. You'd think even sixteen-year-olds would be invested enough in their friendships to help out the guy who'd just been shot and lost his only parent, but no." He gives me half a smile. "So I don't miss them, either, anymore."

Despite his smile, I frown. I can't imagine going through something like that by myself. At least I *chose* to distance myself from the people I was hanging out with.

I decide to go ahead and tell him what happened with that. "I really only had two good friends. I'd actually been dating the guy for a little bit, but I caught him sleeping with the girl the night I turned Light." I look down at my hands. "In fact, that whole thing was the catalyst for...for...uh...." The only thing flashing in my head is *'my car wreck,'* but I won't say that. I'm not going there.

And oh, God, I hope Gabe doesn't ask me how I almost died. I'm terrified of admitting that to him. Maybe Beatrix handled it all right, but...

...well...I like him in a really different way from how I like her.

I realize I need to finish my sentence. If Gabe's anything like his teal-haired friend, he's going to pry into my discomfort any second now, and I can't have that. But since I can't seem to figure out what exactly to say I just gesture to myself, to my Light state, and hope he's satisfied with it.

He sucks in a breath and starts to say something.

Please don't ask. Don't *ask.*

"He—?" is all he gets out. Then after a pause, "Hold on. What?"

I look up from my hands and see he looks confused all of a sudden. I give him a mildly quizzical look, too. "What?"

"He cheated on you?"

Oh, thank you, stars. He's curious about Rafe. I can handle that—as long as he's not curious about what happened after *the thing with Rafe.* "Yeah," I say, clenching my fists in my lap. I think about mentioning where exactly I found him and Audrey, but it doesn't come out.

Gabe doesn't press me about that, though. He says flatly, "That motherfucker is stupid."

And just like that, I'm laughing. It's real laughter, too, not the kind people let out when they're on the brink of an emotional breakdown. "Ah, thanks," I sigh. "And you don't even know the half of it."

He laughs, too. "Well, tell me some more tomorrow." He quickly starts the car, like he's just remembered we're usually on the road by now. "This information is so fucking preposterous I'm going to have to digest it slowly."

"Preposterous!" I echo, laughing again. "Okay, then. Next question."

"Okay," he says slowly, like he's trying to gather his thoughts. As we leave the parking lot he asks, "What's the coolest thing you've ever done?"

"Oh, wow," I murmur, dropping my head back against my seat. As I ponder the question, one thing in particular stands out above everything else in my mind. "When I was seventeen I overcame my massive fear of water to save a little kid from drowning."

"Did you really?" He sounds interested.

"Yeah. I mean, I didn't know CPR or anything. I just got him out of the water. So I know that's not—" I wave a hand lazily, "—it's not an accomplishment like feeding the poor in another country and it's not cool like meeting someone famous." A little quietly I confess, "But it's always felt great to me."

"It *is* great," he says, and I know he really thinks that. "Fear is a really hard thing to deal with. It's hard to look past it. In fact, I think a lot of people would've reacted differently than you did."

I admit, "Yeah, there were others around who didn't help." But then I shrug, feeling my skin flushing. That whole thing isn't something I brag about. It's just something that silently makes me feel nice.

He snorts a little. "That's exactly what I mean. So you're scared of water?"

"Bodies of water, yes."

"They can get pretty crazy. God only knows what's out in the oceans and stuff."

"Yeeeeah." I'm getting anxious just thinking about it.

I think he can tell, because he moves on. "What's something you think would be fun to do but that you'll never actually do?"

After some consideration I say, "Be an extra in a movie."

He chuckles. "Why won't you do that?"

"I suspect it'd end up being pointless. I mean, I'd be able to say I was in a movie, but what would they really catch me doing? Standing by a wall?"

"Yeah, exactly," he says encouragingly. "It's not like they'll turn you down for something like that. You should go for it."

"Ha!" I turn my head to grin at him. "Thank you, Gabe, for believing that I have what it takes to stand by a wall."

Also grinning, he glances at me. "Don't thank me, Marienne. Just give me a little bit of the twenty bucks you make."

I laugh heartily at that. I don't know how much movie-extras make, but it's probably not much for the ones that only get half a second of camera time.

When I've calmed down he says, "Speaking of movies, I'd like you to know that I actually watched one last night when I got home from work."

"You did?" I ask cheerfully. Based on what he told me about how he spends his free time, I think this is a pretty big deal for him.

Indeed, he looks like he's proud of himself as he says, "*The Breakfast Club.* It was on TV and edited all to hell, but I watched it."

I wrinkle my nose, feeling a little dejected because I don't know much about that movie. "I've never seen that."

"It's a good one. My mom would call it a classic—a must-see."

I'm glad Gabe can talk about his late mother so easily. I can't do it. It's really pretty awful; the torture of being suffocated by that pain isn't something I'd wish on anyone.

Maybe someday I'll come to terms with my parents' deaths, too. Maybe I'll be able to tell someone about them without feeling like a strong, cold hand is closing around my throat, keeping the words in so they can rattle around all sad in my head.

Or maybe not, since Gabe's mom died at the hands of a criminal, not at the hands of her own kid.

I shut that thought down fast and tell him sincerely, "I'm happy you did that."

He nods. "Me, too. Thanks for putting the thought in my head."

I smile at him even though his eyes are on the road, and then I turn to look out my window. I realize that for the first time in days, there isn't any snow falling whatsoever.

"Favorite song?" he asks shortly.

"Oh, that's a difficult one." There's definitely no way I can choose which lyrics I love the most, or which beat, or which voice. I think the easiest thing to do is offer up the song I've been listening to the most lately. "I don't think I can pick, honestly. But for the past month or so I've been playing the daylights out of 'Edge of Seventeen' by Stevie Nicks."

"Hmm. I don't think I know that one."

I grin and look at him again. "Oh, I bet you do."

He smirks and glances at me. "Yeah? You don't think I'd know it by its name?"

"I think a lot of people our age probably don't because it's kind of old."

He puts his eyes back on the road. "Bet me."

"Okay. I'll play it for you, and I bet you a quarter you've heard it before."

"What good is a quarter going to do me?" he asks, laughing. "Bet me a dollar. That'll at least buy me a pack of Juicy Fruit or something."

I snicker. "Fine, I'll bet you a dollar, but don't get too attached to your future gum purchase. I'm the one who's going to win."

"I really think it's going to be me," he disagrees.

"I don't."

He points a finger at me and says good-naturedly, "You and Wes should stop underestimating my gambling skills."

"What? Me *and* Wes?"

He nods. "I've got a bet about Beatrix going with him. Twenty dollars."

"Oh, man."

"Yeah, you're both in trouble."

"We'll see."

"*You'll* see."

The boy better be glad he only has one dollar at stake with me. I know I'm right.

When we get to the apartment he tells me to run in and get "Edge of Seventeen" for him to hear. I do, and then I cross my arms and watch his face as he turns the song on. The opening guitar filters through the speakers, and his forehead creases just a tiny bit. When the singing starts, he presses his lips together against a smile and turns away.

"Gabe," I say knowingly, cutting the volume down some.

His shoulders shake with poorly-stifled laughter as he stares out his window.

A grin spreads across my face. "I told you."

Even as he laughs he says, "I've never heard this."

"Yes, you have."

He turns to face me again and holds a hand out, trying to look serious. "You owe me a dollar."

I lean toward him a little and stare right at him. "Gabe."

His seriousness crumbles and he grins widely— *guiltily*—at me. "Marienne."

"The dollar," I prompt him.

"Yeah, exactly. Hand it over."

"Oh my God!" I laugh. "Admit it! You know this song and I know you know it, so deliver unto me the dollar I've won fair and square."

He laughs, too, and then sighs dramatically and slides a hand into his pocket. "Fine, I'll give you the dollar, but only because you asked nicely."

"Pff."

"It absolutely won't be because I've heard this song before. That hasn't happened a single time." He holds the money out to me and bites down on a smile. "*Definitely* not a hundred times."

I take the dollar and smile, too. "Whatever you say."

"Thank you." He nods at me like he appreciates my cooperation.

I laugh and shake my head as I take my CD from the stereo. "Will I see you tomorrow?"

He says, "Yes," without hesitation, and that single word is infinitely more serious than anything else he said just now. It does something funny to my stomach.

It's just a word, Marienne. A regular-ass word. Calm down. It's a no-go. My cheeks start warming, so I get out of his car again. "Okay, well, I hope you find some white Radiances in the meantime."

"Thank you." Then, "Hey, before you go...."

For all my nervousness I can't help bending down to look at him again, so I'm grateful when the frigid wind blows my hair across my stupid flushed cheeks. "Yeah?"

He smiles at me. "I've always thought the last verse is the best verse. What do you think?"

Even though I'm not surprised by his admission to having heard "Edge of Seventeen" before, I *am* surprised that his favorite part is my favorite part, too. The lyrics remind me of my parents without completely breaking my heart every time I hear them. I wonder if the same is true for him.

Giving him a smile that I hope doesn't look sad, I say, "I think that, too, actually." Then I give him a little wave and shut the door.

The apartment is delightfully quiet. Claire is a social person, so on her time off from working three days a week from 5:00 A.M. to 5:00 P.M. she is frequently out of the apartment. Today is one of her workdays, though, so I have three-ish hours to myself before she gets here.

It's weird that I can be so averse to being alone with thoughts of my parents and at the same time be really happy that I actually am alone in the apartment. I guess encountering Claire is just that painful. At first it was because of what I did to our parents, but add to that my knowing she's the one who let Rafe into my room that morning, and I have absolutely no interest in being around her.

Not like she wants to bother with me anymore. All she is these days is a poised and beautiful ice woman. Even though I've known for forever that she's the opposite of tempestuous when she's angry, I never really felt it until after the car accident. She doesn't keep her fury on ass-blast all the time, doesn't come home and start screaming at me and following me around to assail me with insults. Instead, her rage sits still and silent and solid all over everything. It tenses her body when she's around me, hardens her gaze when she looks at me, chills the quietness when she doesn't talk to me, cuts across her tone when she does happen to speak to me. It even weighs down the atmosphere in the apartment when she and I are both simply in it. And it's torturous.

So I'm grateful for the hours I don't have to suffer her. When she *is* around I do what I can to ignore her, like listen to "Edge of Seventeen" a bunch of times. Or I'll finally get tired of the tension and go to Grove Lane.

Presently, just as I'm about to turn the song on in my room, I hear the front door slam.

I stop moving.

And now for the Scary Moment Reaction Deliberation we always see in horror movies. I can stay where I am and hope that's not anyone who's going to walk in here and see me and murder me. Or I can run out there and hope that's not anyone who's going to see me go past and catch me and murder me.

I hear a sniffle and a miserable-sounding, "God, what is wrong with me?"

A simultaneously relieved and unhappy sigh leaves me. It's only Claire in there, home early from work for some reason. It's not a burglar or rapist or killer. But now I have no time to prepare myself for her being around, and that's a huge letdown.

I decide not to turn Stevie Nicks on because I don't want to get bitched at, even though when Claire's friends come over for get-togethers (as they try to call them all posh-like) they run the apartment through with the worst rap and pop music ever. And to think they call themselves classy.

After a minute I hear what sounds like vomiting from the other end of the apartment, where Claire's own bedroom/bathroom combination is. She's sick, then, I guess. Definitely a good thing I didn't turn my music on.

Part of me feels bad for her and wants to go see if she needs help. I know, though, that she won't accept anything from me—that she'd just tell me to go fuck myself, except not quite like that because that's not her style. So another part of me hopes she'll just lie down and sleep the day away, get herself some rest and save me from potentially running into her.

And I guess that's what she does, because I don't hear anything else from her all afternoon. I don't hear her dragging around looking for a cup of water or crackers. I don't hear her watching TV in the living room, which is something she always did when she was sick back when we were still living with our parents. I don't even hear a sneeze leave her bedroom. I go to bed later with the apartment as locked up, still and silent as it was when she got here.

But I wake up in the middle of the night to desperate, bloodcurdling screaming.

"Claire!" I yell through the darkness. I fully expect my cry to go unnoticed, and it does. She screams and screams and screams and I run to her as fast as I can, flipping on lights as I go. When I make it to her room and get the light on I find her thrashing around in her bed, eyes squeezed shut, face red and contorted by horror. I race to her side, my heartbeat going insane. "Hey! Claire!"

"Please don't do this to me!" she wails, arching her back. Her veins are standing out against her skin. "Please *don't!* I'll do anything!"

"What the hell is—?" I start to shout. And suddenly I realize she's still asleep. I bend over and put a hand on her forehead, which is burning hot and slick with sweat. "Claire, it's me!" I say over her cries. "It's Mari! Wake up!"

Just like that, she's motionless and quiet. Her eyes snap open and find mine and I see the whites are completely red, turning her irises a strange color.

I yank my hand away from her. "Jesus! Are you okay?"

Her expression blackens, twisting a look I never dreamed she could manage onto her face. It is the starkest look of hatred I have ever seen. She starts panting, her eyes clouding over with pure, unbridled, un-Claire-like wrath that is so ominous it halts my heartbeat for a second, steals my breath from my lungs, sends panic straight into my bones. If she could kill me with a look, this would be my last second on this earth.

Something is way wrong with her.

Before I can consider what the hell I should do, she sits up in her bed, her lips peeling back to bare her teeth to me, and lets loose a hand. Her fingernails rake viciously across my cheek, digging into my flesh and lighting it up with pain.

"*Claire!*" I shout, stumbling away.

She slinks over to crouch on the edge of her bed like a feral beast, her fists aggressively gripping the sheets as if she's about to throw her whole body at me. "Get out," she says, and underneath the guttural tone is an unnaturally sharp one that gives her two voices instead of one. That coupled with her violent gaze disturbs me all the way to my center.

I get out of her room faster than I've ever done anything in my life.

Back in my room, I shut and lock the door. Then I grab my pillow and blanket and phone, and I lock myself in my bathroom. Only after I've curled up in my bathtub do I let myself even think about freaking out.

What the fucking fuck is wrong with my sister?

I gasp unsteadily and dab at my face as tears run over my wounded cheek. The scratches burn something fierce, and for the first time I wonder what they look like. But I can't look—not right now. I'm not sure my legs could support me for another second, especially if the cuts look bad. Unfortunately, though, when I pull my blanket back I see blood on it.

"Oh, God," I moan around the aching tightness in my throat.

I've never seen Claire like that. She's never hit me before, even when we were younger and I occasionally pissed her off being the annoying little sister. The woman never even cusses. What brought it on? Her being sick? Was the combination of that, her nightmare and her resenting me so much enough to bring such violence out of her?

Maybe, I try to tell myself. *Maybe. Maybe I was just in the wrong place at the wrong time.*

All I know is that was the scariest expression I've ever seen on anyone's face, and it was directed straight at me.

For what feels like forever, I try to decide whether or not I should call someone. My options are pretty limited and none of them sound particularly enticing: 911, Beatrix and Rafe. I don't think this is really an emergency—Claire hasn't come busting into my room threatening to kill me— so I don't want to call 911. Rafe...well, he's really close by, but I don't want to even talk to him. And I think I'd be a huge asshole to bother Beatrix at 3:36 in the morning, which is the time my phone is giving me. I don't think she'd mind, but what would I say? Definitely not, *'Hey, it's Mari. I'm calling because I'm scared. My big sister freaked out and scratched me like some kind of wild animal and I can't figure out why, even though she's been having a pretty rough time lately.'* That's lame as fuck.

So I don't call anyone. I sit quietly in my bathtub and keep my ears open (don't have to *try* to keep my eyes open because I'm so on-edge). I wait and wait and wait, trying to figure out what I should do the next time I run into Claire. I don't come to any solid conclusions, though, other than that I should be prepared to duck.

It's 8:55 when I finally leave my bathroom. I'm ready for training except that I need some clothes. My hair is already pulled back, my teeth brushed and my scant black eyeliner touched up. I also tried to clean up the deep, angry claw-marks on my left cheek, but they still looked gruesome even after I got the dried blood off of my skin. Claire's nails really did some damage.

Once I'm appropriately dressed, I quiet down and listen hard for Beatrix's knock on the front door. I haven't set a toe outside my room yet and I don't plan to until it's time to go. Once she's arrived, I tiptoe out into the silent apartment. It's Saturday, so Claire doesn't have work; I feel pretty sure she's still asleep in her room. There's no way in fiery, torturous hell I'm going to risk waking her up—thus my very dramatic For God's Sake, Don't Make A Noise gesturing when I ease the front door open.

Beatrix looks confused at first, but she nods compliantly. And then she sees my cheek, and her eyes widen in horror. And then she's pissed.

"Who the *fuck?*" she demands despite my frantic attempt to push outside and shut the door. "No! No!" she says, reaching around to shove the door back open. She must understand that I'm trying to keep her quiet and out of the apartment because the culprit is in there somewhere. "Who did it and where are they?"

"Beatrix, come—" My whisper-yell cuts off in the middle of my sentence because, upon glancing into the parking lot, I see that Claire's white Prius is nowhere in sight.

Is she gone?

I hurry into the apartment just as Beatrix appears from the direction of my bedroom. "Mari, baby, make this easier on your girl," she says, eyes blazing, "and tell me where the fuck I'm supposed to be looking."

Wordlessly and full of curiosity, I lead the way to my sister's room. Now that I'm with a veritable badass I don't feel so afraid of Claire, if she's even here. (I realize that makes me something of a sissy, but ask me real fast if I care.) Indeed, her door is open and the room looks void of human life. I walk in and check her bathroom to find that it, too, is vacant. And as I look around I realize there's not an item out of place in the whole area. There's not a single tissue in the bathroom trashcan or on the nightstand, no pajamas on the floor. Even the bed is perfectly made.

Everything looks chillingly normal.

"What the fuck?" I ask, dumbfounded. I fully expected the place to look like a physically ill and emotionally distraught woman spent the night here. It's weird enough that she got out without me hearing her or without her stopping by my room to give me hell with her suddenly crazy ass. Now this? It looks like nothing out of the ordinary happened for even a second—no sickness, no nightmare, no violent outburst.

"Sweetheart," Beatrix says from behind me, "why don't you just tell me what happened?"

I frown and turn to look at her. "Gladly."

Maybe during her time on this earth, between being a smart woman and a Defender in the Lightforce, she's found a way to understand craziness.

8
Gabe

Time sure is strange. It's the one thing in existence that never ends, even when you think it should or that for a single instant it has. And the passage of time is just as strange as its perpetuity. There are sixty seconds in a minute, sixty minutes in an hour, seven days in a week, twelve months in a year and each one seems to operate independently from the others. One hour can feel never-ending while days come and go like a breeze.

That is what's happened since the Friday I lost that little bet to Marienne (by the way, that song is yet another thing my mom used to love dearly. I never could remember the name of it, but it got played a lot). Six whole days have sped by despite how many of those hours crept along so slowly it was painful, like snails crossing a hot sidewalk. Those were usually a couple of the morning hours I spent Gathering alone, away from Janssen and Wright, during which my mind wandered into places I didn't really want it to go. Namely, the places where memories of Em's life and death dwell. But for the most part, things have been great.

No, they're more than great. They're better than ever.

If anyone were to look in on my life from the outside, they wouldn't see that big of a difference between who I was two and a half weeks ago and who I am now. The only thing that's noticeably different is the raven-haired addition to my circle of friends. My job and my relationships with Wes and Beatrix are as important to me as they ever were. To me, though, the difference *is* big. Knowing Marienne has done something big *to* me.

The more time I spend with her, the more she tugs at my attention when we're apart. So, basically, she's on my mind constantly. It's not like I walk around daydreaming about her face, exactly, though I'm pretty partial to her face. Sometimes I'm just going along, doing my job, and I remember something she said the day before and I can't help but laugh out loud. Sometimes I'm randomly reminded of a cool song she got me to listen to from a band I didn't think I'd like. Sometimes just her name drifts into my head and I find myself wondering for the umpteenth time how she even exists.

And that's the thing about her I like the most: she truly is real. She's got a real personality. She's courteous, but she holds her own. Though she isn't really an introvert, she doesn't feel the need to talk all the time. She makes me laugh, and she laughs at anything *she* finds funny—even if that means laughing at herself or at something no one else seems to find amusing. She doesn't mind talking about herself, but she wants the rest of us to do the same thing. And when we talk to her she listens, and cares, and pulls us all in even more.

I've fallen into a new routine since last week. I check in with my new Gatherers and then spend the mornings searching for white Radiances alone, and I don't find them. When I spot Hellions I call Wes and he comes to take care of them, and then he and I eat lunch and go to the Sanctum. He retrieves Beatrix so they can do Defender work together, and I drive Marienne home. Then I meet up with Janssen and Wright so we can work together until dinnertime, after which I hang around town for another few hours before going back home.

Like Wes told me that one day, I'm not the only one who's grown fond of Marienne; in addition to her general adoration of the girl, for the past day or two Beatrix has been especially pumped about her training sessions with her. She swears up and down that Red was on to something when he said proper instruction would go well with the fearlessness Marienne demonstrated on Blossombranch. Unfortunately, any time Wes and I have gone into the training room after lunch we've only caught her doing her cool-down stretches—if that. And despite Beatrix's enthusiasm we never really hear about what goes on in there. We get next to no details.

So when we arrive on Friday and realize their session is still going, we're interested as hell. But we haven't been watching for five whole seconds before our interest morphs into admiration.

Even Wes says, "Goddamn, look at her go."

You can't tell by just looking at Marienne that anything smolders within her. You can't really even tell by talking to her, unless you get her started on her ex-boyfriend (I did get all of those details, by the way, from him having sex with that girl in Marienne's bed to him paying her a visit at the crack of dawn, which only confirmed that he's a huge fucking asshole). Since I met her I've only seen the fiercer side of her that one time, when she attacked those Hellions. But I see it again now, and again I am stunned.

She's sparring with Beatrix and she's lost in it. Her movements are measured and steady, but it's obvious that something has a tight hold on her and that she's containing whatever it is only barely. She lets loose each jab of her fake dagger and throws each punch with a sound as angry as her laugh is pretty. Her kicks are as forceful as her usual bearing is mild. When she blocks a move, she does so both confidently and desperately. And she isn't fazed any time Beatrix does land a hit. She just continues on and finds another opening. She doesn't stop or slow down or take her eyes off the woman who is acting the way her enemy might act.

I'm so captivated by it that when Beatrix calls out, "Time!" I actually jump.

Marienne's stance relaxes. She drops her head back and lets the fake dagger fall to the floor. Beatrix touches her shoulder and says something with a smile on her face. Then she turns away from her and notices us, and her smile grows.

"Looks like we have fans, Mari," she pants.

Marienne takes in a deep breath that feels jagged even to me, and then rolls her head toward us. Her eyes find me and she smiles even though I suspect she's still stormy on the inside.

Beatrix has already made her way to Wes, and they greet each other cheerfully. I hear him say, "That was great. Is that just the way she fights, or did you piss her off on purpose?"

I miss her answer because Marienne stops a few feet away, hands on her hips and eyes still on me. "Hey," she says easily.

"Hey," I echo. "That was amazing."

She shrugs. "She got me more than a few times."

"That's okay."

"Only because it's her. If she'd been a Hellion...." She rolls her head around in a slow circle. I catch sight of her left cheek, which is healing nicely.

And what a weird situation *that* was. As soon as I saw the wound she filled me in on what happened, and I was as mystified and concerned as she and Beatrix were. But it got even more bizarre the next day when Marienne informed me with wide eyes that when she saw Claire that morning, the woman insisted she didn't talk to her at all on that night, much less attack her. Like, she flat-out said Marienne must have been on something because that wound had nothing to do with her. And as far as I know, she hasn't wavered on that over this past week; she seriously believes someone else scratched the hell out of her sister's face.

But Marienne says she hasn't done anything else scary since then. We're all hoping it was just an ugly reaction to her bad dream and whatever sickness she was suffering from that night, and that her denial is just the product of some kind of black-out.

I tell Marienne, "That's true, but don't sell yourself short. You were on fire."

The smile comes back again. "Thank you," she murmurs.

A hand appears between us, and I look over and see it's attached to Wes. "Mari," he says, "great job. Whatever you're doing, keep doing it."

I notice that something in her smile changes when she turns to him. I can't figure out what's different, though, as she shakes his hand. "Thank you. I've been working hard."

Beatrix snickers. "Uh, correction: she's been working *at a laudably ordinary pace*. She's just a natural, even more so than most new people. She doesn't have to *learn* fighting. It's already in her."

Marienne shakes her head a little. "Oh, I don't know."

Beatrix takes her face in her hands. "Cupcake, *I* know." She looks at me. "Gabe, don't you agree with me?"

"I do," I say promptly.

"And so do I," Wes says. "But that doesn't mean you haven't accomplished a thing or two, and nothing says, *'Good job!'* like having dinner cooked for you. Am I right?"

Beatrix's eyes widen and she lets go of Marienne's face. "Oh, hell yeah."

Marienne looks at the pair with confusion. "Huh?"

"Dinner at our house tonight," he clarifies. "You're coming." He glances at me. "So are you."

I chuckle. "You don't have to tell me twice."

Beatrix grins. "Right?"

A slow smile comes onto Marienne's face. "You're going to cook me dinner?"

All the way from the girls gathering up their stuff to the four of us stepping out into the back parking lot, Beatrix and Wes babble about how magical the dinner is going to be. They're so excited that we have to convince them to leave The Room already so they can finish working and actually get started on the plans.

"You have the best friends," Marienne says when we're finally on the way out of the parking lot.

"Yeah, they're special. But they're your friends, too, you know."

She sighs a little. "I hope they think so."

"They do." I tap my fingers against the steering wheel. "I'm glad you're going to dinner tonight. Don't know if you could tell or not, but they're excited."

She laughs softly. "There's no way I'd miss it."

I don't have to look at her to know she's looking at me. I can feel it. I can feel it the way I can feel the heat from the vents fanning across my fingers.

She says, "Hey."

I wait for her to continue, but she doesn't. I turn my face in her direction just a little bit, keeping my eyes on the road. "Yeah?"

Several more moments tick by in silence. I'm just about to glance over and make sure she's not passing out or something when she finally speaks up. "Could you, um...*not* take me home?"

The question surprises me, and I frown a little. "Why, is something wrong? Is it Rafe? Or your sister?" No telling, I guess.

"Well, no, not particularly," she replies. "I just— there's this place I go sometimes to be by myself, and I'm just feeling it all of a sudden." She clears her throat a little. "Well, I mean, I *usually* go by myself, but I wondered if today...if you...uh...."

Oh.

More than a little thrilled, I glance at her. She's looking out her window and tucking her hair behind her ears, which makes me smile as I look at the road again. She messes with her hair often and at first I just thought it was kind of cute, but I've started to wonder if it's her nervous tick. Given what she's trying to ask me right now, I decide that it probably is. "I'd like that," I tell her without making her finish her sentence.

"It's outside, though. It'll be cold." Underneath her heads-up, I hear relief.

"Not a problem. I'm a cold-weather person, remember?"

After a beat, I hear a soft laugh. "I remember."

She starts giving me directions then, and I follow them. Surprise touches me when she has me turning down Blossombranch. Before I can ask what we're doing here, she tells me to continue on down the street. Then to slow down. Then to turn left on Grove Lane. Then to go all the way to the dead end.

After I've parked in the driveway of one specific blackened house, I look at her, confused. "This is where you go to be by yourself?"

She nods, looking out at the remains of the house almost reverently.

For a few moments I consider keeping my question to myself because I don't want to disturb her. But it's bouncing around inside my head and I have to know: "Why?"

"It's peaceful," she murmurs.

I tear my eyes away from her so I can look at the house, too. I try to feel the peace, but I can't.

She seems to realize that and says, "Let's get out."

If it weren't for the quiet sureness in her tone and the very way she looks at the place, I'd laugh.

Last week's snow stopped falling on Saturday, but it started up again the day before yesterday. It's been light, so around town you can hardly see it unless it's falling right on you, but here it has remained untouched. It still feels...yeah, peaceful. It crunches quietly under our feet as Marienne leads me to a gap in the privacy fence, a gap I wouldn't approach if I hadn't seen her step through it with such certainty.

I follow her through. She steps aside just enough to avoid me bumping into her, and then she stills. I could swear even her breathing changes as she looks around the backyard.

It's a big yard, but the only thing in it is the enormous, commanding tree that stands guard near the back. An old tire swing hangs from one of the tough branches, looking lonely under whatever dead leaves are still clinging to the tree. The privacy fence loops around entirety of the place, unbroken except for a few places near where we passed through it.

I turn my head and study the dead house this yard sits behind. Eventually, my trepidation starts to lessen. At first glance—at first thought, even, Grove Lane feels scary and dangerous. But standing here now with Marienne, who does not appear to be afraid or to feel threatened, I'm touched by a strange sense of calm.

It feels like whole minutes have passed before she asks, "Isn't it nice?"

"Yeah," I admit. I look over at her. "It's so still."

Her eyes lighten a little when she glances at me. "And quiet."

"Very quiet. You never see anyone here?"

She shakes her head. "No one. I rarely even see animals." She looks at the gigantic tree. "I do hear birds a lot."

"What do you do when you come here?" *Please don't say you go into what's left of these homes.*

"I sit in the tire swing."

Oh. "Really? It's still in good shape?"

"Yep."

My eyes flicker to the swing, then back to her. "That's all you do? You just sit over there?"

She nods. "That's all I do. I think it's my favorite place to be."

"Your favorite place to be," I murmur. After a moment I get the weirdest urge, and a smile creeps across my face. "You must really love it."

She makes a soft noise of agreement.

"So what would you do," I wonder, "if someone were to try to steal it from you?"

"What?" She turns to look at me curiously, but smiles when she sees me smiling.

I nod toward the swing with a chuckle. "I'm thinking about commandeering your tire swing."

She grins now. "But if it's *my* swing, I think you need *my* permission to use it."

"Nah."

Her eyebrows lift, and she's smiling so much now that I almost can't handle it. "Well, what decides who gets it?"

Feeling a hundred times bolder than when I attacked those Hellions by myself, I take a few steps toward her. She doesn't move an inch, not even when I stop right in front of her and lean in a little bit. She just looks up at me and lets her eyes drift keenly over my face; their gorgeous light blue color is lightened even more by all this snow, and from up this close I can see they're run through with hints of silver. They leave an invisible trail of fire in their wake.

I can't stop my own eyes from flickering to her mouth even though I'm sure she'll catch the movement.

This isn't the first time a fleeting daydream about kissing her has zipped through my mind, but something about this instant is different. This time, on the heels of one such daydream comes the arresting feeling that I'm just steps away from something else. Some edge that is as attractive to me as it is unfamiliar—an edge I could go sailing over at any minute, with no way of going back.

The insane thing about it is I'm almost certain I wouldn't mind.

I draw in a deep breath and belatedly manage to tell Marienne, "Whoever gets there first."

She looks like she, too, has just been brought out of her thoughts. Momentarily she's back with me and her smile grows impossibly brighter, but I only see it for a second before I'm gone.

"Gabe!" I hear her laughing as I sprint across the yard toward the tree, freezing air smacking me in the face. After a moment I turn around to jog backwards, knowing I'm faster than she is and that it's not quite fair. But I laugh loudly, surprised and impressed, when she barrels into me with a shriek. My heartbeat stutters when her arms go around me, pinning my own arms to my sides. "You are *not* getting there first!" She tries to tug me back the other way.

"Looks like I am," I disagree playfully, twisting around in the hold she has on me. "I'm in front of you, so I'll be there before—are you on my *back?*"

Her arms are draped over my shoulders, knees pressing to my sides, hands flattening against my chest. She says, "Um, no," on a chuckle, but the words are spectacularly close to my ear.

Holy God, she is.

I have never loved my life so much.

I wrap my hands around her legs and take off running again. "Well, thanks! This is way easier without you dragging your feet."

"What! This is such shit!" she complains loudly. "How are you still so fast?"

"You weigh next to nothing."

"Is that right?" As quickly as she jumped onto my back she flings herself off, slipping out of my grasp. But she doesn't let go of my jacket, so I stumble sideways with her.

"Marienne!" I laugh.

"This was your idea!" she reminds me, releasing me at just the right second. I tip toward the snowy ground and she dances out of the way before darting toward the swing.

I might be faster than she is, but that doesn't mean she's slow. By the time I've steadied myself and dashed after her she's only a few yards from the swing. She actually leaps into the air in excitement, and I'm positive she's thinking, *'I can't believe I beat him here!'*

I can't believe it, either.

"Will you go on a date with me?" I suddenly shout.

Marienne trips to a halt, and then turns around to look at me. Her fingers fly to her hair to move what isn't in her ponytail behind her ears.

Slowing to a stop in front of her, I flatten my palms against my own hair. Her eyes follow the movement and she tries to hide a smile. I'm sure it's because my hair looks ridiculous, but I can't find it in me to worry about it when her eyes touch mine again.

"Yes," she says.

Elation soars through me and I don't even try not to grin. God knows I hadn't been planning on asking her out when she invited me here, but that doesn't matter. I like her. I like her a lot. "Great. Awesome. Thank you."

Her shoulders twitch with a breathless laugh. "Thank you for asking." She crosses her arms against a cold breeze. "When do you want to go?"

Right now. I put my hands in my jacket pockets. "Tomorrow night?"

She nods. "Okay."

"What time? Like, 7:00?" *Wait, did I just suggest the evening? No. How about first thing in the morning?*

"Sure." Her smile brightens. "Halloween, right? We should go trick-or-treating."

I laugh. "I don't have a costume."

"We can go by the Halloween store and pick up a couple of masks." She shrugs. "Unless you'd rather do something else. It doesn't matter to me."

"No, that sounds fun," I tell her, and I mean it. "We can run over to the store after we leave here, if you want."

"Yeah?"

"Yeah."

"Okay."

"Okay."

She takes a step away from me and murmurs, "Thank you for coming here with me."

"You're welcome. I like it here."

"Really?"

I nod. "I hope you'll invite me back."

She twirls around lazily and looks at the ground. "I'm sure I will, Gabe." She comes to a stop and then twirls back the opposite way. "But you're the only person I've ever brought here, so...you know, just...remember that."

Not likely to forget this day.

"I'll remember."

She nods a little. "You know what I just remembered myself?"

I'm about to ask when her eyes dart up to mine. She bites down on a smile and takes another step back, and I suddenly remember, too.

We dash for the swing at the same time.

She's a little closer, but I'm a little faster, and we both smack our hands against the tire without a moment between us. It's a tie.

$\backsim$

"Are you sure you don't need help?" Marienne asks Beatrix later.

"Oh, dear love, I'm sure," she says as she wipes her hands on her skull-print apron. "You just go sit in there on the couch and turn on a movie or something."

"Come on, they've got *The Crow*," I tell Marienne. "You said you haven't seen it, right? I promise you'll like it."

Beatrix tips her head back to laugh loudly. Then she straightens up, points her whisk at Marienne and says, "Now there's *absolutely* no way I'm letting you help cook. Go and don't come back until you can tell me what poem Eric is quoting in the pawn shop scene."

Marienne mumbles something about feeling like a lazy guest, but she goes into the other room with me.

Once I've turned on the movie and sat down beside her on the couch, she leans toward me. "What's the poem?"

"Not telling."

"I'm not asking for cheating purposes," she tells me. "I just love poetry. I'm kind of on the edge of my seat here. How far in is the pawn shop scene?"

I let my eyes drift over her. Between me dropping her off after the Halloween store and picking her up for dinner, she took a shower and changed clothes. Now her hair hangs down her back and over her shoulders, and she has on a pair of gray jeans and a loose white sweater. We took our shoes off in the front hall per the house rules, and instead of wearing plain white socks like me, she has on hot pink socks that appear to have little white flamingoes printed on them.

"Gabe?" I hear her say.

I look up at her face, at those eyes. "Yes?"

"Are you okay?"

"Just fine. I like your socks."

She smiles. "Oh, thank you. They're pretty nice, huh?"

"Very nice. And the pawn shop scene is—"

"'*Suddenly there came a tapping,*'" someone cuts me off, "'*as of someone gently rapping, rapping at my chamber door.*'"

Marienne gasps a little. "Edgar Allan Poe."

Wes nods as he heads toward the loveseat. "Yes, ma'am."

I chortle. "We were supposed to let her find out by herself. Don't tell your wife."

"Baby!" Wes says loudly. "Gabe told Mari about the poem!"

Marienne and I both laugh, but I still hear Beatrix shout, "Fucking seriously, Gabe?"

Wes laughs, too, and admits, "No, it was me," though not nearly loud enough for her to hear.

"Thanks a lot," I say.

He waves a hand. "I'll confess later on. Sweet-talk her into not being mad."

"Yeah, okay." As long as I'm not the one getting smacked upside the head, I'm good.

He leaves after another minute, and Marienne grows interested in the movie. Before long she's leaning forward with her elbows on her knees, eyes glued to the TV. She doesn't make a single comment until the scene where Eric is reliving his memories of Shelly. Then she turns around with wide eyes and says, "This song is my ringtone."

"Really?" It's a great one: "Burn" by The Cure. "Good song. It was actually written for this movie."

"Oh, wow! I had no idea. How weird is that?" She smiles at me and turns back around. Nothing else is said until the next time we see Wes and Beatrix, when they're coming to tell us dinner is ready. "Aw, just in time," Beatrix says when she sees that Eric's recitation of "The Raven" has just passed. Then she glares at me and amends, "Well, nevermind," clearly remembering that someone (her husband) ruined the trivia she assigned Marienne.

I raise my eyebrows at Wes, who just hides a grin and waves us all into the dining room.

The food really is fantastic. There's filet mignon, green beans that have a little kick to them, loaded mashed potatoes, and rolls glazed with some kind of honey butter. If I died right now I'd be perfectly fine with it—surrounded by outstanding food and good friends. Wes and Beatrix are looking at each other like they truly are glad they married the other one. Marienne is looking at the food like she'd like to marry *it*.

Conversation picks up soon. The girls discuss Marienne's training and when she should get her hands on a real weapon. Wes wants to know how my training with Janssen and Wright is going—and it's going well, really. Both men are used to working on their own, so even being new to Gathering they aren't in constant need of my company. They're also both smart and capable of taking down Hellions if a serious situation arises (though it hardly ever does for a Gatherer). In theory we're all sure they'll do fine when a white Radiance shows up, but I still told them to call me when they spot one so I can make sure everything goes okay.

Wes and I have just cleared our plates when I tune in to the girls' conversation. They've finished eating, too, and are leaned toward each other like they're best friends or something.

"...doesn't really hurt. Dr. Roterra is good at his job," Beatrix is saying. "So that's pretty much all you have to do—let him draw your blood—because after that it's all up to Red. And that is a process I know *nothing* about, so if you're interested in how he mixes the blood with the metal and all of that, you'll have to pay him a visit."

"Wow," Marienne says. "I don't know if I want to bother him with a bunch of questions, but it does sound like it'd be cool to know." As if she knows I'm paying attention to her now, she glances over at me. "And I'll get a dagger, right?"

Beatrix gets up from the table, reaching for everyone's plates. She gives me a look that says she's handing the chat over to me, so I tell Marienne, "A dagger and a few vials of red powder, which is what we call dried Light blood."

"Yep, those are the basics," Wes speaks up. "But we can put our blood in damn near anything: bullets, arrowheads, shurikens—"

"Shurikens?" she repeats.

"Ninja stars," I clarify.

Her eyebrows go up and she snorts. "Oh, God. Do you guys *have* things like that?"

I chuckle. "I don't. I'm not obsessed with special weaponry like he is."

He laughs, too. "Come on. We're in the ass-kicking business. May as well have fun with it."

"*You're* in the ass-kicking business."

"So are you, man. You switched to Gathering, but I know you know how to lay those sons of bitches out."

Marienne gives me a look that says she agrees with him. "I did find you fighting those Hellions by yourself, and before I interrupted you were winning."

Wes taps the table. "Exactly. Thank you. Now can you imagine how awesome he'd have looked sinking ninja stars into their foreheads?"

She bursts out laughing.

"I wasn't using anything on them when she saw me," I remind him, "not even my dagger, so ninja stars were way out of the question."

"So you were whipping their asses by yourself with no weapons in your hands, after years of living the quiet life?" He grins and shakes his head. "And still trying to say you're not into being impressive."

I nod toward Marienne. "I think she's the impress—"

"Jesus!" She jumps a mile and bangs her knees against the underside of the table.

"What?" Wes and I both ask.

"Nothing, just—I forgot this was on me." She twists around in her chair and produces her vibrating cell phone from her back pocket. She silences it. "Believe it or not, it rang and scared the...." Her eyes widen in confusion when she sees the screen. After a second she shoots me an apologetic look. "I'm sorry. My sister just called and it looks like she's been texting me for an hour already. Just a second." She gets up and hurries into the living room.

Beatrix appears from the kitchen with a chocolate cake in one hand and clean dishes in the other. "Who wants dessert?" she chirps.

"Whoa, baby," Wes says, taking the dishes from her. "I'll take a fork, but what'd you bring the rest of these dishes for? All I need is the platter the cake's on. Not gonna dirty up four plates for no reason."

She snorts and puts the cake on the table. "Whatever."

He grins up at her. "Huh? This is all for me, right?"

"Oh, of course."

"I thought so." He tugs on her ponytail and she bends down. "You're the best."

"No, you." They kiss quickly and then she straightens up and looks at me. "Where's Mari?"

"In the other room. Her sister called."

"Oh." She sits down, frowning. "I hope everything's okay. I can't say I trust the woman."

"Yeah." On top of the whole face-mangling thing, Marienne says her relationship with Claire is in pretty bad shape. The most I've learned about the situation is that it stemmed from the event that turned Marienne Light, but I still haven't heard what exactly that was. I haven't pressed her about it, though. Whether it's something she caused or something she couldn't help (like my own near-death event), I'm sure she has a reason for not bringing it up.

Beatrix starts cutting the cake. I listen to her and Wes talk about some problem they've been having with their kitchen sink until Marienne comes back. She sits down, looking distinctly aggravated, and says, "Gabe, I'm so sorry. Really. You were in the middle of your sentence and I ruined it."

"No, you didn't. Don't worry about it." I take in the faint flush in her cheeks. "Are you okay?"

She glares at the table for a few moments, and then she sighs. She looks like she's trying to pull herself together. When she meets my gaze she gives me a little smile. "I'll be fine. Thank you." It looks like she means it.

"Okay, then." I return the smile.

Beatrix stands up and starts dishing out the dessert. "And, doll, believe me when I say this cake will speed up the healing process."

Marienne looks at the cake and then up at Beatrix, her smile growing with approval. "Oh, *yes.*"

"Working already?" I ask with a chuckle.

"It really is," she says. And I notice it again: the way her smile changes when she looks at me. I notice it and still can't figure out what it is that's different.

Then she mimes throwing a little plate of cake at me, and I decide to contemplate those kinds of things later, when I'm alone instead of sitting next to the girl herself.

9
Marienne

After Gabe drops me off at home, I walk in thinking I've had a pretty good day. I did well in training and Beatrix thinks I'll be able to obtain my real dagger soon. Gabe asked me out. I watched a good movie and ate some kick-ass food.

There's always *something*, though.

Trying to never encounter Claire means there's so much distance between us that she has no way to talk to me when something important comes up. Apparently a thing or two *has* come up tonight and that's why she was blowing up my phone while I was out. She wouldn't tell me what the deal was, though. All I got was snappy insistence that I get home right then because we needed to have a talk and nothing I was doing could possibly be more important than that.

I might've done what she wanted if I wasn't still a little bothered by her trying to claw my face off and then insisting that didn't happen. Oh and yeah, if I hadn't heard Rafe in the background telling her I was probably out with *'that fucking bastard guy or that bitch with blue hair.'*

So I didn't hurry home whatsoever. When I find them both waiting for me on the couch, I'm not surprised that they're glaring daggers at me.

"Where have you been?" Rafe demands.

I drop my purse and coat onto the couch. "Out with friends."

"Friends," he echoes with a humorless laugh.

Claire's glare burns into me. "I told you to come home immediately."

"I was having a nice time *with my friends.*" I look at Rafe and silently dare him to mock that again.

Before he can, Claire snaps, "Did I ask if you were having a nice time? No. I didn't even ask if you were with those people. I *told* you to come home."

I love how she says *'those people'* as if they're pieces of shit, when the guy *she's* been seeing for over a month has never even set foot in our apartment.

"Okay, what is this even about?" I want to know. "Why are you two together? Claire, you don't give a shit about me or what I do." I point at Rafe. "You give too much of one."

She shoves a manicured hand through her bob-cut raven hair. Not for the first time in the past week her typically smooth disposition is gone, and it's really starting to weird me out. "I'm here because Rafe told me about some guy in a silver Honda who comes over every day, and some woman with blue hair who's been in here. You better explain yourself. You better explain right now why you've been letting strangers come over to my house."

Okay, cool. So Rafe has been creeping on me and Gabe every afternoon.

I'd still like to hear *her* explain why she let that son of a bitch stand in my room and watch me sleep.

But I cross my arms and say, "Did he mention to you that Beatrix has only been in here for less than five minutes, and that Gabe has never even gotten out of his car?" I raise my eyebrows. "Even if that weren't the case, it's not a crime for me to invite my friends over because, in case you forgot, I pay half of everything here, Claire. And again, it's not like we come in here and party and mess the place up."

"That guy is just some random—" Rafe starts.

"I'm already *really* tired of hearing you talk," I interrupt him curtly.

"Fix your attitude," Claire says warningly. "Your recent behavior is unacceptable and you will hear us out about it or I will kick you out."

'Unacceptable'? Oh, Jesus Christ. Pots calling the kettle black, both of them.

Rafe seizes his opportunity. "I was fifteen when I first saw you," he says. "I'm not going to dance around it: you were hot. And now we've grown up and you're even better-looking, but I'm not the only guy who sees that. Younger guys than me see it, older guys, nice guys, douchebag guys, everyone. They all see what I see and that's not good."

I look at him quizzically, unsure of where he's going with this.

"The problem is that you don't see yourself that way. You're too humble and innocent and you just wander around not knowing how—" he shoots Claire a look that almost seems apologetic, "—how *appealing* you are."

I laugh once. "Uh...so, what, you want me to act like I'm—like I'm at the top of the Maxim Hot 100 list?"

He sighs. "What I'm trying to say is that girls who know they're gorgeous—yes, like the ones on the Maxim Hot 100 list—they know that they don't only attract decent guys. You have to be even more careful because you've never been like that. You're naïve, Mari, and maybe it's because you didn't date around a whole lot, I don't know, but it doesn't occur to you that some of the guys who approach you shouldn't be within a mile-wide radius of you." He frowns. "So you can imagine how worried I got when I saw you talking to that guy the other day, and how much more worried I am now that he's over here so often. He's a fucking stranger."

It'd probably be easier to believe all that if jealousy wasn't audibly dripping off of it.

I rub at the side of my face. "Well, this really is the end of our conversation. Thanks for your concern or whatever you want to call it, but I'm done."

Rafe looks at me incredulously. "*I'm* not done until you give me an explanation."

"My explanation is that I'm an adult." I shrug wearily. "I can do whatever I want with whomever I want."

"You can't do whatever you want if it's harmful to you or someone else."

"Okay, is this coming from *you?*" I ask loudly. "Really?"

He stands up from the couch and demands, "What do you do with him, Mari?"

"It's none of your business."

"Your safety is my business."

"Hardly, and I'm not in danger, anyway."

His eyes widen and he laughs in disbelief. "The other day you were in the middle of a run-down neighborhood with him and he was looking at you like you're the greatest thing he's ever seen! Tell me how you knew he wasn't dangerous, that he wasn't going to yank you into one of those empty houses and rape you!" He points at me. "How do you know *now* that he's a trustworthy person?"

I bite down on my tongue to keep from screaming, *'Because he doesn't look like he's just walked straight out of hell!'* And after a few long moments I just shrug unconcernedly. "I knew then and I know now."

"Don't. Don't fucking say that. That's so stupid, Mari." Rafe shakes his head. "Just tell me what's going on with you—tell me why you shut me down at Applebee's. Tell me why you've been so distant and reckless. Was it the accident? Because ever since your car slid off that goddamn bridge—"

"Stop," I say flatly.

"—you got your parents killed, I know, but people die," he continues indifferently. "Peoples' parents and spouses and children die. It's a part of life. When are you gonna understand that?"

"*Stop!*" I shriek, because all I hear is him talking about the death of my parents as if he had no hand in it— as if he didn't even know them.

Claire says, "Rafe, I think I need to talk to Mari alone, but I really do appreciate all your help."

To my immense surprise, he doesn't say another word. He just brushes past me, an intense look on his face, and disappears out the front door.

"I can't believe this," I say when he's gone. "I can't believe you let him come in here and say whatever he wants. You're my big sister. You're supposed to protect me from the people who hurt me!"

"And what am I supposed to do when *my* sister hurts *me?*" she asks coldly.

I stare at her, baffled for more than one reason.

"He isn't the problem," she continues. "Your current behavior is the problem."

I blink slowly. "I already told you I'm not doing anything bad, and no matter what Rafe makes it out to be, I wasn't hooking or doing drug deals in that neighborhood. If you want to talk about unacceptable behavior, let's talk about him spying on me!" I throw my hands up in the air. "Jesus, Claire, it's not against the law for me to change my interests. I'm not permanently bound to the people I used to be friends with."

"Oh, please," she snaps at me. "This isn't about some innocent change you've undergone, Marienne. This is about how your poor choices affect the people who *are* innocent."

God. She's acting like Rafe cheating on me neither started this whole thing nor was an absolutely awful thing to do. Talk about innocent people getting fucked over.

I wish I could explain to her what's really going on with me. If only I had a way to prove that my choices have been smart, not stupid, she would understand everything. If only I could explain that Gabe and Beatrix aren't bad because they're like me, and that she can trust them because their job is to help protect people, Claire would understand that she has nothing to worry about and that Rafe really is overreacting.

I can't do these things, though, so she doesn't get it. She just thinks as badly of me as she did when she heard about the car accident. Thinks I'm being selfish or childish or whatever.

Then again, I'm not wholly convinced that she's in her right mind these days, so maybe it wouldn't matter if I could explain myself, anyway.

At length she says stiffly, "We have gone through a hard couple of months. I'm still very upset. These kinds of things are supposed to get better with time, and if that's true, I need a whole lot more of it. And maybe you do, too. Maybe this irresponsible phase of yours will fade off someday. It would be wise of you to try to hurry that day along, because you being insufferable is really wearing on my nerves and here before long, I'm going to have too much going on to tolerate it."

Oh, nuh uh. I'm Light—I'm *different*, not irresponsible, and I'm not going through a phase like some little kid. And *'insufferable,'* seriously? It's bullshit for her to say those things, and I suck in air to tell her so.

But she holds up a hand and says, "There's something else I need to tell you."

Well, praise God, it's a fucking miracle: something in her tone hints that this one might not be about me.

Instead of letting out yet another counterattack, I raise my eyebrows in acknowledgement.

She straightens up and inhales deeply, folding her hands into her lap. She speaks upon exhaling. "I'm pregnant."

Huh? My eyebrows dip down into a frown. "Pregnant?" I repeat.

"Yes."

I blink slowly, bewildered. "Who got you pregnant?"

She gives me a withering look. "Shaun. Who else?"

"That *assbag?*" I ask before I can stop myself.

Her eyes widen disbelievingly. "Okay, that is *enough!*"

But I may as well go ahead and finish the thought. "Claire, he doesn't even knock on our front door when he comes to pick you up for dates. He just honks and expects you to hurry outside."

She glares at me. "He's a good guy. You know nothing about him."

"Yeah, you've never introduced me," I remind her, "probably because he never gets the hell out of his car when he comes over."

"No, you want to know why I've never introduced you to my boyfriend?" she snaps. "It's because I don't know how to explain you to him! *'Shaun, this is my sister Mari. Don't get too close to her, though, because she's been known to kill people I love.'* I don't think I could stand for you to even be in the same room with him!"

"Oh, you love him now? You love him more than *me?* Mom and Dad are gone and you're just going to abandon—?"

"Don't talk to me about them, goddamn it!" she screams. As if the shrill cussing isn't shocking enough, she jumps up from the couch with livid eyes and gets right in my face. "You have no right! Thanks to you, Daddy won't be at our wedding to walk me down the aisle! Mama won't be here to teach me how to be a mother myself! All I have is you and you're the one who ruined everything! *I don't know* how *to love you anymore, you unimaginable* fucking *bitch!*"

The room and my head both ring with her ear-piercing scream even after the words leave her mouth.

My heart swells painfully in my chest.

Whoa.

Tears are suddenly burning like fire at the backs of my eyes.

Whoa, whoa.

My bones ache. I can't breathe.

I stare at my sister. Her face is full of anguish, like I really have single-handedly demolished everything her life used to stand on.

My chest tightens uncomfortably. *Breathe. Breathe.* I try, but the air is full of her razor-sharp words. Every time I suck in a breath, it feels like my lungs are being shredded to bits.

After what feels like forever, I croak, "Okay."

She shoves one of my shoulders and I stumble back. "Could you just fucking congratulate me?"

I grab my stuff from the couch with shaking hands. "Congratulations." I'd say I hope she keeps the baby because I've always wanted a niece or nephew, but why bother? After what she just said, I don't think she's going to let me anywhere near her child.

When I get to my room I shut the door and lock it. I put down my coat, retrieve my phone from my purse and connect it to the charger with trembling fingers. I try to change into pajamas, but I only get one shoe off before my legs give out. A sob escapes me as my knees hit the ground, and then I burst into tears. I cry so hard it hurts me. The sorrow is icy and invasive, and for a moment I think I'm going to throw up.

Then, so abruptly it steals my breath, the agony turns to rage. I pick up my shoe and heave it as hard as I can against my wall, screaming at the top of my lungs. Then I wrench off my other shoe and throw it, too. I'd throw something else, but nothing is within my reach and I hurt too badly to move. So I crumple onto the carpet and cry some more, unable to fight the crushing weight of the guilt descending on me, smothering me, spotting my vision with black.

It's the one thing I don't think time will heal me of.

c

I have a headache when I wake up. And a sore throat. And an aching neck.

Daylight is coming in through my window, so I guess I slept the night through on the floor. That explains the neck pain, and reminds me of why the rest of me feels like such shit.

But the day is coming no matter how I feel, so I sit up and reach for my phone. I'm relieved to see that it's only 8:15. A little late for me to be waking up, but it means I didn't sleep through Beatrix showing up to get me for training; she probably would've freaked out if I never came to the door. Would've tried to call, which I probably would've slept through as well since I never turned my phone's ringer back on. Then would've called Gabe in a wild fit of worry even though he's got as much of a way into my apartment as she does (none).

Ah, Gabe. My stomach flutters like crazy. *I have a date with him tonight, don't I? A date!*

The excitement doesn't last long, though. Within a minute I have my head in my hands, feeling like the least dateable girl currently walking the earth. My emotions are a huge jumble, I slept on the floor in my clothes and without brushing my teeth, and my face feels like a puffy mess because I cried myself to sleep. Oh, and I'm a life ruiner. Who wants to date one of those?

No one's perfect, I try to tell myself.

Only a small portion of me thinks that's worth anything.

My hot shower makes me feel a little better—I'm clean when I get out, at least, and some of my aches are gone. But I don't have much time to get ready, so I get the basics done and then twist my wet hair into a bun even though that's my least favorite hairstyle ever.

Claire is already out somewhere, so the apartment is silent and still. I'm grateful for it because I don't think I could handle bumping into her right now, but it also makes me sad because it's an 1100-square-foot representation of the utter nothingness that our relationship has become. I try to distract myself by eating a bagel and it works okay, but it gets better when a cheerful Beatrix arrives. Once we're in her car she turns on an upbeat rock song, and I have to hand it to myself because I don't think she can tell what kind of mood I'm in.

But somewhere between her turning on Breaking Benjamin in the training room and me practicing my dagger-wielding moves on a dummy, I give myself away.

My fake weapon does no damage to the dummy whatsoever. I know this because when the ferocity hits me, I start trying to stab the fuck out of him. Once I realize I'm getting nothing out of doing that, I drop the dagger and start in with my bare hands. That at least knocks his head to one side, shakes his entire frame, and makes me feel like I really am laying into...

...well, I don't *know* who I'm trying to beat the daylights out of. Myself, most likely. But Rafe and Claire and even Audrey are possibilities, too.

I do this for whole minutes. Minutes that are long and full of played-back conversations and crying and a car flying off a bridge and glares and angry tones and a cheating boyfriend and two shiny black caskets.

When I finally can't do it anymore, I sink to my knees. Hot and panting, I stare up at the dummy and his turned-backward head.

Beatrix turns the music down and asks very carefully, "Better?"

I try to catch my breath. She was right all those days ago when she told me training is good for getting rid of anger, but some of this anger feels like it's actually a part of me—like it's in my muscles and ligaments and bloodstream. It's the kind of anger that isn't easily purged. I gasp out honestly, "I don't know."

I fully expect her to ask me if I need to talk about it. But she says, although still kindly, "Well, let's keep at it until you *know* you feel better." And I think that's even cooler than lending an ear.

It's an intense training session. I sweat a lot and yell a lot, push some of my limits and overcome some of my obstacles. Three months' worth of negative emotions keeps me going, keeps me from slacking or being hesitant or worrying I'm going to hurt someone or something. And when I'm sparring with Beatrix herself, she keeps up with me blow for blow; she never flinches or complains or tells me to calm down, which proves how truly badass she is because I'm not holding anything back.

When it's time to call it she drops her hands onto her hips and asks breathlessly, "How do you feel now?"

I nod and reply in kind, "Better."

"Awesome." She starts toward the water jug and I follow her. "Heads up: I'm going to ask you to try something different tomorrow."

I work on getting my breathing under control as I get myself a drink. I don't bother asking for details before I say, "All right," because I'm in a Give It All You've Got mood. Whatever she's thinking, I'll go along with it. Good practice for the real world, because sometimes you don't have the freedom to say, *'I think I'll pass on that one, but thanks.'*

She seems to get where I'm coming from. She says, "Great," and gets a cup of water, too.

After another minute of winding down, I realize Gabe and Wes aren't here. I bend over to stretch my back out and I sigh when something pops. "Where are the guys?"

"They aren't coming by today," she says, doing a few cool-down stretches of her own.

"Why? Is something wrong?"

A smile creeps across her face. "Nope. I'm meeting Wes after I take you home and Gabe just wants to see you later..." the smile is huge now, "...when he picks you up for your date."

A flush erupts across my skin. "Oh," I try to say casually, but I'm smiling now, too.

Beatrix actually giggles.

Later, after a nap (the hard work I put in today caught up to me while I was sitting in the car), I feel even better than I did. My head is clearer. The hell I've felt since last night is finally slinking off to hide somewhere. And happiness about going on a date with Gabe—even if it *is* just trick-or-treating—is digging its heels in.

Since I'm still the only one here, I decide to turn on a random music mix and do some housework. I straighten up my room, start a load of laundry, load the dishwasher and vacuum the apartment. Then I seize the opportunity to turn the music up way loud and take another shower.

I'm not a good singer, but I sing Matchbook Romance at the top of my lungs as I wash my hair. At one point I even bust out the air guitar, and that's how I know I'm really feeling better.

"Total Eclipse of the Heart" comes on as I'm getting out. I sing along to it, too, as I dry off, get a bathrobe on and head into my room to find something to wear later. I'm thinking about keeping it simple since the mask I got at the Halloween store—a glittery pink and black thing that goes over my eyes—is so glitzy. Eventually I decide on a long-sleeved black maxi dress and a long chiffon scarf that's just about the same color pink as my mask. And that's enough pretty stuff, I think; I toss my old black Chucks toward the outfit and go back to the bathroom.

I'm a pretty simple girl when it comes to beauty products. I usually just do something with black eyeliner and call it done. But since it's Halloween I decide to go a step further: black eye-shadow. Oh, fine—*sparkly* black eye-shadow. It takes me a while to get it right, but when I finally put my mask on to see how it looks together, I'm pretty damn pleased. So pleased that I'm sad to take the mask back off, but it's only about 5:00; I'm not going to wear the thing around for the next two hours.

Doing my hair is by far the easiest task because I was blessed with naturally compliant hair. I don't use any extra-special products on it, so all I have to do once it's dry is choose my hairstyle. Tonight I'm leaving it down because I think I look the best with it that way, and I want Gabe to think I look nice.

Claire gets home at 5:30 and announces very frostily that in about an hour I'm going to have to turn my music off (off, not down, because she never was a fan of The Dear Hunter in the first place). Apparently she's cooking dinner for Shaun and some of their friends tonight to celebrate her being pregnant.

But I'm not going to let her or the memories of last night's argument bruise the good mood I'm in now. So I sing along to "Black Sandy Beaches," put my shoes and dress on, and knot the scarf around my waist so that the ends flow prettily behind me. And when I look at my reflection in the bathroom mirror, I smile at her.

When I turn my music off per Claire's orders, I hear loud female chatter from the other room. After a minute I hear a screechy, "I can't believe I'm gonna be a godmother!" Claire's best friend Ashley is in there, I guess. What a thing for her to sound excited about, considering she's the vainest person I know. She's the kind of woman who won't go anywhere near a baby because she's afraid of projectile spit-up. Seriously.

"So where are these guys?" a female voice I don't recognize asks.

"I don't know. They're just late." Claire sounds like she's trying not to be frustrated with the father of her child, but I know better. No matter who you are, if you're not punctual you're getting on her nerves.

Around 7:00 I decide to go wait for Gabe in the living room. Mask on and trick-or-treat bag/purse in hand, I step out into a conversation between Claire and her friends about whether or not Shaun is good in bed. Thank God they shut up about it when they notice me. I'd be pissed off if I barfed all over this outfit.

"Well, look who it is," Ashley remarks. She tosses back her glossy auburn hair and looks me up and down. "And aren't *you* dressed up? What's the super special occasion?"

"I'm going out."

"Little Halloween party? How cute." She smiles at me like I don't know what condescension is.

I start to say something back when a knock sounds at the front door. I know Gabe is on the other side of it because my Light mark is growing faintly warm on my wrist. I hurry over and open it.

My pulse does something funny when I see him. The breath he sucks in makes me wonder if the same thing is going on with him. His gaze lingers on my eyes before drifting to my hair, and then to the rest of me. He whispers, "Wow."

Ashley doesn't get so much as a backward glance from me.

I step out into the cold evening, and as I shut the door behind me I look up at Gabe in the porch light. My voice goes soft when I tell him, "Thank you. I think *you* look 'wow.'" He's dressed in the black outfit he had on the first day I talked to him on Blossombranch. A white phantom mask hugs part of his face and above it his hair is unruly, as it seems to always be.

He smiles happily at me. "Thank you. Ready to go?"

You have no idea, beautiful. "Yep."

Once we're in his car with the heater going, he asks, "Are you hungry?"

"Yes, I am."

"Me, too. What should we have?"

I shrug. "Let's say what we want on a count of three."

"Okay. One...two...three."

We both say, "Chipotle." Then we both say, "That was easy." And then we laugh.

An excellent way to start a date, if you ask me.

On the way there, we ask how each other's day was and listen to Snow Patrol. I only know one or two of their songs, so I'm glad when Gabe plays some that I've never heard and I find myself enjoying them. He has good taste in music. If I weren't so hungry I'd be sad to get out of the car and go in Chipotle when we arrive—that's how much I like these songs. But I haven't eaten since lunch, so.

After we get our food and sit down amid other costumed customers, we take a minute to discuss places to go trick-or-treating. Then we start talking to each other just like we always do. We talk about how much fun we had with Beatrix and Wes last night, and how good that chocolate cake was, and whether or not Wes ever told Beatrix he's the one who ruined her movie trivia (that one remains to be seen). After a little bit Gabe asks if things are okay with Claire, what with the phone call I received and all.

I don't really want to relive all of it, but I decide to answer and just keep it simple. I say Rafe was waiting for me with Claire and that he's really worked up about me spending time with people he doesn't know, especially Gabe (he's already up to speed on Rafe wanting to date me again, so he rolls his eyes just like I do when I mention his jealousy). Then I tell him Claire and I had an argument and she's pregnant by her jackass boyfriend—and briefly, why I think he's a jackass.

I think he senses how touchy that topic was, though, because instead of asking for more details he just smiles and says, "Well, that's exciting. Kids are fun." It's much appreciated. I don't want to burden him with my broken-family problems, and if he asks anything else about them I might not be able to shut myself up.

We continue talking for a long while, the way I suspect we would have if time had been on our side all those afternoons he drove me home from training. It's fun like I've never had before. I mean, yeah, I've been on dates before and had a few boyfriends over the years and I thought Rafe was a serious thing, but this feels different. *Gabe* is different. I don't know why, but he works for me in a way other people don't.

When we finally decide to leave the restaurant, we start toward one of the nicer neighborhoods so we can trick-or-treat. When we get there he parks at one end of a well-lit street teeming with trick-or-treaters. Then he kills the engine and turns to look at me.

"So, this is off the subject, but I just want to go ahead and say that if we see any Hellions while we're out, we're going to pretend they're not there. Completely ignore them and leave them be. If we come across one that needs taking care of, we'll call Wes and Beatrix. You and I won't be doing any fighting." Even with his phantom mask on, his expression is serious.

I nod just as seriously. "Yes, sir."

His eyes lighten. "Okay, don't call me that."

I hold up my hands. "I just meant that I'll do what you said. And you're older than me, anyway." I say the last part teasingly.

"Right, yeah." After a pause he asks, "Are you ready to go trick-or-treating, then, young lady?"

We don't last two seconds before we bust out laughing.

"Gabe, that's...no...." I wave my hand in a Don't Ever Say That Again way.

His shoulders shake with his laughter. "See? It's weird."

"That was a terrible one. I'm not *that* much younger than you," I remind him.

"Exactly, so don't be so formal with me."

"I was trying to be respectful because you've been doing this for *eight years*." I wave my fingers in his direction. "You're important. You're a Gatherer of aimless Light people and the first time I ever saw you, you were successfully fighting two monsters alone without any weapons. I'm still pretty new to this and I know it. Still just a girl. I'd be crazy to think—to think I was...."

My words get stuck in my throat as he leans over the center console toward me. He comes forward slowly, clearly trying not to startle me, but I *am* kind of startled because I don't know what he could possibly be doing. I highly doubt he's going to kiss me—

—ohhh, God, now *that* glorious thought is in my head. *Fuck.*

He stops moving, his face level with mine and only some inches away. A slant of light from a nearby light pole falls across his eyes, making them look more brilliant. For a few moments there is only silence as those eyes move over my face.

Then he says softly, "Marienne, it behooves me to tell you that you are *not* just a girl."

It's a good thing it isn't really up to me whether or not I breathe. If it was literally *my* responsibility to make sure I never run out of air and die of suffocation, I'd be failing horribly right now because all of my attention is on Gabe.

He's so damn unassuming. I haven't seen him act conceited a single time since I met him, despite the fact that he's strong and skillful and funny and generous—and beautiful. He's beautiful all the way from the obvious parts of him, like the way he carries himself, to the parts you have to really look at to appreciate, like the little scar that cuts downward, thin and faint, from the left side of his bottom lip. And some guys would start laying it on thick in a moment like this, with us being on a date that's going so well, and him being so close in the near-darkness of his car. Not him, though. He just looks serious. He isn't charming me on purpose.

When I figure out how to talk again, my words are just a murmur. I still go for a half-hearted joke, though. "Where've *you* been all my life?"

He says just as quietly, "I could ask you the same question," but amusement glints in his eyes.

It's so nice that he understands my sense of humor.

You know what else I've found to be nice? His hands. His left one is curled around the steering wheel and his right one is resting on the center console between us. They're a little bigger than mine, and stronger.

His hair is nice, too...

...and the light scruff dusting his jawline...

...even his skin is nice. And I bet it feels—

My breath catches when I realize one of my hands has just inched in his direction. I jerk it back and close both hands into fists. Then I blink slowly and say, "Let's go get some candy," before my fingers have a chance to do anything that might humiliate me.

Gabe's gaze meets mine rather hastily; apparently I wasn't the only one off in La-La Land. It takes him a few seconds to say, "Yes, let's." Indeed, he sounds as distracted as I feel.

Getting out into the cold air seems to help—that, and all the children hurrying around shrieking at the scary house decorations. The farther we get from the car, the more I see how far a lot of these people went to make their homes look horrifying. And I'm aware that it's all supposed to be for fun, but each time a kid yelps all I can think about is the possibility of him or her being in real danger.

We go to collect some candy from a house with cute paper ghosts hanging from the trees. The woman at the door looks at us like we're too old to be doing this kind of thing, but she drops mini Snickers bars into our bags anyway. I'd be irked if my mind wasn't on something that actually matters.

I know Gabe told me not to worry about Hellions right now, but I can't help it. It's not that I plan on convincing him to do anything if I see one; I just can't act like they aren't out there somewhere. They probably eat up Halloween festivities like cupcakes. So, yeah, these children running around shrieking in the dark has me on edge.

After we stop by two more judgmental houses, he asks, "What's on your mind?"

"Monsters," I say. On cue, a horrible (albeit automated) laugh booms from down the street, sending several children screaming and running away from a house draped in black cobwebs. I move toward Gabe a little.

He moseys closer to me, too, leaving little space between his arm and mine. "Don't be worried. I'll take care of you."

It's a lovely thing to hear, but I frown. "Will you? I thought you said we aren't going to bother with Hellions if anything happens."

He grins and actually winks at me. "We aren't. I can run very fast, though, even carrying you."

With my own wink I ask, "Then why didn't you beat me to the tire swing?" I press my lips together to keep from laughing. How does he cheer me up so easily?

His eyes get so big that it cracks me up, though. "That doesn't count," he protests with his own laugh. "You distracted me."

"*You*," I raise my eyebrows, "cheated right out the gate."

"I might've." My skin tingles when his fingertips hesitantly brush against the back of my hand.

My fingers twitch up to graze his. "No, you did."

He says teasingly, "Well, I'll admit to it, but I won't apologize." Despite his tone there's softness in the way he looks at me, and I figure I know what he's thinking even if he doesn't say it out loud: *'Because look where it got me.'*

I have to agree. And, truly, the scarier things in the world bother me a little less—at least for right now.

Even though literally all of the people handing out candy in this neighborhood look at Gabe and I like we're lame, we have a lot of fun. Some of the people in the next neighborhood we visit are a little better. One very nice lady thinks we're delightful and tells us our costumes are romantic (I guess she didn't see my Chucks). And at the last house we hit up for the night, two girls a little younger than me who are dressed as sexy Disney princesses are too busy being fascinated with Gabe to be rude.

"That mask really shows off your eyes," Slutty Belle says, smiling and tilting her head to the side.

Slutty Cinderella settles the candy bowl against her hip and smiles, too. "Oh, it really does."

"Perfect outfit, too. Black is *so* your color."

Lame as they are for flirting with a guy who's out with another girl, I can't help but look at Gabe to admire him right along with them.

I'm pleasantly surprised to find him already looking at *me* with admiring eyes. I'm even more surprised when he reaches up and takes a piece of my hair in his hand, like he's done it a thousand times before. He runs his thumb down the length of it and replies reflectively, "Yes, it is."

A shiver skips all the way through me. I manage a smile.

"*Lucky*," one of the girls stage-whispers.

"I fucking *know*," the other one whispers back.

Gabe returns my smile just before he looks at them and says, "So, about this candy."

When we finally get away from them, my smile turns into a grin. "You should've autographed something for them, Gabe. It would've made their entire lives."

190

"Are you kidding me?" he asks with a chuckle. "The only reason I even stood there as long as I did was so you could get candy from them."

I snort and hold my bag up. "Well, thanks, but they *fucked* me on—"

"Ahem!" an older woman exclaims as she nears us with a boy dressed as Luke Skywalker. He isn't very young and doesn't seem to care about my cussing, but the woman still glares at me and hurries him away. Gabe tries to stifle his laughter and fails.

It makes me laugh, too. "So anyway, you have way more candy from those girls than I do. They loved you a lot and they weren't fair with candy distribution at all."

"But you," he catches one of my hands in one of his, "have way more of *me* than they do."

Like my pulse doesn't feel like it's on fire or something, I slant toward him and muss his already-wild hair with my free hand. "True. All they have is a fleeting memory while I get to see you every day."

He grins down at me and asks a little randomly, "What do you think about my hair?"

"I like it."

His grin widens and he bumps my arm with his. "I like yours, too."

My mind plays back how he touched my hair before. Mmm, mmm, mmm. I happily tighten my hold on his hand for a second, and he returns the pressure.

It's 9:45 by the time we drive out of the neighborhood. "What now?" I ask as he turns the heat up.

He pulls up to a stop sign. "Well, I think the trick-or-treating is pretty much over, but I'm having a really fun—"

Music bursts to life from somewhere on him, and he stops talking to pull his phone from his pocket. Then he looks at me apologetically. "I should get this. It's Janssen."

"Not a problem." I know the Gatherers he's training are supposed to call if they spot anyone with white Radiance. Maybe that's what's happened.

From what I can tell by listening to Gabe's end of the call, that's *exactly* what's happened. He tells Janssen how to approach the guy, says he'll be there soon, and hangs up.

"Work beckons?" I ask.

Looking disappointed, he nods a little. "It does."

"Well, if you need to drop me off at home, that's okay."

He slides a look over to me. "I probably do, but I don't want to."

Even though I don't want him to, either, I know how important Lightforce business is. I lift my shoulders and give him a little smile. "White Radiances are good things, though, huh?"

He looks out the front windshield and sighs theatrically. "Oh, I guess you're right."

I chuckle. "I'll see you tomorrow, won't I?"

His tone is lighter already when he says, "Absolutely."

When we arrive at the apartment, there are no empty spots in front of the door. He has to park three cars down from Claire's Prius, by Shaun's yellow Corvette. He reluctantly turns down the music and looks over at me. I take a second to just look back before I say, "I've had the best time with you."

"So have I, Marienne." He gives me a shy half-smile. "I want to do it again."

I wonder if he can see me blushing. "Me, too."

"Yeah?" He hesitates. "Do you think I can have your number?" He looks genuinely nervous, like I might tell him no.

As fucking if. I nod and actually laugh a little, and he relaxes, smiles more easily.

After we've traded numbers he says, "Call any time you want to and every time you need to."

I murmur, "You, too, okay?"

He nods. "Okay."

And now it's time to go.

As I get out of the car I say, "Good luck with the white Radiance."

"Thank you." He leans over so he can smile at me. "Bye."

"Bye." I smile back and shut the door. And suddenly I feel way colder than I did when we were outside trick-or-treating just fifteen minutes ago.

He waits for me to open the door to the chatter-filled apartment before he starts driving away. I wave and back into the front hall. Once he's gone I shut the door, and I jump a mile into the air when I take another step backward and bump into someone.

I turn around, shoulders hunched in embarrassment. "Oh, I'm sor—"

A startlingly loud gasp swallows the rest of my words as my eyes lock with a set of eyes that are full of nothing but moving white smoke. Without my permission my gaze sweeps over the person's form, which is made up of bone and muscle that's visible under webby pitch-black skin. Shock and horror spike through me, rapid and scorching and crippling like an electrical current. My body temperature soars skyward, and then plummets into the ground.

"Hey, you don't need to go look in your car. I found it," a familiar female voice says. A moment later Claire comes into view, and my wide eyes meet hers. Her expression turns stony, but she says nothing to me. She just casually looks at the monster in front of me and takes his arm. "Come sit back down, Shaun. I found the book of baby names."

Oh my God. Oh my fucking God.

I'm going to throw up.

I drop my gaze to the floor and squeeze my way past the pair, unable to school my features into an even expression like I did with the guy at Applebee's. I hear him ask my ignorant sister, "Who issss thissss?" in a hissing, inhuman voice.

My entire body is quaking. *No, no, no, no, no.*

"My little sister Mari. Even if she had her manners about her," Claire's voice is sharp and I know she's glaring at my back, "you wouldn't benefit from talking to her."

I'm already to my room when I hear Shaun call almost playfully, "What a fine ssssurprisssse meeting you hassss been, Mari. Truly."

My complete horror is the only thing that keeps me from vomiting long enough to shut my door and lock it. Then I drop my stuff, fly into my bathroom and lose it.

Shaun, the man my sister is dating and whose baby she's carrying—and who is in my apartment at this very moment—is a Hellion.

And I've probably just given myself away to him.

10
Gabe

"It's not a problem," I tell Janssen as I cruise down a lonely street. "Sometimes they get away." He called me back a minute ago to tell me not to bother driving to him after all because the new Light guy is gone now.

"Yeah, I'm sure," he says, "but it's still disappointin'. All this time spent lookin' for white Radiance, and then we find one and it disappears on us."

I roll my shoulders back and sigh. "I know how that goes. All we can do is keep an eye out for it, now that we know for sure it's around."

"I guess so." Janssen yawns. "Well, again, I'm sorry for callin' you over here and then losin' the guy."

"Nah, don't apologize," I say. "In fact, call back if you spot him again."

"Will do. Have a good night, Gabe."

"Later."

When I hang up, the first thing to pop into my head isn't that I need to drive around and look for the white Radiance myself. It's that I dropped Marienne off early for damn near no reason.

As I pull up to a red light I think back on our date.

Dramatic makeup and splashes of hot pink and sneakers under a long dress.

Easy conversation.

Me having the urge to kiss her more than once, and for a different reason each time.

Her not seeming to notice any time the song in my car described her perfectly.

The way she got me to have fun asking strangers for candy.

Me not being too terrified to touch her...and her touching me back.

I think I'm in trouble.

My phone rings yet again as the light ahead turns green. I pull myself out of my thoughts and let off the brake, answering the call without seeing who it's from. "Gabe Elias."

"Gabe, oh my God!" a terrified voice bursts through the phone.

I don't need to ask who it is. I'd know that voice anywhere, especially that voice saying my name.

"What's wrong, Marienne?" I execute a U-turn. My phantom mask clatters out of the passenger seat and onto the floorboard.

"There's a—there's a Hellion in my house!" she gasps out.

For a single second, everything flashes red. My thoughts, my vision, the rest of the world.

Then I come back, and I ask, "Are you hurt?" in a dangerously calm tone. She better not be hurt. If he laid a hand—

"No."

Some of the tension coiled around my ribs loosens. "Is he where you are right now?"

"No, I'm in my closet and he's in the living room with my sister—it's her boyfriend." Her voice is wobbly. "He's here to celebrate the baby with Claire and her friends—"

Oh, Christ. My eyes widen. *Her sister is pregnant with a Hellion's child.*

"—went in the house after you left and I wasn't watching where I was going and I ran right into him and I just—I just—"

"Okay. It's okay. I'm already on my way over there."

She starts sobbing. "What do I do? I think he knows that I—that I *know*—"

My stomach twists violently, because I can only imagine what her reaction to seeing him was.

I think fast. "Be ready to leave for the night when I get there. Less than ten minutes, okay?"

She sucks in a shaky breath. "Okay."

"I'll call you when I'm at your front door. Don't leave your room until you get that call. When it's time, you get outside to me without looking at or talking to anybody, not even your sister."

"Okay."

"Less than ten minutes," I remind her.

"I'll be ready."

We hang up and I immediately call Beatrix. She answers after a few rings. "Gabe, darling! How was—?"

"Can Marienne stay the night with you? It's an emergency."

"I—yes, of course," she says, her gaiety disappearing. "I'll fix the couch up for her right now."

"Thank you. We'll be there soon." I hang up.

I focus on getting to Marienne as quickly as I can without being pulled over by a cop. It's difficult work because it's Halloween and I know they probably expect extra-wild behavior from people tonight. There's no way in hell I can go the speed limit, though. Or stop at stop signs that no other cars are approaching. Or sit at red lights when there are parking lots for me to zoom through.

I prepare myself for any encounter with the Hellion I might find myself in. I don't mind a fight, but one thing is for sure: if I can get Marienne out safely and avoid actually killing the Hellion, I need to do that. It goes against the urge sitting deep in my chest that tells me to just wipe him off the face of the earth, but I know it'd be stupid to kill him if an apartment full of his friends might see. If it comes down to it, I'll just get a good slice on his leg with my dagger—that'll slow him down.

When I pull up to the apartment everything is as quiet and still as it was before—no meeting the Hellion out in the open, then. I park next to the yellow Corvette again and leave the motor running as I jump out, pulse pounding, fingers already dialing Marienne's number.

Half a ring goes off before she answers. "Coming."

I step up to the door. "Remember what I told you."

"I remember." She hangs up.

I put my phone in my pocket and wait. I prepare to go in and get her if I have to.

An acceptable amount of time passes before the door flies open, but when Marienne steps through it she looks much more horrified than she sounded just now on the phone.

A woman inside yells, "When did you turn into such a little cunt, Mari?"

Before I can get upset about that, Marienne whispers quickly, "Gabe, he's trying to talk to me and they're mad that I ignored him. He's headed this way."

I turn her toward my car. "Go. I'm right behind you."

Two men round the corner at the end of the front hall. One is utterly normal. The other is not.

I step toward the wide-open door as the normal one says suggestively, "Oh, I get where she's goin' now," and points his beer bottle at me.

I grab the doorknob.

"Why don't you share, you lucky son of a bitch?" He grins wickedly. "She is *hot*."

"Fuck off," I deadpan, pulling the door toward me.

"I'd check your attitude if I were you, boy," the Hellion says in his unnatural voice. Within a second he's closing one repulsive hand around the door.

I don't check shit.

With all the power I can muster, I wrench the door forward and then immediately kick it back. It violently collides with the Hellion, and before it springs forward again I see him stumbling backward into the other guy. It's good enough. I jerk the door shut and bolt for my car, which Marienne is already in and which is still running— with my door open, which is not how I left it. That must've been her doing. How helpful.

I swing into my seat and slam the door closed at the same time. Then I'm reversing, and then shifting into Drive, and then zooming away.

"Seatbelt?" I ask as I buckle myself up.

"Yes," she says breathlessly.

I keep my eyes on my mirrors as I put one mile between us and the apartment, and then two miles, and then three. I see nothing alarming—no suspicious cars, no Hellions, not even a police car. By the time we've gone six miles and are only a few minutes from Beatrix's house, I feel confident that no one is following us.

I turn down the first dark and empty street I see and park the car.

Marienne sighs shakily from beside me. "Ohhh, God."

I look at her. She's staring straight ahead with her hands knotted in her lap. "Are you okay?"

"Um. No. I don't know." After many seconds her shoulders slump. "I'm not hurt, but...."

But your sister is pregnant by a monster. "Yeah."

"What's he doing with her? What's he *going to do* with her?" Her tone is frail and breathless. "Will my first niece or nephew be a monster? Is Shaun going to—is he going to kill my—?" She covers her face with her hands.

Softly I ask, "You really want to know the answer to that?" It's not fair for me not to tell her what she wants to know. The question is whether or not she actually wants to know it, because it isn't pretty.

"Yes. No." She inhales deeply. "Yes."

"You sure?"

She nods a tiny bit.

"This is how Hellions reproduce. They have sex with human women."

She seems to stop breathing.

"They create either a normal child or a Hellion child. If the first happens, the father will either corrupt it or kill it. If it's born a Hellion...well, you know."

A sound of dejection leaves her, and I know she's comprehended what I didn't say outright: that either way, there's no hope for that baby. "And—and Claire?"

My hands seem to be going cold. I ball them up and cross my arms. "If the child is normal, she's up against the same risks as any other pregnant human woman. If she's carrying a Hellion, the risks are significantly greater. You've seen adult Hellions—just imagine what it's like to have that growing in your body." My throat tries to constrict and keep my next words in, but it's something Marienne needs to be prepared for. I clear my throat. "Sometimes the woman can't handle...sometimes she doesn't *get through* the...."

It turns out I can't say it out loud. But judging by the way Marienne wraps her arms around her stomach and curls in on herself, I think she understands that, too.

For a while we just sit in silence. She stays balled-up and I sit here and let her have this time to think, or mourn, or whatever she has to do. I don't know what to say to her, so I say nothing. I don't know if touching her is a good idea or not, so I keep my hands to myself.

Eventually she straightens up. For the first time all night, she tucks her hair behind her ears. "Are you mad at me?" Her voice is quiet.

I raise my eyebrows. "No. Why would I be?"

Her fingers smooth back her hair. "I called and interrupted your work."

Oh, God. How can she worry about something like that right now? "You didn't, actually," I tell her. "Janssen called back pretty fast to say he lost the guy."

She curls her fists around the ends of her hair, and her eyes flicker hesitantly over to mine. The Halloween mask is gone and she's wearing jeans and a hoodie now, but her makeup is still in place—pretty miraculous, considering the crying I know she was doing. "Really?"

I nod encouragingly. "Really."

She grimaces and finally lowers her hands back to her lap. "I'm sorry. That's sad."

"We'll find him at some point."

Her teeth absently graze her bottom lip as she looks at me. My own teeth are jealous of them.

Talk about thinking about shit at the wrong time. Thus why I decided to take her to Beatrix's house instead of mine.

I shut down the lip-biting thought, albeit with some difficulty, when she says quietly, "Thank you so much for coming back."

I want to assure her that I will always go back for her, but I don't. I just gingerly hold my right hand out, palm up, and say, "Of course."

She spreads her left hand out against mine. It's smaller and cooler and more delicate than mine is. But I can't be fooled; I know what those hands are capable of. I've seen what she can do with a dagger—real *or* fake—in her hand, and she told me about how she punched Rafe one time.

After a while she touches her fingertips to mine and asks, "It's not safe to live there now, is it?"

"Well," I sigh, still inspecting the way our hands look together, "once you get your weapons you'll be safer no matter where you are. I wouldn't recommend staying there, though."

"Where, then? The Sanctum?"

"That would be the best idea. It's late, so Mark's not there right now to get you down for a room, but that can be done tomorrow when you go for training. Tonight you can stay at Beatrix's house."

She sinks her fingers through mine. "Okay."

I'm struck by how good it feels to hold her hand. I fold my fingers around hers and relish the perfect fit. After a second I hear a soft breath leave her, and I look over to see she's looking at our hands with a tiny smile on her face.

But the smile doesn't help with how tired she looks. I suddenly feel bad for not having her at Beatrix's already; the discovery she just made about the father of her sister's baby is exhausting, no doubt.

I squeeze her hand before I take mine away and finally get us going again.

I'm in the middle of considering turning music on when I hear her say, "*'Hope was but a timid friend; she sat without the grated den, watching how my fate would tend, even as selfish-hearted men.'*"

The words are a sad, soft melody, like poetry. I glance at her and see she has her head turned toward her window. Her hands are limp in her lap. "What?" I murmur, looking at the road again.

"It's a poem. Emily Brontë."

It *is* a poem. The girl has poetry memorized.

Today must be my goddamn birthday.

"Do you know more of it?"

"I used to know the whole thing by heart. I had to study it extensively for a college class I took..." after a beat she sighs, "...before. I don't know if I remember all of it now or not."

"Will you tell me what you know?" *Please. Please.*

She doesn't speak right away, but when she does it's more languid poetry that leaves her mouth and fills up my car. "*'She was cruel in her fear; through the bars one dreary day, I looked out to see her there, and she turned her face away!'*"

I can't drive like this. I park my car on the side of the street and stare out into the night.

"'Like a false guard, false watch keeping, still, in strife, she whispered peace; she would sing while I was weeping; if I listened, she would cease. False she was, and unrelenting; when my last joys strewed the ground, even Sorrow saw, repenting, those sad relics scattered round....'"

Silence falls for many seconds. It's so perfect that I can hear the tremor in her breathing.

"'Hope, whose whisper would have given balm to all my frenzied pain...'"

My eyes find her. She's still facing the window. I want to touch her again, but can't make myself do it.

"'...stretched her wings and soared to heaven...'" she inhales thinly, "'...went, and ne'er returned again!'"

A minute passes before I can manage, "Marienne...."

She clears her throat and rolls her head around to look at me. Her eyes are cheerless. "Looks like I do remember the whole thing."

"That was amazing," I tell her.

She says nothing else, just looks at me. I look at the sadness marring her face and wish it didn't have to be there. But I know there's nothing I can do about it, not really. There's no changing the path her sister has started down. All I can do is try to keep her out of the way.

For tonight, at least, I have succeeded there and I find solace in that. And I want her to find some peace, too. I want her to feel like not everything is in shambles. So I say, "Hey, do you want to know something cool?"

She looks startled by my abrupt question, but nods a little. "Okay."

I point out into the night. "Did you know that some of the stars in the sky have been burned out for years and years, but we don't realize it because they're so far away?"

Curiosity touches her features as she glances outside and then back to me. My guess is that she didn't know this bit of information.

I shift to face her better. "The time it takes for us to learn about a star's activity is related to how far away from us it is. If it's six hundred light-years away, when it burns out we won't know it for six hundred years. In fact— have you ever heard of the Pillars of Creation?"

She shakes her head. "No."

"Well, they're not actual pillars. They're just collections of dust and gas out in space that look columnar to us. NASA got a picture of them, and since then some scientists have said the Pillars were actually destroyed *thousands* of years ago—dead and gone a very long time before we first found out about them." I let out a soft laugh. "They're just *that* far from us."

Her eyes are wide. "That's...incredible."

"It is." I give her a smile. "The wonders of our universe."

She breathes out, "Wow." And I don't expect her to smile back at me, so when she does it's even more fantastic than usual.

I'm so pleasantly distracted by it that I don't register her movement until she's an inch away and I can smell her hair and her hand touches my shoulder—

She presses a soft kiss to my cheek, and my breath catches in my chest. I wasn't expecting this.

A look of unabashed admiration is on her face when she draws back. She looks right into my eyes and whispers, "Thank you for that."

I can't say or do anything. I just stare at her with my heartbeat stuttering and my skin burning deliciously where her lips touched it.

She gazes back at me, still so close, still wearing that look on her face.

Kiss her, a voice in my head abruptly commands.

Oh, God, I could.

And not on the cheek, either, even though that was superb. I could do it for real, the way a guy *should* kiss a girl he's crazy about: like he means it. Like she deserves to know the effect she has on him, and like he wants her to feel affected by him, too.

As if she knows where my thoughts are, her eyes flicker to my mouth. And there it is: the look that tells me she would not stop me.

I could do it. I want to do it.

Do it, the voice whispers.

If only I could fucking move.

Suddenly there's a frown on her face and she's leaning away. "I'm—I'm sorry." She tucks her hair behind her ears and then unnecessarily does it again. "That was too much, wasn't it? I'm sorry."

Fuck. *Fuck.* She's misinterpreted my reaction.

I manage to shake my head a little, but she holds up a hand, looking like she understands—which would be great if there were anything *to* understand. "Let's just go, huh?" she says with almost-nonchalance. "Beatrix is probably wondering where we are."

Yeah, probably so, meaning my chance to do this thing has come and gone and is flying farther and farther away by the second.

But maybe it's better this way, anyway, right? Maybe this is the universe's way of saying, *'Gabe, how about you* don't *wear out your welcome? Your date went well, but Marienne has just received some pretty unfavorable news, so just take her to a safe place and call it a day.'*

It's a pretty sound piece of advice if I really think about it.

Still...she was *right there.*

I get us back on the road and decide we definitely need music. It's more Snow Patrol because I'm still incapable of asking if she'd rather hear something else. Not really a bad thing, though, since she liked it earlier.

As Marienne predicted, Beatrix is peeking out her front window when we pull up. The curtains fall back into place and she's out the front door before we're out of my car. "What happened?" she wants to know, reaching for Marienne's shoulders as soon as she's close enough.

"I'll let her tell you about it," I say as I approach them. "I should get home."

Beatrix looks at me a little strangely, but she'll probably call me later and ask what the deal is, so I don't feel the need to elaborate right now.

Marienne looks distinctly embarrassed, though, and...well, that's not really fair.

I look at Beatrix. "Can you give us a second? I'll send her right in."

She nods and releases Marienne, smiles at her. "Yep. Let me go make sure everything's set up for you, babydoll." Then she disappears into the house and we're alone again.

Marienne reaches for her hair. "Okay, listen, I want you to know I *really* wasn't trying to be weird—"

"It wasn't too much," I finally get out. "It wasn't too much, it wasn't weird, and I'm not upset about it whatsoever. It was great. You're great. Don't be nervous."

She manages to look surprised and furrow her brow at the same time. "Nervous? No, I'm—I'm not—"

I fight a smile. "You worry the living hell out of your hair when you're nervous. I know this."

Those eyes of hers look up at me, partly shy and partly mystified. She lets go of her hair and puts her hands behind her back. "I just want you to know I wasn't trying to be...um...a scary girl."

Now I do smile. I don't know why I froze up back there, but it wasn't because I was scared of her. I assure her, "I know."

She gives me a little smile of her own, and then she clears her throat. "Well, good. So I'm...I should...." She gestures over her shoulder toward Beatrix's house.

"Yeah, go," I agree. "Get some rest. I'll see you tomorrow."

"Thank you again," she murmurs.

"Any time."

She backs away. "Goodnight."

"Goodnight." I watch her step into the house and take hold of the door, then shut it tight. And then I turn and get back in my car.

As I drive away, I wonder how it is that out of all the extraordinary things I've experienced in the past eight years, it was this girl that finally overwhelmed me.

∽

Beatrix calls later like I assumed she would. She asks everything I expect her to ask, from how my date went to how sure I am that the Hellion didn't follow me to her house, or to my own.

For a second I consider asking if Marienne mentioned our weird kiss thing—for an even smaller second I consider asking when a good time to kiss her might actually be. But our call ends with me having kept both questions to myself, because I know I don't really want an answer to either of them.

That's not to say Beatrix isn't smart. She knows about these girl-type things. I don't doubt she'd be able to offer good advice if I ever asked for it—or, as she's demonstrated before, even if I don't ask. But I take it as a good sign that she hasn't felt the need to warn me about Marienne the way she did with Ella.

I met Ella five years ago, shortly after Beatrix joined the Lightforce, and she was not Light; she was just a girl, as Marienne tried to dub herself earlier this evening. From the start she and I were very different—we had next to nothing in common and she was extremely superficial, which annoyed me—but she was hot and expressed an interest in me, and I was lonely. She worked at a coffee shop I found in Little Rock on one of my traveling stretches and she flirted with me every time I stopped in, which was often. She had a way of touching her choppy blonde hair and looking me up and down with her dark brown eyes that made me feel like our differences didn't matter.

But they did matter because they weren't all *little* differences. No matter how much I thought I needed a girl, there was no ignoring that I was Light and Ella was not. Us living in two different worlds meant she couldn't really know my mind, my profession, my interests, and thus could never really know me. She couldn't be my equal. I didn't fit with her.

At least, that's what Beatrix told me.

I'd called the Sanctum one day to check in with Grayhem and she answered the phone instead of Mark because he was away from the desk. She asked how I was doing, and the thing with her is she asks those kinds of questions because she sincerely wants to know the answers. She asked how my work was going in Little Rock, so I told her. She asked if I'd had any fun, and I told her I met Ella. The first thing out of her mouth was an excited, "You found a Light girl your age?" But as soon as I answered no, she was zero percent thrilled and one hundred percent advisory.

I didn't want to hear that stuff from her, though. I didn't want to hear that I shouldn't be having fun with a girl who wasn't exactly like me. I just wanted to be a normal guy and enjoy a girl and not have to worry about how completely and utterly wrong for me she was.

So I kept trying with Ella, spending eighty percent of my time searching for Light people and the other twenty percent with her. But that's a big gap even for the casual relationship we had, and she noticed it really quickly. She thought I was seeing someone else, and there wasn't really anything I could do or say to change her mind. How would that have gone? I couldn't have said, *'To prove I'm not always out with another girl, I'll take you along with me for a day so you can see that I spend the majority of my time looking for people who glow. Oh, by the way, you can't see the glow because you're ordinary. I have actually been given a very rare ability, so just bear with me.'* No, there was no explaining the gap.

That was when I first got the feeling that Beatrix was right, but I still didn't want to listen to her.

The second time was on the night Ella got drunk and found the only vial of red powder I'd brought with me, some of which I always carry in case of a Hellion emergency. When I wouldn't tell her what it was, she smashed it on the floor and said if it wasn't important enough to explain, it wasn't important enough to have. That left me with only my dagger for a weapon, which wasn't that bad, and it meant I'd have to go give more blood to fill up a new vial, which *was* bullshit. But I still didn't listen to Beatrix's advice.

It wasn't until Ella interfered with my speaking with a new Light person that I finally understood it couldn't work between us.

I'd insisted on going to the mall in case someone of interest to me was there. I hadn't spotted anyone with white Radiance in forever, partly because there are so few of them anyway and partly because I'd been trying to spend more time with Ella. To my immense relief, while we were moseying around the place I spotted just the kind of person I'd been looking for: a man cloaked in a brilliant white glow. He was walking in the same direction as me, so I had to follow him.

Ella had one manicured hand looped around my arm and the other holding her cell phone to her ear so she could gossip with some friend of hers. I tried to mime to her that I was going to the restroom, which wasn't true, of course. She quickly bid her friend goodbye and suggested with a wink that she come along with me. Despite the short skirt and high heels she had on that day, my attention was on the man, who was getting away; he was several stores down from me at that point. So I faux-confessed that the bathroom thing was a ruse, that I was actually planning to buy her a gift and wanted it to be a surprise. I told her I needed to leave her behind for a few minutes.

Ella actually screeched with excitement, but she didn't let me go. She begged me to tell her what the gift was. I had no answer because I wasn't actually planning on buying her anything, and I was losing the man, so I tried to evade her inquiries as I headed off in his direction. She literally dragged her feet while I tried to walk. Her high-pitched voice echoed loudly around us, catching people's attention as she whined that she wanted to know what her surprise was, and I tried to tune her out while she made outrageous guesses. I kept my eyes on the new Light man; I was too afraid of losing sight of him to take a second to pry Ella off of me. I couldn't let him slip through the cracks, so I suffered through our snail's pace and prayed to God that he didn't get away from me.

I was awash with relief when he finally headed into a store. I was able to walk in, too, after a minute, but Ella was still clinging to me and harping on about her surprise. She wouldn't leave me alone for a single second. The employees in the store were already starting to look as annoyed by her as I was, so I finally told her to give me a minute to breathe or I wasn't going to buy her anything at all.

That was when she lost it. Right there in the middle of Champs, she started screaming at me. She pushed me with both hands and complained that I was a shitty boyfriend, even though she'd never referred to me as her boyfriend before. She yelled that I'd been cheating on her and the only way she'd ever forgive me was if I bought her something expensive, treated her like a princess, and quit spending time alone. She demanded that I walk her down to Zales and buy her jewelry, and let her drive my car whenever she wanted, and give her the name and number of the other girl I'd been seeing. If I didn't do what she wanted—*everything* she wanted—she would kick my sorry ass to the curb and then kick me again just for fun, heels on and all.

Since I couldn't promise her a single bit of that— since I couldn't even say anything in my defense—she slapped me across the face in front of the customers that had gathered around us, and then kicked me hard in the shin. It wasn't until after she'd stormed out and the onlookers had wandered away that I realized the man with white Radiance was nowhere in sight. I was so horrorstruck that I thought I was going to throw up right where I was. And I finally, resentfully admitted the truth to myself: normal girls, no matter how attractive, truly are nothing but trouble for me. And pain—lots of pain, if they kick me with four-inch heels on.

So I left the mall with nothing but a stinging face and a throbbing leg. Later, after I was back at the Gatherer house I was borrowing, I took note of the weight of it all, of how truly disconnected being Light kept me—not just from anyone I used to know, but from any new people who'd want something from me. I decided then to commit myself to my job because it really was all I had, all I could call my own. I was unspeakably ashamed that I'd let the man at the mall disappear, especially over someone who wasn't even important to me. I hated myself for it.

And Beatrix had been right all along about the romantic aspect of my new life: if I was ever going to devote time to a girl again, she couldn't be just any girl. She would have to be Light like me. If I ever got that far, *then* I could worry about things like physical attraction and shared interests and whether or not I like spending time with her. Until then, it would all be messy and wrong and idiotic.

The experiences I'd had with Light females so far, though...well, they weren't encouraging. Eventually I started thinking it was highly unlikely that I'd find a girl who was both Light and of any notable interest to me. I got to where I was okay with being alone. I became a firm believer in personal space. I turned into one of those people who live and breathe the, *'All I need is what I have,'* mentality.

But life is made up of countless moments that each hold an atomic bomb's worth of potential. You can never know what the moment you're in means. Is it only meant to propel you forward? Is it one of the ten-and-counting moments you have left before you die? Is it the last moment of the routine you've grown used to before everything changes? The last lungful of air you'll draw before something happens that will make you forget how to breathe?

That day on Blossombranch Lane, right after Marienne killed those Hellions when she took the time to just look at me, my thought process changed. In that moment I realized I didn't know everything, hadn't seen everything, wasn't already in possession of everything that was meant for me in the world. In that moment I was reintroduced to possibility I'd stopped thinking was out there; even if it ended up that me and her weren't quite right for each other, I still had proof that girls like her exist.

But somehow, things with her only got better from there.

I wonder if that's how Wes felt when he first met Beatrix: like it was too good to be true, only nothing bad ever happened to confirm that. Oddly enough, I've never asked. I know how they met and I attended their tiny wedding and I know they love each other immensely, but I've never asked my friend to *explain* what he has. I've never asked him what it's like.

Maybe I will someday, because *I* sure as hell don't know anything about love. My mom was a single parent and whatever I had with Ella was inane. All I've known is friendship—which does count as love, I guess, but whatever.

My phone rings right as I'm climbing into bed. Part of me hopes it's Marienne because I like talking to her, though I don't like the possibility of her calling because something else is wrong. Another part of me hopes it's Janssen or Wright, bearing the news that they've come back across that white Radiance.

Turns out it's just Beatrix again. "Hey, I forgot to tell you something," she says.

I get comfortable in my bed. "What's that?" I turn my lamp off.

"Mari is doing excellent in training, but so far she's only worked on the dummies and sparred with me. Except for the time she saved your ass, that is." Her tone tells me she's still judging me for that.

I snort. "Okay."

"Okay," she echoes in a goofy voice that is, I guess, supposed to sound like me. "So before I take her out to kill an actual Hellion, I want her to spar with you."

My amusement flickers out and is replaced with interest. "Really?"

"Yeah, I think it'd help her to fight someone besides another woman. Hellions are male and almost always bigger than girls, and you're stronger, taller, and more experienced than her. Even though you wouldn't be trying to kill her, the practice would be extremely beneficial."

I won't lie: the idea of being that close to Marienne is enticing. But the Gatherer/former Defender in me is most impressed with the idea. "That's some really smart thinking, B."

"I know! So how about tomorrow? It can be the last thing she works on. Just show up a little earlier than usual."

Tomorrow? Jesus. I only took her on a date and almost kissed her *today*.

Oh, grow up, I chide myself, and I know I'm right. This isn't about me. This isn't even about me and her. This is about her being prepared to fight a Hellion, and being strong enough to win.

"Sounds good," I tell Beatrix.

"Awesome possum. I'll see you tomorrow, then."

"Later."

We hang up and I drop my phone onto my nightstand, and in the darkness of my room I start thinking about what I'm going to do in this spar. It's been several years since I did something like this with anyone other than the actual enemy; I'm way more used to killing than practicing. For what feels like an hour, I mentally flip through attacks I could work in that wouldn't really harm Marienne but wouldn't be considered slacking.

Eventually my mind grows tired, and my bed starts feeling way more comfortable, and my body decides it's time to rest.

As I start drifting off, I wonder something: why didn't Beatrix ask her Defender-training husband to spar with Marienne? Why did she ask me?

It feels like whole minutes pass before the answer floats up to me. The thought is quiet, sleepy, and a little amusing: *Just for entertainment, probably.*

$\sim$

Starbucks is weirdly busy on Sunday morning, but not a single one of the customers is glowing. I don't even see a Hellion. The crowd is made up of nothing but totally normal people. So when I take my place at the end of the long line I let my mind wander away from the extraordinary and just listen to the chatter of the people around me.

"They said on TV that we're probably gonna see a bad ice storm soon," a woman says.

"They also said on the TV that the end of the world is coming," a man responds, "but that doesn't mean it's true."

"Snow is a little bit different from the apocalypse, Dave."

"What I'm saying is that the people on the news don't always know what they're talking about, *Miranda*."

The words of a much crosser man than Dave float over that conversation. "Hutchison, I told you to submit those two days ago," he snaps. "What do I have to do to get you to do your job? I can't just check up on you all the damn—" He pauses, clearly on the phone with someone who is now trying to defend themselves. But then he shouts, "*You didn't finish your work because some character on your favorite TV show died?*"

Several people in the area chuckle at that, including me, but then my own phone vibrates in my pocket. I pull it out and see that someone is calling me from the Sanctum.

"Gabe Elias," I answer.

"Gabe, it's Grayhem. I need you to come by the Sanctum first thing. We need to have a talk."

The greeting is so grave that it actually chills me. Still I say, "All right. I'll be there after I get my coffee, if that's okay."

"That's fine. Goodbye, now." I see he's not solemn enough to leave off his typical parting words.

I stand in line for another twenty minutes before I even make it to the counter.

The girl taking orders has bright blonde hair and way too much makeup on. When she looks away from the woman in front of me, who is complaining about the shortbread cookie display being empty, she waves a manicured hand at me. Her voice is high-pitched and flirty when she says, "Hello again, sir! My name is Heather, just in case you forgot. How might I make your coffee wishes come true this morning?"

She reminds me of Ella, from her appearance to her voice to her place of employment. How annoying. And her greeting is weird because I don't remember seeing her here before. But whatever. I tell her, "I need a venti vanilla iced coffee, please."

"Would you like a tasty breakfast food item this time?" She tosses her ponytail in the direction of the food case.

"No, thank you."

She taps my order in on her computer. "The Cinnamon Swirl Coffee Cakes are delicious. You should try one."

I'll admit it: that does sound good. Plus my stomach is a bit more anxious than usual because of Grayhem's call. I say a little absently, "Okay, yeah, I'll take one of those."

She grabs the coffee cake for me and then winks. "Can I talk you into anything else?" More lowly, "Maybe something that involves me being off work tomorrow night?" Her red-glossed lips curve into a smirk.

"You sure your name isn't Ella?" I grumble, handing her a ten-dollar bill.

One of her eyebrows goes up. "I'm sorry?"

"Nothing. And I'm just interested in my breakfast, so...." *You are nowhere near my type.*

"Well, what's the name for the order?" The look in her contact-lens-green eyes says that she's not letting me leave without giving her something to work with.

I take my change and the coffee cake from her, say, "Harry Potter," and walk away to wait for my coffee. After what feels like forever they call the name out, and as I leave more than a few wide-eyed people are asking where Harry Potter is. I can't help but laugh a little.

When I get to the Sanctum, Mark is on the phone behind his desk. He waves at me as I come closer. "Yes, I wrote it down. I'll make a copy of it for you." Then, "Gabe just walked in. Do you want me to tell him to head your way?" After a moment he gestures for me to go on, so I give him a nod and move through the door that leads to the offices.

I get to Grayhem's office and see he's still talking to Mark, his bespectacled eyes on his computer. "...try to figure this thing out," he's saying when he spots me. "Gabe's here. Goodbye, now." He hangs up and sighs at me.

"Morning," I say as I step through the doorway.

"Hello there. Close the door, will you?" I do, and then sit down in a chair across the desk from him. He takes his glasses off and rubs at his eyes. "So, I'll just get right to it. Em wasn't the only member of the Lightforce to meet an untimely and particularly violent end in Dallas. In fact, he's one of about fifteen to die down there in the past few weeks."

The information hits me weird. I don't know what I thought he wanted to discuss with me, but I didn't think it had anything to do with Em, and I especially wasn't expecting a discussion about a city in another state. At length I clear my throat and say, "Go on."

"The Director there—name's Bartholomew—has been sending updates on these deaths to me and the Director from El Paso, since we both had a man die in his city. He says things have been unusually violent for him lately: more regular citizens have been dying or going missing or what have you. And that's bad on its own because it means Hellions are causing a lot of trouble, right? So now add in that they're also taking our Light people out in handfuls."

I frown. "Right."

He lays his glasses on his desk. "The three of us have agreed that Dallas needs to be checked out before things get any worse. Bartholomew's asked me and Young if we have anyone who'd be capable of helping with that, and I'd really like for you to head down there sometime this week for me."

Emotions swell in my chest. There's anger still clinging to Em's murder, and sorrow for the other Light people who died too soon, and a desire to take down the Hellions that are to blame. Responsibility for the Light people who are still alive and for the human lives we're supposed to be protecting. Gratitude for the chance to help make things right. And a dark gray feeling that has nothing to do with the matter at hand and everything to do with having to leave a certain girl behind.

I try to get my mind around that last one.

"Is it just me going?" I want to know.

"I plan to ask Wes, too." Grayhem puts his glasses back on.

That dark aversion lessens a little bit. Wes going with me means Marienne wouldn't be all by herself; she could stay close to Beatrix. I take a long drink of my iced coffee and then say, "All right. If you need me to go, I'll go."

He nods. "Great. Like I said, I've still gotta get Wes in here and fill him in. Then I'll need to settle a few more things with Bartholomew. I'm thinking you'll drive down on Tuesday or Wednesday—plenty of time for everyone to figure their plans out."

"Okay."

He stands up, so I do, too. "Thanks, Gabe. You're a respectable man and a strong member of the Lightforce. I know you'll lend a lot of assistance to the other branch."

I nod once. "I'll do my best. Anything else?"

"That'll be all. I'll let you know details when I straighten them out." Then he holds up a hand. "Actually, I do want to know how your two new Gatherers are doing. Any luck finding white Radiances?"

"Oh, not yet," I sigh, deciding to leave out the guy from last night. "Soon, though, I'm sure."

Grayhem gives me a patient smile. "Agreed," he says. "Goodbye, now."

I head out with a wave. When I step into the receiving room I exchange a few words with Mark, who is merry as always. Then I walk back up into the cold daylight so I can see about getting some work done, and then have lunch with Wes, and then come back here to pretend to be a Hellion trying to kill one fierce and lovely girl.

11
Marienne

My heart claws its way into my throat as my car bursts through the rail on the side of the bridge.

The sound of the impact is horrendous, but the scream that leaves me is worse. It's unlike any noise I've ever heard myself make. It feels and sounds like my vocal chords are being pushed past their limits, furiously straining to alleviate the panic suddenly invading my entire being.

They do not succeed.

My car sails downward, heralded only by the beam of the one headlight that isn't shattered. It drops, drops, drops even though I'm screaming for it not to and desperately clutching the steering wheel and wildly kicking my feet.

My hairs stand on end as my mom shrieks my name from the backseat. My dad bellows hers from beside her. I realize we'll be hitting the rocky, uneven ground any second now. My eyes burn with tears and my stomach lurches with dread and my heart thrashes around in places it doesn't belong and my soul is shot through with agony, because I know we're all going to die.

We're going to die in this car and I'm the one behind the wheel.

Nothing flashes before my eyes. I relive nothing from my childhood. I envision no surreal images of me in the future. I have no sudden thoughts about what I should've done or said in my life, or shouldn't have.

All I know is terror. It's such a part of me that it feels like it's burning through my synapses—

"Mari, wake up!" someone says right in my ear.

I gasp so violently that it hurts me.

"It's okay! It's okay," they say quickly. A hand brushes my hair away from my face. "It was just a nightmare, sugar. You're okay."

My eyes open and I find a blurred figure swirled with bright teal stationed close to me. It takes me a few seconds to recognize that color, that voice, that gentle hair-brushing. Still, even as Beatrix's face comes into focus and I remember where I am, some part of me tries to tell me that I was dying just seconds ago, that my car was just falling through thin air and I'd just been hearing my parents screaming.

She smiles tenderly. "Hey."

I try to say something to her, but I'm suddenly choked by sobs.

"Oh, honey," she murmurs, pulling me to sit up. "Come here. Come here." She sits down next to me on the couch and lets me curl into her side and cry. Her arms are comforting around me—exactly what I need, what I've missed, what I don't really think I deserve. I accept them greedily.

It hurts me to know I'll probably never get this from Claire again. Not only do I not know how to fix what I did to our relationship, but also there's no way I can be around her if there's a chance Shaun might appear.

But what if her baby is a monster and it kills her from the inside out? What if she dies with this chasm still between us and I never get the chance to really talk to her about it?

Or what if the baby is a monster but Claire lives through the pregnancy? Maybe I'll be able to try to talk to her, but would it do any good? Would the baby corrupt her somehow? Would Shaun? Would they kill her?

What if her baby is human and normal and precious, and Shaun does something to it? Would he kidnap it and be gone for good? Corrupt it and then have to do the same to my sister? Kill it and then try to stick around to father another potentially evil child?

I shove away from Beatrix and run from the room, knowing I'm about to be sick.

I spend several minutes in the bathroom, vomiting and crying and feeling helpless. When Beatrix comes in she gets right back to taking care of me. She ties my hair back, dabs at my face with a damp washcloth, offers me water and a few crackers. When I think I'm done being sick, I rinse my mouth and let her take me back to the couch.

After I've gotten covered up and settled in again, she makes herself comfortable on the floor beside me. "Need to talk about it?" she murmurs.

My throat hurts when I say, "I don't even know what to say."

"Say whatever pops into your head."

I gulp and wrap the blanket tighter around me. "I was dreaming about my car wreck. It was exactly like it happened in real life." My pulse speeds up, turning my next words a little breathless. "My parents were screaming in the backseat. I can't believe that's the last thing I ever heard from them. It was *so*...." There isn't even a fitting word. I press my trembling lips together.

She starts stroking my hair again. "You were screaming in your sleep," she whispers. "That's why I ran in here."

"I'm sorry," I whisper back.

"Don't be, sweetie."

I shake my head. "But I am. To you, my mom and dad—Claire—*Rafe*—" My voice falters.

I'm still so angry with Rafe. I still can't wrap my mind around what he did, or why he's acted the way he has since that night. Such a big part of me blames him for my parents being dead, because if he hadn't cheated on me in the first place....

But now that I'm telling someone else about it—now that it's not just lurking in the back of my mind—the truth winds itself around my lungs. Rafe was only part of the problem. He may have started the whole thing, but he didn't directly turn me into an idiot driver. He didn't cause the wreck, the death, the cracking apart of my family.

I did that.

I shut my burning eyes. "Have you ever just *hated* yourself?"

Beatrix inhales a little sharply, like she didn't expect that from me. She doesn't freak out about it, though. Just takes her time answering. When she says, "Yes," I know she's being honest.

"I hate myself so much," I whisper.

"Maybe you do," she allows, "but listen to me. It's important for you to remember *you didn't do it on purpose*."

"Not on purpose," I moan, "but because I was so *careless*." The night flashes back to me all over again. "I was having a party and everything was going great. Friends everywhere and good music and I'd just fixed myself this awesome-looking drink I'd wanted to try for the longest time. And then I found Rafe and Audrey and I got *so*—I don't even know what I was." I press a hand to my eyes, which are tearing up again. "Then my parents called and needed a ride home because it was their anniversary and they'd had drinks at dinner, and I ran out to get them because I had to get as far away from that party as I could or I was going to lose my mind. And Rafe was yelling after me and then calling and texting and finally I got so fucked up about it that I started reading his texts, and that's all it took, Beatrix! Just looking at my phone for two seconds and my car was going off the bridge and—and just look what...." I draw a slow, pained breath. "Look what that cost me."

Look what it cost the people I love.

I cry much more quietly this time, but it doesn't hurt any less. Again Beatrix comforts me, whispers kind words about me that can't possibly be true.

At length she murmurs, "Sometimes even our worst mistakes bring us things that are beautiful. Do you ever think about that?"

"No," I say, my voice wobbly and weak. Why would I think about something like that? *How* could I?

"Well, you've gotten true companionship and a very special lifestyle out of that one mistake. You have the chance to protect people from the worst things in the world, and as if that's not a wonderful gift all on its own, you've also been given the gift of people who care about you and truly understand you."

My heart feels weak in my chest. "That...that sounds so nice, but...."

"Mari, it's true," she insists, reaching over to squeeze my hand. "Baby, you might not have thought about it this way, but your parents would've died anyway.

If you weren't involved it would've happened some other day, in some other situation."

Even though I know she's right, I whimper, "No."

"Yes. We'll all die. The only surprise about it is the timing. Maybe they would've died later that night in some way that had nothing to do with you—or say they'd tried to drive themselves home even though they'd been drinking, and they died like that. Would you have blamed yourself for not being able to stop it?" She shifts to look straight at me, her eyes bright with gentle conviction. "It's healthy for you to feel guilt, but do your best not to let it consume you because the truth *is* that you still have a purpose to fulfill. You made a mistake and that's okay, even if it's ugly, because it just happens. You just have to remember it was an accident, and that your parents loved you. They still love you, honey, wherever they are, and I know that they forgive you. They're probably as pissed off at Rafe as you are."

My heart aches at the very thought. I hadn't even told my parents Rafe cheated on me. My mom would've been appalled, and then pissed, and then optimistic. *'One day he'll realize what he did wrong, and he'll be sorry,'* she would've said in a tone that was somewhere between bright and resentful. My dad would've hugged me and told me to keep my chin up, and then every time he saw Rafe afterward he would've given him that flat, disapproving look no one *ever* wanted to get from him. It would have made me feel better, knowing my parents were on my side.

I've always heard parents are supposed to love their kids unconditionally. I hope that's true. I hope Beatrix is right. Because the idea of them hating me for what I did as much as I hate myself is *agonizing*.

Beatrix seems to know what I'm thinking. "You have to learn to forgive yourself. Trust me. This pain is hard to bear and I know it, and maybe it'll take years for it to simmer down, but I also know you *will* be fine if you learn to accept the things you've done. What if this was just your fate? What if this was just what had to happen in order for your life to be what it's supposed to be?" A soft laugh leaves her. "Because believe me, darling, we're glad you're here. You're good for us. We love you already."

Hot tears leak out of my eyes as I gaze up at her. I choke out, "I love you, too," as I painfully remember what Claire said about not loving me anymore.

Beatrix smiles more radiantly, but only for a moment. Her expression goes gentle and she curls her fingers against my temple, like she's checking to see if I have a fever. "Have you talked to Gabe about all of this?"

Oh, God, no. No.

She sees it on my face. "I think you should."

"He'll never talk to me again," I protest sadly.

"Yes, he will."

I shake my head. "You don't know that."

She pats my cheek now. "Well, I *do* know that," she disagrees, "but if you want to do it this way, allow me to say *you* don't know he'll never talk to you again."

I sniffle and frown at her.

Her shoulders lift a little and then go back down. "Just saying."

"I guess," I mutter. I sigh and dry my face off with my shirt sleeve.

"Just be honest with him. It'll be good for both of you." Her words turn into a yawn.

"Oh, God, what time is it?" For the first time it occurs to me that I might've woken her up with my freakout. When I look over at the window I'm at least glad to see some daylight coming through the curtains.

"A little before 8:00, I think."

I moan. "I'm so sorry if I woke you up."

"Nah, I'd just seen Wes off when you started screaming. So it's just me and you here and I was already awake." She gives me a patient smile. "Do you need to go back to sleep for a bit? You've got some time now that I don't have to pick you up for training."

"I don't know," I mumble. I don't feel so hot, but maybe it'd be better for me to just greet the day. Have a shower and some coffee or something.

"Well, do what you want, okay?" She stands up. "I'm going to take a shower, and if I come back and you're asleep I'll just wake you up after a little while."

"Okay. Hey!" She freezes mid-turn-away, one hand in the air like she'd been about to scratch her head or something. I tell her earnestly, "Thank you."

She relaxes and looks at me tenderly. "Of course, but you don't have to thank me. I'll always try to take care of you guys." She snorts. "Maybe even when you don't want me to."

I sink back into the couch and give her a look. "I can't imagine such an occasion."

She winks at me. "I accept the challenge. And speaking of challenges—" she points at me, "—I hope you'll still be up for what I want you to try in training later."

Yesterday's training session feels like it happened a week ago. It takes me a second to remember her mentioning that she wants me to try something different today. "I will be," I assure her, and I mean it just like when I agreed to it before.

"Great. Now take your time getting your thoughts together," she backs away with a nod, "and I'll see you soon, lovely."

I can't help but feel a twinge of amusement, because only she would call someone that after a morning like this.

ᘓ

I feel okay after I've showered and had breakfast. I got in some thinking about my night with Gabe, too, and that cheered me until I remembered the end of the night. Then I felt humiliated about that all over again.

That whole car situation was just something else. First I felt like my world was falling apart at the seams, and then I was in some half-miserable, half-awed state because of Gabe's cosmic talk, and then I was suddenly so rocked by him that I had to do *something* to let him know it. And that turned into some wild time-freeze thing during which I thought he really might kiss me, and God, I'd hoped he would. I really hoped that. And then I realized he was actually probably just too traumatized to do anything but stare at me, and that it might not be kiss-related at all.

He said it didn't freak him out, though—in fact, he said it was great (said *I'm* great!)—and I decided to believe him because I trust him to tell me the truth. I wouldn't have minded a smidgen of explanation, but I didn't really get it and there was no way in hell I was going to ask for it. So I just said, *Fuck it,* and called it a night.

And anyway, in the grand scheme of things it's not really that big of a deal, is it? If he still likes me as much as I like him, he'll do something about it. If he doesn't....

Well, among other things, I got fucked over by my best friends, survived a horrific car accident, and killed two Hellions without an ounce of knowledge about what I was doing. I don't think a simple case of It Just Isn't Meant To Be would destroy me—hurt, maybe, but not destroy.

Though if anything's going to mess up what we have, it's that I'm responsible for the deaths of two people.

My conscience won't stop whispering about Beatrix's advice. *Tell Gabe. Be honest with Gabe. You owe him that. He's an awesome guy. Don't let this go any further without the truth.* I can't shut the shit up. I can barely shove it to the back of my mind.

At the Sanctum, Beatrix and Mark help me obtain a room. It makes me happy to officially have somewhere to live again, and I'm told I can bring my stuff in any time I want. I plan on stopping by the apartment later to see if I can get in and get out without any problems.

So I'm not in that bad of a mood when we start training, but as usual it's this time that helps me the most emotionally. Like yesterday, I push as hard as I can. It's intense and tiring and I get so, so hot, but I persevere because I know by the end of it I'll be thanking myself. Indeed, when the long hours come to an end and my skin is slick with sweat and I'm humming with vitality and the distressed half of my mind has quieted down, I feel like the world sucks less than it did this morning.

Something else that happens at the end of the session: I realize I haven't received any unusual directions from Beatrix yet. Once she starts her cool-down stretches, I wonder if she worked the stuff in on the sly so she could say something like, *'You already did what I wanted you to do! You just didn't notice it because you were taking everything in stride, and that is an important skill to possess. Lesson learned.'*

But then she levels her gaze on me and says, "Okay, Mari. Ready to try this?"

Oh, whew, I didn't miss it. I stop rolling my shoulders and nod. "Yeah, I'm ready."

"Great." She nods at something behind me. "Spar with Gabe."

My heartbeat does something funny, and it has nothing to do with the rigorous workout I just went through. I turn my head and see him walking up, looking like he already knew about this idea. He gives me an encouraging smile and crosses his arms—probably unknowingly showing off his forearms, which are uncovered because the sleeves of his black shirt are pushed up, and which are pretty damn appealing as far as forearms go.

(So, I'm supposed to be getting ready to spar with this man, and what am I doing? Not assessing the advantages he has over me, or mentally planning out how I can make my height and weight work in my favor. No, I'm thinking about his fucking arms.)

Well, that's enough of that, I resolve. *I didn't slack yesterday or today and I'm not doing it now. Handsome opponents be damned.*

"Fake weapons or no?" I ask Beatrix.

"Yes." She hands hers to Gabe. "Whoever lands a solid killing blow with it in their hand wins."

"Gotcha," he and I say at the same time. I pick up the fake dagger I'd been using.

She starts backing away. "Calling it on in five..."

Not wasting any time, I see.

We inhale deeply and look at each other.

"...two...one...go."

Despite my tiny mental pep talk and my determination to try something different, for a few seconds I just look at him. And he looks back, normal as ever. And I wonder what the hell I'm actually supposed to be doing with him right now.

After another moment his eyes seem to grow tighter. I get the feeling that he's trying to convey something to me with that gaze—*'You have to pretend I'm not me,'* perhaps. Then I watch his form tense, his shoulders square, his knees bend a little and his arm curve around to hide his dagger behind his back. His expression closes off and those eyes turn hard and focused. And even though the serious air works for him, it's also unsettling— he still looks like sweet Gabe on the outside, but what I can't know is what he's like on the inside right now. What he's planning. What he's capable of.

Just like a Hellion, my mind whispers. *To most people they look normal, but underneath it they're dangerous. Evil.*

Shaun pops into my head, and then my pregnant sister. My mom. My dad.

Some switch in me is flipped. The torment crashes over me again, and my very bones ache to fight it. I *have* to fight it.

I have to fight it or it'll kill me.

I fly forward, ducking when Gabe swiftly swipes his dagger hand out. When I'm up again I throw a punch with my free hand, and his catches it to yank me closer. We both aim our daggers at the other's throat, but the attacks block each other. He sweeps his arm away from mine, and just as he goes to curve it around me to ostensibly stab me in the back I whirl around and down to the floor, throwing him off balance because he's still holding on to me.

And for I don't know how long, this is all that happens.

The spar is intense and fast and full of tricks and we don't go easy on one another by any means, but we get nowhere. Neither of us gets our dagger into a killing blow position long enough for it to count because the whole encounter is just one big dance. I send a jab of my dagger his way and he deflects it before shoving his elbow at me, which I veer away from so I can whirl toward him a strong kick that he catches easily. Cyclically it goes on like this: a swift attack met with a smart counter that opens the door for a good hit that is fated to be avoided, too.

At one point I get some decent space between us and I'm determined to make it work. His free hand is around the wrist of my empty hand, and I've just spun away from his dagger hand like we're a couple of ballroom dancers. I think fast, and before my chance disappears I throw my dagger at his chest. He dips and swerves away from it, looking mildly startled for the first time. Before he can straighten up again I've stepped forward, cocked a foot back and aimed it at his head. Unable to block me worth a damn, he takes the kick, and the collision is just powerful enough to make him stumble and loosen his hold on my wrist.

In one move I yank my hand back from him, spin around full-circle and swing a leg out, fast and strong, at his feet. They leave the ground and he falls backward, gasping loudly just before his back slams against the floor. His dagger tumbles out of his hand.

I'm on him in what feels like half a second, planting my left hand firmly on his chest while my right hand grabs his dagger. As I settle the fake blade against his throat, an amazed expression brightens his face.

"Done!" Beatrix yells.

I did it. I'm suddenly panting. *Oh, God, I did it. I won.*

Relief mixed with triumph burns through me. I relax, drop the dagger back onto the floor, and crawl just far enough away from Gabe to lie down flat, too.

I hear Beatrix chattering with someone—Wes, probably—but all I can really focus on is what I just accomplished. I stare at the ceiling and try to catch my breath, my hot skin tingling and my mind going wild with exhilaration.

After a minute I realize Gabe hasn't said a thing. I turn my head to look at him and see he hasn't moved except to gaze at me, too. I'm sure I look like absolute hell, because *he's* sweaty and flushed and out of breath and he hasn't been in this training room all morning like I have. But he doesn't seem grossed out or anything—at least, not enough to look away.

He reaches over to touch my sweat-dampened hair, which I can feel is falling all over the place, so I guess he doesn't find me too terribly repulsive.

"Are you okay?" I ask him. Not like I think he's fragile or anything, but he did take a hard fall right onto his back.

"I'm great." His fingertips leave my hair to trail down the side of my face. "How are you?"

I can't help closing my eyes against the touch. "I'm great," I echo.

That's all we have time to say because Beatrix's voice sounds from my other side. "Excellent spar. Gabe, honey, you doing okay? That was quite a fall." She tries to say it teasingly, but I can hear some big-sister worry in there.

My eyes reopen, and he smiles at me before finally looking away. "I'm fine. I might be a little sore later—" he groans as he sits up, "—oh, yeah. But you're right. That was kick-ass. Literally."

Wes says, "Yeah, good job, both of you." Then he nods at Gabe and says, "Hey, man, walk with me." The two of them head toward the water jug as I get up, too.

Beatrix beams at me. "Babydoll, I think you're ready for the next step."

I can't help but smile, too, as I start my cool-down stretches. "Yeah?"

"Yep. I think we should let Dr. Roterra take your blood tomorrow. Then we can drop it off with Red and maybe he'll have your weapons ready on Tuesday."

"Sounds good." I catch my reflection in the mirror and roll my eyes. I look as crazy as I imagined—so crazy that before we head out to the receiving room, I stop by the bathroom to rinse my face off and put my hair back up.

During the walk out of the Sanctum, Beatrix fills the guys in on my new living arrangement. I stop paying attention once we get outside, though, because the cold weather feels fucking wonderful. "Oh, Lord Almighty," I breathe when a breeze seeps through my hair and clothes, feeling arctic and glorious.

I manage to participate in the goodbyes, but another breeze drifts through on the way to Gabe's car and I'm distracted again. I hold my arms out to my sides in satisfaction.

"We can walk instead of drive if you want," he teases.

I chuckle. "There's no way I'm walking home. I need music on the trip and I'm a terrible singer."

He laughs, too, and we get in the car. "I need music when I'm on the road, too. But there's something I need to talk to you about this time."

"I'm listening."

"Well," he sighs as he gets us ready to go, "remember me telling you about Em?"

His Gathering mentor/friend who died. "Yes," I say sympathetically.

"Grayhem's been looking into his death. Not just his, actually—there have been way too many Light people being killed in Dallas, on top of normal Hellion activity. He and a few other Directors think it needs checking out, so Wes and I have been asked to drive down and meet up with some other people to see what's going on."

I can't help a frown. "Oh." After a beat I clarify, "You've been asked to check out a dangerous situation that a bunch of other Light people haven't walked away from."

It's not a question, but he still nods in response. "Yeah," he says slowly, "but I'm not overly concerned about it. I don't know that we'll be doing any fighting."

I chuckle even though I'm not very amused. In fact, a rather troubled feeling is settling in my bones. "I'm sure you will. He's sending you because you're the best *at fighting*. He wouldn't ask you and Wes to drive several hours there and back if all he wanted was for you to glance around."

Gabe shrugs. "I mean, he's known us a while. He trusts us and knows we're not idiots. And yeah, if a fight were to come up I'd bet on me and Wes, too." He pauses. "But for the record, I'm not the best."

I drum my fingers on my legs. "Yeah, whatever you say. When do you have to leave?"

"Middle of the week sometime."

Well, at least it's not tonight or tomorrow. "Okay."

He pulls up to a red light and grips the steering wheel. "I just wanted you to know as much about the plan as I know so far. I don't know how long we'll be gone or where we're staying or anything."

I swallow hard and stare out my window. "Okay. Thank you. Just...come back in one piece." I purse my lips. "Well, and come back alive. I like you being alive."

He laughs a little. "I'll come back alive and in one piece. I promise."

If only promises like that could always be kept.

There's no sign of Claire's Prius or Shaun's Corvette at the apartment, but we agree that Gabe should go in with me, anyway. I leave him to look around the still and silent apartment while I pack my stuff up. All I absolutely need are the details because there's furniture in the Sanctum's living quarters, so it doesn't take me too long. The only mildly difficult part is deciding which clothes are going and which are staying, because I can't take them all.

When I go to grab my phone charger from my nightstand, I see a slip of paper with my name written across it. I open it and read the slanted writing slung down the page:

What a shame it is for such a delectable girl to possess such an unsavory gift.

Your sister considers you not being a social butterfly something of an affront, but I'm quite all right with it. Rest assured that if there's one thing I'm willing to engage in with you, it isn't conversation.

Take care, won't you? I'd love to see you again. In fact, I'm planning on it.

No name at the bottom, yet I'm sure I know who it's from.

I say, "Um, Gabe?" but the words aren't very loud.

He hears me anyway, like he heard my gasp that first day on Blossombranch. Pretty quickly I hear him say, "Yeah?" from the doorway.

I turn around and walk the note over to him, and then hurry to finish packing my stuff.

After several seconds he asks, "You found this in here?"

"Yep." I struggle to zip up one very full bag.

"So he really does know you know what he is, and he's not planning on letting it go unsettled."

"Sounds that way. Damn it all!" I yank my pinched finger away from the un-zipped zipper.

I hear him walking toward me. "I'll get this bag. You okay?"

"Fabulous," I grumble, moving to stuff a few more last-minute things into my other bag.

"Hey, I know this note is scary—" I hear him zip the bag cleanly closed, "—but he's not going to hurt you. You proved today that you can handle someone stronger than you, plus B will be with you if I'm not around."

Even though things seem to be getting more and more frustrating for me, I can't help but smile a little at the thought of our spar. "While I'm thinking about it, I'm sorry I tripped you back there."

"Nah, you did what you had to do."

"As someone who was in the middle of a fight, yeah. But since we're not actually enemies, I'm sorry I tripped you."

"It's fine. And congratulations. I forgot to tell you that earlier."

I close this bag with no problem. "Thanks, I guess. I kind of feel bad about it."

He laughs. "Don't. The point of the whole thing was for you to beat me."

"Still." I turn to look at him just in time to see him touch a sketch I hung on one of the walls. It's really simple—just a picture of a lone toddler sandal I spotted on the floor in the mall years ago—but for some reason I loved it enough to hang it up.

"Did you draw this?" he asks.

I smile at the memory. "Yeah, at the mall one day with Audrey. She was shopping for something I didn't care about whatsoever, so I was sitting on a bench outside a store and saw that."

"It's great," he says with an easy laugh. "One lost shoe. Kids are funny."

"They are," I agree. Then I think about Claire's baby and all the things that can—or *will*, I guess—go wrong with it. Then I think about Claire herself and the giant mess I've gotten myself into with her. And then I decide I'm done standing around in her apartment. "Hey, grab that off the wall, will you? I think we should get going."

With an endearing amount of care, he takes the sketch off the wall. Then he picks up the bag I don't have in my hands, and we head out.

Just before I shut and lock the front door, it occurs to me that I should leave something for Claire even if she does abhor me. I put my stuff in the car and tell Gabe, "I'll be right back." Then I hurry back into the apartment to write her a note of my own.

Claire, I've decided to stay somewhere else for a while. I'll be safe. I've got my phone if you need to call.

Mari

I don't know if she'll care that I'll be safe, or if she'll really call if something happens, or if she'll give a shit that I left a note in the first place...or even that I'll be gone. But I have to try. I put the paper on the kitchen counter where I'm sure she'll see it.

And then I walk out the front door for what I expect to be the last time ever. I leave behind the possessions I couldn't grab, and the sheets I've grown used to, and the living room that I've been helping Claire decorate for Christmas every year since I moved in when I was eighteen. I'm not sure how well it'll work, but I try to leave the bad times behind, too: her attack on me and the arguments and tears and nights I lost sleep over what I did to our family.

Even though I know this is what needs to be done, my legs feel heavy as they carry me to where Gabe stands against his car, waiting to take me away.

And I remind myself as we leave the parking lot that there's something else I need to do before the day is done. Something that won't be as easy as sneaking out of my sister's life while she's out of the house.

I have to sit this guy down—this guy for whom I fall more and more every time I'm with him—and admit to him that I have blood on my hands.

12
Gabe

Marienne is remarkably quiet on the ride back to the Sanctum. The only thing I get out of her is, "No," after asking if there's a particular song she wants to hear on the drive. I chalk it up to her being upset about Shaun's note and leaving her sister—maybe even about the news of my trip to Dallas. She didn't seem to like that a whole hell of a lot.

I don't bother her about her silence, though. I care how she feels, but I've never been the prying kind. Sometimes people just need a minute to themselves.

We've just unlocked Room J on the Sanctum's quiet residential hall when she says, "Hey, do you want to come in and sit down for a minute? I need to tell you something."

If it weren't for her solemn tone, I'd be exultant she asked me to stick around. Still I say, "Sure." Whatever's on her mind must be important.

She nods and leads the way into the room. We both take a second to look around; I've never been in any of these private rooms before. It's pretty nice—not huge, but not limiting, either. There's a full-sized bed, a nightstand, a dresser with a TV on it, a bookcase, and a desk and chair. A few lamps and an alarm clock, a closet and a bathroom.

"Not bad, huh?" I ask, putting her bag on the floor by the dresser.

"Yeah, it's nice." She puts her stuff down, too, and takes her coat off. Then her fingers immediately start in on her hair. "So, sit?"

I go to her desk chair and sit. We look at each other, and I wait patiently for her to speak.

She clears her throat, crosses her arms, walks toward me but looks down at the floor. A frown creases her forehead and she opens her mouth to say something, and then closes it again. After a few seconds she mumbles, "Um."

"Take your time," I tell her gently.

"No!" she snaps. Then quickly, "I'm sorry, I don't— it's not *you*—this just has to be said right now." A humorless laugh leaves her. "Oh, who am I kidding? I should've said this a long time ago. I'm just a sissy."

I try not to smile. "No, you're not."

"Oh, but I am." Her grimace deepens and her voice grows softer. "It cost me so much the first time around.... I haven't wanted to give up anything else, especially not you, but I have to say it."

My amusement dimming, I lean forward in the chair to study her. She looks like she might be trembling, but I'm not quite close enough to tell.

Why? Why would she have to give me up?

I wait, and wait, and wait some more for her to tell me what's wrong.

Finally she looks up at me, her eyes misty. She really does seem determined to see this through, but she still struggles to get the words out. "I turned Light because—because I—"

She looks so uncomfortable that I almost tell her she doesn't have to do this. But I know she believes otherwise, so I don't say it.

Her right foot taps a nervous beat against the floor. "I was reading text messages," she gets out, "and my car went off a bridge."

A frown comes onto my face, but before I can fully process that bit of information she sucks in a breath to keep talking.

"I'd never texted while driving before because I'm a very cautious driver. I believe in people handling cars with care. But I wasn't thinking straight. I was extremely upset because I'd just found Rafe cheating on me with Audrey and I left the party and I didn't want to talk to him, but he wouldn't stop trying—" She suddenly grabs her head with both hands and lets out a noise of frustration. "Jesus *Christ!* No! That's not the important part! Rafe is not the important part! What's important is that no matter how much I like you, you deserve to know that my parents were in the car with me while I was fucking around and not paying attention and when my car went off the bridge and hit the ground, *they fucking died!*"

The wild words ring out around the room. I blink, my brain moving slowly all of a sudden. I look at her and she looks back, now very visibly shaking, tears getting ready to spill out of her eyes. Her breathing is unsteady as she waits for me to react to her confession about the night she became like me—the night that, in the back of my mind, I've considered to be a blessing.

But for a minute, I don't really know how to react. I don't know how to process what she's said.

At length she stammers, "Ok-kay, Gabe, if you have to go, just—just do it. I unders-stand." She wipes at her cheeks, which are wet now.

The details finally click together in my head, and I fully understand what's going on.

She got her parents killed because she was being an irresponsible driver. That's why her sister hates her, why she doesn't have a car, why that poem from last night made her so sad. It's probably why when she's fighting she goes from being the Marienne I know to a girl who's so turbulent with pain and anger that she can lay a guy like me out on his ass.

"Hey, look," she whimpers, "don't sit there and—and ponder how terrible I am. Just get it over with. *Please.*"

And she thinks her being honest about it means I don't want anything to do with her anymore. That's why she thinks she's giving me up. She thinks the truth is too much for me.

I try to tell her I'm not going anywhere, but all I manage is a soft, "I...."

When I can't figure out how to finish my sentence, she sobs weakly, "I get it." She takes a step away from me, and then another.

I shake my head. "No, I—hold on—"

Her breathing quickens as more tears slip down her anguished face. "I appreciate—" she gasps out, "—you not telling me to my face how sickened you are—" she puts a hand over her heart, "—because Claire did that and it hurt—so—goddamn bad."

I stand up. "I would never do that to you."

"But you don't have to try to be nice," she chokes out. "I *beg* you not to try to be nice. Just leave and that'll be that and—"

"Okay, do you actually *want* me to leave?" I ask over her.

"Of course I don't! I just don't want to stand here and be handed some line like, *'I think I need some time, Marienne—'*"

"Why would I say that?"

"Because I'm a l-life ruiner."

"No, you're not."

She looks at me like I'm crazy. "Yes, I am! Ask my sister!"

"No, you're not," I repeat loudly, "and I don't give a fuck *what* your sister thinks!"

"Well, would you share some of that with me?" she yells. "Name your price, Gabe! I'd give *anything* to be able to disagree with her!"

I stare at her, suddenly at a loss for words. Part of me empathizes with her and can understand how she feels that way about herself. But she can't possibly think I feel that way about her, too. She hasn't ruined *my* life. She's made it better. And that leaves most of me wondering how she can hate herself when I think she's so amazing.

She stares back at me for many long seconds, and then a soft, wry sob of a laugh huffs out of her. And I know that just like every other time I couldn't figure out what to say, she thinks I'm thinking the worst about her. Even when everything I've said and done before speaks to the opposite.

Her fingers brush at her cheeks and she murmurs, "I'm sorry. I don't want to fight with you. I just want you to know what kind of girl you've been spending your time with." She shakes her head and hunches her shoulders a little. "She's not all music and trick-or-treating and poetry and...and whatever. She's an idiot and a murderer." Her hands fall limply to her sides. She gives me a long, miserable look, like she really thinks this is goodbye, and then she turns away from me.

And I'm suddenly right behind her, taking her arm in my hand, turning her back toward me. She barely gets out a startled gasp before I kiss her so insistently that she dips backward. My other hand catches her waist before she falls, and she grabs my jacket with both hands as I pull her back up. Then we're steady and she's kissing me, too, her fervor matching mine. Even though I figured that's what she'd do when this moment came—and even though this isn't romantic and I didn't plan it out and we weren't so much as smiling before—I feel like I could just melt.

It feels exactly right.

I don't indulge myself for long, though; after a few seconds I drag back so I can look at her. My pulse is running wild. Still I manage to inform her carefully, "I've been spending my time with Marienne Rose Connor. She's cute and hilarious and *so* beautiful and tough and smart...." I take my hand off her arm to lay my thumb on her bottom lip. "That's you. That's who you are." I shake my head a little. "So I appreciate your honesty, but for me, *one* mistake doesn't eclipse everything else. I don't see you the way you do."

She looks up at me timidly, her still-damp eyes ringed with red. "But...it was such a bad mistake, Gabe."

Her lips brushing against my thumb makes me want to kiss her again. Ha—*again*. Why exactly was it so hard for me to do it last night? "It happens. Listen to me, okay? If you were a monster, you wouldn't..." my eyes rove over as much of her as they can with her being so close to me, "...you wouldn't look like this. You wouldn't look *anything* like this."

A nearly inaudible laugh leaves her, drifts unbelievably lightly against my thumb. "You're too kind," she says, even as some of the distress seeps out of her eyes.

"Am not. Everything I said is true."

"Are, too."

One corner of my mouth turns up. "I am not, but if you want we can agree to disagree." The smile fades back down and I regard her intensely. "Believe me," I beg her. "Trust me. Trust what I'm telling you."

At first she just returns my look, but eventually she smiles a little bit, too. It falters when she whispers, "Gabe, I'm...I'm really sorry. I mean, for yelling at you and everything."

That's it. My thumb is officially causing trouble. I move it to her cheek, my fingertips to her temple. "I forgive you."

Her eyes soften and she swallows hard, like that really means a lot to her. "Thank you."

"Mmhmm."

She falls silent and looks up at me, seeming to take in the details of my face. Her gaze touches my mouth more than once. I wonder if she knows how alluring she is, even after training this morning and freaking out just now. Her ponytail is a little mussed, her cheeks a little pink. And *God*, does she feel good under my hands, even though only one of them is actually touching her skin.

But that's not all I find attractive about her. She's also unpretentious—she's *sweet*. She felt like she had to be honest with me even if it put her being happy at risk. That kind of selflessness gives her an understanding of the fragility of things, of the real possibility that her being responsible for herself might mean losing joys she holds dear. And that's mature of her—kind of inspiring, even. Many people would rather live a lie than make the necessary sacrifices to preserve their well-being and that of those they care about.

God only knows what she was envisioning in her head. Evidently it had a lot to do with me being disgusted by her and leaving her, and perhaps then Beatrix and Wes would've sided with me, leveling everything Marienne knows about life in the Lightforce. Maybe she'd have had to find a new Defender trainer because we wouldn't want to spend time with her anymore. Or just move to another city and try to start over with the thin hope that any friends she made there wouldn't react like we did.

I'm as wounded by that line of thinking as she had been. I look down at her now and I'm glad I told her that I'd never treat her that way. It was so true. Her showing me what she's hiding on the inside even though she doesn't like it only makes *me* like her more.

My admiring her is interrupted when she murmurs, "I think *you're* beautiful." She lets go of my jacket front, which I realize she's been grasping all this time. Looking a little shy, she curls her fingers along the edges of the pockets instead. "It's unfair how beautiful you are. And you're so much more.... You crack me up and you teach me things and you're good at being Light."

Halcyon warmth creeps into me, drifts along every inch of my body.

"Thank you for being so good to me," she says. Her gaze absently drops away to random points between my eyes and collarbone. "Sometimes I don't think you even know you're doing it. It's just you. *You* are just...good."

I drop my face closer to hers, deciding this is too much. "I'm also about to kiss you again," I warn her lowly. "This is your chance to get away."

She inhales softly, and then shakes her head a little. She tugs me closer by my jacket pockets and mumbles, "This is *your* chance to get away."

Fuck no. I'd say it out loud, but the only thing my mouth wants to do is get back on hers.

This time we kiss slower, more deliberately. It's *so* good. My senses have time to register more than just the fact that she's with me on this, like that her height, though shorter than mine, is pretty perfect. Her lips taste faintly like fruity lip balm. She smells kind of like sweat, but also like vanilla. I move my one hand from her waist to her back and I hear her breathing turn a little unsteady when my other fingers leave her face to slide up into the underside of her ponytail. I feel a shiver dance through her and her lips leave mine just barely...and then I feel her move closer yet to wrap her arms securely around my waist, and she fits our mouths back together. And I am all hers. I'm hers in a way I've never belonged to anyone else.

I don't know what I ever did to earn this. Enigmatic as it is, I don't want to question it. I just want to fall into it, into *her*, and not resurface until I absolutely have to—until the outside world can't stand our absence a second longer and yanks us back. I want to be this warm and at peace and enraptured for as long as I can be.

That's not nearly long enough, of course; eventually it has to end. When it does she barely breathes out, "Just wow," and gives me a look that says I'm not the only one who's disappointed that it's over.

I curve my hand around the back of her neck and murmur, "I know." Then, "Go out with me again. Tonight."

"Okay. Where?" Her voice is so soft that it makes those two ordinary words sound gorgeous.

"Anywhere." I don't care where we go or what we do as long as I'm with her. Then, less willingly, "Think about it, okay? I need to go for now. Need to stop by my house before I meet up with Janssen and Wright."

"All right. I hope a wayward Light person wanders across your path."

"I hope you do okay unpacking those two bags bursting with your belongings," I tell her a little teasingly. And then more seriously, "Also that you feel better about everything soon."

The corners of her mouth turn up. "I'm feeling a little better already. You and your too-kind ass really know how to cheer me up."

I can't help laughing, and that brightens her smile, and *that* is always a good sign.

Unbelievably, it turns out that she was on to something. After I've gone home for a shower, I convene with Janssen and Wright and we find a white Radiance huddled in an empty corner of Barnes & Noble.

He's sitting on the floor with a graphic novel in front of his face, but it's not lifted high enough to shield his eyes from my view—eyes that, luckily, are warily following a Hellion perusing the literature a few aisles over. Really I guess it's more likely the Hellion is perusing the two teenage girls standing a few feet from him, who *are* looking at books. I consider this lucky because Gathering is a little easier if the new Light person has already noticed the Hellions. Sometimes they don't think we're completely out of our minds if they've seen the perplexing creatures with their own two eyes.

He lowers the novel to turn the page for pretend-reading purposes, and I see that for only the third time in the past eight years we've found a guy who can't be more than a few years older than me. And even though that means he'd probably relate better to me, I can't let this opportunity pass my new Gatherers by. We decide I should spark it off myself and then call them over to take control of the situation while I observe and make sure everything goes well. While I head over to the guy, Janssen calls Wes to let him know about the Hellion.

I can't say I know a whole hell of a lot about graphic novels, so when I get to him I go with the only conversation-starter I've got. I cross my arms, slide a look over to the Hellion and murmur, "He's a scary bastard, isn't he?" And he is. He's tall and milk-white with thick black liquid steadily dripping from his drooping eyes. Hard muscles stand out on his bare arms and chest, and metal spikes protrude from various points on his body, even out the sides of his neck and through the legs of his pants.

"What?" the guy tries to ask casually, but I can't be fooled. Indeed, when I look at him I find he's lowered the graphic novel again to regard me with both hope and disbelief.

I nod toward the Hellion. "That man over there with the spikes all over him."

The guy gets up off the floor, glancing between the Hellion and me. "You can see him?" he asks slowly. "I mean...you see how fucked-up he looks? It's not just me?"

I shake my head and assure him, "It's not just you, man. Trust me."

"Holy shit," he whispers. "So, dude, why doesn't anyone else look worried?"

Awesome. He really is one of the ones who are willing to listen to me. "They're just normal people."

The guy's eyebrows go up. "And...we...are not?"

I chuckle. "Not anymore. So, look, my name is Gabe and I've got all the answers you need, but I'm training a couple of new guys—long story—and I'd like for them to talk to you, too. That okay?"

"Uh..." he runs a hand through his dirty-blonde hair and inhales deeply, "...yeah, dude, okay. As long as someone tells me what the hell I've been going through lately."

"Oh, we will. Don't worry about that."

"Sweet. And I'm Trenton, by the way."

I tell him sincerely, "It's good to meet you, Trenton. Let me grab these guys."

Their first official encounter with a new Light person goes smoothly. Trenton is an open-minded guy and he gets along with the ever-serious Wright as well as he does with me and Janssen. He receives some of the information with a look of shock on his face, but mostly he seems to think this new side of his life is incredible. He even thinks our Light marks are awesome, like Marienne thought.

We learn that he's twenty-six and saw his first Hellion a week ago, when he left the hospital after a nearly fatal night of partying. After that sighting he shut himself into his house for three days, scared out of his mind. Then he decided he couldn't stand being cooped up and went a couple of places, determined to ignore the Hellions if he saw any. He'd nearly walked right into the one in this bookstore, but since the creature was eyeballing the teenage girls Trenton was able to hurry away and hole up in this corner without raising any suspicion.

Commendably, Janssen and Wright say everything that needs to be said. They include the responsibilities of us Light people and end with our obligation to give him time to think everything over. He agrees to meet them back here tomorrow.

Then we notice the Hellion has wandered away, and Trenton says, "Oh, thank God he left." He holds up the graphic novel. "This wasn't even the piece I wanted. I found it lying around and was on my way to the collection when I saw that creep. Now I can get what I really want and get the hell out of Dodge."

Janssen and I laugh while Wright nods politely. Then we bid Trenton goodbye and he hurries off.

As the three of us follow, Janssen punches the air victoriously. "That was somethin'. And what a nice kid."

"You both did very well. Your speech was great."

"Aw, thanks, son. You taught us right."

Wright agrees, "That did go very well. Good job."

After Wes drops by to kill the Hellion, the three of us decide to hit up a few more places around town. As is tradition, we don't spot another white Radiance for the rest of our time together. They're in a good mood, though, so we part ways for the evening feeling optimistic about Trenton.

When I arrive to pick up Marienne, she's cleaner and much cheerier than she was earlier. Her mood improves even more when I tell her about Trenton, and she tells me she wants to treat me to something fun. We agree that we should eat something, so we go by Chipotle again. And then we somehow end up at the bowling alley.

I haven't been bowling in probably ten years. She said she's done it more recently than that, but she's as bad at it as I am. It's hilarious, and we have a great time. The place is full of lights and music and people (normal people, that is) and laughter. And, of course, our abysmal scores make our sparse triumphs all the more exciting. On one of her turns she knocks down more than two pins, and she's so happy about it that she throws a hug on me. And I'm so happy about the hug that I lift her off the ground and spin around a little when I hug her back. And that makes her laugh, which I love.

And then a Hellion walks through the front entrance and I have to call Wes again. That leads to extending a bowling invitation to him and Beatrix, and *that* turns out to be entertaining for all new reasons. Once the Hellion has been taken care of, Beatrix confidently bets me fifty dollars she'll have a higher score than her husband at the end of our game. Then Wes kicks all of our asses and I get fifty free dollars from his wife, who can't stop laughing even though she's trying to be mad.

It's a damn good night, even when some inebriated guy trips and spills his entire beer on me as we're leaving. I finally realize Marienne's smiles are brighter and happier for me than for everyone else—that's the difference I was unable to place before—and to top it all off, she kisses me despite my being damp with beer the second we're shut into my car.

c⁓

Late the next afternoon, after Marienne's training and her letting Dr. Roterra take some blood from her, she and I go to Grove Lane. After a minute of deliberation we decide to walk around and see what the rest of the neighborhood is like. We've only made it to the end of the driveway in front of her usual house when Janssen calls to say Trenton is joining the Lightforce.

I tell Marienne after I hang up, and she gasps. "Congratulations!" She holds out a hand for me to take.

I grab it and grin at her. "Thank you, but the other guys did all the work."

"They did all the work *you* taught them how to do," she says, not unkindly. "It's a success for them because they got someone to join, and it's a success for you because you trained them for that all by yourself. See? I told you you'd be great at it."

What a compliment. And that's on top of the news about Trenton and just being with her in the first place. It makes me really happy and I feel grateful for it, for *her*. I pull on her hand as I step toward her, bringing us chest-to-chest. A smile flashes onto her face and even though it's glorious—even though it makes me smile, too—I spare only the smallest moment for it. Then I steal a kiss from her.

It's not that stolen, truthfully, despite my intentions. Each time I kiss her anew my body hums her

258

name a little bit more, and it's hard to give up. Especially when she can't seem to kiss me back without having both of her hands on me, like she wants to keep me firmly where I am for as long as she can. Right now, the one that isn't wrapped in my hand drifts up to my waist and I can feel it like there's not a jacket, a hoodie, *and* a long-sleeved shirt under those fingers of hers. It has me curving my free hand against her check as I continue kissing her, not ready to let go of her yet.

I wonder if she feels this way about me.

When I finally draw back from her I decide to ask. "How do you feel when I'm kissing you?" A cold breeze drifts through and flings a piece of hair across her forehead, and I move it for her.

As unusual a question as I know that is, she doesn't look bothered by it. She just looks at me while she contemplates it. Finally she says, "I feel—I feel special, honestly. And overwhelmed, in a good way."

I decide those are good ways of describing how I feel. I nod in agreement.

"What about you?" she wants to know.

"Both of those, and...." I take a few seconds to sort the rest out in my head. "And happy and distracted."

She smiles at me, and that turns into a breath of laughter. "I dis—I distract you *from things,* or you're distracted *while* you're kissing me?"

A laugh leaves me, too. "Okay, the first one, obviously."

"You sure?"

"I'm absolutely sure."

Before I know it she's caught me up in another kiss, wrapping her lips around my bottom lip, and the gesture is soft and innocent and it makes my breathing stutter. Warms my skin against the freezing air. Makes me think something in the universe has either gone horribly wrong or gone right by complete accident, because I am utterly colorless compared to this girl. I don't think she's even trying—no, I'm pretty damn sure she's not trying—and she still just—

"Tell me how tall you are," she says against my mouth.

"What?" I barely get out.

"How tall are you?"

What does that matter right now? "Um." I lay my hand over where hers is on my waist.

"Hmm," she muses. "Either you don't know your own height or I really can steal your attention just like that."

That puzzles me for a moment. And then I figure it out, and I lean back to give her a look.

She chuckles, looking both flattered and embarrassed.

I shake my head and say with mock-melancholy, "There I thought you were kissing me because you like me or something. But it was all a ruse."

She laughs more. "No, that *is* what I was doing it for." A few of the inches between us disappear again when she leans closer. Like it's a secret, she whispers, "The test was just an excuse, Gabe. I believed your answer in the first place."

I laugh, too, and kiss her on the cheek. "I am six feet and one inch tall."

I feel her smiling under my lips. "Good to know."

"And you?"

"Not quite five and a half feet." She pulls back a little to look up at me. "So I hope you're prepared to get stuff off the highest shelves for me and whatnot."

"Nope," I tease her. "You better learn to jump."

She laughs. "Yeah, much better idea. I'll work on it. Ready to walk around?"

"Sure. I want to see if any of these other houses have playground equipment I can claim."

Marienne snorts and steps back from me. The air feels downright arctic as it fills the space she'd just been standing in, and I can't help a shiver.

We mosey down the street from one decimated, blackened structure to the next, our hands still knotted between us. There's a rusting metal swing set in one backyard, a trampoline *and* a swing set in another, and one yard just extends way back and ends in a forest. Something about a cluster of the trees looks unusual to me and I stare for a few seconds, trying to figure out the incongruity despite the distance. Then I realize what it is and I look at Marienne. "Do you see that back there?"

She peers in that direction and shakes her head. "I don't know. What does it—?" A little gasp cuts her words off. "Hold on. Is it a tree house?"

I smile at her. "I truly think it is."

She smiles excitedly and we start toward the shaded, snow-topped tree house. Once we're a few paces from the forest we stop and she breathes out, "Oh, man. I've never even seen one of these in real life." Her head is tipped back so she can look up at it. "Have you?"

"Nope."

"Well, this one meets my expectations. It's ours now."

I chuckle. "Okay, but you know we're not going up there, right?"

"Oh, I know. But you said you wanted to claim some playground equipment, so I was just helping out." A gust of wind whirls up from behind us and she hunches her shoulders against it. "Holy...." She usually keeps her hair up after training, so it's up now and I'm sure the exposed skin on the back of her neck does not appreciate the icy wind. She reaches behind her head, ostensibly for a hood, but nothing she has on right now has one attached to it.

I walk over until I'm behind her, hopefully blocking the wind. "Does this help at all?" I ask.

She peeks over her shoulder at me and smiles. "Yes. Thank you."

"You're welcome."

She turns to look at the forest again, and her hands reach back toward me a little. I take both of them in mine, and for a little bit we just stand here together and listen to the nothingness of this snowy, abandoned neighborhood. It's amazing how she (and I, thanks to her) can see the beauty in something most people don't appreciate at all.

"We can walk up a little closer," I tell her at length, "if you want a better look at it."

"Yeah, okay. I wonder how big it is."

"Only one way to find out." I let her lead me leisurely toward the massive trees, her hands still in mine. We drop it down to one hand once we start into the woods, though, and pick our way across the frozen ground until we're standing under the tree house. "And," I say slowly as we look up at the excellent view, "it's pretty damn big."

"Jesus. How many kids did these people have to...?" Marienne's words trail off, and after a second her hand tightens around mine. She stares alertly up at the tree house.

"What?" I ask, my voice lower than before.

She speaks more quietly, too, her eyes still stuck on something up there. "I...don't know."

I carefully step up against her to try for her vantage point. My eyes search for whatever has caught her attention, but only when I'm directly behind her and bent down a little can I see it. "The hell is that?" I murmur.

She shakes her head in a silent, *'No idea,'* and we simultaneously step farther forward so we can try to get a better look.

The entrance to the tree house is a good-sized circle at the top of a fancy wooden ladder someone attached to the trunk. Looking up through the circle and a little bit back from it, I can detect movement, but it's not a person or an animal. It's just...well, it's just blackness, and it looks like it's writhing. Like extremely dense black smoke, but unlike smoke it's not moving around freely. It's just sitting in that one area.

And it doesn't sit well with me, whatever it is.

I whisper to Marienne, "I'm going to climb up there, okay? You stand right at the bottom of this ladder where we can see each other."

"Okay," she whispers back. She grips my hand as we tiptoe forward, working on being extra-quiet even though I think we'd already know if there was something up there we didn't want to attract to us. I let go of her hand and start up the ladder and she says, "Be careful."

"I will. Don't move."

The ladder looks a little old, but it's of good quality and it doesn't give me any trouble as I ascend it. I keep my ears open for even the tiniest noise coming from above me—boards creaking or muttered words or anything like that—but I hear nothing. That does a little something for the tension in me.

And then I reach the top of the ladder and get a good look at what's in the tree house, and the tension zips right back into me. I throw a mystified look down at Marienne, and then I look back at my deathly quiet surroundings. There really are no people or animals in the open room. There isn't even any stuff—no toys or empty snack wrappers. The only thing in the whole gigantic space is the tall rectangle of twisting blackness looming near the wall not too far in front of me.

It's several feet wide and the top of it grazes the high ceiling of the tree house. The shape hovers off the floor a few inches, and each edge shimmers faintly like the whole thing is a mirage; though I don't know what it is, I feel pretty certain it's not an illusion. But I don't dare go toward it, so for a minute I just look from where I am. I inspect the pitch-colored interior and find I can't see through it no matter how much it shifts.

The thing is fucking creepy.

After another minute of me not having any ideas about what it could be, I get a picture of it with my phone and decide to get back down to Marienne. I tell her what I saw and show her the picture. She's as perplexed as I am.

"It's floating?" she asks.

I nod. "Floating."

"And you didn't hear anything coming from it?"

"No, nothing. Not even a hum. The whole place was completely—"

I shut up when a thud sounds from above us. Instinctively I grab Marienne and swing her away from the entrance. Rhythmic clunks move across the floor of the tree house now, and she whispers anxiously, "Gabe?"

"I don't know," I whisper in response to her real question: *'Why do those sound like footsteps?'* The whole place was empty a mere minute ago, except for that strange black...

...*door.*

I realize all too late that's what it is. And we don't make it to a hiding place before whatever came through it leaps down from the tree house and sees us.

My blood runs cold as my brain tries to process the thin, pallid Hellion standing right where we'd just been.

A hoarse voice escapes him. "Well, what do we have here?"

I snap to attention and my mind clicks into Defender mode. I position myself between him and Marienne, and in a matter of moments I've assessed him and how this encounter is about to go. It will be brief and it will end with him dead, of that I am certain, so I start toward him to get it done. If he came through that door with no warning, so might another. He needs to die and Marienne and I need to leave.

He tilts his head to peer behind me at her. "You sure are pretty," he croons in that voice of his. He slowly runs his repulsive black tongue over his lips, and then looks at me again. "I'd say to remember not to bring your girlfriend out to a place like this again, but..." he smiles at me, baring his rotten teeth, "...there won't be a next time for you. Or for her."

It's written on his face that he thinks I'm stupid. Just some guy trying to be a cowboy for the girl I have with me. He thinks he's about to make quick work of me and then do what he wants to her.

But while he was checking her out, I was swiping my dagger out of my jacket and behind my back. Years of being Light, of dressing and undressing with my dagger and slaying Hellions bigger and more menacing than this one has made me very quick, very surreptitious. If only he'd been smart enough to keep his eyes on me.

The distance between us shrinks to mere feet and I duck down to make him think I'm planning on going for a low shot. He bends down, too, and does exactly what I hoped he'd do: lunges at me. But all he manages to land on me is a hand—one hand on my left arm. And with a violence that only surges up in me when I'm fighting a Hellion, I swing my right hand out from behind me and drive my already-unsheathed dagger up into his flesh.

His scream pierces the air and hurts my ears, but I don't stop. I sink my blade into every place on him I can reach, and there are a lot of them. The more I stab him, the more his flesh breaks up—the more he instinctually switches his attention from me to himself. He looks up at me once, though, roaring in fury and agony as his stomach and legs fail him, and he reaches up toward my head to do who knows what. And while his arms are lifted, I shove my dagger into his heart.

His eyes widen for the briefest moment and his bellow trails off, and then he's dead.

In two-point-two seconds I'm back with Marienne, who's as ready to run as I am.

"What the fuck just happened?" she asks as we bolt for the tree line separating us from the backyard.

"That thing in the tree house is some kind of door," I tell her as I stuff my dagger back into my jacket. "I don't know where it goes or how it got there, but that Hellion had to have come through it. There wasn't a goddamn thing in that room while I was up there, and then suddenly there he was."

"And you've never even heard of anything like this?"

We break out of the woods and tear across the snow. "No, I never have." *And I'm not about to keep it to myself. It's too big. We need to talk to Grayhem.*

"Should we tell Grayhem?" she asks.

In spite of the circumstances, I can't help a smile. If I weren't determined to get us the hell out of Grove Lane as fast as possible, I'd take the time to slow down and smile *at* her. Instead I say, "My thoughts exactly."

"Let me just say," she announces as we turn onto the actual street and run toward my car, "that I'm pretty fucking mad that the only tree house I've ever had in my life has some kind of demonic portal chilling in the middle of it."

Now I laugh. It's unbelievable how she can lift my spirits in a situation like this. "I'll build you a normal tree house one day."

"What? You know how to build stuff like that?"

"Not at all. It's the thought that counts, though, obviously."

She laughs, too. "Well, I promise to love whatever wobbly tree house you craft up for me, but if I fall out of it and break my ass, you're in trouble, mister."

I abruptly decide we've run far enough away to pause for ten seconds. My feet slow to a stop. Hers immediately do the same, so I grab her by the hips and yank her to me and confidently take her mouth with mine.

In a second her hands are on my shoulders and she's pressing herself even closer to me. We kiss avidly right here in the middle of the street like we don't have important, unpleasant news to deliver to people. Our lips part because we're a little winded from everything, but neither of us seems to be able to stop at drawing air—our tongues meet, and a groan leaves me at the same time that she breathes a moan into my mouth, echoing bliss through my whole body. I wrap one hand around the back of her head and give her a deeper, bolder kiss, and she gives it right back to me, and I commit these moments to memory. I commit her mouth to memory, and the way her hands feel gripping my shoulders. And the way she looks at me when I drag my mouth from hers and lean back.

I tell her breathlessly, "I would never send you up into a wobbly tree house."

She laughs in kind, and I love the way it sounds.

After a second we step apart and grab hands and take off running for my car again.

13
Marienne

I thought I'd never be able to get that last kiss on Grove Lane out of my head.

It was one of those things that seems to ignite every cell at once and permanently alters thought processes and makes shitty life events feel one hundred percent worth it because they all ultimately led to *that*. I experienced all of those things, and every time I replay the kiss in my head I experience them all over again.

But even that kiss is wiped from my mind when Gabe and I finish telling Grayhem about that bizarre shit at the tree house, and the man says not questioningly but *knowingly*, "You found one of the hidden gateways between our world and the Dark world."

A long stretch of silence falls before Gabe stammers, "Did you—huh? You already knew about it?"

Grayhem isn't a bad guy. Although he's always more professional than fun, I like him pretty well and so does everyone else. But I am rendered totally speechless by how evenly he looks at Gabe from across his desk and admits, "I did."

I look to where Gabe sits beside me. He looks torn between being pained and being pissed off.

"Allow me to explain." Grayhem takes his glasses off to look at both of us intently, but mostly at his chief Gatherer. "All of the Lightforce Directors know about the gateways. I can honestly tell you I didn't know we had one right under our noses—I had no idea there was even one in our state—and I greatly appreciate you coming to me with that information. But I must ask you not to share it with anyone else. There's a reason we've kept this knowledge from the general Light population."

Gabe blinks slowly, and his eyes seem a smokier green than they were before. "Well, with all due respect, what the hell reason is that? Shouldn't we know about things like *gateways* between the regular world and a world full of *monsters?*"

Grayhem doesn't look offended by his vexation. He just asks patiently, "What is the purpose of the Light community?"

Not so patiently, Gabe says, "To eliminate Hellions from this world."

"At all costs, yes?"

"Yes," he almost snaps.

"People fall away from their families, sever their friendships, learn new and dangerous ways of living to ensure that our purpose is fulfilled. It is an all-consuming existence—but the number of people who know it is painfully small. Each Light person is immeasurably precious because they are one of so few." Grayhem leans forward a little. "Can you imagine what such dedicated members would do if they knew we had direct links to the Dark world? Can you imagine the urge they'd have to step through the gateway and launch an attack on the Hellions?"

The words send a hot tremor through me. I'm still way new to this, but I'm not ignorant. My sister is in love with and pregnant by a Hellion, for God's sake. So I can definitely see how strongly going in with guns blazing would appeal to people who have been doing this for years and years and years. And one look at Gabe tells me he is one of those people. His fists are clenched, his veins standing out on the backs of his hands, his breathing a little tremulous. His eyes are full of the same determination I saw when he and I sparred, and just earlier in the woods when he turned away from the deteriorating body of that Hellion, his dagger still clutched confidently in his hand.

Grayhem notices this, too, and says softly, "We cannot allow that, Gabe, and I know you understand that. You as *you*, not just as a Light person—you as the intelligent, benevolent, practical man I care for and trust—I know you understand the severity of this situation. I know you understand how imperative it is that our people be protected from their own passion, because if they storm into the Dark world instead of keeping both feet on the ground they are meant to protect, they will be overpowered and *stamped out*."

A deep frown creases Gabe's forehead. His fists open a little and his shoulders drop the tiniest bit.

"Believe me," Grayhem continues, "I know how incredible it is to realize the gateways exist and how infuriating it is to find you've been kept out of the loop about them. But this is something that *must* be kept secret." He looks at me earnestly. "Mari, dear, do you understand where I'm coming from?"

The question has me gripping the armrests of my chair. I take a few seconds to push past the desire I already have to do my utmost to protect people, especially those I love, from the Hellions. I do see Grayhem's point. Eventually I nod. "I understand."

"Do I have your word that you'll keep this to yourself and that you won't try to go through the gateway?"

"Yes, sir," I promise him.

Gabe lays a hand over mine where it sits on the armrest between us. His skin is hot and he's trembling a little bit. I look at him and see he's already looking at me, his expression damn near unreadable because of all the emotions flitting across it.

I turn my hand over so our palms are pressed together. I understand his struggle, but I try to tell him without speaking aloud, *'This is a secret we can keep. He's right. We can't suicide ourselves all over the Hellions' doorstep.'*

And I think he understands me somehow. He looks at Grayhem and breathes deeply. "You have my word on that, too."

The Director regards him with what looks to me like respect. "Thank you."

Gabe nods and, to my pleasant surprise, gives the look back to the man. "Of course."

Grayhem looks toward me. "Mari, my dear, would you mind giving me just a minute with Gabe? I need to fill him in on some details about his upcoming trip."

I stand up. "Yeah, I'll just...." I motion to the hallway with my free hand and look down at Gabe. He gives me a smile as he lets go of my other hand, and I smile back. Then I step out of the office and shut the door behind me.

I wonder if he's going to tell Grayhem we kind of, sort of, a little bit animatedly already told Wes and Beatrix about the gateway.

The instant I lay eyes on my dagger on Tuesday afternoon, something in me shifts. It hits me harder than ever that I am not the girl I used to be. As I look at the weapon, the notion of something in the universe looking at *me* and deeming me worthy of this responsibility makes my throat tighten with emotion.

And when I actually take it from Red, that emotion hits me in the stomach and almost makes me cry. This thing was literally made for me. My hand fits around it like my skin fits around my hand. It's an extension of me; it's the extraordinary power in me made into something tangible. It will help me save lives.

"Whatcha think, Mari?" Red asks with a knowing grin on his face.

"I love it," I say promptly.

"Beautiful, ain't it?"

I give him a smile even though *'beautiful'* doesn't cut it.

He laughs. "Just wait'll ya kill a Hellion with it. It's a damn divine experience, I'm tellin' ya."

"When do I get to do that?" I feel only the tiniest twinge of nervousness. Mostly I feel good, excited. Having my dagger in my hand makes me feel even more powerful than I felt that day I used Gabe's.

"That'll be up to Beatrix, but my guess is it'll be sometime today."

I honestly don't know how I'll be able to wait another minute.

I make it through another minute, of course. In fact, I make it through many minutes because when Beatrix comes back from the restroom she's got both Wes and Gabe with her, and they want to chat with Red briefly and ooh-and-ahh over my dagger like they don't have their own. And then, once the four of us have bid Red farewell and started back down the hall, they announce that they've got a gift for me.

They present me with a brand-new, absolutely beautiful, absolutely badass black jacket. It's made of smooth wool and has pale blue polka dots on it. I get it on and find it fits me like a damn glove. On the inside are special pockets that are meant specifically for my Light weapons, and I slide my dagger and two vials of red powder into them. Their fit is as perfect as the jacket on me.

And this time I can't help crying. I just cannot help it.

"Oh, Mari!" Beatrix yelps, throwing a hug on me. "Don't cry! It'll make *me* cry!"

"I'm sorry. I'm just so happy," I tell her. "You guys are the best. Thank you so much."

"You deserve it," she assures me, sounding teary, indeed.

When she pulls away, I sniffle and duck my head rather than look at the guys. "Thank you, Wes and Gabe," I say as I try to pull myself together. I clear my throat and wipe at my eyes. "Don't worry. I won't cry all over you two."

All three of them laugh and I feel Gabe tug on the end of my ponytail. "We're glad you like it," he tells me. I can hear the smile in his voice.

"So now that you've got this jacket and your weapons," Wes says energetically, "I personally think it's time we let you loose on a sick son of a bitch or two."

"Oh, God, I wish I could watch," Beatrix says, sounding melancholy.

"Why can't you?" I finally feel okay enough to look up from the floor.

She gives me a smile, but it looks apologetic. "Honestly, darling, I was going to get in as much time with Wes as I can before he leaves."

Oh, that's right, I remember. *They're going tomorrow.*

"We thought I could take you out," Gabe says to me, "if that's okay with you."

A chuckle escapes me. Like I'd be upset about spending time with him, especially when he's about to be gone for who knows how long. I say, "Of course that's okay." Then I smile at Wes and Beatrix. "I hope you two have a great time together."

She gives me a grateful smile and curls both of her arms around one of his. Even though they're always touching one another, I pick up on the sadness lying under this particular gesture. She isn't a fan of this trip, either.

I don't want to take up another minute of their alone time, so I take a breath and look at Gabe. "Well, I'm ready whenever you are."

I think he must feel how I feel because he says easily, "I'm ready."

As usual, the four of us walk up to the parking lot together and say our goodbyes. Beatrix tells me she'll be here in the morning to see Wes and Gabe off, so she'll see me then. And then we go our separate ways.

"Where to?" I ask once we're in Gabe's car.

"First things first," he says as he looks at me sunnily. "Congratulations on getting your weapons."

I try not to smile too widely. "Thank you."

"And that jacket looks awesome on you."

The smile inches further across my face. "Thank you."

After a second of hesitation, "And I got you something just from me."

"What?" The smile drops away and my fingers fly fretfully to my hair, but my face flushes because I'm as thrilled as I am nervous. "No, you didn't."

"Yes, actually." He reaches into the backseat.

"You don't have to buy me things," I tell him earnestly. "I'm not that kind of—"

My words die off when he hands me a box of the thin, simple, This Is Jewelry variety. My pulse skips.

Again he hesitates before he speaks. His words are quiet. "I know. But aside from telling you about the Lightforce, I haven't done a single thing with you or for you because I felt like I had to. Only because I sincerely, entirely *wanted* to."

I want to say something in response to that. I really do. But I come up with absolutely nothing. So I drop my eyes to the box and open it, my fingers trembling slightly.

Inside lies a necklace. A tiny round gemstone that is so dark blue it nearly looks black hangs from a delicate white gold chain. The piece is understated and pretty—it's *flawless*. It screams my name. It screams *Gabe's* name. It makes my heartbeat trip over itself even more.

"Do you like it?" he whispers nervously.

I drag my stare from the necklace to his face. "I—I *love* it," I whisper back weakly.

He looks so happy that it's heart-wrenching to me.

"Can I put it on?" I ask, suddenly aching to get the necklace out of its box. "Can I wear it right now?"

"Yes," he says promptly. "Yeah, yes, please put it on. I'll *help* you put it on."

I don't fight him on it. I need the help as much as he wants to give it to me. Once he's got the necklace in his hands I turn away from him and move my ponytail. He bends over to me, so close that his breath drifts over my hair and across my skin, and carefully loops the necklace around my neck.

"There," he says after a few moments.

I face him again and gently tug on the short chain to get it in place. It's so lightweight that I don't feel it after I take my hand away. "How does it look?"

"Perfect." He gives me a bright smile. "It looks perfect on you."

I know the smile that comes onto my face mirrors his. "Thank you so much for it." The words are barely out of my mouth before I press my lips against his, and he immediately returns the soft pressure. It's the first time we've kissed since he dropped me off at my room last night, and he seems to have missed it as much as me. As he touches his knuckles to my jaw, I briefly—*selfishly*—wonder how I'm going to get by without this while he's gone.

When the kiss ends he says, "You're very welcome." He leans back enough to look at me and sighs heavily even though his eyes are untroubled. "We need to go find you a Hellion to kill."

He traces my jawline with one fingertip and I have to fight not to let my eyes flutter closed. He's right. I'm a Defender now, and I have a job to do. "Okay."

The fingertip moves to drift along my bottom lip, along with his gaze. "We can pick back up on this later if you want to," he murmurs.

Something about the unassertive way he said that is downright sexy. And it's a no-brainer if I ever encountered one. "Yes."

Even after hearing that, it's all over his face that he doesn't want to lean back into his seat yet. But he does, giving me a soft smile as he goes. "Then let's go find some good-for-nothing bastard and dirty up your pretty new dagger."

That mental image appeals to me quite a bit.

He can tell, and his smile widens. He gets us on the road, but not before he adds, "I know. Sounds fun."

Even though there may not be a Hellion within eyesight twenty-four-seven, there's no shortage of them. And, really, there's no place they won't go; bad people are everywhere, even in schools and churches and daycare centers. So our objective today isn't to find just any Hellion and go after him—we need to find one that is on his own and in a place that doesn't hugely risk exposing me when I attack him. Gabe tells me to keep my eyes open for stray Hellions as we cruise down street after street. He tells me about the one he and Wes found a week or so ago that was sneaking into some alley with a teenage girl. His point: they could be anywhere doing anything.

We end up zeroing in on one hanging around the edge of the U of A campus, next to a cluster of buildings that look rather lonely. He's not wearing anything but a pair of tattered shorts, so I am afforded the stomach-turning sight of something meandering around under his gray skin like a long, scaly snake. He's pacing between a truck that looks broken down and a building with a realtor's sign in the front window, staring at two girls in the distance who are talking with their arms full of books. We park and creep up on foot to spy on him from behind, and before too long one of the girls wanders off toward the heart of the campus, leaving the other to start toward us.

After a minute we deduce she's heading for a car parked a few buildings away from us on the other side of the street, right in the Hellion's line of sight. The closer she gets, the more he lingers around the truck next to him, maybe trying to look like he's having vehicle trouble. Who knows if the thing even belongs to him—what we know for sure is that he's got his eyes on the girl, her blonde hair fluttering in the cold wind like a flag.

"It's time," Gabe speaks lowly beside my ear. "You need to attack him from this direction and get him on the ground. The truck will block the fight from anyone else's view. First use your red powder and then finish him off with your dagger. B told me she explained this to you."

I nod as I draw both of my weapons out of my jacket. "She did."

"Great. So pour a little red powder into your hand—" he waits until I've done it to continue, "—and plan out your attack on him."

I survey the Hellion as I seal the vial and pocket it, and I do some quick thinking. He's bigger than me, unsurprisingly, and could probably pick me up and snap me in half with little effort. I need to avoid him so much as seeing me. And Gabe's right: he needs to be on the ground.

The second he goes down is the second I need to end him. And this can't take a long time, so I need to cut right to the chase—no trying to look impressive.

"Got it," I say as my strategy clicks into place.

"Then go. If you need me, I'll jump in."

Not unkindly, I tell him, "Won't be necessary." Then I sweep away from him.

The college girl is paying her surroundings very little attention. She seems preoccupied with not slipping on the snow and dropping her books, so the Hellion has no reason not to keep his eyes on her. This means he has his back squarely to me, not doing much more than shifting his weight from one foot to the other while he likely plans out how best to ensnare her. I'm as quiet as the engine of this truck as I approach him, adrenaline seeping through my veins, my mind and body preparing for anything. Preparing for him to start walking off, or turn around and see me, or call out to the girl and cause *her* to look this way and see me.

None of these things happen, though. So the instant I'm in place, I go for him.

I throw my red powder directly onto the backs of his legs and he immediately erupts into screams. He has no time to figure out what's attacked him before his flesh starts giving out and he dips toward the sidewalk. My foot comes up to slam against his back and hasten his fall, and I use my full weight to stomp him down flat. An enraged growl bursts from him as the thing slithering under his skin starts racing like a snake through water. But the most he accomplishes before I crouch down on his back is flattening his palms against the ground to attempt to push up. And then I'm stabbing the place where his heart should be, and then again a few inches up, and again a few inches beside that.

And then it's over.

My pulse is flying as I leap away from him. He breaks up into chunks and fluttery bits of disgustingness, and I'm prepared to take care of that gross snake thing if it managed to survive. Nothing else happens, though. The remnants of the Hellion just scatter across the sidewalk in the wind until they're gone.

'Divine experience' *in-fucking-deed, Red.*

Breathing deeply, my body alight with triumph, I look around me. The blonde girl is obliviously shutting herself into her car. There are no people, normal or otherwise, peering at me suspiciously. There is only me— and Gabe. I turn to find him leaning against the building I left him by, arms crossed, hair growing extremely messy in the wind. There's a grin on his face.

"What do you think?" I ask as I walk up to him.

"It was great, just like I knew it would be. I really enjoyed watching you kick him down to the ground."

I chuckle and hold up my dagger, which actually isn't dirty at all despite what he said back at the Sanctum. It isn't even distressed. "What's up with there not being a blessed thing on this blade?"

"It's a mystery," he says, reaching out to run a fingertip along the gorgeous metal. "Can't smudge it, can't scratch it. But Hellions don't bleed because they're not really alive, right? So no blood from them. Some of them have pus or really nasty ooze on them, so that'll get on your dagger, but it just washes off."

I wrinkle my nose. "Pleasant."

"You know it."

I sheathe my dagger and put it in my jacket. (God, do I love this jacket. And my dagger. And the fact that I just killed a Hellion all by myself.) "So I did okay, then? You didn't see anything I should improve on, or...?"

Gabe shakes his head. "It was perfect."

"You just saying that?"

He levels a serious look on me. "I would never, especially not about something this important. If you'd done something wrong I would've noticed it and told you about it so it doesn't happen again."

I believe him. I give him a smile as we start back to his car. "Well, what now?"

He smiles back. "I was thinking we'd go over to the Greek Theatre for a little bit. See if we can spot anyone of interest to us."

"Ah, man, I love that place." I've loved it since the second I first laid eyes on it back when I was experimenting with college classes. I miss it almost as much as that poetry class I took.

We drive over to it and see several (normal) students sitting on the stone benches, which have to be freezing cold. Everyone is dressed warmly, though, and some people are even laughing or chattering in groups—proof that even this weather can't stop college life.

As Gabe and I mosey across the stage area, I think back on the time I spent here. I was just like the other students, just like every one of my friends—just like pretty much anyone, really. I was still considering the question, *'What do you want to be when you grow up?'* Still trying my damnedest to figure out my answer.

I've always wondered why people ask little kids that question. Do they ask it hoping they'll say something cute like, *'I want to be the person who cooks the Mickey Mouse pancakes at Disneyland!'* or something ambitious like, *'I want to deliver food to hungry people in other countries!'*?

Or do they ask it to try to gauge what their kid's future might actually look like? Would the parents of the Mickey Mouse pancake girl simply laugh because what kid *doesn't* want to be around Mickey Mouse pancakes all day, or would they take the answer seriously and start making plans for her to attend culinary school? If another child stomped around his house in his daddy's shiny black shoes screaming, *'I object!'* to everything, would his parents see that as some sign that he's destined to be a judge like his father, or would they record a few funny videos and chalk it up to simple and probably temporary imitation of the man of the house?

I don't really remember my parents asking me what I wanted to be when I grew up, but I suppose they probably did. I wish they were still here to tell me what I said. Was I cute or ambitious? Was my answer that of a daydreamer or of a young girl determined to be classically important?

While I was here I took several different classes to get a feel for what interested me. Nothing really did deeply interest me, though—not enough to start thinking about it for a career. Or maybe I just didn't take that one earth-moving class, since I only took two or three each semester I was here. Nevertheless, being here now makes me think again about how I never really picked a profession, how I can't seem to remember ever declaring that I wanted to be a doctor or a sculptor, or anything.

From one of the corners of my mind creeps out something Beatrix said to me the other day. Something about the Lightforce being where I was always meant to end up. And I let myself wonder for a few dreamy seconds if there really is such a thing as fate, and if it was behind my never figuring out my future while I was normal.

"This really is an awesome place," Gabe comments. We stop walking to look up at the words engraved between the stone pillars: *Knowledge, Integrity, Courage, Culture, Intelligence.* Then he turns to look out at the sea of benches curving around the stage. "Imagine performing something up here in front of hundreds of people."

"What would you perform? Would you play the piano?"

"I don't know," he says thoughtfully. "Would you recite poetry?"

I chuckle. "Maybe."

"I'd clap the loudest. And yell your name, too, while waving around a sign with your name actually on it."

My chuckle grows into a real laugh as I imagine him standing up and cheering for me with everyone else sitting there wondering about his mental health. Before I know it I'm dropping my head back and laughing heartily.

"What?" he asks. I feel his hands drop gently onto my shoulders and I straighten up to find him right in front of me, smiling. "You think I'm kidding?"

"No. Actually, I was picturing what that would look like." I sigh. "Cracked me up."

He chortles and seems to study me, not taking his hands off of my shoulders. I seize the opportunity to enjoy the view for myself. I don't think I'll ever get tired of looking at Gabe; every time I see him I feel like he's gotten a little more irresistible. And sometimes it's just silly, like when I first saw him today at the Sanctum and I couldn't quit thinking his shoes looked good on him. At this particular moment his way-mussed hair is mesmerizing me, and I'm in the middle of debating whether or not I should reach up and run my fingers through it when he asks, "Can I call you while I'm in Dallas?"

I blink as my thoughts leave his hair. "Uh—I—yes," I stammer like a moron. "Of course you can."

"What if I call you every day?" He doesn't bother trying to play that off as purely hypothetical.

I shrug a little and tell him unabashedly, "I hope you do. I'm used to *seeing* you every day."

"And if I call twice a day?"

I reach up to touch his hands where they still rest on my shoulders. "Do it. You won't hear me complaining."

His hands move up to gently cradle my face. "Then I'll go ahead and warn you: I'll be calling you twice a day."

"I have been warned." My eyes flicker to his mouth of their own accord.

Having caught that, he gives me a flirty smile and bends down to kiss me, but before he can a voice says, "*Mari?*" from behind him. And it actually *does* sound warning.

Gabe looks as confused as I feel. I cover his hands with mine before he lowers them so we can look around to see who sounds so aggravated with me.

Aaaand it's Rafe. Of fucking course.

I blink slowly and wonder 1) how the hell he even came across me here, and 2) why he thinks he has any right to interfere with me and Gabe. Which, by the way, is what the entirety of his body language says he's trying to do.

"What?" I don't ask nicely.

He gestures to Gabe. "Are you fucking kidding me with this? Did I or did I not talk to you *specifically about* him?"

Gabe straightens up a little and lets go of my hands.

"We need to talk," Rafe says, jabbing a thumb back the way he came. "Again. Now."

I laugh humorlessly. "Uh, absolutely not. Leave me alone."

He strides over to us, his eyes flickering angrily between me and Gabe. "You're a fucking idiot to ask me to do that. You have no idea what you're doing and it's my—"

Gabe's arm shoots out between me and Rafe, who quiets and stops walking. "That's enough," he says, his tone even. I don't have to see his expression to know he's not pleased.

"You will not tell me," Rafe says slowly, his eyes flashing, "how to behave when the girl I love is in danger."

My mouth falls open. Gabe's hand curls into a fist and Rafe glares at him with absurd defiance. For several seconds none of us say anything else. And then I find my voice and say, "Rafe, if you don't step off within the next five seconds, I'm going to beat the ever-loving hell out of you."

His eyes snap to me and soften the tiniest bit. "Mari, this guy—"

"Is this the guy who cheated on you?" Gabe interrupts him.

I say, "It is," and Rafe turns livid.

Gabe lowers his arm and turns to look at me. I'm surprised to see he's fighting a smile. More quietly he says, "This guy who says he loves you is the one who cheated on you, and even though he cheated on you in *your* bed—" his eyes light up and he presses a hand over his mouth to hide his growing smile, "—he thinks that *I* am going to hurt you."

His amusement is contagious. I can't make good on my threat to beat Rafe's ass, or even feel a twinge of pain over what he did, because I'm totally distracted by Gabe. I try to stifle a giggle, but I fail so I press my lips together and nod, my shoulders shaking with chuckles.

He lets out a laugh and reaches up to caress one of my cheekbones.

"Don't you touch her, you son of a bitch!"

He does it anyway—draws a long, tender, promising line across my skin. Then he drops his hand from my face and turns back around to Rafe. "Here's the thing," he says, his amusement audibly fading. "I will leave Marienne alone the second she asks me to, but whether or not that happens has nothing to do with you. *You* need to worry about how many boundaries you've overstepped and figure out how to avoid continuing to do so."

"No, fuck you!" Rafe shouts, his voice echoing around the Greek Theatre, probably garnering the attention of anyone not already interested in this stupid fucking argument. "I haven't done anything but try to protect her even though she broke up with me! Three months isn't long enough to make me forget about her! Yeah, I fucking cheated on her, I get it, but that's none of your goddamn business and neither is she!"

I almost start giggling again at how he's just *announcing* his stupidity to these strangers.

But then he's moving toward Gabe with balled-up fists and violent eyes and an angry, "Let's just settle this right now." And I'm not tickled anymore.

In half a second I'm between them, my back pressed against Gabe's chest and my own chest heaving with a new rush of anger. "Rafe, get back," I growl right as he cocks a fist back.

He almost isn't able to stop it from flying forward. "Mari, get out of the fucking way! I'm handling this whether you like it or not!"

He has the gall to lay a hand on my arm to move me, and it enrages me. I knock his hand off and shove him back with my free palm. Then with both palms. Then I slap him across the face and *then* I backhand him so hard the bones in my hand scream in pain.

"Mari, what the fuck! *Stop!*" he shouts.

I point a finger in his face and say wrathfully, "*You* stop. You stop this shit right now, or I will hit you in the face for every single maddening thing you've ever said and then put on some giant-ass costume jewelry rings and hit you again for every unacceptable thing you've ever done."

He stares at me with eyes so wide I don't know how they're still in his head.

"And that is a long list of things," I inform him before I turn around and stride back to Gabe.

Rafe says nothing as we leave. A few people seated on the benches giggle and one girl says, "You're a total badass, girl!" But I don't say anything back or even look at anyone, not even Gabe. I just walk and walk and walk, my hand wrapped in his, my heart racing with everything from anger to satisfaction to embarrassment.

We're in the car in no time at all and as soon as the doors are shut I'm talking. "I'm so sorry. I'm so sorry about him. I don't know what his problem is, but I guess he's crazy and I can't believe he talked to you like that and actually tried to hit you. I'm—I'm just—" The end of the sentence won't even come to me, and I still can't look at Gabe.

At length he suggests, "Maybe we should just go back to the Sanctum. You killed a Hellion like we wanted. We can find something to watch on TV."

I nod way too many times, worry running wild in my mind.

And then I remember he doesn't even watch TV.

Oh, please don't let this be some kind of This Is Goodbye Because Fuck Your Drama thing, I beg God. *Please don't let Rafe have run him off from me.*

Hey, he didn't freak out about your car accident, I remind myself. *Surely he can handle a dumbass, jealous-ass ex-boyfriend.*

We don't say anything on the drive. We just listen to music. I let myself get lost in "Echo" by Trapt (I love when Gabe and I turn out to like the same songs) and try not to get too overwhelmed by everything. Like the excitement of my first official Hellion kill, and the stress of having discovered the gateway to the Dark world, and the sentiment behind the gifts I received today, and what just transpired with Rafe, and Gabe being directly confronted by him, and the fact that Gabe is leaving tomorrow for a Lightforce mission that feels dangerous to me.

He and I end up in the lounge on the residential hall. Even though I've been told a couple of people live at the Sanctum like I do, I never see them, not even in the laundry room, so the lounge is lonely. We take our jackets off and sit side by side on one of the couches (that's encouraging, at least) and flip through the channels on the TV. I try to care about what's on, but I don't do very well. Gabe settles on something, but then he says, "Marienne," and when I look at him I see he doesn't look like he cares, either. I briefly wonder if he even knows what program he picked, since he's so unused to watching TV.

I try to swallow my nerves. "Yeah?"

"I need to tell you something."

Don't be nervous. Don't be nervous. "Okay." The word is barely a whisper.

He mutes the TV. "Well...so...I—I know I bought you that necklace," he stammers, "and I know I've taken you out and kissed you and—and we agreed that we'd talk on the phone while I'm gone and everything."

As painfully as my stomach twists, I can't take my eyes off of him. I just nod a little. "Mmm."

He looks right back at me even though he's clearly nervous. "But I want to be very honest with you. I need to just say it because I need you to understand that this isn't—that *you* aren't—especially after what happened back there—"

"Um," I mumble, my hands flying up to my hair.

His hands close around mine. "Marienne, I—"

"Is this not what you want?" I blurt out. My heart is suddenly racing and I don't want to look at him while I ask this, but I still can't look away. "Is that what you're trying to tell me? That you've had fun with me, but you don't want me to get the wrong idea and Rafe was too much and you don't have time for this anymore?"

He doesn't say anything.

Mother*fuck*—

"No, that's not what I'm trying to tell you." His tone is suddenly lighter than it was, and upon refocusing on his face I see his expression is calmer. "I'm...I'm trying to tell you this *is* what I want."

The tension strapped around me loosens, but that's all I can comprehend because he leans closer, seemingly having more to say. His gaze moves easily over my face.

"I'm trying to tell you that I *mean* everything—the necklace, our dates, all of that—they're not empty gestures. I don't feel like this is a fling or whatever. I don't *want* it to be, and I want you to know it so that...." He sighs a little. His hands are cool but steady as they release mine to frame my face, and his voice drops softer. "I want you to know how I feel because if you don't feel the same way—just—if you don't want me to keep falling for you, for whatever reason, you gotta tell me right now."

I think my heart misses a beat.

"If it's just me, I'll—I'll try to work on it or something. Friends, maybe...?" He frowns. "Just be honest with me. Please."

Peace and wild hope and happiness and longing hit me like great waves in the ocean. They leave me without a clue about what I should say after something like that. But I try to think of something. I try and try and try— because I have answers, I just don't quite know how to piece them together to form a coherent sentence.

His hands on my face tremble just a little. "Marienne?" he says unsurely.

Not unsurely, I manage to say, "Gabe." And then words are coming out of my mouth in a stream I can't control. "Oh, God, I do feel that way. I do *not* want to just be your friend. I adore you kind of a lot. And I appreciate you saying you'll leave me alone if I ask you to, but I don't want to ask you to leave me alone because this isn't a fling for me, either. It's—it's—*you* are significant. I haven't stopped tripping over you since I saw you fighting those two Hellions. And in case you didn't notice, I physically assaulted *and* threatened someone today because he was trying to hurt you and it made me—"

His mouth on my mouth cuts me off, firm and warm and perfect. I instinctively curve toward him and he shifts to face me better, kissing me hard, like he's missed me even though I haven't gone anywhere. And while I kiss him back and let him draw me closer I try to memorize him and how this feels, because he *will* be leaving.

Oh, God, I don't want him to go.

I've just lifted a hand to his hair when he pulls away so he can look at me. His expression is radiant and amused. "When you jumped between him and me," he says, "I almost busted out laughing just at the thought of the ass-kicking he was about to get. And I don't think he knew what hit him even after you bitched him out."

I smile and feel another flutter of satisfaction, but mostly I'm awed by how he's looking at me. "Yeah," I say slowly.

"I wanted to tell you how amazing you were, but I couldn't get it out. I was too dazed." He pauses. "And too distracted by how hot it was."

My eyes widen in surprise, and I don't think there's a single place on me that escapes a flush.

Faint color touches his face, too, and he laughs a little. "You're the only person who's ever stood in front of me like that. It's not my fault I think it's awesome. It was awesome on Blossombranch, too."

I grin at him. No, I don't imagine he ever *does* need anyone to fling their body between him and danger—especially not little things like me. But he's right. Whether the situation involves Hellions or angry guys, I can't seem to help myself.

I close my eyes as he presses a kiss to my still-blazing cheek. Then more slowly he kisses my temple. Then his lips move closer to my ear and I'm pretty sure I'm in danger of melting.

He sounds a little more solemn when he mumbles to me, "No one has ever said they adore me before."

I draw a breath as slowly and quietly as I can. It's not easy to do. My lungs are starving for the air; God only knows how I didn't realize sooner that I was holding my breath. I sound a little raspy when I say, "I don't know how that's possible, but...I'm happy it was me."

His arms coil strongly around me and pull me into a hug. I move the hand I don't have in his hair around to the space between his shoulder blades as the words, "So am I," rumble through him to me. For a minute we just hug each other, and I can feel both of our heartbeats, and I love it from the top of my head to the tips of my toes. It's another thing I'm going to miss when he leaves.

Eventually we untangle ourselves from the embrace just enough for our mouths to start moving together again. Something about it is more intimate than any other time we kissed. We kiss each other languidly and tenderly, still chest-to-chest. He holds me against him like I'm precious to him, but he's the one who's exquisite. I hope he can sense how deeply I believe that, because he needs to know it. Even if he never boasts it to the world, I want him to know it for himself.

We stay this way for a long time, and the way we treat each other is unlike anything I've ever experienced. It's almost lazy, even when our kisses are open-mouthed and deep. Just easy, like breathing. Neither of us pushes the other farther or kisses any faster, even when one of my legs moves up to drape across his lap. He just bends his hand around the back of my knee and keeps me close, and I let one of mine graze against the light scruff on his jawline, down his throat to the curve of his collarbone. He smiles against my lips and I have to smile back, and I know that the Marienne Rose Connor of the Now Times is the best version of me the world has seen so far.

I've never been promiscuous, but I had one nice boyfriend a few years ago who I went all the way with, so it's not like I've never made out with anyone before. But Gabe makes me feel like that's not quite true. With him I feel better, lovelier, more important, like the past doesn't matter very much. He makes me feel like a color-by-numbers picture that others have left blank because only he understands how to fill it in. I decide I need to tell him that, so I do, and a warm laugh reverberates through him to me. He tells me that might be the best thing he's ever heard. Then he presses a kiss to my bottom lip and tells me more quietly that I color him in, too, big places and tiny places alike. And that touches my heart.

The memories stay with me through the night and into the next morning. And as Beatrix and I watch Wes and Gabe drive away for Dallas, I reach for those warm echoes—and for those of the days before—instead of giving myself over to the foreboding feeling scratching at my insides.

14
Gabe

On the drive, Wes and I have a decent time. When I'm not lost in memories of making out with Marienne, we enjoy some good music and discuss the situation in Dallas, and we even talk about the Hellion gateway (which includes me stressing again how he and Beatrix *cannot* let slip to Grayhem that they know about it). In the silent stretches, though, I feel kind of...weird. I can't place why that is, but I don't mention it. Eventually I chalk it up to the long drive and me feeling grumpy about leaving Marienne. Neither does it help lighten the atmosphere when Wes zones out and charges the air on his side of the Jeep with silent longing for his wife. I don't think he's ever been this far from her.

We told the girls we'd call them when we arrive at the Sanctum in Dallas, but that doesn't quite happen. We don't have a free minute between spotting the little family-owned store disguising the local Lightforce headquarters and being rushed into a meeting once we're underground. The Texan Light guys were ready and waiting not only to catch sight of us but to help us out of the Jeep, get us through the store, haul us through their own passcode-protected doors and then downstairs and into a conference room. They don't even give us time to put our stuff in our temporary bedrooms. We're offered a bathroom run, but told to be quick because we have a lot to discuss.

Although I don't take my time, I do take an extra second after washing my hands to text Marienne, *'Here and safe and already being pulled into a meeting. I'll call you in a little while.'* It's pretty lame; I wish I could hear her voice already, or even just text her something better than this. I wish I could tell her I can't quit thinking about how much I love that necklace on her. Or about how, even though she's smaller than me, her hugs make me feel like nothing else is allowed to touch me. Or how I've relived yesterday in my head three thousand times already because I've never kissed or been kissed like that, like time and the world outside were non-issues because we were learning each other and that was all that mattered.

But these are things that will have to wait. They'll have to rattle around in my chest until after this meeting.

It's only a little after 2:00 when we all sit down, but everyone acts like they've been waiting for me and Wes for forever. We meet the people involved in this thing: first Bartholomew the Director, Lon from Armaments, and the Defender trainer Reibek. Then five of the Defenders from this area: Delaney, Thompson, Smith, Cates and Simon. Then Torrance and May, the two Defenders from El Paso. Wes introduces himself as the Defender trainer from Fayetteville and I as his colleague and Fayetteville's Gatherer trainer. A couple of the men look at me strangely, but I just smile at them. They'll find out soon enough that being a Gatherer doesn't make me useless.

"All right, men," Bartholomew says, crossing his arms. "Here's the plan...."

And what a plan it turns out to be. He's apparently been putting it together for some time, so he's got locations, times, transportation details, maps and even extra weapons for the ten of us who are involved. Because as it turns out, this isn't an investigation like Wes and I were told—these guys have *been* investigating.

We're here to help them handle the Hellions, just like Marienne predicted.

I'm mostly torn between being surprised by this change and amused by her intuition. But something else pokes at me the whole time Bartholomew explains things to us. It takes me three whole hours to figure out it's that strange feeling I had in the car. It creeps further and further into me the longer I sit around this table and sink into the details of the attack.

It's just nerves, I try to tell myself. *Nerves and new people and a new place and not knowing how long this is going to take. Calm down.*

Except that my job hardly ever makes me nervous; when it does it's because I don't understand what's happening, like when Marienne and I found the gateway. This is different, though. I know what's up here. Even though I didn't think we'd be fighting when we got here, I've gotten used to the idea since then. I've been listening to a very long explanation on what's going on and what's expected of me, and I'm with a bunch of other people.

And that's another thing: new people don't make me nervous, either. I'm a Gatherer. My job deals exclusively with people I don't know. I've also traveled a ton, so unfamiliar places don't freak me out. The length of our stay here is a detail I'd appreciate knowing, but I'm not so worked up about it that it justifies my stomach feeling this unsettled.

So what's wrong with me?

I look at everyone else several times during the meeting. A few look somber, but I can't tell that any of them feel quite the way I do. Except for Wes: he doesn't look wholly comfortable. That at least makes me feel a little less crazy. I still make a mental note to discuss it with him after we're dismissed. Then I try to tune back in to the confab.

By the time we're done with the meeting it's 6:30. We're told to grab some food and be back in two hours so we can leave and carry out our plan.

Wes and I find a pizza place easily. After we order we sit down in a corner booth to talk privately. Before I can even say anything he says frankly, "I feel fucking weird about this, man."

"That makes two of us," I assure him. "But I can't figure out why."

He shakes his head. "I can't, either. Something just feels...off."

I frown, and even though I don't believe it I ask, "Is it the people here?"

"Nah. I mean, I don't think so." He sighs. "Maybe it's just the situation. I personally haven't ever heard of more than maybe five Hellions causing trouble at the same time. These guys think we're gonna encounter anywhere from fifteen to twenty-five tonight. Maybe the fact that we've been called into this at all is what's so bizarre."

I nod slowly and thump the straw in my glass of water. "Maybe. So let me get this straight, because honestly, I zoned out for a bit."

He chuckles in understanding.

"This group of Hellions has been meeting up every night for the past several days on some piece of land outside the city. Our guys figure they're directly responsible for the recent killings of both Light people and regular people around here, since they've been heard speaking openly about it and even brought in a couple of people and violently murdered them at this place. Both normal people, we're told."

He nods.

"So our plan is to sneak out there and ambush them. Take them all out. Leave."

He nods again. "That's my understanding."

Saying it out loud like this lessens my anxiety a little bit. "Well, I wonder why they haven't mentioned when we can go back home. For as many details as they've dug up and planned out, it seems pretty straightforward."

"Yeah, no shit," he agrees. "Maybe they're just trying to leave some breathing room for us. Maybe once we actually do it they'll be like, *'Done and done, fellas. Thanks. Now go back to your own city and take your girls out on a nice date because one of them is having a birthday this weekend and she's not gonna like it if her husband isn't there.'*"

I laugh. "Speaking of the girls," I say, my heartbeat doing something crazy just at thinking about yesterday, "Marienne and I encountered her ex-boyfriend yesterday at U of A. He got belligerent and came at me, and she jumped in and started beating his ass."

Wes's eyes widen and he chokes on his water. After a few seconds he laughs. "Are you serious?"

"Yeah, she went all Defender on him. He tried to push her out of his way so he could hit me and she didn't take it for a second." I can't help but grin widely at the memory. "Knocked his hand off her, shoved him back, slapped the piss out of him and then turned around and backhanded him."

He laughs, tipping his head back. "Oh my God. I wish I'd seen it. I wish *B* had seen it. She'd be so proud."

"*I* was proud. It was fantastic."

I get a knowing look from him. "Mmm, so B was right. She's crazy about you. Started whipping wholesale ass right there in front of people because she wanted to protect you." He flutters his eyelashes.

"Whatever," I say on a chuckle. "I mean, yeah, maybe. But I don't think it was just that. I think it was that he's caused her a lot of stress and pain already, and *then* went after me." I shrug a shoulder. "Even if I'd been some random stranger I'd have enjoyed it." After a beat, "In fact, the random strangers who saw it *did* enjoy it."

"No doubt. She's an excellent fighter. By the way, how was her first go with her weapons?"

I wish I could say she laid out a bunch of Hellions with them—well, kind of. I really like that the day turned out like it did. So I just say a little vaguely, "Just as great as her training. She's good."

"Cool. Hey!" He looks like he just remembered something exciting. "Did those guys from El Paso say they brought guns?"

We talk about the extra weapons mentioned in the meeting until our food comes. Thanks to what happened when I was sixteen, I've never shot a gun before and I don't know a thing about them, so I'm intrigued but not drooling about it like Wes. I let him daydream about getting to shoot one tonight, hoping no one expects me to do the same. I'd probably do more harm than good; I'm inexperienced and a bullet's a bullet, whether or not it's got Light blood in it.

Our food is good, but it's gone too quickly, along with our time. We get back to the Sanctum with about twenty minutes left before we have to rejoin the others, so we take our stuff to our rooms. I glance around at the blank walls and simple furniture and plain colors as my fingers find Marienne's number in my phone.

She answers after two rings. "Hi, Gabe." Her voice sounds a little different on the phone than it does in person, but it's still like music to me. I still love the way she says my name and I can still tell she's smiling.

I'm reminded all over again how lost I am to her.

"Hi, gorgeous," I say, picturing that smile.

She laughs, sounding happy and bashful at the same time. "That's nice, but you don't know what I look like right now. You're a little too far away."

"I can see you in my head," I inform her as I sit down on my bed. "And you look gorgeous."

A softer laugh meets my ear. "You look even better in *my* head. I promise you that."

"Impossible." I smile and lean forward to put my elbows on my knees. "Hey, I'm sorry it took so long to call. They accosted us the second they saw the Jeep and since then..." I sigh, "...we've just been bombarded with information."

She says, "It's okay," like she means it, but her next words are more careful. "What do you have to do?"

"Well...let's just say it's a good thing we didn't bet on whether or not I was coming to kill Hellions. I would've lost pretty badly."

I hear her groan. "Shit."

"They've got it all figured out, though, and Wes and I know exactly what we're supposed to do. And they didn't tell us it'll only be a one-night thing, but we can't see how it could go any longer. It's a simple plan."

"Are you the only two going?"

"Nah. There are eight other guys going with us." I pause and try not to sound like the weird feeling is prickling at me again. "There are quite a few Hellions. They've been meeting in one place for several days. That's where we're going."

"Gabe...." I can hear the worry in her voice.

"We're all very capable," I promise her. "It'll be fine. We've even got extra weapons."

She sighs a little. "When do you have to go?"

I don't want to waste time looking for a clock, so I say, "Really soon."

A few seconds of silence fall. Then, "Look, I didn't want to say anything before, but I have to now. I don't feel right about this thing you're doing, and neither does Beatrix. I've tried not to dwell on it, but it's been jabbing at the backs of my eyes and it's worse now that I know for sure you're not just there to have a look around."

I drop my head into my free hand and feel my shoulders slump. "Well, if you want to know the truth," I say slowly, "Wes and I kind of agree."

"What! And you still went? Why didn't you tell Grayhem you thought it was a weird idea?"

"It didn't get bad until we got here and actually heard about everything." I rub my forehead.

"Okay, well—" she draws a deep breath, and I know she's working to calm herself down, "—just please be careful. I know you're a badass, but holy shit. I can't explain to you this feeling I have."

As amused as I always am to hear her talk me up like that, this time I can't muster up much more than a weak smile. I just wish like hell I was there to touch her and make her feel better—make *myself* feel better. "I'll be careful, Marienne," I say softly. "We both will. And this really shouldn't take long. We really are hoping to leave tomorrow or something."

She makes a blubbery noise with her lips. "Okay. I'm sorry. I'm not trying to be a...whatever."

"I don't mind. Just don't run yourself insane. Think happy thoughts. Go kill your own Hellions with B."

"Oh, we've been doing that," she assures me. "We killed ten in two hours alone."

"Christ," I groan, sitting up again, "I wish I'd been there to see that."

I'm relieved to hear her smiling when she says, "I'll admit it was fun."

"Keep doing it." Then more seriously, "But don't go back to Grove Lane, all right? Not for anything, not even the tire swing. And definitely not for the gateway. I don't care how helpful a killing spree is for your nerves. Don't go back."

"I won't. I promise." She doesn't sound the least bit disappointed by the directive.

"Thank you."

"Mmhmm. So what's it like in Dallas?"

"Not a speck of snow on the ground," I say. "And the people here are fucking terrible at driving."

She laughs. "I guess the weather knows what it's doing, then, huh? Snow would just make it worse."

"Right," I say with my own laugh. "The whole city would be a car accident."

"That sounds terri—aw, man," her voice drops quieter. "Hellion alert."

"Yeah? Where are you?"

"I'm at Applebee's with Beatrix. She's been outside talking to Wes, so I'm sure she saw this bastard walk in."

It's less than willingly that I say, "Well, I'll let you go, then. You've got work to do." I remember too late that I wanted to voice those thoughts I was having before the meeting. Guess I'll have to tell her later.

In kind she says, "Yeah, you have work to do, too." Then she reminds me, "Be careful."

"I will." And even though I know she'll be fine with Beatrix I add, "You be careful, too."

"Oh, Gabe," she sighs. "If there's anyone who needs to watch their ass on our end, it's this Hellion. He's going to regret eyeballing that little girl in the ballerina tutu."

That's my girl.

Out loud I say, "I'll call you when I get back from this thing."

"Okay." She sounds like she wants to say something else, but ultimately just clears her throat and says again, "Okay."

"Okay," I echo. "Bye."

"Bye."

I miss her voice the second I hang up.

Thankfully, I'm saved from that by a knocking on my door. I walk over and open it to see Wes. "Hey, man," he says, looking a little less stressed. I guess speaking with Beatrix made him feel better.

"Hey, what's up? You ready to head out there?"

"Whenever you are. If you're busy, you've still got maybe ten minutes left."

"Nope. I'm good." I make sure I've got everything I need on me, and then I step out into the hall.

Back in the conference room we find that everyone has already returned from dinner. Reibek decides we'll be okay to leave now, so we quickly check and double-check everything. Before long we're piling into three dark-colored vehicles and hitting the road to kill these Hellions.

I'm in a Civic that's just like mine, except this one's black. I'm riding in the backseat with Wes and two Dallas guys are in the front: Delaney driving and Thompson riding shotgun. They seem to be early thirties, maybe.

"Hey, man, change the station," Thompson complains. "Fuck country music."

"Dude, you live in Texas," Delaney counters. "You're in the wrong state to be hatin' country music."

"That's the dumbest logic ever."

"No, it ain't."

Thompson turns around to look at us beseechingly. "Seriously. This warbling shit about a woman wearing cowboy boots, or Staind?"

Wes and I say, "Staind," at the same time.

"Aha!" Thompson turns around and points at Delaney.

"Dude, they're from Arkansas. They don't count."

"Bullshit!"

The guys seem nice enough—even Delaney with his country music—but all I can really think about is this attack we're about to stage. It really should be a flawless encounter. I mean, I have to admit that Wes and Marienne were right the other night: I was fighting those two Hellions on Blossombranch with my bare hands just because I didn't want to kill them and be done that fast. With all the things we've got going for us tonight, a quick and painless win is pretty much guaranteed.

Each of us has our own dagger and at least one full vial of our own red powder, but we've been given an additional dagger and more red powder, courtesy of a few guys who offered up the extra blood. The two El Paso guys really did bring guns, and one of the other Dallas guys used to do a lot of hunting with a bow, so he's got that and some special Light blood arrows on him.

I don't know why the portentous feeling is plaguing me, but all it's doing is taking up space in my head that I need for helpful things. I decide I'm done being concerned about it. I mentally go over our plan once again, and make sure my weapons haven't disappeared into thin air, and start preparing myself for anything.

When I suspect we're getting close to our destination, Delaney says, "So, not that I'm fond of the idea, but I'm leavin' my car key in here while we're out. That way, if anything unfavorable happens we can get gone quicker."

We all make noises of acknowledgement. I especially appreciate the information. I already knew I wouldn't have problems driving the car if it comes to that because it's just like mine, and knowing the key will be in the ignition only further bolsters me.

"You guys got any questions?" he asks.

"Nope," Thompson says.

Wes and I say, "Nope," too.

He doesn't press us, doesn't even ask to go over the plan again. I imagine it's because he doesn't actually care about those things. I personally don't question a whole hell of a lot when I fight a Hellion. I figure out the differences between him and me, assess my surroundings and go for it. These guys are probably the same way—I know Wes is, for sure.

So the rest of the drive passes in silence, except for the terrible music.

We're a fair distance from the lights of the city when the car starts creeping down a lonely road that leads into deeper darkness. Delaney turns the headlights off before long, coloring everything around us black. I don't have time to be concerned about his ability to determine where we're going because a tiny metal building with a light above the door comes into view out of nowhere. We pull up in the shadows next to it, and the other two cars creep up as we're getting out.

Once we're all together, Reibek says lowly, "Check your weapons."

Rounds of bullets are examined. The whisper of daggers being unsheathed fills the air. Everything seems to be in order.

"All right, get in your groups and let's get going."

Even though Wes and I rode here with Delaney and Thompson, our attack group is a little different. We'll be with Delaney and May, one of the Defenders from El Paso. Thompson will be with Cates, Smith and Torrance, the other El Paso guy. Reibek will be with Simon, the Dallas Defender with the bow.

After we're clustered up Delaney, Reibek and Cates all turn on some very dim lanterns. Then our groups split apart and we set off on foot.

My group goes through a field full of some kind of grass so tall it reaches my shoulders. I take care to absorb as many details of my surroundings as I can. To my left the field is expansive and rippling in the wind. To my right is a forest, through which Reibek and Simon are sneaking. Behind me, in the direction of the cars, are faint city lights. I make a mental note to aim for those lights when it's time to get back to the car.

No one speaks as we traverse the mile and a half from our meeting spot to the meeting spot of the Hellions. It's ideal for me. The night is cloudy, so I listen for thunder. I also listen for laughter or car tires, and gunshots or screams, since we know these Hellions have brought victims out here before. But I hear nothing. At least not until we get closer to the spot, which is just an abandoned metal farm building of some kind. Then we start hearing voices, and I know it's the Hellions because some of them sound like ass. They seem to just be chatting with one another.

Per our strategy, the four of us get into a line and get low to the ground. Then we creep forward just enough to see the Hellions, and the lights around the place allow me to count them. Fifteen are in the clearing, but some are coming and going from the building, so who knows how many aren't in sight.

The plan is to start with our ranged attacks. To avoid the Hellions just running off to hide, Simon is going to step out in plain sight to shoot his bow; he mentioned that that'll help with his aim, anyway, versus trying to stay low and hidden. We expect the Hellions to charge him, and when they do Torrance and May will keep firing their guns and the rest of us will dash out and fight up close and personal.

The cue is a quick text sent to each leader. Delaney sends out his two, and when two come back to us, we know we're good. "In five, May," he tells our shooter.

Breathe.

My hand closes around my extra dagger.

Breathe.

I get ready to move.

A somewhat muted shot echoes through the air. Then one from our distant left, where the other group is. Two Hellions hit the ground, and then a third as an arrow zips into him.

Some Hellions run toward the gunshots, but most run toward the forest where Simon is. "Two of you, go!" Delaney says, and Wes and I bolt away.

I'm interested in the damage Simon is doing, but I don't dare look. I set my sights on a tall Hellion racing that way on what look like hooves. When I'm close enough I grind my own feet to a halt and fling the dagger at him. It spins and glints before it digs into his back, and he stops running to let loose a howl and strain an arm back to pull it out. But it's a no-go for him, and by the time he spins around to see where the dagger came from, I'm upon him and already driving my own blade forward. One solid stab and another for good measure, and I'm done.

I yank both daggers out of him and don't stand around to watch him crumble. I just turn to face the Hellion charging me from the left, and I've sliced him down with both blades in no time.

Shots are still being fired. I go for a Hellion that takes an arrow to the thigh right as I'm getting to him. He manages a punch to my ribs, but I take it in stride and roundhouse kick him in the head, then throw an uppercut at him, and then slit his exposed throat. I snatch the arrow up and whirl around to find my next target...and see that there really isn't one.

We have kicked total ass.

I spot Wes swerving away from the fist of the Hellion he's fighting. Then he lets loose a roundhouse kick of his own and finishes the Hellion off before he even hits the ground. I head over to see what he thinks about our victory. He spots me and starts jogging my way, a grin forming on his face.

And then something slams powerfully against my entire backside and my feet are taken completely off the ground.

I sail through the air like a leaf blown helplessly along by a breeze, and I lose sight of Wes as my vision blurs. My stomach seems to drop out of me and my mind explodes with confusion and shock. My limbs flail wildly, coming in contact with nothing but air. Under the sound of the wind in my ears, I hear faint shouts. I think one of them belongs to me.

And then I'm colliding with something unyielding, and the air whooshes out of me with painful violence, and my vision flashes black.

I'm aware of my body rolling a few times, and when I stop I'm facedown on something cool and scratchy. I slump against it in exhaustion; I feel like I've just been hit by a speeding car. It's overwhelming. Dizzying. My breaths are coming in short, pained gasps. My skin is stinging, my entire body aching, blood pounding, vision spotting, lungs starving for air.

And then suddenly, all of that disappears to leave me feeling numb and weightless.

I feel as close to death as I did the night I was shot in my own house.

No. No, my mind slurs. *I don't want to die.*

"You have all made a very foolish mistake," a sonorous, menacing voice says. The words are eerily loud and fill the night and my head like its owner is standing right beside me.

The scary numb feeling ebbs away, and even though I'm elated to still be alive, I tune in to my skin crawling and my muscles twitching. The pain and dizziness come back and weigh me down and make me feel tired and a little nauseated. I realize I'm lying in and surrounded by the tall grass, and the fragrance isn't helping me any.

And what did that person just say?

What the hell is even going on?

"Although it is adorable," the syllables glide slowly along the air, "that you thought you could march in like heroes to save the day and amusing that you thought you had the upper hand, *the power*...it was most unwise of you to come here tonight. Here, you are not heroes. Against me, your power is useless."

And what the hell does *that* mean?

The words tap frantically against my clouded mind, beseeching me to understand them. I try to replay them to myself, blinking slowly against the pain trying to dominate my attention. After several long seconds I think I begin to grasp their meaning: it sounds like this person— this man—knows my comrades and I are gifted, and even though that should concern him, for some reason it doesn't. And that sends anxiety creeping through me, lucidity hot on its heels.

Why wouldn't he be afraid of us? We just killed all those Hellions. If he's here with them, doesn't that mean he's *like* them? And if he's like them he should know we're a threat to him...

...except that I didn't throw *myself* through the air just now.

Was he what picked me up and tossed me around like I was nothing? Like I wasn't a person, a man, a fighter?

How could he have done that?

A wave of pain shudders through me. I moan and the sound is pathetic. My attempt to push myself up off the ground is even worse.

In his chilling voice he drawls, "Yes, adorable and amusing, indeed. You have fought back against us with little trouble for many, many years, but the hour of your weakening approaches. And it is long overdue."

Growing more unsettled by the second, I decide I *really* need to start trying to move. I use every ounce of strength in my body to roll over onto my back, gritting my teeth against the ache and disorientation. Once there's open air in my face I try to get my breathing right, and I find it's much easier now. As my lungs drink in the oxygen, my mind feels a little clearer yet.

Whoever this guy is, he definitely knows we're Light. He knows what our purpose is. But 'hour of weakening'*...? Is he serious?*

"Perhaps you think this cannot be," he says like he knows my thoughts, "but you will not be so ignorant for very long. You have cut down a few of our soldiers, but there are more standing and more on the way. The armies we are amassing in your human world are only growing stronger, and they are chomping at the bit to flood your streets and escort you to your ends."

O-fucking-kay, my mind claps nervously. *Weapons. Where are my weapons?*

One of my hands is lying out to my side and the other is across my stomach. I wiggle my fingers and clench my fists, and realize they're empty. My arms are heavy as I move them to pat at my jacket, which feels flat. "Oh, fu...." I barely breathe out, closing my eyes in frustration.

I don't have my weapons.

I don't have anything.

But this man is obviously different from regular Hellions. Why do I even think having my dagger would help me at all?

Right. Yeah, this is good, I tell myself. *I don't need to waste time thinking about a fight. I need to think about everything else.*

Something is clearly very, very wrong. I need to stay hidden, stay in one piece because I have to find out just what this very wrong something is. That way, when I get out of here I can take the information with me— because, oh yes, I *am* getting out of here.

I have a girl to get back to.

Her face drifts into my mind. Perfect light blue eyes, soft black hair, a soul-searing smile—

"You are all so very small," the dark, velvety voice cuts in, "so very weak, and clueless about what lurks on your doorstep."

The words are unlike anything I've ever heard, and they worry me.

Marienne's words from yesterday drift through my head like a prayer: *'I don't want to ask you to leave me alone...you are significant.'* And I remember us on that couch, her fingertips on my skin and my hand holding her leg across me while we kissed, both of us having just admitted the importance of what we have together.

"But we are almost ready to bust down the door, and when we are ready we will announce our presence to your pathetic little world, and take it from you."

Trepidation is quickly overwhelming my pain.

But no matter what this person says about our deaths being around the corner, there's no way I'm letting myself die *here*, in some goddamn Texas grass, while Marienne sits at home waiting for me to come back for her. I'm not going to leave her alone. Maybe I didn't say it out loud to her that one night, but I know I thought it to myself: *I will always go back for her.* And that's all there is to it.

So I force my body into action. I try to block out the aches and discomforts as I crawl at a snail's pace toward the man's voice so I can find out what the hell is happening. The wind blows cold, and I'm glad for it because it moves the grass, masks my shuffling through it.

"We will watch as you all try to run, and smile as you trip clumsily onto the ground, and laugh as you attempt to crawl away. You will be humiliated and terrified when you realize that your resilient days are over, and we will enjoy every second of bending you until you break."

It feels like ice-tipped fingers are scratching down my back.

From my left I detect movement that has nothing to do with wind. It halts my advancement toward the voice, tenses every muscle in my body. I slide my gaze in that direction, and as the commotion creeps closer I reach a hand into my jacket with the grasping hope that some red powder survived the fight I got into with the ground. I've got nothing, of course. Nothing but broken glass mixed in with the powder. *Fuck.*

I'm just trying to decide if I should grab as much powder as I can, anyway, when a scratched-up but familiar face melts out of the grass. *Oh, thank God,* I think as Wes's expression alights with relief at the sight of me, and then with fear. "We have to go *now,*" he mouths.

I point toward the voice, which is saying something else about how we won't stand a chance against what's coming. "Who is that?" I mouth back.

"I don't know."

"We have to look."

Though he hesitates, he appears to want information in spite of his apprehension, like me. We proceed slowly and as silently as possible.

"Well, now, are none of you brave enough to face me?" the voice calls out mockingly. "You were all so eager for battle just minutes ago. I am but one man, and still you all cower from me? Have I scared you off so easily?" The laugh that leaves him is abysmal. "What warriors you are."

As intent as I am, my heartbeat is going crazy with dread by the time I peek out of the grass.

I see two Hellions standing by the door to the building. One has what appear to be shards of glass jutting out along his arms and shoulders. The other has barbed wire wrapped around his torso and each of his limbs and even around his head, and what flesh I can see is red and puckered. Out in the middle of the very empty clearing stands a tall man with white skin, wide black eyes and a gaping black mouth, and he's covered in red tattoos.

They're on his muscular arms and legs, his chiseled stomach and thick neck, his face and the top of his hairless head. The only scrap of clothing on him is a black loincloth-looking thing.

His appearance is frightening to me in a way Hellions' never have been. He looks almost normal compared to most of the monsters I've seen; indeed, he looks...*separate* from them. More dangerous than simply gruesome.

Those black eyes of his scan the forest. My stomach curls at the thought of them edging in our direction. But my thoughts on what I would do to protect myself are interrupted when he lifts a hand at the trees and says solemnly, "Come to me. Let us see what exactly you are made of." After a moment: "Yes, there we are. Come to me."

I could laugh. There's no fucking way anyone is going out there to—

My twisted amusement flickers out as a figure drifts out from the woods, slow and awkward. After a few seconds I realize it's a man...a vaguely familiar man...*Delaney*. I stare at him, shocked and horrified. *Why* is he doing what the enemy wants? Surely he's not actually going to confront him after all of this? And why is he moving so strangely? Why isn't he at least running or—?

Oh. My. God.

My eyes are suddenly stuck on the ground below Delaney's boots—the ground he's not touching. The ground that is several feet below him.

The fear I felt before is dull compared to what's blasting through me now.

"Gabe," Wes chokes out almost inaudibly.

I can't speak.

That tattooed man is bringing Delaney to him against his will. Straight through the air. With...his mind?

So he *is* what sent me flying earlier. Goddamn.

"And you," he croons, holding up his other hand. My eyes snap to the forest, out of which someone else comes floating. Torrance.

We have to go, my mind blares. *No more hiding here. We really have to go.*

Delaney's body drifts to a stop in front of the tattooed man. In the light from the building I can see his chest is heaving violently, his eyes are wide, and his face is slick with tears or sweat or both. As I watch, his eyes start bulging and his face turns a different, darker color.

Now. Leave now.

His mouth opens in a silent scream and one of his eyes spurts out of its socket. Then the other. My stomach rolls as his body arches mid-air, his veins standing out against his purpling skin. I can see him trembling even from here.

A laugh like low thunder leaves the tattooed man.

My comrade continues to be bent in the wrong direction. His head approaches the heels of his feet inch by inch by inch—and then his body folds in half completely. A sickening crack echoes through the air and broken bone jabs out from his center, sending out a spray of dark liquid.

My mind goes blank.

When it comes back to me I'm in the middle of rocketing through the grass away from the clearing, my body bent low and my legs moving faster than I ever imagined they could.

My desperate mind urges them. *Go. Go. Go. Go.*

Wind whips past my ears. The sound of Delaney's body snapping in two echoes in my mind. My feet pound the ground even harder and faster, trying to outrun the memory. The grass whistles as I fly through it. My lungs gasp angrily for air.

Yet I hear the monster laughing like he's running right behind me.

Don't catch me, I silently beg him.

On the heels of that thought is the command, *Go faster. Don't slow. Keep going. Don't look back.*

My body hates me. I don't care. I dare to straighten up and push myself past what I thought were my limits until I feel like I'm going to blow up.

Don't catch me.

My eyes zero in on the Dallas city lights in the distance, my point of reference.

Keep running! Go! You can make it! Go!

Don't catch me. Don't catch me. Don't catch me. Don't catch me! Don't catch me!

The mile and a half is nothing. My body surges into the space we parked the cars in and I can't stop it from crashing straight into the black Civic. I barely feel the impact. I roll down the frame until I get to the driver's side door, both wondering how I got here so fast and bemoaning that it took so long.

I hear my name as I get behind the wheel. I know that voice, and deep relief bursts through me. In a flat second I've got the car started and Wes is in the passenger seat. "Go!" he roars.

I go.

Fast.

Too fast.

Way too fast.

So fast it scares me.

But I don't stop until we're back in Dallas and there are lights everywhere and I've found a hiding spot I'm quite literally betting our lives on and no one is around to hear us explode into a million demands and obscenities and questions and shouts.

And then we call Grayhem.

                                ᘓ

Back at the Dallas Sanctum, chaos is ensuing.

Ten of us went out to the clearing. Six of us returned, by some miracle. Delaney is dead for sure and the others say Torrance is just as gone. Smith and Cates are uncertainties.

And not a single one of us has any idea what that tattooed man was all about.

"What the mother*fuck* was that?" Simon is shouting. "Why weren't we prepared for that?"

"You're asking the wrong people, Mitch!" Reibek shouts back. "We didn't know anything *about* that! You know we've never seen that son of a bitch before!"

"Well, where could he have possibly come from if no one has seen him before? And what was he doing to our men? Was that *magic?*"

Thompson yells something indistinguishable from behind his hands, which are pressed to his face. It sounds obscene, whatever it is.

I say nothing. I got all of my freaking-out over and done with in the car with Wes. He sits as quietly as I do, listening to our Texan colleagues ask questions no one has any real answers to.

A couple of people are arguing about the absurdity of the tattooed man using magic on Delaney and Torrance—and on the rest of us, for that matter, though that was harmless in comparison. Wes and I already agreed it had to have been some kind of Dark magic. There's no other explanation for him holding two grown men off the ground like that, no other explanation for how Delaney was killed. And, really, why is it such an irrational idea considering the kind of life we all live already?

Bartholomew has to do *a lot* of shouting to get everyone to quiet down.

Once the conference room is ringing with deafening silence, he looks at me and Wes and then at May. "I have no words, men. I have absolutely no words for how sorry I am that you came that close to death. It's true that we expected nothing but a group of Hellions to be there. But I hope to my bone marrow that you three will stick around a few more days and at least help us think of something to strike back with. You absolutely do not have to stay to carry out anything we come up with—I will not ask for that much, won't even think about it—but the brainpower would be invaluable."

"That bastard killed my brother-in-law," May croaks out. It's all he manages because he bows his head and starts crying, but we all know what he meant: *'That bastard killed my brother-in-law and I'll do everything I can to help get revenge.'*

Bartholomew nods and inhales deeply. I'm sure he's thinking about Delaney, as well as the other two men of his who aren't here. Then he looks at me and Wes again.

He and I look at each other.

I take the time to form my own opinion in my mind before I ask him hoarsely, "What do you think?"

His voice is just as worn-down as mine. "I think I miss my wife, and after the bullshit we just went through, the only place in the world I wanna be is where I can touch her." He clenches his jaw. "But I wanna be able to keep her safe from whatever we saw out there...and will I be able to do that to my utmost ability if I don't try to find out what exactly we're up against?"

So he feels how I feel.

When we spoke to Grayhem on the phone he told us our next move would be of our own choosing, not a directive. He heard us breaking down over what we saw; he understood that our escape was nothing short of a miracle—that had we waited five more seconds we might've been the next to die.

The three of us agree that whatever the tattooed man was on about was neither a joke nor close to being over, and we'd be morons to believe otherwise. We figure that the things he said match up with what's been happening: so many Hellions meeting up in one place, the mounting violence in this city including the deaths of Light people like Em, and maybe even the feeling that something about this trip wasn't right. Grayhem said any additional information we can gather about the man and his unprecedented powers will only benefit us. Even if we stay just long enough to remember what all was said before he started crazy-murdering our men, writing the words down and bringing them home for observation will still be helpful.

As badly as I want to get the hell out of Dallas, I can't deny my sense of responsibility. Even though I'm not used to being afraid of anything—and I am very afraid of what's going on here—I know I can't run from this. It's true that my body overtook my mind back there and I bolted, but it's different now. Now I'm at the Sanctum and I have room to think. And I need to do it.

I choose to be of as much use as I can stomach being.

I don't want to go home and look Marienne in the face and tell her I brought nothing back with me to help keep her safe. I don't want to have to tell her I ran away before I even *tried* to understand what went on in that clearing. I don't want to curl up with her somewhere, all defeated and ignorant, hoping nothing that man said will come true and that nothing will find us.

No, I want to be standing upright, confident and as prepared as I can be. Like always.

I set my jaw and give Wes a nod.

He nods back and then looks at Bartholomew again. "We'll stay."

15
Marienne

Beatrix and I are lounging on her couch in our pajamas. We thought it'd be fun (less lonely and sad, that is) if I stayed with her while the guys are gone. It's nearing midnight and we've just finished watching the end of *Fight Club* on TV, which was way less awesome than usual because of all the editing, but whatever. It helped with our mood. And now we're just sitting quietly; I'm thinking about Gabe, and I'm sure she's thinking about Wes.

I decide now's a good time to ask, "How'd you meet Wes?"

She twirls the end of her ponytail around one finger. "On my second day in the Lightforce I was checking out the CD collection for the stereo in the training room, trying not to be nervous about learning how to fight the most terrifying creatures I'd ever seen in my life. Wasn't working so well. I was jumpier than hell."

"Mmm," I hum sympathetically.

"First words I ever heard him say: *'How did you know blue is my favorite color?'*" She holds her hair up a little. "I was worked up already, you know, and there he'd snuck up on me, so I turned around to say something bitchtastic and saw he didn't have a shirt on. An incredible sight, believe you me, but what really got me was that he had the words *'I'M ALIVE'* tattooed across his chest." She drags a fingertip from right to left, just under her collarbone. "And I didn't say anything shitty after all. I just said, *'Nice tattoo,'* and showed him mine." She tugs the left sleeve of her hoodie up, where *'I'M ALIVE'* swirls prettily along her forearm.

I have one of those moments where you think, *Ohhhh, okay,* like you know what the hell's going on even though you don't actually understand. So I take a second to replay her words in my head, and then it clicks and I feel my eyes widen. "Hey, are you serious? You guys had the same tattoo?"

Beatrix nods and smiles. "Bam."

"That's fucking awesome."

"We thought so, too." Her shoulders hunch and she tilts her head to one side, like a love-struck teenage girl. "It was a pretty coincidence, but there's no doubt in my mind now that we're just soulmates. Wes is like...." She holds her breath and looks up at the ceiling, like it might have the perfect description of her husband written on it. Then she releases her breath and drops her eyes back to mine. "The sun. He's like the sun. Powerful and bright and hot—" she winks at me, "—and if he ever went away, I'd just...I'd...."

Just like that, her face is shadowy. She taps her labret piercing with one fingertip and gnaws on her bottom lip. She doesn't have to say aloud what's on her mind, because I get it.

"Gabe seemed really confident that everything would go well," I murmur.

She sighs and nods. "Oh, I'm sure. He and Wes are both outstanding fighters and they're smart. I just don't...know. I just don't know." Her hand falls away from her face to smack against her thigh. "I don't know where this weird-ass feeling came from and I'm not a fan of it."

"I feel you," I assure her with my own sigh. "But maybe they'll call soon. Gabe said he'd call me when he came back."

As if on cue, my phone rings on the coffee table. Gabe's name lights up the screen. I grab it up and answer, "Hi," unable to hide my relief.

He says, "Hi," back, and he sounds absolutely terrible. It's not like him and I don't care for it, but I suppose he just fought hard. Big group of Hellions and all.

"How'd it go?" I ask as Beatrix's phone rings. She runs out of the room with it. "Did you kill the Hellions?"

A laugh leaves him and the sound is all wrong. It's almost derisive. "Most of them, yeah. Only a few from that group are left."

I sigh a little sadly at how hoarse his voice is. "Well, that's good. When can you come back?"

He audibly draws a breath, but doesn't say anything.

After several moments pass in silence I frown and say, "Gabe?"

"I'm so sorry," he says, sounding like he means it all the way to his bones, "but I can't come home yet— probably not for another few days. Something...something went really wrong out there. We think it might've been what killed Em and all those other Light people. We're staying to find out what we can about it."

Even though his tone concerns me greatly, I command myself to stay calm. "What went wrong? I thought you said you did what you went to do."

"We did. We did a great job with the Hellions, but there's something else." He hesitates before he says dimly,

"Marienne, there's something *worse* than the Hellions here."

A chill skates over my skin and burrows into my flesh.

Don't freak out, I order myself even as my breathing turns unsteady. *Shut up. Don't freak out. He doesn't need you to freak out on him right now.* "Tell me," I say with remarkable evenness.

He doesn't speak right away. I know he's still there, though, because I can hear him breathing. Every inch of me is growing more and more anxious by the second, leaving me unable to imagine how he must feel already knowing what he knows.

Finally he says, "We came in strong and laid the Hellions out easily. We were well-prepared and quick. Then all of a sudden we were soaring through the air. Like, literally soaring—something just knocked us off our feet out of nowhere and we were all catching air like we were fucking soccer balls or something. And then I hit the ground and it hurt *so* much. I couldn't even move, so I just laid there—I felt worse than I ever have, Marienne. I wondered if I was dying. That's how bad I felt. I can't even...."

I suck in a horrified breath.

He thought he was *dying?* Something hurt him that badly?

My vision starts blurring.

"I didn't know what was wrong. I didn't know what had happened. But then this guy started talking about how we'd all made a mistake going there. His voice was fucking awful, and *loud*—it went everywhere like he was talking into a microphone or something. And the things he said…honestly, it took me a minute to even figure out what he was talking about. I was confused as hell at first, but the more I listened…." He expels a breath. "He was talking about us—about Light people, and he didn't say good things about us. He said really *bad* things about us, and he knew exactly what he was talking about. He knew about us being what kills Hellions."

Hot tears spill down my cheeks and I shove the sleeve of my shirt across them.

"He said we've had power over them all this time, but that that's about to change. He said there are *armies* of Hellions building up where we can't see them and that they're planning to wreak fucking havoc on us. And he was serious." Gabe hesitates, and when he speaks again his words are strained and nervous. "I don't really know what he was, Marienne, but he's stronger than any Hellion I have ever fought. He had actual *powers*, supernatural powers, and he killed two of our guys with them. I only saw one of them die before I took off running and it was the worst fucking thing I've ever seen—and I swear to God, he didn't even lay a hand on him! He did it with his *mind* or something."

My heartbeat is wild. My breathing is erratic. My thoughts are taking off on a panicked rampage.

"And more are coming," he repeats, sounding a little stunned. "He said they're going to just overtake us and—I don't know, kill us or corrupt us or something and there won't be anything anyone can do. Not even Light people."

I frown so deeply it makes my head hurt. "What?" I finally ask. "How is that? We're—we're *built* to kill them."

"I know we are, but I don't know how to kill something like him," he confesses. "How could we possibly...? I mean, what the hell do you do to defend yourself against that?"

Defiance bursts through my distress like a firework through a black sky. I shake my head even though he can't see it. "No. *No*. There has to be a way to do it. Light blood is the Hellions' weakness and it might be their *only* weakness, but it's what maintains the balance. There *is* a balance, Gabe, so there's no way we're doomed to be unarmed and helpless against this. It's worse than the Hellions, but it's just something else evil, right? There has to be something that will help us balance *that* out."

He's silent for a few seconds before a long sigh leaves him. I must have annoyed him. I start preparing my defense, but then he says softly, "Marienne Rose, I love that mind of yours."

The defensiveness drops away as quickly as it popped up. Something much warmer seeps through me; leave it to Gabe to make me feel better when everything seems to be headed toward hell at warp speed. "Thank you, I guess."

"No, thank *you*. That really helped me. I mean, I knew talking to you at all would help me deal with all of this, but you did me one better." A short, much more Gabe-like chuckle drifts through the phone. "Reminded me who I am and what I do. What my life's about. All in, what, fifteen seconds?"

My throat tightens painfully, and I can't help the weak request. "Please don't go back to that place, Gabe. Please stay where you're safe."

"Oh, no, don't worry about that," he says gently, and I know he can hear my struggle not to burst into tears (again). "We're not going back there. We're just going to sit here at the Sanctum and try to sort out what happened and what was said. Things like that." After a long pause he murmurs, "I won't go back even for a second. I don't know how I got away the first time. I could still hear him laughing and I was terrified he was chasing me or going to see me running somehow and just...."

My chest aches and my body tenses up, wanting so badly to cry. "I don't even want to think about that."

"I don't either, but I can't seem to stop," he says sadly. "It's like waking up from a nightmare and remembering what happened in it, only these details haven't started going away. They're just stuck in my head. All of them."

I take a deep, shaky breath. "I'm *so* sorry you went through that. I wish I could help more." For a second I debate whether or not to say it, since he hasn't even been gone twenty-four hours. Then I decide, *Fuck it,* because this was no ordinary trip and apparently anything can happen. I admit, "I wish I was with you. I miss you."

Not sounding weirded-out at all, he tells me, "I miss you, too. I really do." Then he sighs. "My first impulse after I got away was to come right back to you. Fuck Dallas and fuck this turned-ass-backward plan."

I smile, but it's frail. "Yeah."

"But I would hate myself for coming back with nothing to go on. I owe you that. Wes owes B that, and we both owe it to everyone else."

I want to tell him he owes me nothing, but I understand what he means. It's not just for me—we're all in the Lightforce *together*. We're in the business of taking care of people who need to be taken care of. It doesn't matter if those people are Light or just human. So I just say, "I gotcha, Gabe."

He says delicately, "Yeah, you do."

My free hand scrambles to touch the necklace he gave me. The chain feels even more fragile in my trembling fingers. "You've got me, too."

"Thank you," he murmurs. "I wish I had you in my hands right now."

The ache that slinks through me is as warm and delightful as it is painful. "I wish that, too. Soon, huh?"

"Yeah." After a second he adds, "Not soon enough."

No fucking joke.

∽

"I can't believe this," Beatrix says, wiping her nose with a tissue. "The one time he gets away from me and something horrendous happens."

She was on the phone even longer than I was, and that was quite a while. When she finally shuffled back into the living room her eyes were red and she looked horrorstruck. Now we're curled up together on the couch, both sad for the loss of more Lightforce members and beyond worried about our own two guys.

Oh and yeah, confused as hell about the evil monster-man who murdered two people in mid-air with his mind.

I stroke *her* hair for a change, and find it's softer than I thought it'd be what with the bottom half being dyed teal. "Gabe said they won't be going back to that place," I

331

remind her. "They'll be safe at the Sanctum. I highly doubt the Hellions know where it is."

"You think?"

"Yeah, of course. They'd have attacked it long ago if they could have."

She sniffles. "I guess you're right. I'm just freaking the fuck out." She sounds like she's about to start bawling all over again.

"It's okay," I murmur. "They'll be okay. They'll be back in a day or two. Seems like forever, but it's not." I make a mental note to think back on my own words in thirty-six hours when I'm running up the walls with fear and impatience.

She lays her head on my shoulder and sighs, and I wish I could help her better. I won't pretend to know how she feels—Wes is her *husband*. I'm not trying to discount how I feel about Gabe, but we're not married to each other and haven't been together for years.

So there's not a lot I can do. I just brush her hair with my fingers and let her come to terms with the situation in her own time.

After a while she says, "Mari?"

"Hmm?"

"I..." she clears her throat, "...well, I wondered if you'd do something for me."

"Sure I will."

She shifts a little. "Could you sing me a song?"

Whaaaat. "You want me to *sing* you something?"

I feel her nod. "I always wanted siblings, you know, and I never got them. I kind of got a brother with Gabe, but I never thought I'd get a sister. And then we found you and I really love you so much." She takes a second to calm her wobbly voice. "And for as long as I can remember, one thing I wanted me and my sister to do is sing to each other. I always imagined it would be so nice. Something we did together when we were sad or happy."

My eyes are burning again, so I close them. It takes me several seconds to rein in the tears that are threatening to fall; I don't want to cry anymore, and I don't want to make my voice sound worse than it already does when I'm singing. When I feel stable I open my eyes again and say, "Okay, lay your head down and I'll sing you a song. But I'm not very good."

"I promise I'll love it." She moves to lay her head in my lap, facing away from me. For a moment I'm rocked by a weird, shifting, backward déjà vu thing. First I feel like we really are sisters, only I'm the older one, the strong one, the one taking care of the other. Then I imagine that she's Claire and I'm me as we were before our parents died, even though Claire and I never sang to one another.

I clear the thoughts and try to figure out a song. Soon I decide on, "Hello, I'm In Delaware" by City and Colour. It's sad, but it also feels hopeful to me. I sing the lyrics slowly and with less enthusiasm than I do when I'm by myself with the song turned way up. I don't try to make my singing sound any better, except that I forego the higher notes and stick to singing them lowly and more evenly. And while I sing I braid a section of Beatrix's hair, the way a sister should.

I get through the whole song. After I'm done I actually feel better myself. I'm not crying or anything. A few times I thought Beatrix might have been, but by the end of the song she's quiet and still except for her breathing. "How was that?" I whisper. But I figure out quickly that she's asleep. Something tells me it's because I helped her, not because I bored her, and that makes me smile a little.

I drop my head back against the couch and close my eyes. I try to think optimistic thoughts.

We'll take care of each other until Wes and Gabe come back.

They'll be back soon.

They're safe.

We can all get through whatever this is together.

Everything will be okay.

It at least works well enough to lull me to sleep.

<p>

Two days later, it's looking like training is as good for sadness and worry as it is for anger.

Beatrix has been appointed the temporary Defender trainer since Wes is out of town, meaning Thursday sparked off Trenton's training sessions. Even though I'm no longer in training myself and I'm of little help to the guy, Beatrix has insisted that I stick around while they're working. I'm guessing it's because she wants to keep an eye on me rather than let me walk around and kill Hellions by myself, and I don't fight her on it. I just chill in a corner of the training room and get some exercising in. I figure being done with Defender training doesn't mean I should slack.

We talk to Gabe and Wes a few times a day. Most of their time is being spent going over and over and over the event from the other night. I'm interested in the discussions, but I don't like to press Gabe about them because I know it's all still very raw for him. So we try to talk to each other about things that don't involve death, too.

Even though being in the training room and knowing Gabe is safe helps me not to lose my marbles, I'm starting to suffer from Loveliness Withdrawals. It's frustrating. I keep my phone out at all times so I'll know when he's trying to reach me, which means I spend a lot of time waiting for it to ring and it doesn't. When I sleep I have nightmares that something's happened to him, or that Wes dies and Gabe comes back and Beatrix hates me for it, and when I wake up I'm even more worried than before. But I don't know what's worse: having nightmares, or lying awake one night for what has to be whole hours because my wistful mind won't stop replaying every second of how he kissed me the day before he left.

On Saturday morning I wake up to a media message on my phone. It's a picture from Gabe, of him lying in his bed seemingly after recently waking up. Though it's mostly a picture of his head resting sideways on his pillow, I can see he's wearing a white t-shirt and I can't help thinking it looks nice against his skin. Then I move on to his face and it hurts me to see that it's scratched in more than a few places, that there's a scrape on his forehead and a bruise blooming on one cheekbone. But his eyes make up for it; they're soft and gorgeously green, and the gold lamplight adds a little bit of brightness to them. He's looking at the camera like he'd look at me if he was here. There's even a faint smile curving along his lips. It makes me want to cry.

I don't let myself cry, though. I just snap a similar picture of myself and send it back.

I don't know if he'll be able to call soon or when he'll even see the picture, so I don't wait around. I get out of bed and get dressed and then make a little bit of breakfast for me and Beatrix. My phone rings as we're leaving the house for the Sanctum and my pulse leaps with excitement, but it slows back down when I see the caller is Rafe.

"What's wrong?" Beatrix asks quickly, seeing my expression.

"Rafe's calling me," I sigh.

She rolls her eyes and turns on the heat in her car. "God only knows how this boy's balls are so big. Seriously. How is it possible he can't take ninety different hints?"

I chuckle and stuff my phone into my hoodie pocket. "I don't know." Rafe has been blessedly quiet and absent since I saw him at the university. I haven't gotten so much as a text from him, nor have I happened upon him again while out with Beatrix. I have to say I'm more than a little annoyed that he's picking back up on bothering me when I have so many other things to think about right now.

And damn him for trying to reach me *all day long*. By the time Trenton's training is over I've got twenty missed calls and fifteen unopened text messages from Rafe. That's thirty-five different times I thought Gabe was getting back to me, so each time I saw it wasn't him my disappointment grew and my irritation sparked hotter. So when Rafe calls for the twenty-first time as I'm walking into my room in the Sanctum, I answer with an explosive, "Holy *fuck*, why have you been blowing up my phone all day?"

"What the fucking hell, Mari!" he shouts into my ear. "What is your problem? How hard it is to answer even a single text message? I've been trying to get a hold of you all day!"

Immediately on the defensive, I snap, "Call me crazy for not wanting to hear you moan and groan about the other day like you always do! I'm pretty fucking tired of it, Rafe!"

"That's not even what I've been calling about! I've been calling because something's wrong with Claire!"

That shuts me right up.

He seizes the opportunity to keep bitching at me. "Oh, yeah, remember her? Your sister? Are you listening now? Do you care what I have to say now? You're so fucking pathetic, Mari, and selfish and I don't know why I've been trying this hard to get your attention. I should've just let you find out on your fucking own."

"What are you talking about?" I try to bite out, but his words are too foreboding.

"Your sister has been acting extremely strange for the past few days," he informs me. "At first I just brushed it off because she's looked sick and I know you two haven't been getting along as it is, and I thought maybe she's just upset that you jumped ship. But this morning she up and abandoned her apartment, including her furniture—didn't even lock the door behind her—*and* her fucking car. I caught her leaving with that dude with the yellow Corvette and I tried to talk to her about it because she looked like shit, not even happy or anything. And the whole time I was talking to her she was like a damn zombie. She wouldn't look at me, and the one time she did she clocked me in the fucking mouth."

"*What?*" I exclaim.

"I'm not repeating all of that," he says exasperatedly, like I even asked him to do that. "Fucking exercise that brain of yours for once."

"Oh, shut up about my decisions already. I don't need that from you right now."

"Well, yeah, you're right," he agrees hotly. "What you *need* is to find out what the hell is wrong with Claire, because maybe you don't give a shit about *me* anymore, but *she's* your family!"

I could rip my hair out, he makes me so mad; he doesn't know half of what I'm going through with Claire. It takes me several long seconds to clear my head enough to think about her instead of him. "So she renewed her lease last month and then this morning she bailed? Just walked out and left with Shaun?" *That dirty, no-good son of a bitch.*

"Yeah, so I'm telling you, something's wrong with her. She looked god-awful. Paler than usual and there were huge bags under her eyes—and her eyes looked really weird, by the way. I don't know what it was about them, but they were fucked. And she didn't say a single thing to me. Not even when she hit me."

"Ugh," I moan to myself.

"I don't know what's going on with her," he says, "but if anyone is gonna find out, it's you. Drag your pretty little eyes away from that bastard from the other day—"

"Rafe."

"—had his hands all over you like he has any right—"

"Shut the fuck *up!*"

"No, fuck that! I don't like him!"

"I do not care," I say slowly. "Now back to Claire. She said nothing to you at all?"

"No, and don't change the subject! You and that guy are—"

I hang up and call my sister. It rings and rings and rings and rings. Soon it hits her calm and collected voicemail recording, but I don't bother leaving her a message. I just change into clean clothes and go back up to the training room, where I left Beatrix.

I tell her what Rafe said. She agrees with me that Claire's behavior is weird, on top of how she attacked me before all crazy-like and then vehemently denied it. Beatrix says she'll drive me to the apartment to see if maybe Claire is there, and even though I absolutely *do not* want to risk running into Rafe, I take her up on the offer.

"Have you spoken to Wes today?" I ask her on the way over.

She inhales deeply and shakes her head. "Not really. He texted me that he loves me this morning."

"Aw. I got a little text, too." Thinking about Gabe's picture makes my chest ache. And my fingers, too, because *God*, what I'd give to be able to touch him right now.

I hope I don't humiliate myself when he gets back—or hurt him on accident. I like to think I'll be able to refrain from throwing such a big hug on him that I end up knocking him down, but honestly, there's no way to tell at this point.

Claire's Prius is in front of the apartment and the sight of it makes my stomach flip. Before I can decide what emotion is hitting me the strongest—relief or dread—I remember Rafe said she abandoned her car and left with Shaun. She's not here. I let loose an equally confused sigh and get us into the apartment.

Rafe was right about this, too: almost everything is where it should be. After taking several minutes to walk around the place I notice that only certain things are gone, and they're her personal items. Her closet and dressers are damn near empty. Her jewelry, perfume, and hair products have been swiped. Things that she might be able to find at Shaun's house—bedding, furniture, dishes, movies—are all still here. If Hellions even have normal houses, that is.

I cross my arms and stare at the pictures of Claire and her friends that are sitting on the mantle above the fireplace. "Huh," is all I can say even though my mind is full of questions and obscenities and fears.

"Sooooo," Beatrix says from beside me, "do you want my opinion?"

"Sure." I chew on the inside of my cheek.

"I think your sister is pregnant with a Hellion child."

My blood seems to suddenly have shards of ice in it.

"I think that's why she's been acting and looking so strange. Not just to Rafe, but to you—I think it's why she tried to claw your face off and then forgot about it. And didn't you say she was uncharacteristically angry during that last fight you had?"

I shrug a shoulder. "Yeah, but...I mean, I figured it was just her letting out all her pent-up emotions from the car accident."

"Very likely," she agrees. "Still I'd be willing to bet she's also being taken over from the inside. Sickness and mood swings are expected with pregnancies, but carrying a Hellion child isn't like carrying a normal one. We know what Hellions are like. We know they're nasty and how they operate and what their goals are and that they are capable of anything. And given how she left—" she gestures around, "—I'd say that Hellion she's with is more than a little bit responsible. I mean, she left behind some nice-ass electronics *and a Prius*. I think he's controlling her somehow, which especially makes sense if part of his evil is in her."

I swallow hard. Close my eyes. Try to let this sink in.

My first reaction is to insist that she's just got a regular pregnancy going on. Being sick and intense and emotional is part of the deal—Beatrix just said as much. It doesn't mean she's got a demon baby in her uterus.

But she hasn't been pregnant for very long, and look how bad she already is. I'd guess that carrying a Hellion child would ramp up the disadvantages of pregnancy in both intensity and pace.

The biggest factor in this whole situation is Shaun. Even if this baby is normal, I doubt he's going to brush Claire off. He'll probably keep trying until he gets what he wants out of her. He's malevolent, and his intentions are never anything but that. And as long as they're together Claire won't be herself.

"What do I do?" I finally ask.

"What *can* you do?" Beatrix asks back.

My heartbeat skips as an enticing thought touches me. "I can kill Shaun." *Oh, God, it could fix all of this.*

She links our arms together. "Excellent plan. I'm on board." She inhales deeply and exhales loudly. "Except that I don't know where he is. Do you?"

My body sags in disappointment. "Fuck no," I grumble.

"Have you tried calling your sister? Maybe we can work something up if we can get a hold of her."

"I called earlier and she didn't answer. I'll try her again." I do just that (and also notice Gabe hasn't called or texted while we've been pondering Claire's abrupt and bizarre domicile desertion), and the same thing happens as before. Goes to voicemail. "Nothing again."

"Hmm. Well, while we're here, do you need anything?" She starts wandering toward the kitchen, and I hear her open the refrigerator. "She left tons of food. Maybe we should take it with us."

"May as well," I say as I head to my room. "It doesn't look like she's coming back any time soon."

We package up a bunch of food and I grab an armful of stuff from my room. We head back to the Sanctum so I can drop off my belongings, and we put the food in the lounge for the time being. Then we leave again to do some Defender work.

Gabe calls while we're wandering around the mall. As has been happening for the past few days, Wes quickly follows suit, so Beatrix and I give each other some space while we talk.

After we greet each other he says lowly, "So, that picture you sent me. Is that what you look like in the mornings?"

The tone of his voice makes me blush. Ordinarily I'd be worried the picture turned out to be a bad idea, but he doesn't sound like he thinks that at all. I try not to sound too nervous when I say, "Um, yeah."

"Seriously?" He sounds kind of breathless. "Jesus Christ."

I fiddle with my hair. "I'm sorry."

He laughs once. "No. Don't apologize to me for being the best fucking thing I've ever laid eyes on."

I somehow manage to choke on my own air. I hold the phone away from my face and cough into the bend of my other arm, eyes watering and skin burning like it's on fire. *Holy dumb fuck,* I think. I can feel people staring at me like I'm in the process of turning into a zombie or something.

"Are you okay?" I hear Gabe asking when I get my phone back to my ear.

"I'm fine," I say, gulping past the sudden soreness in my throat. "I'm sorry. I'm fine."

"I didn't upset you, did I? I didn't mean to." He sounds genuinely concerned.

Now *I* laugh a little. "Uh, no—surprised me, yes. And I really loved your picture." I'm tempted to look at it again, but fuck that since I'm actually on the phone with the boy.

"Yeah?" he asks, sounding less worried. "I don't know why I didn't think to send you one sooner."

"That's okay. And yeah, it was wonderful even though seeing you hurt made me sad." I try to take a calming breath. "Every time I look at it, I feel like you're looking at me really."

A few moments pass before he says, "That's how I feel when I look at yours. Like you're right here in front of me."

"Like I could reach out and touch you," I agree, the words just a murmur.

"And kiss you," he murmurs back. "God, Marienne, it's a problem how badly I want to kiss you."

343

That's a problem I can identify with. I'm starting to think that if he values his personal space at all, I should warn him not to be alone with me for more than five seconds when he comes back. He's in another state and I can still practically feel his chest against my chest and his hands gripping my waist and his breath mingling with mine—

"Oh, God," I mumble.

"What?"

I remember our last visit to Grove Lane like it happened five minutes ago. How he took hold of me in the middle of the street and kissed me like I was his to kiss whenever and wherever he wanted. How we both moaned, not just me, when the kiss ramped up. How his fingertips dug into my hair while we both tried to own each other's mouth with our own. I breathe out, "Nothing," and sound unconvincing even to myself.

"No, what?" he presses. "Are you okay?"

Trying to think past my sudden insanity, I say, "No. Yes. Um." I rub at my face, which is growing hot. "You just...you shouldn't have mentioned kissing me, because now I can't quit imagining you doing it."

He exhales softly. "Is that what you're all worked up about?"

I scrunch my face up in embarrassment. "Mmhmm."

"Wow." His voice is starting to sound more like mine. "Think you'll still feel the same way about it when I come back?"

"Oh, yeah, you might want to keep your distance," I inform him weakly. "It'll probably be even worse."

"No, I won't want to keep my distance. That's for damn sure." His voice drops lower. "I'm already tired of distance. I'll want to grab you up and get you alone somewhere so I can remind my hands of what you feel like and kiss you better than you've ever been kissed in your life, even by me. I want to make you all breathless in person because through the phone isn't good enough. I want to see that for myself. I want you like that right in front of me."

I spot an empty bench at the exact moment I realize I'm in the *way* wrong place to be having such a leg-weakening conversation. I hurry to sit down and then drop my head into my empty hand, trying not to picture all the ways that scenario could play out. I'm ridiculously unsuccessful. "So," I murmur, "it turns out the middle of the mall isn't a good place for me to be having these kinds of thoughts. I seriously had to sit down just now."

A moment of silence falls and then he laughs throatily. "You're in the mall right now? Are you blushing like crazy? I bet you are. I bet your hand is going crazy in your hair, too."

I tune in to my fingers raking through the hair falling over my shoulder, and I yank them back with my own laugh. "Oh, God, you're omniscient or something."

I can't get enough of his laugh. I love it. I can picture with perfect clarity his grin and the way his shoulders are shaking. "I'm sorry," he finally says. "I'll stop voicing my daydreams to you while you're in public." He chuckles again.

"I'm as guilty as you are," I assure him, trying to subtly fan my warm cheeks. "But I have some not-wonderful things to say about my sister if you want to hear them."

"Okay, good idea. Take my mind off of you for a minute."

I smile, but it goes away when I start telling him about Rafe's call and my visit to the apartment. Then I tell him Beatrix's opinion on the whole thing.

When I'm done he says, "Okay, Marienne, listen," and his amused, sexy, not-worried attitude is gone. "Are you listening?"

"Yeah, of course," I say, hoping he's got some good ideas. I need some pretty badly.

"*Do not*," he says slowly, "try to hunt Shaun down."

16
Gabe

Nothing snaps me out of the peace, warmth and deliciousness of Marienne Land quite like a Hellion.

She says, "What?" and her surprise is audible.

I concede, "Not without me, anyway. Don't go without me."

"Why not?" The question sounds more curious than exasperated. "I wouldn't go by myself. Beatrix would go with me."

"I think he's too dangerous."

"But I'm a Defender." I can practically see the quizzical look on her face. "Beatrix even more so."

"You're right," I agree, "but he's clearly the calculating type. He's a Hellion who has been *dating* your sister. And think about that note he left you. I wouldn't put it past him to be waiting for you—expecting you, even—to come after Claire and that's not good. That means he could have something planned for if you show up."

"Well, if I just call Claire and tell her I want to talk without him there...."

I shake my head even though she can't see it. "I hate to say this to you, but we have to assume she's on his side now. I think it would be most unwise to trust her with anything, especially your safety."

I can hear the air whoosh out of her lungs. "Are you...really?" She sounds crestfallen.

"Really," I tell her softly. "That might make you angry and even though I don't want that, I'd understand because she's your sister. But you know we can't trust

Hellions, which means we can't trust Shaun. We can't trust him not to have some kind of influence over her that he could use to harm you—I mean, you and B have already agreed he's gotten into her head somehow because she took off with him like she did."

"I...yeah...."

After many moments of her not saying anything else, I start feeling bad. I'm not trying to order her around or anything, nor am I saying she's stupid or wrong for wanting to go after Shaun. I just don't want her playing into his hands, even with Beatrix there.

"Hey, I'm sorry," I tell her sincerely. "I'm not trying to boss you around."

"I know," she murmurs. "You're just thinking more clearly than I am."

I frown. "Well, I understand where you're coming from with all of this. And, honestly, if you'll just wait for me to get back, I'll go with you if you still want to. Shit, all four of us can go."

Sounding hopeful, she says, "Really?"

"Yeah, really. I just don't want you girls going when Wes and I are more than three hundred miles away from you."

A little laugh reaches my ears. "Again with the practical thinking. I'm starting to feel like an idiot."

"Oh, no," I say quickly. "Don't. You're not an idiot at all."

"Not even a little bit?"

"Not even a little bit."

I can hear her smiling when she says, "Okay, then."

Feeling more at ease, I lie back on my bed and ask, "How is Trenton's training going?"

"Fine, I think. I kind of zone out while I'm in there. I saw him do a backflip this morning, though."

"A backflip?" I repeat. "That sounds awesome. Maybe he can teach me how to do one."

"You mean to tell me you can't already do one? I thought you could do everything."

I make a puzzled face like she's here to see it. "I never claimed to be able to do everything."

"Well, no. I just thought that."

"You thought wrong," I say with a laugh. "I can speak a little bit of French, though."

"Huh? Do it!"

"*Bonjour, mon nom est Gabe et j'adore le fromage.* That means, '*Hello, my name is Gabe and I love cheese.*'"

Marienne bursts into loud laughter. It warms me and makes me laugh, too.

"Oh, man," she says. "You gotta teach me some of that."

"I'm still waiting on a drawing lesson," I tease her.

"Okay, okay," she says brightly. "When you come back, I'll teach you how to draw something and you can teach me how to say something in French."

"It's a deal."

"Awesome." She breathes deeply before she asks, "How are things going there?"

Disappointment skates through me. "Not that great. I mean, no one's gone back out or anything. We just haven't come up with anything new to add to the list."

Smith and Cates still haven't come back, and even after a couple of days we have only the barest of details about the tattooed man. We put everything down on paper, from what he said, to our thoughts on what he could be planning, to where he might've come from. We noted that he's stronger than normal Hellions at least power-wise. We wrote out our thoughts on the warning he gave us. Although we agreed that we should take him seriously, we aren't afforded many proactive courses of action—the best we can do is plan for more encounters with Hellions since he said there will be a lot of them around. Lon from Armaments has been working like crazy to create new weapons. And, at least at the Dallas Sanctum, plans have been made for those who don't know how to shoot a gun or who simply need a license to get those things taken care of.

It occurred to me at one point that a Hellion gateway probably had something to do with the arrival of the tattooed man, especially since everyone insisted they'd never seen the likes of him before. When Wes and I spoke to Bartholomew in private about it, he seemed to think it was a plausible idea except that he's not aware of a gateway around here. We tried to tell him it could be hidden somewhere like the one in Fayetteville, but that was when he shut us down. "Even if there is one here," he said, "I'm not sending anyone out to look for it. It doesn't matter how he got here—only that he *is* here."

But we couldn't, and still can't, help thinking it *does* matter. If he came through a gateway, there's no guessing what might follow him or what might come out of the gateway at home—or *how many* what's.

I tell Marienne, "It's frustrating to be as in the dark as we are."

"Well, I think you've done a great job," she says.

"How?" I ask in soft disagreement. "We've got hardly anything to go on."

"That's because you spent hardly any time with that man. No one expects you guys to know everything there is to know about something you encountered for five tiny minutes."

The optimism brings a little smile to my face.

"You've got that list, right?" she continues. "That's a hell of a lot more than what you'd have if you never came across that guy. And didn't you tell me yesterday that Bartholomew wants to contact as many other Directors as possible to fill them in on what happened? That would be a huge help, too, Gabe."

"Yeah, you're right," I concede, wishing I could look into those eyes of hers while she's talking sense to me. "But that tattooed man seemed really sure that shit's about to hit the fan and we wanted to at least have an idea of what'll happen. And we have *no* idea. I mean, if he's walking around with powers like that, how can we make any kind of prediction? And what if the other Directors aren't happy with such incomplete information?"

"It won't always be incomplete, Gabe. I still think it'll come to us." Her voice comforts me. "I still think we'll figure it out. Maybe it'll just take a little bit of time—Rome wasn't built in a day and all that. And a tiny warning is better than no warning, by the way. I'm sure other Light people would agree."

I chuckle. "How are you so calm?"

"I'm far from calm." She sighs. "I just know that being Light has fit with me like a puzzle piece and I don't believe it can be discounted this easily."

I sigh, too. "I don't believe it, either. This is all just so...weird. And scary." I stretch out on my bed and my sore body protests. "But I guess I should be used to it by now.

Lately I've been learning that I don't have everything figured out like I thought I did."

"Yeah?"

"Yep." I relax my body again and my eyes drift closed, and I abruptly realize how tired I am. "Started the day I first saw you."

"You were scared of me?" Although teasing, her voice is softer and slower, like she's thinking sweet thoughts. Or like she can tell I'm about two minutes from falling asleep. "That's no good."

I smile and admit, "You know what? I *was* a little scared." As soon as she took off running, I feared I'd never find her again, never even get to know her name.

She laughs quietly and then asks, "What time do you have to go back to the meeting?"

"Um...5:30."

"Okay, well, it's almost 4:00 now. Why don't I let you go? You sound like you could use a nap."

Mmm, she knows me so well. "But I like talking to you. It's all I've got. Unless you count my thoughts, and they're pretty enjoyable, but the real you is way better."

"Oh, I know what you mean," she assures me, "but we can talk later tonight. Get some sleep."

The phone is already feeling heavy in my hand. "Mmm...okay."

"Okay, babe," she murmurs.

Ohhhh, sweet, she called me...or...did she just say my name...? Some part of my brain makes the executive decision to ask her later. "Bye, gorgeous."

I think I hear her laugh again, and then the call is over and I'm drifting off.

When I wake up it's 4:42 and someone is knocking on my door. Even though I'd like some more sleep, I feel better than I did and I get off my bed without complaint. I find Wes on the other side of my door, and he tells me someone brought pizza for everyone and that it's in the conference room.

We head over there together and I ask him, "How's B?"

"She's fine. She said Trenton's doing well in training and Mari is doing well holding *her* together."

"Huh?"

He smiles. "She said Mari is, like, the sweetest thing. She gets up and cooks breakfast every morning and she actually sang B to sleep the night we called to tell them about all this shit. My woman was flipping her fuck and Mari calmed her down."

"Oh, God," I moan, "is there anything about her that's not awesome? How is it possible that she's so *awesome?*"

He laughs now. "Well, I'm sure you'll find *something* about her that'll annoy the piss out of you. B annoys the piss out of me when she leaves wet towels wadded up on the bathroom floor. Like, goddamn, woman. At least spread the fucking thing out."

I snort. "Not much of a deal-breaker, there."

"I didn't say it's a deal-breaker. I said it's not awesome." He claps me on the shoulder. "But she still goes with me. Maybe Mari just goes with you, man. It happens."

I can't admit out loud to him how much that thought thrills me, so instead I ask, "Was B on your mind all the time when you first met her?"

"*All* the time, dude." He rolls his eyes, but he smiles. "Not always pleasant, especially when I was trying to get shit done and all I could think about was me and her...uh..." he clears his throat, "...nevermind. She's like your sister and you probably don't wanna hear it."

I chuckle. "Ugh, yeah, keep it to yourself." I don't want to hear about their sex life. I already have to suffer their PDA—like the time I went with them to shop for a new bed and they made out on every single mattress in every single store we visited. I shudder now just thinking about it.

"That happening to you?" he asks obliviously. "Mari putting up a permanent residence in your head?"

I nod slowly. "It's the weirdest and coolest thing ever."

"I heard that." He sighs. "It gets better and worse, I'll go ahead and tell you that now."

"How do you mean?"

He shrugs. "Well, I don't even know if I could explain it. It's just how it goes. The good parts turn incredible and the bad parts have the ability to fucking cripple you."

We're back in the conference room now, so I say, "Oh." I don't really know what else to say, anyway. It sounds like something you just figure out for yourself.

The cool thing about having so many guys in one place is that we're easy as hell to feed. Several large pizza boxes are open on the conference table, full of food. No muss, no fuss. Wes and I both get a big plateful and kick back in our chairs to wolf it down. I don't know if it's the food or the need to spend our break not thinking about the issues at hand, but the room is quiet even though most of us are in here.

Rather quickly the time approaches for us to start the meeting, but I'm not too disappointed. I feel pretty good, circumstances being what they are. However, there's a certain amount of tension in the room when we all get settled, and I glance around to see where it's coming from. Wes and I are pretty relaxed and May seems to be lost in his thoughts. One good look at Thompson, Simon and Reibek tells me it's them.

Indeed, Reibek crosses his arms and says, "So, look. I think it's time we go back."

Bartholomew clarifies, "Back to the farm building?"

Thompson speaks now. "The three of us agree we have too little information and that if we go back with the intention of listening in, not fighting, maybe we'll find out more."

"I don't think that's smart," I politely disagree.

"It's our only option."

"Not true. We can just wait and see what happens. We don't have to purposely endanger ourselves."

"Look, man," he says a little irritably, "we *don't* have any other options. You're kidding yourself if you think sitting here hashing everything out eighty times is going to benefit anyone. And it's kind of our job to handle the dangerous parts, remember?"

"And what if you get out there," Wes interjects, "and you don't come back? You're *really* not gonna benefit anyone if you're dead."

Thompson shrugs. "We don't think they'll expect us to come back after what happened."

"Or maybe they *are* expecting it. Maybe they're thinking—and they wouldn't be wrong—that those of us who survived are having a hard time making a sandwich out of the breadcrumbs they tossed us."

Reibek speaks up again. "Hey, if you and your buddy don't want to go, don't go. But *I'm* going."

Thompson says, "So am I."

Simon nods his agreement, but says nothing.

"May, what are your thoughts?" Reibek asks.

The man sighs tiredly and shakes his head. "I don't think going is a good idea."

"Aw, come *on*," Thompson groans. "I thought you wanted to fight for your brother-in-law!"

I say, "Just because he doesn't want to take a stroll through where the guy died—"

"No, you know what?" Reibek talks over me, holding up his hands. "This is just fine. It's fine. This is our town, anyway." He gestures between himself and his other two guys, all three looking stony. "I don't expect *you* to be willing to do everything you can for it."

Wes laughs wryly from beside me. "Don't insult us, man. We're not opposed to this because we don't live here. It's got nothing to do with that."

"Yeah?" His eyebrows lift. "I bet if all of this was happening in Fayetteville and your pretty little wife was in immediate danger, you'd man up and do what had to be done."

Wes's forehead creases with a frown. He leans forward and drops his elbows onto his knees, looking at the other man like he's fifteen instead of older than him. "Difference of opinion, fella," he says. "I don't believe walking into our enemy's front yard is a smart move this time, so I'm not gonna do it. And if you wanna bring my wife into it, I assure you this decision *is* me manning up. I'm pretty goddamn sure she doesn't want me risking my life for something that I *don't* feel has to be done, on top of it hardly being worth what it might cost me."

"You think she'd agree with you on every bit of that?" Reibek still looks unconvinced. "You think she'd agree that her husband should just sit by idly when he could be doing his job as a member of the Lightforce? A job that only the people in this room have the ability to do?"

Wes stands up and pulls his phone out. "Call her and ask her," he suggests. "And put her on speakerphone because I wanna hear the verbal ass-beating she's gonna give you when you imply that I'm sitting here in fucking Texas doing nothing like a lazy piece of shit instead of being at home with her."

I lean an elbow on the armrest of my chair, trying to subtly cover my grin with my hand.

Bartholomew finally speaks up. "Let's all calm down." He turns to Reibek. "Maybe it's for the best that the room is split like it is. That way we've got people going and people staying here. Both are useful."

Reibek shakes his head but says nothing.

Wes sits back down and Bartholomew looks at him, then at me and May. "I told you the other day I wouldn't try to ask you to go along with any extra recon, and I meant it." His expression says he's sorry for his guys trying to force us into it. "Your decisions are yours to make and I respect them."

I nod once at him, and Wes says, "Appreciated, sir." May says nothing.

Bartholomew sighs and addresses the rest of the room. "If you want to go back I won't stop you, but I ask that you hold off for another hour or so." He clears his throat. "I've spoken with several Directors in the Ark-La-Tex area over the past day or two. Even though I didn't have much information for them, they did appreciate that I reached out to them. They're informing their members and other Directors they know, creating more weapons, bringing in extra food and water just in case it's needed— even if this all turns out to be a whole lot of nothing, none of us see the harm in trying to be prepared. Like us, they all say they've never encountered a man like this, but one Director did say he's been having a bigger problem with Hellion attacks than he's had in the past...."

He continues on like this for a little while. I consider it favorable news. I agree with Marienne that telling people what we know is a good idea, and I'm pleased that they're receiving it well. I can only hope that we're over-preparing—that even though I'm sure it won't turn out to be *'a whole lot of nothing,'* maybe the tattooed man is bluffing. Maybe he's just trying to scare us. Maybe he can't actually use those powers all the time, leaving us mainly with Hellions we already know how to defeat. Or something.

Fear is an effective weapon—a poisonous one, a deadly one. And if anyone knows how to use it, it's someone from the Dark world.

A little over an hour passes before Bartholomew finishes talking. He gives Reibek, Thompson and Simon the opportunity to figure out their plan. They seem to have most of it worked up already, and before long they're moving out. Once they're gone Wes stands and says to me,

"I'm thinking we should have a drive-around and kill some Hellions."

I'm about to say that sounds good when May speaks up. "Care if I go?"

"If you're up for it, we'd be glad to have the company," I tell him.

"Yeah, man," Wes agrees.

He got out of the clearing the other night with both his dagger and the extra one he received, so he hands the latter to me. May has his dagger, too, so we head out within minutes.

We're not even to the Jeep yet before we start noticing Hellions. They're relatively spread out from one another; one is following a teenage boy who's too busy listening to headphones to notice, and a couple of others are just lingering by storefronts. One seems to be studying a Mercedes someone parked in front of a nearby bank. Though there aren't that many compared to what we found at the farm building, it's a noticeable change.

May says quietly, "I don't remember there being this many the last few times we came up."

"Yeah," Wes says slowly, "that's because there *weren't* this many before."

So, yeah, the tattooed man meant it when he said we'd see an increase in Hellion numbers.

We quickly decide who's going where and then we split up. Wes gets in the Jeep and drives off to park out of sight. I head down toward the bank on foot and May wanders to the other side of the street, where the teenage boy is pulling out his phone and slowing to a stop, still unaware of the Hellion lurking behind him.

The one I'm headed toward is trying to look inconspicuous next to the Mercedes, but I've been watching him alternate between glancing at the bank entrance and peering into the empty car. He's going to try to steal it, I'm sure—not the worst crime I've caught a Hellion committing, but that means nothing to me. So even when he starts wandering innocently away from the car, for which a well-dressed man is heading after leaving the bank, I follow him down the otherwise boring sidewalk. A cold wind blows, and in what I assume is an effort to seem harmless he crosses his arms against his chain-bound chest and says to no one in particular, "Damn, I can't believe how cold it is out here!"

I think he's lame, but I take a leaf out of his book and act like I'm not up to anything. I cross my own arms and start walking a little faster, like I want to get where I'm going as quickly as possible. I even keep a fair amount of distance between him and me so he won't think I'm following him if he turns around.

But he doesn't turn to glance around, and it would've benefited him to be sketchy enough do so. He's trying too hard to look normal, so he doesn't see me snake the dagger out of my jacket and, at the last second, step sideways so that I'm right behind him. He senses my presence and tenses up all too late, right as I drive the blade into him. It's one of my quicker kills; he's dead in a second, not having made a single sound.

I step around his disappearing body like it's nothing more than trash on the ground and keep walking.

Wes calls after a few minutes to say he and May cleared out the others we spotted, and I tell him I killed that one plus another I saw around a corner. The two of them show up in the Jeep and I get in and we start off again.

After almost an hour we've got fourteen kills between us. By 8:45 we're at twenty-six. After we hit thirty-five I call Grayhem.

"You need to really keep an eye on things there," I tell him. "The Hellion-to-Light people ratio around here is way off. Three of us have killed thirty-five Hellions in two and a half hours. Maybe it's just Dallas since this is where the tattooed guy is, but the tree house where you are is what concerns me."

"Funny you should call and tell me this," he says, not sounding very amused. "Beatrix and Mari just walked out of my office. They've also seen an increase in Hellion kills in the last few hours. Not quite the number you've got, but still."

Hearing her name makes me ache.

"And I don't know if it has anything to do with that or not," he continues, "but our new Gatherers have found two white Radiances since last night."

I blink slowly. "*Wow.*"

Speaking of white Radiances, I look out the window and see the familiar glow of one walking into a gas station. I tap Wes on the shoulder and point the person out, and he gets his phone out. After a few seconds I hear him say, "Hey, it's Wes Avery. You've got a white Radiance at the gas station on the corner of...."

I tune in to Grayhem saying, "We're doing fine here, Gabe, so if you two need to keep working there I understand. But if things are going to keep picking up, I may be asking you to come on back pretty soon."

"I'm not sure how much longer we're planning to be here, anyway." I fill him in on the Dallas guys' insistence that we need to investigate the farm building more, and tell him what Wes's and my stance on that is. He agrees that going back there wasn't the best idea he's ever heard, and that truly maybe we've lent as much assistance as we can right now. After another reminder that he'd be glad to see us back any time, he calls off. I hang up, too, to find that Wes and May have spotted a group of six Hellions and are trying to plan out how the three of us can handle it.

We expect it to take a little longer than our other kills, and the expectation is met. We come out of the fight with a couple of bumps and some really terrible-smelling stuff on my jeans from one of them, but it's a victory. And that leaves us at forty-one dead Hellions.

I feel glad that we're preventing forty-one Hellions' worth of bad shit from happening until I remember there are many more than that still walking free.

$\sim$

We get back to the Sanctum at 10:45 and are just filling Bartholomew in on our evening when Reibek, Simon and Thompson walk in.

"How'd it go?" Wes asks.

Thompson levels an annoyed look on him, and then on me. "Well, we're not dead."

"I can see that," Wes says.

"Can you? Good. Just making sure you caught on that nothing went horribly wrong like you two were convinced it would."

I roll my eyes.

Bartholomew looks interested, though. "What did you find out?"

Thompson's annoyed look stays in place, but he turns it on the ceiling. Simon says, "Nothing. No one was there at all."

"That's right," Reibek speaks up, jaw working. "We snuck out there extra-carefully, didn't see a thing, decided to wait a little longer." He shakes his head. "Nothing."

So they were just sitting in the dark out on some farmland while the three of us were fighting a stupid number of Hellions. That's cool.

"I wonder why the place was empty," Bartholomew muses.

"Probably because every Hellion in Dallas was crawling the streets instead of hiding out," May deadpans.

The other Defenders look at him questioningly.

But Bartholomew says seriously, "Yes, now that you say that, I'm sure that's why."

"What are you talking about?" Simon asks.

The Director motions to us. "They decided to do a little headhunting while you three were out. They killed...well, how many was it again?"

"Sixty-two," we all say together.

The others stare at us. After many long moments Reibek says, "What? Seriously?"

"Wouldn't dream of making that up," I promise him.

"Didn't you see them when you went up?" May asks. "Obviously there weren't sixty-two of them outside our building, but the ones that were there weren't exactly hiding."

Thompson scratches the back of his neck, looking confused. "No, I...I don't guess I was paying attention." The other two don't look like they're in any position to disagree.

I can't help but laugh. Though I don't guess it's really funny, it blows my mind that not only did these guys run off on a boneheaded and utterly fruitless quest, they also completely ignored their real and immediate duties in the process.

"What's funny?" Reibek snaps.

I chuckle and shake my head. "Nothing. I'm tired. I'm going to bed."

Wes shuffles out of the office behind me. Bartholomew calls, "Good work tonight," after us, and we wave our thanks and continue on.

"How fucking long were they gone?" Wes asks when we're out of earshot of the others. "As long as we were, right? And they spent all that time just sitting out there?"

"Guess so."

"*Dude*," he groans. "So not worthy of those attitudes they've got going on."

"I don't even know why they're mad at us. I mean, shit, when we left home we didn't even know we were coming here to fight. And here we are catching glares because we don't want to go offer ourselves up to the enemy a second time."

"An enemy like none we've ever faced."

"Exactly."

"Well, I stand by my instincts. And I'd say it's a damn good thing I stayed here—and you, too, and May—

because if all of us had gone back out there…I mean, we took out *sixty-two* Hellions in just a few hours."

I nod. "I wouldn't have stayed out there all that time, though. I don't know why they didn't call it sooner."

"No shit."

I'm glad when my room comes into view. Despite the nap I took earlier and our lack of strenuous physical activity over the past few days, I'm tired. It's probably leftover fatigue from that night in the clearing plus stress and, of course, this night we had tonight.

Like he knows how I feel, Wes yawns and says, "All right, man. See ya."

"Later."

I take a quick shower before I call Marienne. My bed is even more comfortable than it was earlier, and I wish it wasn't so. I don't want to be tired while I'm talking to her, especially not for the second time in one day.

When I tell her about my night, she gasps loudly. "Are you kidding?"

"Not even kidding," I say.

"God. And I thought me and Beatrix kicked ass."

I laugh. "You did."

She laughs, too. "I may not be good with numbers, but I know sixty-two is bigger than twenty-five or whatever we got."

"Come on. It's not a competition. And I'm *glad* you aren't being overrun with Hellions like these people."

"Mmm, and I wish you weren't there to deal with all of them."

I smile. "Well, I'm ready to come back to Fayetteville. I'm going to see about leaving tomorrow."

"Really?" She sounds relieved.

"Yeah, I think we've done all we can do here, barring going back to the place from the other night. Which, by the way, the Dallas guys did tonight and it yielded absolutely no results."

"Uh, okay," she says derisively. "If they're going to start up with that, then yeah, just come back."

"My thoughts exactly." I tell her about the tense meeting we all sat through earlier.

She tsks. "I'm sorry they were rude to you, Gabe."

"Not a big deal." I have a thought that makes me grin. "Though I wouldn't mind watching you slap someone else across—"

The room shakes and I stop talking.

"Hmm?" she asks after a moment.

The hell was that? "Uh...." I wait to see if anything else happens. After several seconds of nothing, I shake my head a little. "I'm sorry. I must have imagined—" It happens again more forcefully and I sit up in my bed. "There it is again."

"What is it?"

Again.

I throw back my blanket and stand up out of bed, immediately on alert. "Something's happening." I dash toward my clothes.

"Huh?" she asks, worry coloring her tone. "Like what?"

"I don't know." The floor trembles under me as I pull my jeans on. "All I know is something is shaking this entire place, and we're underground, so...."

I hear shouts in the hallway.

"Shaking the—? Like an earthquake? But Texas doesn't get those, right?"

"I don't think so." I start yanking on my socks.

"Well, I...oh—Gabe." Her voice turns fearful. "Could it be him? The tattooed man? Could he be doing something to the city?"

I freeze for a second as the words threaten to shut down my mind. Then I blink slowly and say, "Oh, *shit*. Maybe. You might be right."

"Wait, no," she says quickly. "I don't want to be right!"

The place won't stop shaking. I'm having trouble stepping into my shoes.

Or maybe that's because *I'm* shaking.

"Well, he said—he acted like they were going to attack us soon, right? And it's been a few—and he can probably *do* anything—" The details are falling into place in my head, but I can't get all of them out of my mouth. I grab my jacket. "All those Hellions! He said there'd be more and there were!"

"Okay, all right! It's all right," Marienne tells me even though her voice is full of alarm. "Just take a breath and try to figure out what you can do—"

Someone starts banging on my door as I'm stuffing my wallet into my pocket. "Come on, man! We gotta go!" I hear them bellow. It's Wes. He sounds frantic.

That is not good.

Over the din I barely hear Marienne say desperately, "Gabe, be careful! Keep yourself safe!"

"I'm coming home!" I tell her as I fling open the door. "Right now!" Wes bolts down the hallway and I race after him with tense muscles and unsettled bones. When she doesn't say anything I ask loudly, "Did you hear me?" Still nothing. "Hey! Marienne!" As I tip sideways from another quake, I look at my phone and realize the connection is gone. "Oh, damn it!"

"What the hell is happening?" Wes demands.

"I don't know!"

We don't encounter anyone else on our way upstairs, but once we burst into the store above the Sanctum other people come into view. I see Simon, Thompson and some people I don't know peering outside. My eyes are attracted to the flickering orange glow outside the building and before I even get to the windows to pinpoint what it is, my stomach drops painfully.

A thunderous boom sounds and the building shakes worse than it did when we were underground, has us stumbling to a stop against the front counter while dust drifts down from the ceiling and merchandise in the store rattles. We're close enough to see outside now and as I look out, my blood runs cold.

The night is *burning*.

Fear grabs me tight with invisible hands that I can't wrench free of.

"Oh, God," Wes says. "Gabe, we have to go."

"Hey!" Thompson interjects desperately. "You can't leave!"

Wes is already starting for the door with me on his heels. "Watch us."

"This isn't some investigation like earlier! This is *real!* You can't bitch out this time, we need—"

The door slamming shut behind me cuts him off.

Wes and I dash for the Jeep. I'm bombarded with sensation, yet I can't focus on anything but running. I can't fully take in the fire, the smoke, the sparks, the lack of autumn chill in the air, the state of the buildings around us, where the next ground-shaking boom is coming from. I can only think about getting out of here.

Almost there. My lungs suck in the pungent air as I run. *Almost there.*

An abysmal, knee-weakening laugh like low thunder reverberates from somewhere I can't place. A laugh I know and wish like fuck I didn't.

My hand closes around the door handle on the passenger side. *Get in! Don't look around! Get in!*

We're in. We're going. Music from earlier is blaring from the speakers. Another powerful boom sounds. My thoughts are deafening. My heart is running at a million miles an hour.

But we both suck in a breath when that unforgettable voice seems to whisper right behind us, "You are not prepared."

An earsplitting blast sounds and the Jeep jerks out of control and—

17
Marienne

Being Light has taught me a very important skill. I have used it many times since Gabe left for Dallas, and before then during my training days. Some part of me felt its presence the day I first saw him, and even the very first time I saw a Hellion back in August, but I didn't know quite what it was then. Now it's an order blaring through my mind.

Fight through your fear.

It's not easy. Parts of me are in direct opposition to standing up straight and getting things done. But there are things that *have* to be done—like telling Beatrix what happened, and calling Grayhem, and getting me and Beatrix dressed so we can leave her house, and actually leaving the house. I even drive her car because she's not in a strong place of her own. In fact, she's in pieces.

No, it's not easy, but I do it. I do everything. And I do it without stopping to curl into a ball and cry.

I don't expect to be able to persevere forever. But I'll be damned if I'm going to let my darker thoughts overtake me before I've done my part.

When we get to the Sanctum, Grayhem is standing in the receiving room with two older men I've never seen. I briefly wonder if they're the ones who live here like me; it would explain how they beat everyone else here. "Ladies," Grayhem greets us gravely as he flips through the channels on the TV. "We're trying to see if Dallas is on any of the news stations."

"Is it?" Beatrix asks desperately, her tear-stained face pinched with worry.

"Not yet, but if it only happened within the hour they may not have had a chance to broadcast anything."

"Do you need me to do anything?" I ask him. "Make any calls?"

He smiles thinly at the TV. "No, dear, but thank you. I called Mark and Red and told them to make a few calls of their own. And Tye and Anton here helped spread the word, too."

I direct a quick wave at the two of them and they nod back politely.

"Did someone call—?" Beatrix starts right as the door opens and Trenton walks in. "Oh, speaking of," she amends with a relieved sigh.

"Hey," he says, looking between her and me as he drops a full backpack onto the floor. "This really happening? I was told to get out of bed, pack a bag with clothes and some food, and get here fast because that warning from the other day might be coming true."

Despite my resolution to be tough, I find that I can't answer him for some reason. Beatrix is just as unsuccessful. So Grayhem says, "Thus far it's kind of like an educated guess. We're trying to catch something on the news about it."

Trenton rakes a hand through his hair and I realize he looks like he really did make haste to get here—one of his shoelaces is untied and his hoodie is inside-out. "All right. Need me to do anything?"

Grayhem shakes his head and sighs. "Not yet."

There isn't much for any of us to do, so we do a lot of waiting. When we finally spot news about Dallas on the

TV, it's 1:30 in the morning and there are thirteen of us in the room instead of six.

"Reports are saying the city of Dallas, Texas is burning," the female newscaster says in her too-calm voice, "and has been for a couple of hours now. Allegedly it began when bombs started going off in the heart of the city—"

A strangled noise leaves Beatrix and she grabs my hand. I squeeze back, trying not to freak out even knowing that the Sanctum there wasn't located in some suburb. It was *in* Dallas.

"—unable to get any information from people inside Dallas itself due to the destruction—"

A video taken from the air flashes onto the screen and pure horror rips through me.

"Oh my God," Beatrix wails as the others in the room gasp or cuss.

Where there should be dark streets and car headlights and lit-up buildings and business logos and billboards, there is nothing but bright, violently blazing fire. Nothing but furious flames of the hottest colors reaching high into the sky and crawling outward and devouring everything. It's unlike anything I've ever seen.

"There we have a clip of the city," the newscaster says. "As we can see, the fires are raging and totally taking out everything. We've been told that emergency services are being called in from other areas to help with the damage as well as the certain injuries and probable deaths of any people caught in this inferno."

They play the video on a loop for minutes that stretch into eternity, and it's like a car wreck none of us can look away from. I stare at the blazes for so long that when a second video replaces the first my eyes still see the billowing flames on the screen, only in inverted colors. It takes me a few long seconds to adjust to the darkness of the new clip. There are actual people in this one, and as I regain my focus my heart leaps savagely into my throat. "Holy—"

Beatrix lets out a choked sob.

The rest of the room falls dead silent.

"This just in, viewers," the newscaster says. "Here we have a very special live interview with some witnesses to the horrible bombings—Greg, are you there?"

The male reporter on the left side of the video looks at the camera with wide, energized eyes and after a few seconds he nods. "Yes, Suzanne, I'm here with quite the opportunity, indeed, to find out what's been going on. In our attempt to get closer my crew and I came across these three watching the chaos from up here." He gestures behind him to where Dallas burns a safe distance away. "Guys, can you tell us about what you've seen?"

The tattooed man has a Hellion standing on either side of him, but I can't even focus on those two. My eyes are only on him and his spine-chilling face. His spiky red tattoos contrast with his white skin and pitch-black eyes and mouth. When he speaks, his voice is every bit as disturbing as Gabe said it was; his bottomless eyes seem to cut through the miles and peer through the TV screen to look straight at me as he purrs, "We have seen what is only the beginning of something momentous."

I feel like I've been punched in the stomach.

"Why do you think that?" the reporter asks.

"I do not think that. I *know* that."

"Where did you get your information from? How do you know what this is? Is this is the work of a random terrorist group or gang? Who was involved?"

The tattooed man lets out a nightmarish laugh. "This is *my* doing," he says, sounding as proud as he can in his terrible voice, "and I am hardly arbitrary. I prefer to think of myself as a spearhead: well-chosen and purposeful."

I catch the subtle flick of his right wrist, which is hanging by the inked skin of his thigh. Then movement to the left attracts my attention and I look at the reporter just in time to see him sinking downward, his neck bent in a strange direction, his eyes suddenly blank. And then he's out of the frame.

"Greg?" someone off-screen calls. Then, "He's *dead!*" The camera shakes before toppling toward the dark ground, momentarily coming to a rest at a crooked angle on pale, tattooed feet.

The receiving room bursts into horrorstruck chatter.

A few of us remain silent and frozen, eyes and ears still focused on our enemy, who is crouching down and reaching for the camera. As he lifts it he repeats, "Only the beginning." The camera stops on his ghastly black gap of a smile. "Enjoy your lives while they are still yours."

Then the camera is flying through the air. We get another brief glimpse of the blazing city before it cuts off.

⌒

Mark and Beatrix start getting people down for rooms on the residential hall.

Even though Red's been working on more weapons for the past day or two, Dr. Roterra draws more blood yet so we can further strengthen our armory.

Trenton, Janssen and Wright start moving the food people brought with them to the lounge, where the food from Claire's apartment still is.

I'm helping put the food away, and also trying to call Gabe.

Nothing.

Wes.

Nothing.

Claire.

Nothing.

Rafe.

Nothing.

I don't know what I'd even tell my sister and Rafe. I can't explain to them the blatant threat the tattooed man gave on the TV. Even if they were watching it for some reason and heard for themselves what he said, I wouldn't be able to *explain* it to them. But I still want to warn them to be as careful as possible.

Not that I'm sure Claire would even be worried about an attack like this.

I tune back into the news, which is saying that Rockwall, Fort Worth and Grapevine have seen some bombing (that's what they're calling it, anyway. We know it's probably just the insane power the tattooed man has). And the more fire they show on the screen, the more my mind tries to tell me that people can't live through things like this—that *Gabe* can't live through it. The more I think that, the more I fight to not-think it, which leads to me telling myself he *did* live through it and will come back. Is *on his way* back. Will be here in a matter of hours.

But that is a very, very dangerous thought for me to have.

And knowing that—no matter how badly I don't want to know it, no matter how badly I wish I could just live in blissful ignorance—leaves my whole I'm Not Going To Freak Out attitude balancing on a thin wire. I find myself alternating between being chilled to the bone and flashing hot, between being unable to stand still and feeling like I need to sit down or I'm going to pass out. My brain feels like a wild animal and my skull like a cage. My stomach won't stop twisting with anxiety.

And the time is *crawling* by.

After a little while, once I'm back in the receiving room, I go down my phone call list again. Still nothing.

I look at the TV. They're showing a new video of Dallas being consumed by fire.

'Only the beginning.'

"I need some air," I blurt out in the middle of Trenton asking me something.

"Mari, no!" Beatrix exclaims. "Do *not* go outside!"

I'm already bolting for the stairwell. When I get there the frigid air feels good on my temporarily scorching skin. It seems to only get better the higher up I go, the closer I get to the air outside.

My name echoes up to me, as well as the sound of feet pounding up the steps after me. But I don't stop. I don't even slow down until I get to the door at the top, which will take me to the back hallway of The Room.

I burst out of the stairwell and straight into the wall opposite the door. Even though the exit to the outside world is just to my right and there's a whole cold, empty building waiting for me if I go to the left, I don't walk another foot. I just put my back against the wall and try to catch my breath, try to hold my head above the torrent of unbearable thoughts and feelings rushing through me.

"Mari," Beatrix sobs when she steps into the hallway, "what are you *doing?*"

"I don't know," I gasp. I look at her and feel my eyes widen in distress. "I don't know what I'm doing."

She stares back at me—a married, older, teal-haired, pierced and inked version of myself. "I don't know what I'm doing, either," she whimpers.

Tears are starting to burn at the backs of my eyes. "I'm trying n-not to lose it," I stammer. "But all I can think about is—is—" My hand flies up to my necklace, but I'm suddenly shaking too badly to even grasp it.

She shakes her head fiercely, knowing what I'm trying to say. "I can't think that way. I can't. Wes is trying to get back here. I *have* to believe that."

"Yeah." I nod just as passionately, grasping at her optimism. "Yes. He is. And—"

I can't even say his name. My throat constricts around it. And then my body decides it's time to cry.

Beatrix trips toward me and draws me into a hug, and she cries with me.

"What *is* this?" I sob. "How is this happening?"

She shakes her head. "I don't know, but I'm *s-so* scared."

"Me, too."

And as soon as I say that, I feel bad. I feel humiliated and sad and stupid for being as scared as I am.

Standing next to this woman, I'm a fucking joke. I don't *have* a husband. I don't have that link with Gabe, haven't spent years building a friendship and a romance and a life with him. Here I am falling apart over the probable loss of a future I only wanted, and what is *she* falling apart over? So much more than that—the probable loss of a whole piece of her, of a past she loved and a future she didn't just dream about but intended to have with the man she married. The one man she swore to love until she dies.

I don't realize I've said any of that out loud until she pulls back and fixes the sternest look she can manage on me. "Do *not* say that," she commands me thickly, her hazel eyes ringed with red and still spilling tears. "Do you know how Wes and I got to where we are? Do you know how we built what we have?" Abruptly her face crumples into an expression of heart-breaking sorrow, and she sucks in an aggrieved breath. "We met each other and *felt something.* Just like you and G-Gabe did."

I feel like someone's got their hands around my heart, trying to squeeze it until it ruptures.

"You *have* been building something with him," she gets out, "something that sh-shows on your face and makes him happier than I've ever seen him." She sniffles and grips my shoulders. "Mari, you are not so different from me. You are not stupid. You feel how you feel because you care about Gabe *and this is a nightmare.*"

I can't say anything back and she doesn't keep talking. We just dissolve into more tears. Standing up becomes too much of a chore, so we sit down on the floor with our backs against the wall and let our bodies try to work through the heaviness of our thoughts. It's difficult. I hate everything in my head.

After a little while I start trying to accept that things can go either way—not just with Gabe and Wes, but with all of us. Any of us can die at any time and, honestly, that shouldn't be news to us. We're Light. We've looked death in the eye before. We know we aren't invincible.

An indeterminable amount of time passes with us sitting up here in the cold hallway, and I can't decide whether or not I appreciate the chill, the stillness, the silence around us. It makes Beatrix's confident words about me and Gabe feel warmer. At the same time, I have nothing to block out the very real possibility that he might not come back; the only defense I have against it is to hope he *will* show up. But that hurts, too, because if I'm wrong....

The dichotomy exhausts me faster and more severely than anything else ever has.

Eventually the door to the stairwell opens and Janssen looks over at us. His kind face creases with concern when he sees the state we're in. "Hey, sweethearts," he says gently.

Beatrix says nothing. I try for a polite smile, but I don't feel like I'm very successful.

"I just came up to check on you two, but why don't you come on back down with me?" he suggests. "It's on past 4:00, and you both look ti—"

A huge boom sounds from outside and the building shudders violently.

His eyes widen as he works to keep his balance, and Beatrix and I get up off the floor. For a single moment I'm perplexed.

And then I realize it's happening here.

"Oh, God," I get out as another boom comes. It sounds a little farther away than the first, but everything still shakes, leaving me feeling weaker than ever. A car alarm starts wailing from somewhere nearby.

"Girls!" Janssen exclaims, holding the door open for us.

We're in the stairwell in a second. The door has just shut the three of us off from the hallway when my phone rings in my hand. I'm so immediately exultant and terrified that I feel like my heart is going to burst.

It pains every inch of me to see Rafe's name on the screen instead of Gabe's. But I answer it. "Rafe?"

"Mari!" he yells. "Where are you? Are you okay? Something's going down!"

"I know and I'm fine. Are you? Have you seen Claire?"

"I haven't seen her, Mari," he says, sounding strained, "and I'm okay, but I heard this really loud noise a minute ago and my apartment shook and I looked outside—things are *exploding* outside!"

"Bombs," I lie weakly as I run downstairs with the others. "They're bombs and they went off in Dallas tonight, too—"

"Are you fucking serious?"

I feel like I'm going to fall over at any second. The running and stress and fear and agonizing disappointment that I'm not talking to Gabe right now are draining me. "Yes," I pant. "I—Rafe, I can't talk—"

"No!" he cuts me off. "Stay on the phone with me!"

"I can't," I suddenly sob. "It's too much. Be careful—"

"*Mari!*" he bellows.

I hang up.

I have the distinct feeling I'm about to tumble down the stairs. I only barely get my phone into my pocket to grab the cold metal bannister with both hands before I fall.

The lights flicker and a soft whimper leaves me. I have half a mind to just go slack already, to just sit down right where I am and curl in on myself and block the world out because this is unbelievable.

But some part of my mind yells, *No! Do not bitch out right now! Keep going. Keep. Going.*

With great effort, I listen to me. I continue down the stairs, trying not to be slow even though my legs want to stop moving altogether.

Yes. Go. Fight through your fear.

For a second I stumble, but then I start to move a little faster.

This could be worse. It can always be worse. Don't give up just because things are looking bleak.

Now I only have one hand on the bannister.

Gabe wouldn't give up.

No, he wouldn't.

And if he comes back and asks how I managed while he was gone, I'm not going to tell him I was too upset to even walk down some damn stairs.

I take a deep breath and dash the rest of the way to the bottom floor, even passing Beatrix.

In the receiving room, only Dr. Roterra and Grayhem are around. They look at us when we burst in, and even before we announce that the explosions have started, Grayhem's expression turns knowing. "Us now?" he asks.

"Yessir," Janssen replies.

Grayhem nods and sighs. "All right. Everyone else went on to bed, I think. I'd alert them to this, but it's been a long night and they're sure to get longer. I don't really want to wake them, and I'm certain we're safe down here."

The three of us nod our agreement. "I don't guess there's really much we'd be able to do, anyway," Beatrix says with a sniffle.

"Not much at all," Janssen agrees.

"Why don't you three head on to bed, too?" Grayhem suggests. "Rest is just as good for the mind as it is for the body."

If it'll come to you.

"Okay, well, you come get me if you need somethin'," Janssen tells him. "I'm up for whatever needs doin'."

Grayhem smiles tiredly at us. "Of course."

The three of us leave for the residential hall. When we get there Janssen says, "Girls, I'm just here in Room C if somethin' comes up."

"Thanks," Beatrix murmurs. I just wave a little.

After he disappears into his room I say, "You can stay in J with me if you want to."

"I do," she says promptly. "Let me just brush my teeth and stuff and I'll be right over."

We part ways a little farther down the hall, and I head into my room.

I feel weird almost as soon as I'm shut in. The place feels lonely and mocking, and it doesn't take me long to figure out why.

Gabe was in here just days ago.

He sat right there in my desk chair and spoke to me, looked at me.

He kissed me for the first time right around where I'm standing now.

He stood here and looked my past in the face and said it wasn't dark enough to send him running.

For a minute I remain motionless and silent. Try to separate reality from my imagination, and probability from what I only hope will happen.

I hate this.

How did it get like this? Just days ago things were okay. We were all safe and I was getting used to the Lightforce and Gabe and I were just beginning. We were all happy. And now we're scattered and breaking and hurting and wondering and I want to believe it's going to get better, but what if it isn't? What if this is my life now?

My fears are smothering me. I have so many of them and they are all enormous and so many of them are about Gabe and I can't fight them off. I want him back. My confidence in our ability to sort this situation out will be so much stronger if I get him back. That frenzied craving to have him here to stabilize us—to stabilize *me*—coupled with the awful blindness of not knowing anything about where or how he is...it almost takes me out.

But then I feel a flicker of clarity. It's cold and flat and as ugly as the Dark beings in this world, but it's better than pandemonium and I clutch at it. It's truth. It's control. I need it.

So I close my eyes and draw as deep a breath as I can. My hands clench into fists. While I hold my breath, I try to take control of my thoughts and fears—I bring the worst of them to the front of my mind. I try to fight panic with preparation.

I will never see Gabe again, my mind whispers. *He's dead. He didn't make it out of Dallas.*

The last thing I heard him say before the call got cut off was the last thing I'll ever hear from him.

My breath huffs out of me so hard it hurts. I already want to stop this, but I don't. I have to do it.

He will never be back in this building. He will never set foot in this room again.

I need to get used to him not being around. He isn't going to be around anymore. I can't touch him again, or look at him, or talk to him. All I have now are memories.

All the plans we made for when he got back don't matter anymore. Nothing we even briefly imagined for our future together will come to pass.

Some things only last for a little while, and we were one of them.

A deep sadness winds through me. It weighs me down and makes my eyes burn.

There is no 'we' anymore.

As badly as I want to believe he's okay and he'll come back, I have to do the smart thing: I have to prepare for the worst. If I confront these painful things now and get them out in the open, maybe they won't cripple me later if it turns out he really is gone. Maybe they won't send me to the floor like an unexpected kick to the backs of my knees.

I owe it to myself to be ready for anything, no matter how much it hurts or how ugly it looks or how unbelievable it sounds. I'm not a child, and I shouldn't treat myself like a child. I shouldn't handle my feelings with too much care. It would only be to my detriment if I let myself go on believing bad things don't happen and good people don't die and everything will go right just because I want it to.

So I keep going. I open my fists and take the time to tune in to every part of me, from my head to my feet. I pay attention to how it feels to only have me in my personal space. How it feels not to have his hands in my hands, or his palms curving around my hips, or his fingers sliding through my hair, or his mouth against my mouth. *This is how it's going to be from now on,* I tell myself. *I have to get used my body having nothing to do with his. Things are different now. I didn't always have him. I have to go back to that time. I have to just be me.*

Next I open my aching eyes. Through fresh tears I make myself look at my desk chair until I don't see his tall, gorgeous frame sitting in it anymore—until all I see is an empty seat. Then I do the same thing with the air around me. I notice how he's not to my left like he always was in his car, and not behind me like during those first few minutes we looked at the tree house, and not in front of me like when he and I sparred.

He's not anywhere. All there is now is me.

Change is inevitable. Nothing stays the same.

I take a deep, shaky, excruciating breath and let it back out.

And then I start getting ready for bed.

I change into my most comfortable pajamas: gray drawstring pants and a white V-neck. Then I head to the bathroom. I'm in the middle of brushing my teeth when Beatrix appears, looking as exhausted and sad as I feel. She half-heartedly waves at my reflection in the bathroom mirror and I wave back.

After I'm done brushing I floss, wash my face and brush out my hair. Then I turn my lamp on and the overhead light off and head to my bed, where she's curled up.

"Couple of guys are up watching TV in the lounge," she tells me. "I stopped by to update them and they said some city in Louisiana is getting it, too."

I sigh, not knowing what to say.

I barely even know what to think.

We quiet down and cover up, but we don't do much situating. We just loll here. I feel numb or something and I wish I could just zone out—out of my head, out of reality—but I can't. Even though this has been a long, stressful, emotional day, we lay awake for quite a while.

Eventually she says softly, "I don't know if I can sleep."

"I don't know if I can, either," I whisper. "Don't know if I want to."

"We should, though."

"Shoulda, coulda, woulda," I say although I don't even know what the appropriate time to say that is.

A pitiful laugh leaves her and then she says, "Mari," and her voice cracks.

"Yeah?" I barely get out.

She grasps for my hand. "It hurts me to breathe not knowing if *he's* still breathing."

The words make my stomach ache. "I know it does."

As more dense uncertainty and fear—not just about Wes and Gabe, but about everything—settle on me, I hold her hand in return and close my eyes.

Eventually the numbness turns into me drifting, not quite asleep and not quite awake. It goes on for a long time and not a bit of me appreciates it. But as tired as my mind is, it won't shut off completely, nor will it just go ahead and snap to attention. At one point I'm vaguely aware of Beatrix moving around beside me, then of the mattress shifting, and then I hear her feet padding across the floor, but I don't so much as open my eyes.

My thoughts meander through my head with no rhyme or reason. Some are sad, some hopeful, some angry, some ridiculous. I ponder what that monster's red tattoos mean, if they mean anything. Whether or not my parents are in heaven and, if so, whether or not they're watching me. I wonder what Audrey has been doing since I cut myself off from her; I wonder if she got with Rafe any more afterward or if that was just something she wanted to try on one poorly-chosen occasion. At one point I wonder what the weather is like in Africa right now. And I wonder just why it is that people can't touch clouds when they look so touchable, when they're so breathtaking and unique, when they *deserve* to be touched and admired—science be damned, I want to touch—

I hear, "Oh my God! *Oh my God!*" from somewhere relatively close by and my eyes finally drift open. A little disoriented, I glance around my room and belatedly realize Beatrix isn't in it. I guess I was more out of it than I thought if she left and I didn't notice. That was her voice, though. I know that for sure. I sit up so I can get out of bed and find her.

Just as I'm grabbing a fistful of blanket to move it, the door to my room bursts open. I freeze and my own surprised cry gets stuck in my throat when Gabe swings in.

His eyes find me instantly, but he doesn't come to me. He shifts his weight back against the door, causing it to shut heavily and send a jolt through my bones. And for a few eternal seconds he just stays there, leaned against the door, and looks at me with the most wonderful and most chaotic expression in the world.

My mind is suddenly wide awake and racing, my heart pounding so hard it hurts. I choke out, "Gabriel?"

He sucks in a loud breath and shoves away from the door. His feet carry him toward me. My feet develop a mind of their own and propel me forward even though the rest of me isn't ready to get out of bed. I get twisted up in the blanket and fall and my back hits the floor with absolutely no grace.

But I have only a fleeting thought of embarrassment because he drops onto the floor, too, and I sit up on one hand as he kneels across my lap, planting one knee on either side of me. He grabs my head with both hands just before his mouth collides with mine, burning and desperate. I'm shot through with something unnamable and amazing and it rips a moan from me and a moan leaves *him* in the form of my name and I—

—I am touching clouds.

My free hand clutches the front of his jacket and one of his flattens against my back. He swiftly and effortlessly pulls me away from the floor until I'm sitting up against him, my face tilted way up. He holds me securely in place as our mouths rediscover each other, remember all the things we said and did before, retrieve our future from the jagged edge it very nearly dropped over.

I'm abruptly overwhelmed by the need to look at him again. I have to look at him *now* or I'm going to explode. I drag my mouth from his and pull back to gaze up at him, and my throat tightens. God Almighty, he really is here in front of me—not a picture, not a figment of my imagination. "I need to just—" I barely get out. Since he's holding me upright, I put the hand I had on the floor up against his cheek.

He turns into it and lets out a shaky breath. He languidly kisses my palm, making that one place feel red-hot with glorious, not destructive, fire. Then he looks at me again, and even though his perfect eyes were on me ten seconds ago he looks like he's seeing me for the first time in days all over again. It makes my heart swell.

Those eyes drink me in and he says scratchily, "Me, too."

Seeing the wounds from his picture makes them very real for me, but I decide they're not too bad. I'm sure they looked worse when he got them, except for that bruise, but that'll fade soon. His face is just a little scruffier than normal and his hair is unruly as ever. His gaze is powerful on me, just like always and more than ever at the same time. There are too many emotions in his expression to focus on just one, but together they say the same thing to me: *'I'm alive and you're alive and we are both here right now.'*

He's divine.

Something about him doesn't look quite right to me, though. Momentarily I figure out what it is: part of him is still in fight mode, still trying to stay alive. I can only fucking imagine why that is. But the longer we sit here and look at each other, the more I can sense the tension leaving him. It relieves me immensely. I don't want him to suffer any more than he has to; he went through so much while he was gone and I know some of it isn't going to go away quickly, if it ever does.

I move to slide both of my hands between his jacket and his shirt and then lay them against his back. He exhales, seeming to calm even more under my hands, and slants down so his mouth can pull mine into a long, deliberate kiss.

When he stops he says, "After our call got cut off, I...I thought I would *never* get back here, Marienne. I felt every single mile. And it hurt me so much."

My chest aches even though he's here now. He told me before the attack on Dallas that he missed me and was thinking about me and those kinds of things, but these words are different than those were. These are despondent.

I tell him earnestly, "It hurt me, too." I gently smooth my hands over his back, partly for comfort and partly because he's too marvelous for me not to touch after all of this. Thinking he'd been ripped away from me so soon after I found him...I hated that. But, oh, it hadn't come true. It hadn't. Thank the Lord. "But you did get back."

"Yes, I did." His eyes rove over my face and then down to my necklace, which I haven't taken off since he gave it to me. A flash of a smile touches his lips. He trails his hand away from my face and lays it on my collarbone, warm and strong, looking like he has something to say. But he's only taken a breath before he stops, seeming distracted by something.

If I had to guess, it's the way I suddenly can't breathe right under his hand. I'm trying, I really am, but my heartbeat isn't listening. It's like my body is just now catching up with reality; it can't figure out how to act with him touching me and my necklace like this when before I'd tried to prepare for never feeling his hands on me again. I'd tried to tell my body he was no more and there was only me. And now it's finally grasping how very untrue that is.

He just looks at his hand on my skin, his lips slightly parted, as my chest rises and falls faster than normal. He looks like he can't believe what he's seeing— like he can't believe he can do this to me.

Absurd. So absurd. That delicious, unassuming bastard.

I work on getting a deep breath. I try to calm down, try to slow my pulse, and...

...and then his scorching eyes slowly move up to mine. They lay all of his emotion right on me. And I feel like I'm going to break into a thousand pieces underneath it.

He whispers, "You astound me."

"You astound *me*," I whisper back, "Gabe."

He draws his own deep breath before dipping down to kiss me slowly, his lips pressing and pulling on mine with tenderness that only barely masks intense promise.

I don't have words for how it makes me feel.

I'd told myself he was dead, indelibly gone from the earth and from my life—and worried he really was. The breathless sound he makes as my tongue grazes his bottom lip assures me he is not. Suddenly his hands are flat on the floor instead of on me and I drop back a little, only kept from totally falling because my arms are around him.

"Have I ever told you," he asks unevenly, "that you make me love my name?"

I almost don't get out, "No," before he kisses me again.

I can't help collapsing onto my back now and he follows me, moving a hand down to whip the tangle of blanket away from my legs. When it's gone his hand seizes my hip and he covers my body with his, propping himself up on one arm while the rest of him settles on me and warms me through. And, oh, it feels so right. It makes me sigh out of the kiss. He sighs, too, and I feel it and it's wonderful and his lips graze my lips as he murmurs, "Well, there are a lot of things I need to tell you." But then his mouth is around mine yet again, no longer just grazing, and I suspect I won't get to hear these things right now.

I can't find it in me to mind.

My hands spread across the back of his shirt as my lips part against his. His fingers tighten on my hip and he's in my mouth, reminding me with his that he cares about me, wants to be mine and wants me to be his. As my legs graze his and I hug him to me, I hope he knows that I still feel that way, too. I want him to kiss me like this whenever he feels like it. And laugh at me even when I think I'm being stupid. And tell me he's proud of me when I think I'm not quite good enough. And talk about things like tree houses with me even though we're both way past our childhood days. And get through all of this bullshit going on outside with me.

Both of our breaths catch and my back leaves the floor the slightest bit when his fingers splay shyly over the bare skin just under my shirt. All the nerve endings in my body react to him like they're tiny magnets and he's magnetic, and for a second I'm staggered by how such a tentative touch can affect me like this. And then my hands find the hem of his shirt, too, and move underneath it just as carefully to feel the warm skin of his back. His muscles flex as he inhales unsteadily; I wonder if he feels the magnetic thing, too. He kisses me so unexpectedly sweetly that a shiver dances down my spine, and I think maybe he does feel that way, and as he slides his palm over my bellybutton, skims his fingers over more of my skin, I move my lips from his because I want to tell him he's beautiful.

And then someone knocks on my door.

We go still, and then we both sigh. "Oh, I knew that was coming," he says against my mouth.

Instead of what I was planning on telling him, I say breathlessly, "I guess everything *is* kind of going to hell outside, isn't it?"

He lifts his head and calls, "Just a second," with surprising composure. Then he comes back down to me and we kiss one more time. Two more times. Under my shirt he gently traces something on my skin with his fingertip. Then he pulls back again. "Guess you can distract me from explosions and Dark-magic-wielding monsters as easily as you can distract me from everything else."

It's not very funny, but I can't help a grin.

He grins back briefly and then asks quietly, "But there will be time for that, huh?" His eyes drift over me longingly.

Even though I'm not over this yet, either, I feel my smile softening. "Yeah. We're both alive and well and not three hundred miles apart."

He takes his hand out from under my shirt to touch my bottom lip, then my cheek, and again his smile matches mine. "You are very right," he whispers as I take my hands away from him, too. Then he gracefully lifts himself off of me and straightens his clothes a little. Even though the sudden space and chill is an unpleasant shock to my body, I don't complain because Gabe *is* still here. Still in this room with me, in our Sanctum, in Fayetteville. He helps me up, too, and we head for the door together.

Before I open it I turn to look up at him, and I say hesitantly, "Hey."

He slides a piece of my hair behind my ear. "Hey."

Softly and with more seriousness than I've ever asked anyone anything, I ask him, "Can I keep you?"

He gazes at me, managing to look sincere and alluring at the same time. "Yes." The word is just as soft as mine. His hand leaves my hair to touch my necklace again. "But only if I can keep you, too."

"You can." I swallow hard and nod toward the door. "Ready?"

He drops his hand. "Sure."

I open the door and find Grayhem standing in the hall. "Hello, sir," I say, hoping I don't sound as surprised and embarrassed as I feel. I guess I thought Wes and Beatrix were at the door—though now that I think about it they're probably down the hall in the room she picked for them, going crazy on each other.

Except that in the next instant I hear her say, "Here we are." She and Wes step up next to Grayhem, not looking too disheveled, miraculously. She waves enthusiastically at Gabe and Wes smiles at me, and we reciprocate the little greetings.

Grayhem says, "Oh, wonderful." Then he gives me a polite smile. "Now, good morning, Mari." Then to Gabe with relief, "And to you, too. It's so good to have you back. As soon as Red said he saw you run past, I wanted to get the four of you together..." he turns hesitant and inhales deeply, "...to tell you."

Gabe nods. "Thank you. What's going on?"

"Well, I...." Grayhem clears his throat. "First, allow me to say I know you two haven't been here long and that you're in dire need of rest—"

"Oh, no, stop right there," Wes interrupts him. "We don't mind. This must be important."

"Yeah, don't worry about it," Gabe agrees. "We really are just happy to be here."

Grayhem crosses his arms, and for several seconds he just looks at the four of us. Then he says, "I'll inform the others when the day isn't so young. But I want you to know I've been watching the news for hours, and this thing is growing. It's not just Dallas and us and Baton Rouge that are being attacked. It's happening all over the country."

I blink slowly. The atmosphere between all of us seems to cool. The lovely dreamlike minutes I'd been sharing with Gabe before start dimming. Shortly Beatrix asks, "*Really?*" and I'm right there with her on it. This is news even to me and her, and there for a while our eyes were *glued* to the TV.

He nods. "Yes. It isn't worldwide, I don't think, but the United States is definitely getting it." He looks at Wes and frowns deeply. "I'm—I'm afraid...."

Wes waits a whole second before he asks, "What?"

"I'm afraid...that the unusually powerful Dark figure you two encountered in Dallas is not the only one of his caliber." Grayhem's eyes flicker to Gabe and he finishes slowly, "There are many more just like him, and they are spread out around our states, and they are destroying everything."

Silence falls even colder than before. It's thick and heavy and uninterrupted except for the erratic breaths leaving Wes and Beatrix and me and the guy beside me, whose hand is curling around mine, who saw personally the damage *one* tattooed monster-man can accomplish in mere minutes.

And there are more than one.

I turn my alarmed gaze on Gabe, and he looks back at me with troubled eyes.

At length he cuts through the silence with a quiet, absent, "We'll...figure something out."

I nod just as absentmindedly.

And then the words wiggle their way into some part of my brain that isn't overcome with shock, and it's like an electrical current is suddenly whooshing through me. I blink several times and straighten up a little and look at Wes and Beatrix and Grayhem, who all look just like Gabe does. Finally I look back at him.

Oh...oh, absolutely we'll figure something out.

We'll do just what I said the other day to him on the phone. We'll find the balance between us and them.

We will find it, he and I, because he's with me again. And not just us; the other three standing with us and all of the other Light people we know, and even those we don't know, will find it. Our defense exists somewhere, I *know* it.

I squeeze his hand and echo more surely, "We'll figure something out."

Gabe's eyes lighten after a few seconds, like he's catching on, and his fingers tighten around mine. Then he, too, stands a little taller as he looks at Grayhem again. "Let us get some sleep, and tomorrow we'll look this thing in the face. It's not over for us."

"Fuck," Wes says slowly, "yeah."

Beatrix extends a hand to me and I grab it tightly.

A look of optimism skates across our Director's face as he looks at us. Soon it turns into a small but proud smirk. Finally he says, "I look forward to it."

"So do I," Wes says.

Beatrix nods. "Me, too."

"Me, too," Gabe says.

I'm looking forward to it, too, of course.

And when I glance down at the hand Beatrix is holding, I realize for the first time that the Light mark on my wrist isn't as faint against my skin as it used to be.

End of Book One

Book Two, "Fight," Coming Soon

CPSIA information can be obtained at www.ICGtesting.com
Printed in the USA
LVOW05s1712211014

409813LV00019B/611/P